get me

THE
keatyn
CHRONICLES
get me

JILLIAN DODD

Published by Swoonworthy Books, an imprint of Jillian Dodd, Inc.
www.jilliandodd.net

The Keatyn Chronicles and Jillian Dodd are registered trademarks of
Jillian Dodd, Inc.

Editor: Jovana Shirley, Unforeseen Editing
Photo: ©Regina Wamba
Cover Design: Mae I Designs

ISBN: 978-1-953071-14-9

This book is for

You

Love yourself.
Find control in your chaos.
Follow your heart.
And don't be afraid to wish on the moon.

Books by Jillian Dodd

London Prep
The Exchange
The Boys' Club
The Kiss
The Key

The Keatyn Chronicles®
Stalk Me
Kiss Me
Date Me
Love Me
Adore Me
Hate Me
Get Me
Fame
Power
Money
Sex
Love
Keatyn Unscripted
Aiden

That Boy
That Boy
That Wedding
That Baby
That Love
That Ring
That Summer
That Promise

Saturday, December 17th

WALKED OUT.
WINTER FORMAL

I TRY TO rid my mind of Aiden and focus on the task at hand.

Keeping Eastbrooke safe from Vincent.

I walk toward the room where Cooper and the dean have corralled the press.

As I get to the door, they're both walking out.

Cooper speaks to the dean in rapid-fire fashion. "She lied because she's being stalked. I'm her bodyguard. We cannot let this get out on social media or Eastbrooke itself will be in danger." Cooper points to some students on the dance floor who are on their phones.

"I can handle the students," the dean says. "What I can't control is the press."

"I'll handle them," I say confidently.

The dean walks onto the stage and takes the microphone. "All right. Everyone listen up. Take out your phones. Excellent. I'd like you to delete any photos you took of Keatyn. If any of you posted about her, Abby Johnston, Eastbrooke, or what just transpired, I'd like you to delete it immediately from any and all social networks. At East-brooke, we pride ourselves on our students' security and privacy. Each and every one of you knows security, excellence, leadership, and a sense of community is what keeps Eastbrooke strong. As is always our policy, we will be monitoring your social media to make sure you are showing yourself and our school in the best light. Anyone who publicly speaks of this will face detention and possible expulsion. Do I make myself clear?"

Cooper says to me, "One down, one to go. You ready?"

"I need to make a quick phone call first. While I do, could you find me some paper?"

He grabs a large decorative snowflake off the wall. "Will this work?"

I can't help but chuckle. "Yeah, that will work." Then I call Damian.

"I heard what you did for Peyton," he says immediately. "Thank you."

"Is she okay?"

"Because of you, yes. But she's a wreck. I'm headed to the airport now."

"I have a favor."

"Anything. You know that."

"I'm about to talk to the local press. In order to keep them quiet about me being at Eastbrooke, I need to give them a bigger story."

"Bait and switch. Hollywood does it all the time."

"Unfortunately, I don't have a bigger story to offer."

"But I do. That's why you called me."

"You're right. Damian Moran's date in New York City with his new girlfriend would do the trick. But we'd have to fix Peyton's social media first so Vincent can't connect her to me."

"Of course. We'll do whatever you need. It's the least we can do."

"Aiden walked out when he heard the truth about my mom."

"You told everyone the truth? Peyton was sobbing, so it was hard to follow exactly what happened. She just kept saying you saved her."

"I told them who my mom is, but I didn't tell them the truth about why I lied. I told them it was because I wanted to prove I could act."

"Why didn't you tell them about the stalker?"

"Because there are people here who would call Vincent themselves if they knew the real story. I have to protect my friends. Protect Eastbrooke."

"You should be protecting yourself."

"That's next on the list. Okay, I have to go."

"Let's meet tomorrow to discuss."

"Damian?"

"What?"

"Thanks for always being my friend."

"I love you. I'm pissed and scared that you outed yourself but, at the same time, I'm proud of what you did for Peyton. Seriously, Keats, you've changed. I like it."

Cooper motions for me to follow him.

"Thanks, Damian. I gotta go."

I FOLLOW COOPER into a room where the press, three reporters and two cameramen, have gathered. All of them are young.

And, hopefully, hungry.

I was going to emulate my mother. She handles the press so well.

But my mom didn't go through what I did with Vincent.

I'll just be me.

I smile, shake each one of their hands, and introduce myself. "Hi. I'm Keatyn." After that, I address them. "So, I have a huge favor. I'd like for you *not* to report what you just heard."

"Are you kidding me?" the short, blonde reporter says. "Abby Johnston is big news."

"You're right. She is. But I'm not her. I mean, what would you report exactly?"

"That you're at a boarding school using a different last name than hers. Trying to hide who you are."

I nod, agreeing with her. "Except that my mom and I have had different last names my whole life. Douglas for me. Johnston for her."

"But you lied about it."

"So what? I didn't want people to judge me. I wanted to make friends because of who I am, not who my mom is. Not exactly a scandal. I doubt your editors would even print it."

She looks defeated, but the other reporter narrows her eyes. "Why do I get the feeling there's something more to the story?"

I give them my slow smile, the one that's exactly like Mom's.

"Because you're a good reporter." I turn to Cooper. "I'll take that paper now."

I show them the snowflake and my purple glitter pen. "I'm going to write up a simple non-disclosure agreement. If you sign it and agree not to tell anyone, I'll tell you the truth."

"But we can't talk about it?"

"Yes. The story has purposely been kept out of the press."

They all look at me like I'm nuts.

I start writing, reading aloud as I do. "This says, *I agree not to disclose any details about Keatyn Monroe, Keatyn Douglas, Eastbrooke, or Abby Johnston. I will not discuss what Keatyn tells me with anyone. If the truth comes out before the specified time, I will be subject to a damages lawsuit. This contract will become null and void upon two events: Keatyn's death or when she gives written consent otherwise.*"

I turn the paper around and place the pen on top of it.

No one moves.

"In return for doing me this favor, I will give you two things. The first is that when my story is ready to be shared with the press, you will get that story *exclusively.*"

The looks on their faces tell me they aren't really all that excited about a possible future story, so I dangle the bigger bait. "The second is a story you can use now. One every entertainment reporter in the country has been dying for."

"What's that? Is Abby pregnant again?" the red-haired reporter asks, perking up.

"Are she and Tommy breaking up?" her photographer asks.

"Is it true that Tommy is having an affair with the nanny?" another says.

"If you agree to my terms and sign the NDA, you will get to report on and photograph the first public date of Damian Moran and his new girlfriend. The date will take place in New York City. It will include dinner, a romantic carriage ride through Central Park, and a kiss. Who knows, maybe they'll even window shop at Tiffany's. You'll be given a media packet with pertinent information about the girlfriend along with the story of how they met."

None of the reporters can hide their surprise.

And I'm sure none of them ever thought coming to a

high school dance would net them a story like this.

I hold out my pen to the blonde closest to me.

"I think we can all agree to those terms," she says, quickly signing the agreement.

Once everyone has signed, I turn to Cooper. "Would you please sign as a witness?"

I photograph Cooper signing the snowflake, take another of the document itself, and forward them to Sam.

"Now that the business part is out of the way, I'll tell you my story. If something happens to me, you'll have the inside scoop—"

I'm interrupted by pounding on the door.

Cooper and I share a glance, mine probably more panicked than his.

Could Vincent have found me already?

And would he knock?

Cooper cracks the door and says, "Not now."

"Keatyn, we're not leaving!" I hear Riley yell.

Did he say *we*?

Tears start prickling my eyes. I rush to the door and motion for Cooper to open it.

And that's when I see all of them.

Riley, Ariela, Jake, Dawson, Maggie, Logan, Dallas, Bryce, and even Katie and Annie are standing outside the door.

"We're not leaving," Riley states. He's standing straight and tall with his chin confidently jutting out.

"And we know you're lying," Jake says, surprising me.

"I'm not lying, Jake. Abby Johnston *is* my mom."

"That part I believe. It's the rest of it. About why you came here. You didn't come to act. And don't think you can fool me. I recognize your mean girl character from Drama."

"And you better have a damn good reason for lying to

your best friends," Dallas pipes up.

I look at Annie. Her eyes are full of tears. She mouths, *I'm sorry.*

Cooper moves between us. "They need to go, Keatyn."

I remember being in Malibu and wondering who my true friends were. I close my eyes for a moment and make a decision. "Why don't you all come in and have a seat."

Cooper shakes his head. "I don't think this is a good idea."

"I trust them," I say loudly, as much to them as to Cooper.

I GIVE EVERYONE a hug, ask them to take a seat, and then address them. "I'm about to tell you a secret. It's very important that this secret doesn't get out. If you don't think you can keep the secret, it's okay. We'll still be friends, but I'll have to ask you to leave for a bit."

No one moves, so I go to Annie. "Are you sure?" I ask her.

"I'm sorry for what I said. I was hurt and just reacted."

"I'm sorry for what I said too. While you listen, can you do me a huge favor?"

"What do you want me to do?"

"Take everything off the Kiki Kiki profile. Delete all the photos. Unfriend everyone. Then delete the account."

I take a deep breath as I walk to the front of the room.

Then I start talking.

And don't stop until I've told them every bit of the truth, from the moment I met Vincent until the moment he tried to kidnap me.

"Why isn't he in jail?" one of the reporters asks.

"There wasn't enough evidence to prove attempted kidnapping, so they let him go. Basically, it was his word against mine. He told the police that we were friends. That I invited him to the party. That there was a commotion and he was trying to help. When we were back home, I remembered he mentioned a van out back. The police found a van with duct tape and drugs in it, but it was stolen so they couldn't trace it back to him."

"Sneaky bastard," Dallas says.

"Yeah, well, it gets worse."

"Keep going," Riley encourages.

"So, we were back at home, just trying to wrap our heads around it all. How I knew him. How they could let him go. What it would mean—when a house alarm went off down the beach at my boyfriend's. It was quickly discovered that whoever broke in took just one thing."

"What was that?" one of the reporters asks breathlessly.

"My bikini. The one I was wearing when I first met him on the beach."

"Oh, that's sick," she says.

"He also left us something."

"What?"

"An envelope addressed to my mom. Inside were photos of me. From everywhere. School. With friends. Boyfriends. He'd been following me for months."

"Wow," Maggie says.

"And that's why I was sent here. And why I had to lie about who I am. I'm hiding."

"So, are you going to hide out forever?" Riley asks.

I tell them the rest. About Vincent following my friends. About the break-ins at the rehab centers. About Vincent showing up at the surf tournament and later in Miami. About the nationwide search for the next Abby Johnston. About the photos of Tommy and Brooklyn with their heads blown off.

About going back to the club to see Vincent.

About the girl's death.

"That's why I lied. I wanted everyone to hate me because I need to protect you. Protect Eastbrooke. Because if he finds out where I am, he'll come here. And it won't be pretty."

"What are you going to do now?" Maggie asks.

"I'm fighting back. I'll probably end up kidnapped or dead but, hopefully, he'll end up in jail." I shut my eyes tightly, not loving my odds. I look directly at the reporters. "Either way, you'll have another story."

Cooper escorts the press out of the room while I get hugs and words of encouragement from my friends.

Riley wraps an arm around my shoulder and whispers, "You told me the truth. Mostly."

"Yeah, I did."

"I got it all done," Annie says, handing me back my phone. "You should have told us."

"At first, I didn't know you well enough to trust you. Once I did, I was afraid to put you in danger."

"You were going to take me home to meet your parents," Dawson says flatly. "Your *real* parents?"

"Yeah. I was going to tell you the truth on the plane."

"And I fucked it up. I'm sorry."

"Which really made me afraid to trust any of you."

"Okay," Cooper says, heading back into the room. "I think you should all either go dance or head out. It's getting late."

Dallas narrows his eyes at me. "Coach Steele is being *awfully* helpful."

"After the Miami incident, he was brought in to babysit me. Be my bodyguard."

Maggie gives me a smile and a wink. "Lucky girl. Have a

good Christmas break. Be safe. And I'll miss you."

"I'll miss you too."

"You better be coming back to Eastbrooke."

"If I can't, at least now you'll know why."

Dallas joins the hug. "If you don't, you better stay in touch."

"I will. I promise." I turn to Riley. "Hey, can I catch a ride to the hotel with you and Ariela?"

Riley looks around, seemingly surprised. "Where's Aiden?"

I put my head down. I don't want to say it. My heart hurts.

"Is he meeting you at the hotel?"

"He walked out and didn't want me to follow him."

Riley shakes his head. "Why would he do that?"

"I don't know, Riley!" I snap.

"We'll give you a ride," Ariela says sweetly, comforting as always.

"Thank you. I'll meet you out front in a couple minutes."

As soon as everyone leaves the room, Cooper says, "I'm coming to the hotel with you. And you need to explain to me what really happened."

"Whitney was going to share something about Peyton. It was bad, Cooper. Something that should not have been shared. I couldn't let her do it."

"So you outed yourself for a friend?"

"Yeah, I guess so. It just all happened so fast. In retrospect, I should have confessed to having an affair with you or something like that. We could have dealt with it a whole lot easier. I mean, big deal if you got fired and I got expelled. I didn't tell you this, but I was going to tell Aiden the entire truth tonight as soon as we left the dance. I guess it was what was on my mind. And you don't need to come to the hotel. I'll be fine there. Just meet me at my loft on Monday morning, as planned."

"Look, I know you want to call the shots. I get it. I like your bravery and your boldness, but you need to listen to me and do what I say."

"What do you want me to do?"

"Let me guard you twenty-four seven. I believe it's in your best interest. At least until we know if this is contained."

"You're probably right."

His eyes get big and he laughs. "Did you really just agree with me?"

"Yeah, I did. I don't think I'll be in danger at the hotel. Even if it gets out, Vincent won't know where I am. Everyone else is staying at another hotel near here. It's where all the parties are. Riley and Aiden wanted us to be somewhere . . . nicer . . ." I sigh, thinking about the amazingly romantic night I was supposed to have.

"What's your room number?" Cooper asks, getting out his phone.

"Twelve fourteen."

He calls the hotel and makes himself a reservation, securing an adjacent room. "Don't leave the hotel room without me."

"Aiden walked out when he heard the truth. If he's gone when I get to the hotel, I'll want to go home. To my loft."

"Sounds reasonable. I need to tie up a few loose ends with the dean and break the news to Garrett."

"Do you have to?"

"He has computer experts who can monitor social media sites. They're skilled hackers, which may come in handy. We need to be sure you aren't compromised."

"Yeah, I guess you're right. Don't let him yell at you. It's not your fault."

As I leave, I can't help but glance back at the students dancing to a slow song and wish Aiden and I were still out there.

EPIC, WEED-INDUCED DREAM.
MIDNIGHT

RILEY HANDS ME a flask the minute I get into their limo.

I shake my head. "I'm okay."

"How did you speak so calmly about almost being kidnapped, the stalker, and possibly dying?" Ariela asks.

"It's been four months since it happened. I suppose I'm just used to the facts. I hope I didn't ruin your night."

Riley grins at me. "Some of the events were a bit unexpected but, you gotta admit, it's been an interesting evening."

Ariela nods in agreement. "Was it hard for you to lie?"

"At first, it was easy. All I was really lying about was my parents. But the more I got to know people, became friends with them, the harder it got. That was another reason why I almost didn't come back to Eastbrooke after Thanksgiving break. I felt like I was being eaten from the inside out. I love you guys. It was killing me."

She pulls me into a hug. "I'm glad we know the truth."

My phone starts buzzing. I look down at it, hoping it's Aiden. Instead, I see the name of someone I don't want to deal with.

"Shit, I better take this," I say. "Hey, Garrett."

"What the *hell* were you *thinking*?!"

I hold the phone out as Garrett continues to yell at me. About Vincent finding me. About how stupid what I did was. How he's going to come get me himself.

Riley and Ariela start making funny faces at me.

It feels so good to have them on my side. To not have to hide all this.

I start to laugh.

Loudly.

Like I'm high.

I used to wish I were dreaming. That this whole thing was just some epic, weed-induced dream. But I'm glad it's not. Because I would have missed out on making some amazing friends.

"What the hell are you *laughing* about?!" I hear.

I put the phone back up to my ear. "Nothing. I'm with some friends."

"Did you hear anything I said?"

"Kinda hard not to. Are you done?"

"*Excuse* me?!"

"I don't need to be yelled at, Garrett," I say calmly. "I know what I did was not good for me, but it is what it is. I can't change it. Why don't you take some of that passion and use it to motivate your computer wizards. The dean threatened students with expulsion if they didn't comply, but I need keywords relating to my family and all the students' social media monitored. If anyone posts anything, it needs to be deleted somehow. I need major damage control. Vincent cannot find out about Eastbrooke."

"You know you're not going to be able to go back there now."

"I know I can't. Um, I have to go. I'll text you," I tell him because I don't want Riley and Ariela to hear what I need to say.

Me: *Just because I can't go back doesn't mean I don't want to protect the school. Please monitor it. Please, do whatever computer magic you can to keep it and my friends safe.*

We pull up to the hotel and Riley says, "What are you going to do about Aiden?"

"That all depends on if he's here or not. If he is, I'll try to talk to him. The bitch of it all is that I was going to tell him the truth tonight as soon as we got to our room. Tonight was supposed to be *the* night, and I wanted him to know before we were together like that."

"We understand why you lied, Keatyn. Aiden will too."

"Do you think so? The look on his face. The way he held his hand up, telling me not to follow him. It killed me."

"If he loves you the way I think he does, you'll work it out."

"I hope so."

"Don't forget, we're doing brunch in the morning."

"I won't. We have a lot to plan. Damian decided to do a different song for the video. This one will be a lot more fun, I think."

We take the elevator upstairs, Riley and Ariela getting out on the eighth floor. I get the keycard out of my clutch as the elevator dings.

I walk slowly to my room.

No. *Our* room.

The room that was going to change our relationship; take it to a deeper level.

I'm afraid. Afraid I'll open the door and see that his stuff is gone.

While I'm contemplating if I should go in, the door bursts open and Aiden comes out, carrying a bunch of bags.

My heart sinks.

Or breaks, maybe.

"Aiden," I say breathlessly.

"We need to talk," he says in a very serious, he's-so-done-with-me tone.

All of a sudden, I want to run.

Run away.

Run out of the hotel.

It was bad enough to see him walk out.

It's going to be even worse to hear him say it.

"You walked out when you heard the truth about who I am."

He narrows his eyes at me. "I saw Peyton leaving in tears with Whitney's computer. I went to check on her. It was pretty obvious that whatever Whitney was going to say was about Peyton, not you."

"You're leaving, though," I manage to squeak out, my eyes focusing on his bags.

"These are Peyton's bags. Remember, we let her put them in our room?"

"Oh, yeah."

"Peyton told me what Whitney was about to do. You outed yourself for her. I appreciate that," he says flatly.

This feels so surreal. I want him to hug me. Tell me he doesn't care who I am.

But he doesn't.

"I need to take her bags upstairs. Come with me. I know she'd like to thank you."

"Where are *your* bags?"

"Still in the room," he says, giving me half a flicker of hope.

"Oh."

"It's been a rough night," he says.

"Yeah."

"How did you get here? Is the dance over already?" He looks down at his watch and shakes his head. "I went out to check on her and found her bawling hysterically. She wouldn't tell me why. Just kept crying, rocking, and clutching the computer. Saying she was going to have to tell Mom and Dad. How disappointed they would be. She hadn't told me, but our parents decided to come tonight instead of tomorrow to help take our stuff to New York. Anyway, when we got back here, she told us everything. Half of what she said was hard to understand, but we got the gist of it."

"Riley gave me a ride. How did your parents take it?"

"Better than I did." He hangs his head in shame. "I went to Eastbrooke to take care of her. I should have known."

"It's not your fault, Aiden."

"I was coming back to the dance to get you right after I delivered her bags."

"You were?"

"Boots, I told you that I'd never walk away again. I'm a man of my word," he says sternly. Clearly insinuating that I'm the opposite of that.

I'm a liar.

"You lied for my sister, but you didn't tell the truth. I know you were acting. That wasn't the real you."

"Jake said the same thing."

"Was everyone mad?"

"At first. But I told them the truth. You looked really mad. I was afraid you wouldn't ever talk to me again."

The serious look returns to his face.

"Let's not do this in the hall. Why don't you come with me to deliver the bags, then we'll come back here to . . . discuss."

"Um, okay. Is Peyton doing okay?"

As we head to the elevator, he says, "She's better now."

I nod as he hits the button for the floor above us.

He's silent in the elevator.

My heart is pounding. I feel like I'm being pulled under by a riptide.

Like I'm treading water but losing the fight.

Waiting to drown.

I can picture it. We'll talk to his sister, go back to our room, and he'll tell me that he hates liars. That I should have told him. That we're through.

WE EXIT THE elevator and I follow him down the hall.

He's walking fast.

A man on a mission.

Wanting to get it over with.

Peyton's mom opens the door and immediately throws her arms around me, dragging me into their suite.

Peyton is sitting on the bed. Her dad is looking somber on the couch.

"Thank you for what you did for Peyton," her mom says.

"Uh, you're welcome," I reply.

I sit on the bed next to Peyton. Her eyes are red and swollen from crying and there's not a speck of mascara left on them. I give her a hug and whisper, "Did you really tell them the truth?"

She answers me out loud. "Yes. I told my family everything. It was the hardest thing I've ever had to do, but I feel so much better. It's such a relief not having that secret hanging over my head."

"We're very grateful you stopped Whitney from showing the pictures, though," Aiden's dad says.

A crazy and inappropriate thought flashes through my brain and I'm tempted to say he can thank me by giving me Aiden as payment.

"We're prepared for the worst." Peyton rocks on the bed, holding her knees to her chest. "I know it's not over. Whitney will have backup copies. Best case scenario, she goes to the dean. Worse case, she releases it to the press. We'll deal with the fallout of it together. And even though I told Damian about it, I'm sure this will be the end of us." She starts sobbing. "I can't ruin his career. And as soon as Whitney finds out we're together, there will be no stopping her."

"Whitney will not be a problem."

"What do you mean?" her dad asks. "Of course, she is. We'll have to worry about it for the rest of her life."

"Peyton, after you left, Whitney did try to threaten me, telling me that I couldn't stop her. That she has copies of the photos. But I told her that I could and would."

"How?"

I grin broadly, knowing that—for once—I used my inner mean girl for the greater good.

"I told her if any photos *ever* leaked out—if there was even a hint about them—that I'd release a few photos of my own. Only I wouldn't bother with the press. I'd send them to her parents. Her college. Her boss. Her husband. Her friends. Whoever is in her life at the time."

"What pictures?"

"She's been sending pics to Camden for years. Naked. Partially naked. In a recent one, she was even lying on Coach Steele's desk. She thought she could make him jealous. Make him fall in love with her, maybe. Who knows. But what matters is that Cam has kept *everything*. He felt guilty he didn't tell Dawson about them right away, so he decided to save them, just to use as proof should Dawson ever decide to marry her."

"Wow," Peyton says. "I knew she was obsessed with him. I didn't realize how much."

"Cam warned me that Whitney was planning something. He was worried about you, so he sent me the whole file. And he was right. She's been planning this since that day she sat alone at the lunch table."

"I pushed her."

"I told you it would backfire. There's a big difference between standing up for yourself and tearing someone else down."

Peyton shakes her head. "I'm so stupid."

"Chalk it up to a life lesson. Anyway, I had a couple of the photos on my phone and showed them to her."

"What did you say?"

"That I'd ruin her."

"You and Cam are really good friends. Thank you." She dabs her tears. "Do you really think it's over?"

I give her a hug and say, "Yes."

Aiden clears his voice.

The sound of it makes me jump.

"Since we seem to have everything covered here, Keatyn and I are going to head back to our room. We have some things of our own to discuss."

He gestures toward the door.

I give his parents and Peyton an awkward wave goodbye.

HE'S QUIET ON the elevator, on the walk down the hall, and as we go into our room.

After the dirt, the *No more lying,* and all the *You can tell me anything*s, I understand why.

He has every right to be mad. I should've listened to my heart and told him. I had so many opportunities, going all the way back to that day in the chapel.

"Before you say anything, I need to tell you something," I blurt out.

He takes my hand and leads me over to the chaise, where we both sit down.

He lets go of my hand but I quickly grab it again, clinging to it like a life raft.

"I'm sorry I lied to you. There's a lot more to the story. I understand if you hate me. I deserve it. But you have to know that there were *so* many times I wanted to tell you. Remember the slutty video? When Dawson and I broke up? I was taking him to meet my parents that weekend. I was going to tell him the truth. That's why I was so upset. I was more upset at myself for trusting the wrong person again than I was about us not dating. And that's why, after what happened with Chelsea, I forgave you but wouldn't see you. I couldn't lie to you anymore. I was in deep with you, and I knew that eventually I'd have to tell you, and that you'd hate me for lying. But then you brought me dirt and told me our pasts didn't matter."

Tears stream down my face, feeling cold against my flushed cheeks. "You have no idea how deeply that touched me. And it's why I let you come to St. Croix. I wasn't planning to go back to school. I didn't get closure with B. Everything with him—especially how I had to leave—has been so up the air and I didn't want to do that to you. I was going to give you closure, then send you back to school. And that's why I've been so tired all the time. At night, I'm either learning how to defend myself, or I'm flying back to California to mess with him, or I'm having online business meetings in an attempt to take over his company. It's not my friend who was being stalked and almost got kidnapped. It was me." I stop and mutter, "Shit."

Then I stand up and grab my clutch off the bed.

"What are you doing?" Aiden asks.

I pull out a piece of paper and hold it up in front of him. "This is the script I've been working on. In it, instead of truth-vomiting, I eloquently explain everything to you. I couldn't have sex with you until you knew."

I drop the piece of paper on the chaise, wondering why I'm even bothering.

He's not going to forgive me.

I might as well just grab my bags and go.

But he starts reading my script aloud.

"THE SETTING: HOTEL SUITE AFTER WINTER FORMAL.

AIDEN

(Opening a bottle of champagne)

KEATYN

(Lighting all the votive candles he thoughtfully brought)

(They kiss)

(But then she looks nervous)

I need to tell you something.

AIDEN

(Sits on the edge of the bed)

What?

KEATYN

(Stands in front of him)

I've been lying to you. Actually, I've been lying to everyone about something. And I need you to know.

                          AIDEN

                   (Looks concerned)
                        Okay.

                         KEATYN

    I came to Eastbrooke because I was being
    stalked. My last name isn't Monroe. I'm
    Keatyn Douglas. And my mom doesn't work
     in oil and gas. But she is in France.
        And her name is Abby Johnston.

                          AIDEN
                  (Stands up in shock)"

Aiden stares at the script for a few moments then slowly sets it down. I can tell he's thinking; probably trying to figure out the nicest way to tell me to fuck off.

Instead, he stands up, takes two big steps toward me, and brushes a tear off my cheek. "Life hasn't been following your scripts. You told me that once."

"No, it hasn't."

"If it had worked out the way you planned—if you'd followed your script—right now is the point where life would have deviated from it."

"You wouldn't have stood up in shock?"

"No," he says, caressing my face. "I would have said, *Baby, I already knew.*"

"You what?! What do you mean?!"

"I mean I've known for quite a while who you really are."

"How?!"

"That day at the chapel, when you told me about your friend. I don't know. I just felt like you were talking about yourself. So I started googling stuff. The name Keatyn, California, stalker, famous parents. Somehow, eventually, I put in the right mix of words. About ten pages into an image search, I came across a photo of you and your mom. It was from a kids' awards show when you were probably twelve or thirteen."

"You've known this whole time and you let me lie to you?"

"Yeah, Boots, I did."

"Why?"

"Because I wanted to be the kind of guy you could trust. It's why I backed off. Why I told Riley about Dawson. I didn't want to see you hurt anymore. It's why I've told you *so* many times that you can tell me anything. That you could trust me. What I didn't realize before was that I needed to earn that trust. We had to build a strong foundation. I'm really glad you were planning to tell me tonight."

"But when you put your hand up and told me not to follow, I thought we were over, that you hated me."

"I could never hate you. I could tell by the look on Peyton's face that something was really wrong. I held up my hand to let you know that I'd take care of it. That you didn't need to come. I figured it was just some stupid mean girl thing between her and Whitney. I had no idea it would be so . . . involved. Or take so long." He takes my hands and pulls me back to sit on the chaise with him. His face looks similar to the way it did when he walked out. Apparently, this is his concerned look, not his *I hate you* look. "There's nothing you could tell me that would make me hate you. You need to have faith in us. We're going to survive the kiln."

"I was coming to find you. You made me promise that I always would."

He smiles at me. It's a sweet, loving, blazing smile. One that turns my whole night around.

"You told me that didn't count."

"I lied," I say, teasing him.

"Those reporters took pictures of you. Is the stalker going to find you? Will you have to leave Eastbrooke?"

"I don't know. The dean made everyone delete anything they put out on social media. I told the local reporters that they didn't really have much of a story. That my mom and I have had different last names my whole life. I told them if they signed a non-disclosure agreement that I would give them two stories. One they could use now and one they could use, um, later."

"What do you mean, *later*?"

"I told them the truth about the stalker. Told them they couldn't use the story until either he was in jail or I was dead."

Aiden shuts his eyes tightly. "Dead?"

"Yes. You might as well know that now. If he gets me and no one can rescue me, or if I can't get away, I'm pretty sure he will kill me."

"What story can they have now?"

"Who Damian's new girlfriend is. We have a lot of work to do before then, though."

"Like what?"

"Rework Peyton's social media. Make people think she's just from California. With her age, they could think she's in college. Vincent—that's the stalker's name—knows Damian and I are friends. We don't want him to put two and two together. That's the other reason I didn't want to go back to Eastbrooke after Thanksgiving break. I didn't want to put any of my friends in danger. Because he's about to blow. And when he does, it's going to be ugly."

"Isn't there something you can do, legally?"

"We have to prove he's stalking me. Threatening me.

And, even then, about all you can do is get a restraining order. They said if I went away that he'd forget about me. But he hasn't. You know that nationwide search for the next Abby Johnston?"

"Yeah."

"That's him."

"Wow. He wanted someone to tell him where you were? Is that why you freaked out and told Annie you didn't want to be an actress?"

"Yes. I didn't want him to find me."

"Are you safe here? Now?"

"Yes. Even if word got out. Even if he somehow found out about Eastbrooke and the formal, he wouldn't know I'm here. Everyone thinks we're staying at the hotel where all the parties are."

"We were smart to come here then?"

"Yeah, we were."

"So, can we go back to enjoying our night? Tonight was supposed to be all about us."

"It was an amazing night. Perfect, really."

"Come on. Let's start over," he says with a grin, pulling me out of the room and taking me down the elevator to the lobby.

He lets the door to the elevator shut without getting out, pushes the button for our floor, then pins me in the corner and gives me a steamy kiss.

"I had a great time tonight," he says. "But, I will admit, I've been thinking a lot about what will happen when we get back to our room."

I kiss him deeply and say exactly what my heart feels. "You know the heartbreakingly beautiful love?"

"Yeah?"

"I thought it happened tonight."

"The heartbreaking part is never going to happen, Boots." He wags the key in my face. "And, just so you know, when we get some privacy, the kisses are gonna be a whole lot hotter."

We barely get in the room before he has me pinned against the bathroom door, kissing me hard. Running his hands roughly across my body, all the pent up things he's been feeling coming out in his touch. And the freedom I finally feel from his knowing the truth has mixed up inside me to form something practically combustible.

His hands are behind my back, searching for my zipper.

"Side," I manage to say between kisses.

His hands dance around my cleavage, finally coming to rest on the zipper.

A quick *zip* sends my dress falling to the floor.

I'm doing my best to get him naked as fast as possible.

Unbuttoning his shirt.

Frantically pulling it off.

Unzipping his pants.

Once we're down to just our underwear, he picks me up and carries me to the bed, where he quickly spreads my knees apart and kisses his way down my stomach.

He pulls off my thong as I push off his sliders.

The Titan is ready for action.

I'm tilting my hips toward him, my body begging.

The tip of the Titan is touching the damp, steamy edges of the exact place I want it to go, and I'm waiting for him to move his fingers out of the way and plunge it deep inside me.

Aiden takes a deep breath.

Then stops.

"Boots? Do you want to?"

"Of course I want to."

"I know, but . . ."

"But what?"

He rolls off me. "I just want it to be perfect. The perfect night. When we look back on it, I don't want you to remember crying. I don't want you to remember questioning my feelings or thinking I walked out on you. And after seeing your script for tonight . . ."

"You read ahead?"

"Yeah."

I roll over on my side and run my hand down his chest. "In my script, we did it."

"And it was a perfect moment where we both knew it was right. I want that for you. For us."

"Nothing about us has ever followed a script."

"I don't want it to. And, deep down, I don't think you want it to, either."

"So, what do you wanna do?"

"How about a bath?"

"No sliders?"

He grins. "No sliders."

My eyes follow his naked butt as he goes into the bathroom and turns on the water.

A few minutes later, he brings me out a fluffy robe. I snuggle up to it. "It's warm."

"They have a towel heater."

"Nice."

I follow him into the bathroom and add a bunch of bubbles to the bath.

ONCE WE'RE IN the tub and I'm leaning against his chest, I say, "I'm tired, Aiden."

"I know you are, baby," he says, kissing my shoulder. "Just think. Tomorrow at this time, we'll be back at the loft."

"A day of relaxation before I start to work."

"Do I get to come watch you film?"

"You watched every one of my play practices."

"That's because you're amazing."

"It had to be boring."

"It wasn't."

"I'll let you come if you promise me two things: you won't get jealous and you promise to leave if you get bored."

"Deal," he says, cupping warm water in his hand and pouring it across my chest.

I run my fingers lazily down his arm and notice something.

"Aiden, did you take your wish bracelet off because it didn't look good with your suit?"

He holds up his wrist, chuckles, and shakes his head. "Well, I'll be damned. You were right."

"What do you mean?"

"You told me it'd fall off once I got my wish."

"What did you wish for?"

He pushes my hair off my shoulders and kisses my neck. Then his mouth is against my ear. "I wished that someday you'd trust me enough to tell me the truth."

Sunday, December 18th

THE STORY OF US.
9:30AM

I'M STILL TRYING to wrap my head around the fact that Aiden knew I was lying. It all makes sense now, though. His wanting to be my friend. His sneaky ways of getting to know me. I thought it meant he wasn't interested in me, but what it really meant is that he loves me.

I know he loves me.

I was going to say it to him last night. And he knows it, since he read the script.

Just let things settle down a little. Don't plan it. Just tell him when it feels right.

I think about when might be the perfect time.

Then I frown.

"What's the frown for?" Aiden asks.

"Oh, I was just thinking."

"About last night?"

"Yeah."

"And you're disappointed?"

"A little, yeah. I thought it was going to be perfect."

"It was perfect, until Whitney pulled you on stage."

I smile. "You're right. It was."

Aiden rolls onto his side to face me, gently trailing his finger down my thigh. "Maybe instead of writing the script and getting sad when people don't follow along . . ."

"You remember me telling you that at rehearsal?"

"Boots, pretty much everything you've ever said to me is permanently ingrained in my mind. It's all the story of us."

"As opposed to my scripts, which are the story of me?"

"Exactly. What if we write new ones together?"

"Like, collaborate? Hmm. That might be a good idea. I mean, especially since most of my old scripts were already cast."

"Brooklyn?"

"Yeah. There's still a lot there that's unfinished. At least now you understand why I can't see him. Remember Labor Day when I went to his tournament and how upset I was?"

"You told me that he was stupid. Then you said that you were stupid."

"I was. In lots of ways. It was bad enough to watch him sneak into a cabana and get it on with some girl, but what was worse is that Vincent, the stalker, was there. If Brooklyn hadn't done what he did, I wouldn't have left. I would've been a sitting duck. I went with no security and didn't tell anyone I was going. I really didn't think Vincent would fly across the country on the off chance I'd be there. It was a big blow, both to my confidence and my heart."

I start to say something else, but Aiden kisses me hard.

"What was that for?"

"I don't need to hear any more. I get it."

"What do you get?"

"I need to teach you how to live life unscripted, because we're going to be better than anything you ever imagined." He lets his comment hang there for a moment, then says,

"So, what are you going to do about the stalker, now? Will you be able to go back to Eastbrooke?"

"Definitely not. That's why I lied on stage. So everyone would hate me and, hopefully, forget about me over break. I want all my friends at Eastbrooke to stay safe."

"Do you think he would go there?"

"Yes, I do. He went to Oregon where Cush—he's the guy I lost my virginity to—moved. He visited his school and asked if they had any new students. Any new girls, specifically. He even went to Cush's house and knocked on his door. Thankfully, Cush didn't know anything. So, even though it was hard to just leave my friends without telling them what happened, I know it was in their best interests. And that's part of why I didn't want to tell you the truth. I didn't want you to be in danger. After B won the tournament, a photo was delivered to him. One photoshopped to show him being shot, his brains blown out of the back of his head. It was awful. Vincent sent a similar one of Tommy to my mom."

Aiden studies my face then runs his hand down the side of it. "You're amazing, you know that? I knew who you were, and surmised that you were the one who was being stalked, but I didn't imagine it to be this bad. How have you been handling it all?"

"My acting skills have come in handy. But those times in the chapel were when I couldn't hide it. I couldn't act. Not with you."

"After that girl was killed, Riley said you told him that you were being stalked. Something about a guy in Miami."

"That was Vincent, too. He showed up at the club because he heard Damian was doing a surprise performance. He made me dance with him. He'd gotten a tattoo just like mine, only on his wrist. When we were dancing, he rubbed his tattoo on mine. Said it was like our tattoos were making love. It was horrible. He was going to make me leave with him. Said he had a gun and would shoot Damian if I didn't go quietly."

"Were you going to go with him?"

"Probably. I was running my hands all over him, pretending like I was into dancing with him, but I was really frisking him. I had checked everywhere but his ankles when he rubbed the tattoo against me. I couldn't pretend anymore. I'm sure it was my horrified look that made Riley knock him down. When I told Dallas that I was afraid he had a gun, he panicked because of his situation."

"His situation?"

"Yeah. His dad is a senator and has received threats against his family. The story in his home state is that Dallas was arrested for drugs then sent to military school. Instead, he came to Eastbrooke. Apparently, Eastbrooke's campus is very secure."

"So, if you're supposed to be in hiding, how are you going to be in the movie?"

"What did I tell you about the role?"

"That you got a really small part in a really big movie."

"It's the third *Trinity* movie, *Retribution*. I play Trinity's daughter, who gets kidnapped."

Aiden's eyes get big.

"I know, right? It's crazy if you think about it. I was going to have to leave Eastbrooke in March to shoot the action scenes. They got the cast to sign non-disclosure agreements so that word wouldn't leak out about me being in the movie until it was officially announced. Although, lately, things have not been going according to plan."

"Tell me about your plan. I want to help."

"No. You can't help."

"I want to."

"That's part of why I didn't want you to know, Aiden. I'm very serious about this. You have to promise me, that no matter what, you won't get involved."

"I can't promise that."

"Then I can't see you anymore." I turn away from him, my eyes quickly filling with tears. We made it through all of this. All the lies. But this is a deal breaker.

"Keatyn," he says, trying to turn my face toward him.

I hold my chin firm, then get up. "I'm sorry. I have to go."

He grabs ahold of my arms and looks deep into my eyes. "What aren't you telling me?"

"I told you everything."

"No, you haven't."

"I may look fine on the surface, Aiden, but there's only so much I can take." I pull out of his arms and start shoving stuff into my bag.

And crying.

He grabs me again and pushes me against the wall.

He's strong, but I know I can take him if I have to.

"I don't want to hurt you, Aiden."

He looks like he's going to try to kiss me, but he pulls me into a tight hug instead. Just like he did that night outside my dorm.

Which makes me cry harder.

"You've got to tell me why you're crying," he whispers. "Stop trying to deal with it all yourself."

"Let go of me."

"Will you tell me?"

"Yes."

He lets go of me, so I grab my phone, scroll to a photo, and hand it to him.

"This is why I'm leaving. I can't take having one more person I care about threatened. Zoom in. Look closely at his head. He's in danger because he said he loved me. I can't be seen with you. I can't be with you if you won't promise me!"

Aiden plops down on the bed and studies the photo. "That's horrible," he finally says. "You'll seriously leave if I don't promise?"

"Yes. In all situations regarding the stalker, security, and safety, it's imperative that you do exactly as I say. Not what you think you should do."

He frowns but says, "Fine. I promise to defer to you regarding those issues."

"You always ask me if I trust you, but do you trust me, Aiden? Aside from the stalker issues, if I have an acting career in the future, you'll have to trust me. You'll have to believe me over the tabloids. Because they will say that I'm having an affair with my costar. That our chemistry is amazing. Or that I'm doing my hot bodyguard."

"Will you always tell me the truth? From now on?"

"Yes. In fact, speaking of hot bodyguards . . ."

"Do you have one of those I don't know about?"

"Actually, yes. Coach Steele. Cooper. He was brought in after the Miami incident."

"You've told a lot of lies."

"Surprisingly, I haven't told that many, and I've only lied when absolutely necessary."

I dig through my purse, pull out a little journal, and hand it to him. "It's my Lie List."

Lie List

- I'm Keatyn Monroe. (My name was legally changed though, I think?)

- I didn't recognize you as the goalie. (Aiden)
- B's name is Bradley. (Riley)
- My parents moved to France. (everyone)
- I left my Mercedes at home because of the snow. (Dawson)
- I got in trouble at home. (Annie)
- My parents deleted my social media. (Riley) (Annie)
- When I synced my new phone it deleted all my photos. (Annie)
- No one has ever said I remind them of Abby Johnston. (Annie)(Riley's mom)
- My friend was stalked. (Aiden)
- We sold our house in California. (Dawson)
- I'm a Rockette and my name is Maggie. (Allan the driver)
- My Mom's ex boyfriend was stalking me. (Riley) (Dallas) (Senator McMahon and assorted secret service)
- My friend had a scare. (Aiden)
- Garrett is my uncle. (everyone)
- I went on a backstage type tour for school, came home and told my mom I wanted to

write a fairy-tale movie. (Aiden – on how I got into script writing.)

- My mom is retired but used to work in oil and gas. (Whitney)
- I don't want to be an actress. I want to be a doctor. (Riley's mom) (Drama teacher) Went on to add: I want to be a pediatric doctor specializing in children's cancer, because my cousin died from it.
- I want to be a CIA agent. (advisor) (the dean)
- I want to major in International Studies. (college recruiter)
- That I mentioned that I knew Damian when they were watching his video. (Peyton)
- That I didn't think Damian hooked up with groupies. (Aiden)
- That Peyton and Damian weren't skinny dipping. (Aiden)
- I'm going to France to be with my mom. (Aiden)
- That I probably wouldn't like To Maddie,

with Love. (Aiden)

- That I'm at an all-girls school in the middle of nowhere. (Sander)
- That Cooper is one of Tommy's stunt men. (Sander/friends)
- That Tommy and Brooklyn okayed my using their vehicles. (Car detailer)
- I saw my uncle and talked to him about my mom. (Aiden)
- My mom is working on oil and gas leases in the Ukraine. (Aiden)
- My mom's name is Kathryn Monroe. My stepdad's name is Tom Hart. (Aiden and his parents)
- I lied about being stalked. (Riley)
- I came to Eastbrooke because I wanted to see if I could act. To see if I could pretend to be someone else. I lied because I could. (everyone)

When he finishes reading, he looks up at me and smirks. "So, you *did* recognize me as the goalie that day in the cafeteria, huh?"

"Out of all the lies I've told you, that's the one you're focusing on?"

He pushes me down on the bed, lies on top of me, and

talks into my neck. "You liked me."

"I didn't know you."

"Still," he says, his lips kissing slowly down my chest.

"You were too cute for your own good." I move my hands down his back, loving the feel of his weight on top of me.

"Now that I have you under my control," he says with a charming grin. "I'll ask you about the other lies."

"Like what?"

"My name is on the list more than anyone else's."

"That's because you ask so many questions."

"Tell me who Garrett is."

"Garrett Smith. He owns a personal security firm. The best in the industry."

"Damian hooked up with groupies and skinny dipped with my sister? Those weren't lies to protect your identity."

"Those were little white lies. Like when you told me I was beautiful even when I was really a crying, snotty mess."

"That wasn't a lie."

I roll my eyes at him. "Uh, huh. Whatever."

"Aberly/Abernathy and Fritz?"

"Abby and Tommy. Damian almost spilled the beans."

"When you said you saw your uncle. That's when you went to the club and danced? Then, the next week, the girl got murdered and you went back?"

"Yes."

"I told you that you would fight back. I shouldn't have said that. I had no idea."

"I'm going to continue to fight back."

"Just know that I'll help in any way you'll let me."

"That's what I don't think you understand, Aiden. You've already helped me more than you know. All the times you've listened to me when I was having a meltdown.

Your hugs. The sunsets. They all helped me prepare."

"Prepare?"

"For the showdown. It happens in every story. You know, the battle. The fight. The climax. Do or die. I needed my time at Eastbrooke to figure out some things. To figure out myself."

"I think—" he starts to say, only to be interrupted by my phone ringing.

I grab my phone off the nightstand and look at the caller ID.

"It's Cooper. I need to answer." I hit accept and say, "Hey, Cooper."

"What time is brunch?"

"I haven't heard from Riley yet, but let's plan on eleven-thirty."

"Sounds good. I assume since I didn't hear from you that Aiden took the news well?"

"Yeah, he did. Have you talked to Garrett? Do you know if things were contained?"

"He's my next call."

I end the call and peek at the clock. "I suppose we should get ready."

"I'm gonna go hop in the shower," Aiden says. "Care to join me?"

I glance at the clock again then say, "Definitely."

MEET ME AT THE BEACH.
BRUNCH

COOPER KNOCKS ON our door five minutes before we're supposed to meet Peyton, Damian, Ariela, and Riley for brunch.

Aiden answers the door as I run the brush through my hair one last time and gloss my lips.

"So, what did Garrett say?" I ask Cooper as we're walking down the hall toward the elevators.

"So far, so good. There were a few students who made mention of it, but his computer gurus immediately sent them messages with viruses. As soon as they opened them, Garrett's team got control of their accounts and deleted them. They were up for a very short time. We still have two teams on Vincent, watching him. Just to be sure."

"Is the school calendar something the public can view?"

"No," Aiden says. "You have to log in to see it, remember?"

"Oh, yeah. So he wouldn't know that we're out for Christmas break."

"That's why we're watching him," Cooper says.

My phone buzzes with a text.

Tommy: I just got the revised script for this week. Would you like to get together tonight, have dinner, do a read-through?

Me: I would love that. I'll have Cooper with me. And Aiden too, if that's okay.

Tommy: Aiden is the God of All Hotties?

Me: You better not call him that.

Tommy: How about Goah for short?

Me: Not funny.

Tommy: I'm at Matt's apartment. You remember the address?

Me: Yes. I'm having brunch with Damian. He's staying there this week, I think.

Tommy: That's right. Him, his girlfriend, and her parents. Hmm. Might not be the best place to rehearse.

Me: I have an idea. Have Allan drop you off at Grand

Central Station. If you're being followed by someone, they won't be able to park quickly enough to follow you. Unless there are two of them.

Tommy: *There's just one guy.*

Me: *Get dropped off at the main entrance. Cooper will text you where to meet him. He'll make sure it's safe to bring you to my loft.*

Tommy: *You have a loft?*

Me: *Yeah. I bought one at the beginning of the school year so I'd have somewhere to go when we didn't have school and on weekends and stuff. I needed a home base.*

Tommy: *You needed a home. We never even thought of that.*

Me: *It's okay. The loft is sort of a secret. Garrett wanted it to be a safe place for me to go if I needed to run. Leave school. That sort of thing. I'm really excited for you to see it.*

Tommy: *I can't wait.*

Damian and Riley are already talking animatedly when we get to the table.

"Coach Steele," Peyton says, "what are you doing here?"

"Um, he's sorta my bodyguard."

The look on Peyton's face is priceless. I can tell she's thinking exactly what I thought when I first met Cooper. *He can guard my body anytime.*

"So he *really was* teaching you how to fight," Peyton states.

"Yeah, so I can protect myself."

We take our seats, order brunch, and then Damian starts in. "Okay, so we switched the song for the video. This is a really fun, upbeat song called *Meet Me at the Beach*."

"Let's hear it," I say. "Then we can brainstorm about the video."

Damian sings quietly.

"Sun shining on your face.
Ice cream at our favorite place.
Blonde hair blowing in the breeze.
Baby, spend your summer days with me.

Laying in the sand,
Drinking, getting tan.
Kissing in these heat waves.
Got my Ray-Bans.
Laughing, holding hands.
Crashin' on the beach for days.

I'm thinking 'bout . . .
Venice and Malibu
It's only me and only you.
I love it; you're all I really need.
Baby, meet me at the beach.

Cotton candy, Ferris wheel,
Crazy love is what I feel.
Blasting out our favorite tunes,
Late nights sneaking in your room.

Moonlight on the shore,
Always wanting more.
You light me up like a bonfire.
You make me hit the floor.
That's what lips are for.
Summer nights, we're getting higher.

I'm thinking 'bout . . .
Venice and Malibu

It's only me and only you.
I love it; you're all I really need.
Baby, meet me at the beach.

When it's just us.
I feel the rush of every ocean wave.
And after a kiss,
I never imagined it as good as this.

I'm thinking 'bout . . .
Venice and Malibu
It's only me and only you.
I love it; you're all I really need.
Baby, meet me at the beach."

"Oh my gosh, Damian!" I screech. "That's adorable! I love it! Venice and Malibu. It's only me and only you. It's so cute!"

"I love it too," Peyton agrees. "It makes me want summer to start now."

"It kinda reminds me of an old Beach Boys song. Like an endless summer."

"So, what did you have in mind for the video?" Riley asks Damian, getting back to business.

"Well, that's just it. I'm not sure. It's not like we can film on the beach here in New York in the winter."

"We'll have to make our own beach," Riley says. "Wait, I know!"

"What?" Ariela asks. I can tell she's loving watching Riley's creative process. And that makes me happy. I want him with a girl who knows how gifted he is.

"When we were at the Hamptons this summer, my mom, Grandma, and aunts were watching these old surfer movies from the 60s."

"Frankie and Annette?" I ask. "I love those. They were so bad they were good. The romance was sweet, but the special effects were horrible. It was so obvious they weren't actually surfing."

"That's exactly what I mean. Let's do it like that. Kitschy. Funny. Retro cool."

"I love it," Damian says. "We want it to be something different than your typical party on the beach, spring break crazy video."

"The song reminds me of your date in the play," Aiden adds. "The one that never seems to end."

"You're right," I say, squeezing his hand under the table. "Only, this is the summer that never ends."

"You had rolling backgrounds for the play," Riley says. "There was a beach, an amusement park, even a big moon. All we'd need is surfboards mounted on springs. Do you think the school would let us borrow the sets?"

"We could rent or buy them from the school," Damian says. "We have a budget."

"Money talks," Riley replies. Then he turns to Cooper. "Do you have the dean's number?"

"I do. Would you like me to make a call?"

"Yeah. We'd need to pick them up this week," Riley says. "That way when everyone gets back in town, we can start shooting."

"That's cutting it pretty close," Damian states.

"We can do it," Riley says confidently.

"What about you, Keatyn? Can you do it?" Damian asks me. "Please."

I glance at Cooper, who shakes his head no at me.

I think about it for a second.

I'm not sure how it will all work out, but a promise is a

promise. And let's face it. My original plan has unraveled and gone to shit. Might as well start on a new one.

"Yeah, I'm in."

STRANGLEHOLD HUGS.
7PM

I'M WAITING BY the door for Cooper to get back with Tommy. It feels like it's been forever since I've seen him.

The second he crosses the threshold, I leap into his arms and hug him with all my might.

He hugs me back then says with a laugh, "You and Gracie give the same stranglehold hugs."

I try not to cry, even though I feel like it. My emotions are so everywhere.

I finally let go of him, turn around, and sweep my arms out. "So, this is it. My loft."

Tommy looks around, taking in the wood floors, brick walls, and arched ceiling beams. "The architecture is amazing, Keatyn. How did you find it?"

"I think it found me. I just happened to go online and saw it was for sale. It'd only been on the market for a few days. Aiden," I say, as he walks into the living room, "this is Tommy. Tommy Stevens, this is Aiden Arrington."

Tommy gives me a look. One that makes me think he's going to say something like *I thought his name was the God of all Hotties.*

But, fortunately, he shakes Aiden's hand instead. "Nice to meet you, Aiden. Keatyn says you've been a good friend to her at Eastbrooke. With everything she's been through, you don't know how much her mother and I appreciate that."

"I've just recently learned the extent of all of that. And you're welcome, sir. She means a lot to me."

Cooper, who made sure Tommy got here without being followed, jabs my side with his elbow, then raises his eyebrows and smirks at me like I should be embarrassed.

But I'm not.

I'm totally melting.

I smile at them both and say, "Come see the kitchen, Tommy. We'll get you a drink, show you the rest of the place, and then we can get started."

With a drink in hand, I give Tommy the tour. Cooper and Aiden stay in the kitchen, discussing what we're going to have for dinner.

I show Tommy the bedrooms, including the one he'll be sleeping in tonight. Cooper figured it'd be easiest, since we'll be working late.

"Which one is Aiden's?" Tommy asks teasingly.

I point to one of the bedrooms. The one where Aiden has been keeping his clothes. "He has a bunch of clothes in that one, *Dad*," I tease.

Tommy narrows his eyes at me and I spill my guts.

"Fine. He's sleeping in my room. But—"

"But what?"

"We haven't yet."

"Haven't had sex yet?"

I nod my head.

Tommy's eyes narrow further and he tilts his head. "Interesting."

"Why is that interesting?"

He shrugs. "Just is. You love him, don't you?"

"I do love him. I wanted to tell him after the dance, but then everything blew up. It's hard, Tommy. My life is so uncertain right now. I know you don't want to hear it, but things with Vincent are coming to a head. I can feel it. There's a real possibility that . . . it might not go well."

"Then you should tell him soon."

"But that doesn't make sense. I'm trying to make this easier on him. I don't know what will happen when it's over."

"Keatyn, no one knows what's going to happen. That's why you have to live life to its fullest, whether you have a stalker or not. That's why you make sure the people you love know you love them. So, if you get hit by a bus tomorrow, they will have known."

"I've been trying to protect him."

"You shouldn't. He loves you."

"How can you tell?"

"He laid out his feelings for you when he shook my hand. Men appreciate directness. Fathers appreciate it. It tells them the guy isn't just messing around." He looks at me and laughs. "Or not messing around, in this case."

"Tommy! That's not funny. Why don't I show you the upstairs?"

"Changing the subject doesn't change anything."

"I know," I say with a laugh.

WHEN WE GET to the top of the stairs, Tommy sees our Christmas tree.

"You even have a tree. How did you buy the place and furnish it all from school?"

"I had a lot of help. Sam, the guy who handles my money, took care of all the financial details. Garrett introduced me to a great interior designer who totally got my style. We talked on the phone and emailed pictures back and forth. Garrett installed the security. Really, my job has been to fill up my closet."

"I noticed it looks like your closet at home."

"After Dad died, Mom sold our house. She did one movie after another and said we didn't need it because we'd never be there anyway. We were always on location somewhere. Even when she filmed in LA, we leased a different place with each movie. When you let us move into your house, I finally had a place where I could leave my stuff and it'd be there when I got back. You did more than just become my stepdad, Tommy. You gave me a home."

"A home we basically kicked you out of after you were almost kidnapped."

"I left because I wanted to."

"Doesn't really help with the parental guilt," he says, running his hand through his thick, dark hair and taking a closer look at the tree. "Did the designer do the tree too? All the ornaments are things you love."

I smile broadly. "No, Aiden surprised me with all that a few weeks ago."

Tommy studies the tree some more. "He knows you well."

"All the ornaments have meaning. Like, to us."

Tommy chuckles and shakes his head. "You've known him for four months, and you have enough to fill a whole tree?"

The lights on the tree blur as my eyes fill with tears.

Because we have.

So many of my *Take my breath away* moments have been with Aiden.

"Why are you crying?" Tommy says quietly, moving to my side.

"I promised to give B another chance when I got my life back. I'm going to hurt Aiden no matter how it plays out. If

I die, he'll be hurt. If I choose B, he'll be hurt. Why did I have to meet someone so amazing when my life is such a mess?"

Tommy leads me over to the couch, where we both sit down. He pats my hand and says, "My life was a mess when I met your mother."

"Really?"

"Yes. I didn't have a stalker, but the woman I was seeing occasionally had just told me she was pregnant, I had just found out my dad had cancer, and I had just fired my long-time agent. I didn't even want to be on the movie set with your mom. My part in it was so small, it didn't seem worth my time. But Matt and I were going to start filming the first *Trinity* movie next, and the actor who was cast had to back out last minute. Matt asked me to do the cameo as a favor. He fed me a bunch of bullshit about how it'd show my softer side. About how your mom was romantic comedy box office gold. Honestly, the real reason I did it was to get the hell out of LA for a few weeks."

"But then you met her."

"But then I met her," he says dreamily. "In the midst of all my chaos, there she was. And even though we were both pretty smitten, it wasn't easy."

"It wasn't? I thought sparks flew, you took us to the ballet, and we lived happily ever after."

Tommy chuckles. "Not quite. We both had some big personal hurdles to jump over before the happily ever after happened. No offense—I loved you right away—but, not only was she a widow, she was a mom. Being with her meant taking on a kind of responsibility I never thought I'd have."

"You didn't want kids?"

"I very much wanted children, but I wanted a relationship like my parents'. A good, solid one based on love and trust. I was thirty-five when I met your mom. I had all but given up on that dream."

"Tommy, do you have another kid you haven't told us about?"

"No. Turns out the woman I was seeing just wanted to rope me into marriage. She liked my money more than she liked me."

"You have a good agent now. Although your dad didn't make it. I miss Grandpa."

"I miss him too. He got to spend time with the triplets before he passed, though, so that's comforting. I guess what I'm trying to say is what my mom always used to tell me when things didn't go the way I planned."

"She always says that things happen for a reason."

"Exactly. And she's right. Once I got through all that, my life was better than before. Because of you and your mom. The family we've created. My career skyrocketed to a whole other level with the *Trinity* series. It all worked out."

"You found your calm in the chaos," I say quietly, understanding exactly what he means.

"Is that a yoga thing?"

"No, it's finding one thing to focus on that gets you through."

"What are you focusing on?"

"Getting my family back. My life back. Truth? I was sort of excited to go to Eastbrooke where no one had expectations of who I should be."

"And?"

"I found out that it doesn't matter what my last name is. I'll always be Keatyn Douglas."

"Good," Tommy says, ruffling my hair. "I smell Italian food cooking."

"Aiden is a pretty good cook."

Tommy looks at me seriously. "I don't know when it will be, but I know you'll get your happily ever after, too."

I smile at him. "I hope so. Let's go eat. Then we have lines to practice."

SLOWLY LICKS HIS LIPS.
11PM

AFTER DINNER, COOPER and Aiden play pool while Tommy and I do a read through. I'm doing a good job of focusing until Aiden and Cooper start playing for money.

They joke around loudly and pretend to be pool sharks, both of them donning sunglasses.

"I think it's poker players who wear sunglasses," Tommy says, laughing with them. "Not pool players."

I'm not laughing with them.

Because this is serious.

Aiden is playing pool with sunglasses on.

The ones he had on with his leather jacket.

The night he used his tongue on me.

My body is responding to nothing more than the memory of it.

I consider locking Cooper and Tommy in their rooms so I can dance on the table for Aiden again.

Because I love his bad boy wild side.

Aiden, maybe because he's part god, seems to have the ability to morph into any role. Deal with any social situation. Get along with anyone. He can be the sexy bad boy one minute and the sweetest boy ever the next.

Right now, he's an irresistible combination of them both.

Or not.

I overhear Cooper say, "Is there something I should know about this pool table?"

Aiden can't contain his grin.

"He's grinning because you and I both suck at pool," I say quickly. "And, in case you can't tell, he likes to win."

"I don't suck. I'm just a little rusty," Cooper insists.

As he bends down to make a shot, Aiden looks over his glasses at me and purposefully, slowly licks his lips.

Tommy says to me, "This is when you're supposed to say, *I'm not your little girl anymore.*"

"Uh, what?"

Aiden chuckles, loving that he affects me the way he does. That he can control my body and thoughts with the single swipe of his tongue.

I shake my head and become John Trinity's daughter again. "*Dad*, I'm not your little girl anymore."

Tommy yawns. "I think it's time to call it a night even though you have more memorized than I do."

"You have way more lines. And most of mine make sense. Like what anyone would probably say to their dad or when they got kidnapped."

"You have a good memory. Okay, so we have a six o'clock call. Get to bed. You need your beauty sleep."

"Okay, good night," I say as Tommy gives me a kiss on the cheek and says good night to Aiden and Cooper.

"Who's winning?" I ask, knowing full well it's Aiden.

Cooper rolls his eyes as Aiden grins and holds up a stack of dollar bills.

"He's a shark," Cooper says. "Good thing it's time for bed. I'm about broke."

I almost tell him I know. That I tried to beat Aiden at pool once, too, but he'll probably ask what I lost and I don't want to have to say my clothes.

"I'm going to get ready for bed too. Uh, night, Cooper," I say, hoping he takes the hint. I'm ready to be alone with Aiden. Maybe not on the pool table, out in the open, but behind closed doors, watch out!

Aiden drops his cue stick, says, "Night, Cooper," and follows me into my bedroom.

I'M STANDING IN my closet, trying to decide what to wear to bed as Aiden's stripping down to his underwear.

"I want to sleep with you, but I don't want to offend Tommy," he says seriously.

Did I mention that he's practically naked?

Not that it's affecting my judgment or anything.

"He won't be offended. I told him—you know, that we haven't."

"You told him we haven't had sex? When?"

"When I showed him to his room."

"And how did it come up?"

"He asked which room was yours."

Aiden's shoulders drop. "What did you say?"

"That most of your stuff was in the bedroom but that you usually sleep with me."

Aiden throws on a pair of low-slung jersey shorts and a white tank top.

"Why are you getting dressed?"

"I'm sleeping in this. And we're leaving your door open."

"What?"

"I don't want him to think anything is going on."

I pick up the sexy dice he bought me as a Naughty Santa gift and pout. "But, I thought we could use these tonight. And, besides, you told your parents that we slept together and didn't even tell them that we weren't having sex."

Aiden pulls me into his arms. "My parents are liberal."

"So are mine. B used to—uh . . ." I stupidly say. "I, uh . . . Shit. I'm sorry."

"It's okay. I understand what you're saying, but I'm not comfortable with it. Your choice. I'll go sleep in my room, or I'll sleep in here with the door open."

"I hate when you do that." I pull out of his arms, move away from him, and start taking off my clothes.

"Do what?" he asks, studying me.

"Give me ultimatums," I reply, turning around to face him as I take off my bra.

I'm getting ready to slide a camisole over my head when he pounces. In mere seconds, I'm sprawled across my chaise, pinned underneath him.

I start laughing. "What the hell was that for?"

"I decided the door to your closet can stay closed," he says, his voice deep and sensual, as he glides his tongue down my chest. "You were teasing me and you know it."

"I was changing clothes."

He moves his mouth to my neck and kisses me in a way that makes me giggle.

"Aiden! That tickles," I screech.

"Shhh," he says, covering my mouth with his.

After a thorough kissing, he says, "How am I supposed to attack you on the down low if you're gonna scream?"

I slide my hand down the front of his shorts and whisper, "Let's see how quiet you can be."

A LITTLE WHILE later, we slide into bed together, dressed in our pajamas.

Aiden props his head up on his fist. "Tommy was wrong," he says breathlessly, studying my face. "You don't need beauty sleep. You're already beautiful." He leans down and kisses the side of my face, my forehead, and my cheek.

"I think you're beautiful too." I reply, snuggling closer to him and laying my head on his shoulder. I reach up and touch his face. "And not just because of your perfect face." I glide my hand down his chest, run my fingers across his abs, and then trace down his V-line. "Or your perfect muscles."

"You move your hand any lower and I'm going to have to take you back in the closet."

I slide my fingers under the waistband just to tease him, but then I lay my hand across the left side of his chest. "This is what makes you the most beautiful, Aiden. You have a really good heart."

He smiles at me, kisses the top of my head, and wraps me tightly in a hug.

I close my eyes and fall into a blissful sleep.

Monday, December 19th

MILKING THE FAME COW.
5:50AM

COOPER DROPS TOMMY and me off at a little before six, then heads back to my loft. Tommy told him there was no reason for him to sit around all day. But he and Aiden are both excited to watch the process for a bit, so I know they'll be here at some point. I also know they will get bored. It's going to be a really long day.

I get a hug from Matt, who is already on the soundstage. "Before you go to hair and makeup, let's rehearse the first scene. Since you're still in bed in the scene, it should be easy."

I lie in the bed, cover up, and pretend to be sleeping. Tommy tiptoes in from the left side of the stage, sits on my bed, runs his hand gently across my forehead, and bends down to kiss it.

I open my eyes. "Have a safe trip."

"I will. Are you sure you're going to be okay until Grandma gets here?"

"Dad, I'm nineteen. I don't need Grandma to babysit me."

He smirks at me. "Your being nineteen is exactly why Grandma is coming."

I roll my eyes. "So, *one time,* when I was seventeen and didn't know any better, I had a *little* party when you were out of town. You're never going to forget it, are you?"

"Harper, honey, I saw the video your friend posted on YouTube. You know, the one where the cops kicked the door down? Oh, and then tasered your drunk twenty-four-year-old boyfriend?"

"He wasn't my boyfriend." *Or much of a friend,* I say under my breath.

"At least something good came out of it," he says, ruffling my hair. He reaches in a fake pocket, pulls out a fake wallet, and pretends to put money on my nightstand. "Why don't you go to the mall and find a cute outfit for tonight?"

I laugh at him. "Probably because I'm not doing anything tonight but sitting on my ass and playing cards with Grandma. I mean, I love her and all, but it's a Saturday night!"

He nods his head toward the cash and grins at me. I squint at him, supposedly puzzled. I reach over and grab the nonexistent cash off the nightstand and see what's supposed to be underneath. I let a wide, happy smile spread across my face then throw my arms around his neck. "Concert Tickets? To see Drake? Ohmigawd! You're the Best. Dad. Ever!"

"Did you notice the seats I got you?"

I look down. "Ohmigawd. Third row? Maybe he'll sweat on me!"

"I'm not sure Grandma will like that."

"I have to take Grandma!?" I ask in horror.

"I'm just teasing. Take Michelle. Have fun. Be responsible. Don't talk to strangers."

"I won't. I promise. Have a good trip! Where are you

going, anyway?"

He gives me the vague look that supposedly he always gives me when he's going on a mission. "Just Berlin. I'll be back in a few days."

"Cut. Perfect," Matt says. "All right. Let's go ahead and block it out."

Blocking out is basically planning the physical movements and positioning on set in relationship to the camera. My job isn't too difficult for this, since I don't get out of bed.

After that, I'm sent to hair and makeup. I study my lines again—so I don't screw them up—and have fun listening to gossip about Knox's latest fling.

Halfway through, I'm pulled out for a wardrobe check and when I get back to hair and makeup, Knox himself is sitting in the chair I just left.

"You took my spot," I tell him.

"The early bird gets the worm."

"The early bird looks tired."

He groans. "The only thing I hate about making movies. The early morning calls."

"I was here before six."

"You weren't at the club last night. You should've been."

"No, I was rehearsing with Tommy. I take this seriously."

"So, what's your deal, anyway?"

"My deal?"

"Yeah, where'd you come from? How are you Abby fucking Johnston's daughter and I've never seen your picture anywhere? Last one I could find of Keatyn Douglas was from like five years ago. You don't even have any social media."

"I like my privacy, maybe?"

"Why? You're young and hot. You should be milking the fame cow."

"*Milking the fame cow.* That's one I've never heard. Enough about last night. Are you ready for today?"

"You inviting me to your dressing room to *practice our lines?*"

The hairdresser who's running product through his hair groans.

I stifle a laugh. "Actually, yes. That's not a bad idea."

Knox grins. "I knew you just wanted to kiss me. Story of my life."

"It's that pretty face," I tease. "Girls can't resist."

"Thank god they can't," he says. "Ouch," he yelps and gives the hairstylist a dirty look.

"Sorry!" she blurts. But it's obvious that she's not. At all.

KNOX AND I are ready but the lighting isn't, so I grab the script out of his hands and smack him on the butt with it. "I'm serious about practicing."

He wraps an arm around me. "Call it whatever you want. I'm in."

When we get in my dressing room, he plops down on my couch. "They listen and talk. You know that, right?"

"Who does?"

"Hair and makeup. Huge gossips. I'm really not hung over."

"You're not?"

"Nope, just working on that bad boy image. Speaking of that, we should go out."

"Go out where?"

"Anywhere. Dinner. Club. You like to dance?"

"I love to dance. But I'm seeing someone."

"He in this movie?"

"No."

"Even better. I've been hearing a few rumors myself. About you and me. So we need to get to know each other."

"If you tell me that involves going to bed with you, I'll pass."

He sits up, looking very serious. "I've been acting since I was ten and working on the tabloids' image of me since I was fifteen. I let people see what they want to see. When I was on a family show, I was the good boy. The boy who visited sick kids in hospitals. The boy who took his mom to the Golden Globes. The boy who had a sweet relationship with his on-camera love."

"You two were publicly waiting until you got married, right?"

"I had to be my on-screen character in real life. Well, not real life. Public life."

"I understand what you're saying. I used to date Luke Sander."

"He disappeared for a while. Left as a child star. Came back as an adult. It was a good move. Where was he hiding?"

"Malibu with me for a year and a half. We broke up last spring, but he's still one of my best friends."

"That's cool. Malibu, huh? Do you surf?"

"Yeah, I do. My, um, ex is a professional surfer."

"Your, *um, ex*? Why does it sound like there's a story there?"

"There isn't, really. He left to go on tour. We broke up. Well, sorta broke up. We weren't actually going out. We'd been dating for a while. It ended. Sort of."

"But sort of not?"

"Sort of not."

"So, who are you dating now?"

"A guy from my school. He's coming by later. You can

meet him."

"I'd like that. So what should we practice first? Kissing?" He gives me a naughty grin. "Or should I just take my shirt off again, so we can pretend to fight?"

"I think we should just read through our lines."

"Seriously, though. Have you heard the rumors?"

"What rumors?"

"About us?"

"*Us*? No, can't say I have."

"And here I thought you were connected."

"Why don't you just tell me what you heard, since you're dying to."

"Tommy doesn't want to make any more *Trinity* Films."

"That I am aware of."

"But the studio wants more."

"I am aware of that as well."

"Mr. Moran—your Uncle Matty—told me that you're going to make me a rich man."

"I assume, since you don't die now, that they're going to pay you more?"

He looks up at the ceiling and winces. "Shit. I didn't think to ask for more money."

"So how am I going to make you rich?"

"I think they want us. You and me. To take over the series. Like a spin-off franchise. Or the new cast. Whatever. It's going to be us."

"How? You're a bad guy."

"Have you not read the whole script?"

"Uh, not yet," I say, honestly impressed that he has. Tommy said they just finished re-writes a couple days ago.

"I have a change of heart. *You* change my heart. I fall for you. We have some very touching scenes. You know, in between being shot at and almost getting blown up."

"No one has said anything to me."

Knox studies my face intently. "You look like you're telling the truth. But you're a good actress, so it's hard to know."

"Ahhh, you think I'm a good actress. I'm touched."

"You should be. And, yes, I know I gave you a hard time. But I watched the screen test. We *were* really good together. You've seen *Independence Day*, right?"

"Yeah, of course."

"Will Smith stole the show. Won the MTV award for Best Kiss that year. That's going to be us when this movie comes out. I just know it."

"So, are you a jerk or not?"

He shakes his head. "I just play one sometimes."

I think about Vincent. The upcoming music video I'm doing for Damian. My plan to let Vincent see me everywhere. "Then we'll get along just fine. And, after the holidays, I'll take you up on going to a club."

There's a knock at my door, but whoever it is doesn't wait for me to answer. The door swings open, and a girl looks surprised to see Knox and me sitting on the couch together.

"Oh, um, excuse me. Miss Douglas, they're ready for you in wardrobe."

"Thank you. I'll be right there," I tell her.

As I'm walking out the door, Knox says, "Find out if the rumors are true."

THE DAY IS a blur of rehearsals, hair and makeup, wardrobe, blocking, and shooting. Normally, there's a lot of down time on set—to nap, hang out, eat—but they're trying to cram a lot of scenes in before the holidays to make a preliminary teaser trailer that will air during the Super Bowl.

I see little of Cooper and Aiden, but when I do, they're both smiling. Cooper is happy because he won some of his lost pool money back from Aiden in a poker game.

I shoot a scene where I'm being held captive in a small room. Earlier in the movie, I'm kidnapped by some guys who work for Knox's character. They aren't the smartest, so I'm able to steal one of their phones.

In this scene, I use the phone to call Tommy/Trinity.

We shoot the scene three different ways, Matt trying to determine just how distressed I should be. He wants to see my growth in the film. From the girl who is only worried about the next party to the tougher girl I was in the screen test.

Needless to say, based on what I've been through, none of the versions were much of a stretch.

I'm thinking about my own journey as I grab some food and take it to my dressing room. I have a short time to eat before I have to block out another scene.

When I open my door, I find Knox, Cooper, and Aiden laughing and eating.

I wolf down my food and am quickly back at it.

I'M EXHAUSTED WHEN I finally get back to the loft. Aiden took a cab home after dinner, but Cooper waited for me.

It's past one when I sneak into my room and find Aiden sprawled out across my bed. The remote is near his head and ESPN is playing softly in the background. It reminds me of that night when I went into Bryce's room. His scribbles. *Why should I bother? Because she felt it too.*

It was definitely love at first sight.

But after what Tommy said about him and Mom, I understand what I didn't understand when I first met B.

Love at first sight is only the first step of the journey.

It's the spark that starts the fire.

I tiptoe in my bathroom, thinking about the similarities between my life, my scripts, and the Bachelor Prince play. It feels like they were all just a rehearsal for the big show. And I can't help but wonder if they tell me about what's coming next. Are there parallels between what's going to happen to me in *Retribution* and with Vincent's version of *A Day at the Lake?* Will someone save me? Will I save myself? Or will the bad guy win?

I really need to get my hands on that script.

After washing off my makeup, I set my alarm and slide carefully into bed.

Aiden rolls over and pulls me into his chest. "I just realized one of your lies was that you were going to France for Christmas. Where are you really going?"

"I was going to stay here. I really want to see my family, but I can't risk it."

"No way I'm letting you be alone. Either you're coming to St. Croix with me, or I'm staying here with you."

"I didn't really want to be alone."

"But you were going to be, weren't you?"

"Yes."

"And now?"

"I'd love to spend Christmas with you, Aiden."

Wednesday, December 21st
STUNT PLANNING.
LUNCH

WHEN I GRAB some lunch and take it to my dressing room, I find Tommy, Aiden, and Cooper already in there, eating.

"Aiden was just telling me about his parents' place up in Northern California, Keatyn," Tommy tells me.

"And Tommy was telling me about France," Aiden says.

"That's awesome," I say, but my heart is going *awww*, loving that they're talking.

Bonding, even, maybe.

Matt walks in the room with a plate and sets it down just as his phone rings. "Excuse me; I need to take this."

When he walks away from the table, he flashes Tommy a smile and a thumbs up.

Tommy breaks out in his trademark crooked smirk. The one that leaves women swooning.

"What's that all about?" I ask.

"He's on the phone with Edward Moffett."

"The head of the studio?"

"Yes."

"I take it that's good?"

"It could be very good, for you," Tommy says cryptically. "Gentlemen," he says to Cooper and Aiden. "Would you mind excusing us for a minute? I need to speak to Keatyn privately."

After they leave, I say, "What's up?"

"I have a plan."

"What kind of plan?"

"The kind of plan where we hijack the Moran plane that's going to St. Croix."

"Hijack it? Why?"

"So everyone will come to France instead."

"Really?"

"Yeah, the weather is gorgeous. I ordered barrels of wine. Officially, we're saying it's a late Beaujolais Nouveau Day party."

"That's the day when France celebrates the release of the young wine with all the festivals and fireworks, right? We were there for that a few years ago because it's around Thanksgiving."

"That's right."

"So, officially that's what it is, but unofficially— ohmigawd, Tommy, are you going to propose?!"

"Not *just* propose. We're getting married, too. But it's a surprise."

"A surprise wedding?"

"Yeah. What do you think?"

"What does Mom think?"

"She doesn't know. She thinks we're just throwing a holiday party."

"That's amazing, Tommy. I wish I could . . ."

"I don't give two shits about Vincent. He's not invited. Garrett already has the security in place and will be personally supervising the event. Your presence is required."

I launch myself into his arms and hug him tightly.

"So, Mom thinks people are coming for a party. And the people who are coming for the party don't know they're coming?"

"Pretty much."

"What if Mom talks to Millie about it?"

"She won't. I'm in charge of getting everyone there, and she's in charge of the party."

"If you're able to pull that off, it will be a miracle. You know she and Millie talk daily."

"Cross your fingers that they don't talk about this. And what's the worse case? Millie finds out we're throwing a party and packs warmer clothes. She still won't know about the wedding."

"Yeah, you're right. And you don't have to worry about the paparazzi."

"Exactly."

"But what about a dress?"

"Kym's bringing full wedding attire."

"Mom's going to think that's odd."

"No, Kym told her she's already got designers wanting to dress her for the Oscars and she's bringing them for her to try on after Christmas."

"That's a good lie. So, did you decide how you're going to propose?"

"I loved the *Me and You* idea."

"I liked that one too. Oh my gosh, Tommy. I'm so excited! And I get to see the girls!"

"They're upset you aren't coming for Christmas."

"I know. Are you sure it's safe for me to go? Like, positive?"

"Keatyn, we could all die tomorrow. We're taking precautions and we're going to keep living. We're also going to be very careful about how we get you to the airport. Garrett wants Cooper to take you to the plane before anyone else."

"Okay. What about everyone else's clothes? They will have packed for the beach."

"Matt is in on it too. He's telling everyone it's supposed to be unseasonably cold, even though the weather forecast says otherwise. He's telling them Inga feels there's a storm coming in. Or some other bullshit."

"That's funny."

KNOX AND I go through the choreography of the re-worked scene we did for my screen test and then I go back to hair and makeup to get ready for my next scene.

I'm ready before the camera and lighting guys are, so I go to my room to lie down. I need a nap.

But when I get to my room, Cooper, Knox, and Aiden are playing poker.

"Can you go play somewhere else so I can take a nap?" I ask.

Knox says, "Boo. Party pooper," and Cooper doesn't move.

But Aiden lays his cards down on the table and says, "I fold."

"Awesome," Cooper says, as he and Knox lay down their cards and he wins the small pile of coins.

"We're leaving as requested," Aiden says. "The star needs her rest."

"She's not the star," Knox sasses back.

"No, but she will be," Aiden counters.

His comment and the adorable wink he gives me put a huge smile on my face.

Aiden grabs a set of noise-reducing headphones, plugs in his phone, and hands them to me. "I made you a new playlist."

"Thank you. Are you going to lie down with me?"

He glances at his watch. "I'm going to let you rest."

"Where are you going?"

"Allan invited me to a stunt planning meeting. I think it will be cool to sit in on it."

"That would be cool."

He sits on the couch next to me and gives me a steamy kiss. "What were you and Tommy talking about at lunch?"

"It's a secret."

"I thought we weren't going to keep secrets from each other?"

"Um, no. We're trying not to lie to each other."

"Trying?"

"What I mean is, I want to tell you the secret, but I've been sworn to secrecy. Part of what makes it a secret. Besides, if I tell you, you'd have to lie to your family. And I don't want to put you in that position."

He runs his finger down my arm, leaving a trail of goosebumps in its wake.

"What kind of position do you want to put me in?" he asks sexily, leaning closer to me.

"Hmmm. I don't know. You feel like playing pool?"

He laughs and raises an eyebrow over a gorgeous green eye. "Ah. *That* kind of a position. I don't think that's what we were talking about."

"If I wasn't so tired when I get home, I'd offer to dance for you."

"I'm tired just watching. I never realized you would work such long hours. Or all the times you do the same scene."

"It doesn't help that they're trying to squeeze a lot into a few days."

"So, what's this secret? I won't tell my family."

"Good, because I'm dying to tell you."

He smiles at me.

"I get to spend Christmas with you."

"I already knew that."

"And also with my family."

"They're coming to St. Croix?"

"Umm, not exactly. We're all going to France."

"How's that going to work? We'll all be packed for the beach."

"Yeah, that's the only problem. Just tell your family to pack some sweaters. Say it gets chilly at night or they keep the house really cool or something."

"I'll do that. So, why isn't your family just coming to St. Croix?"

"Because they're planning a big party. And the location is more secure."

"Where is the house? I just realized I never asked."

"Southern France, between Nice and Cannes. It's in the country, up in the hills. You can even see the sea most days. It's really beautiful."

"I can't wait. What's the party for?"

"Just to celebrate our being together."

"Very nice," he says, giving me a kiss and heading out the door. "Get some rest. We have a date with a Naughty Santa gift later tonight."

"We do?" I ask, suddenly perking up.

Aiden smiles. "Yes, we do."

"Which one?"

"I told you, I have a sweet tooth," he replies. "And a sweet tongue."

"You said you wanted me in the candy thong and a pair of cowboy boots."

"And nothing else," he says in a way that almost sounds like a threat.

A really sexy one.

CUSS AND GET LAID.
11PM

I GET BACK to my loft around eleven. Cooper is tired and heads straight to his room.

Thank god.

Aiden's in my kitchen, nothing but a pair of athletic shorts hanging dangerously low on his hips and a candy necklace hanging deliciously around his neck.

I can't even think straight.

He kisses me in greeting and sits me up on the breakfast bar while he opens a bottle of champagne.

Who knew something so simple could be so sexy?

He sets the bottle on the counter and cuts the foil off. Then he untwists the metal topper. Every muscle in his arm ripples with each twist. I see a flash of his clover tattoo.

And I feel lucky just to be sitting here.

"You're wearing a candy necklace," I say, stating the obvious as he pulls the cork out.

He glances up at me as he pours the champagne. "I put it on, but it's up to you decide where you want it."

I gulp.

Imagine the Titan saluting me and wrapped in candy.

He leans across the bar and clinks my glass. "Here's to a sweet night."

I definitely drink to that and follow the hottie god as he takes the champagne into my bedroom and locks the door behind us.

I go into my closet, strip, and put on the candy thong and cowboy boots, as requested.

The candy thong is not particularly comfortable, I might add.

I look at myself in the mirror. The pastel embroidered cowboy boots are the same colors as the candy, so I match. But . . .

"You're taking an awfully long time in there," Aiden says, knocking on the door.

"I look ridiculous."

"Why don't you let me be the judge of that."

I shake my head at myself in the mirror, knowing I'd be ridiculous for Aiden any time if it makes him happy.

And turns him on.

I push my shoulders back, stand up straight and proud, and march my mostly-naked ass to the doorway.

Aiden's standing by the bed, holding two glasses of champagne.

I know I look silly, but I might as well have some fun with it. I lock eyes with him, spread my arms and legs wide, and pose in the doorway.

Aiden immediately sets the glasses down. His eyes are dark and sexy as he strides across the room. He places his hands on my shoulders, moves them out across my arms, and lands on my hands, which are braced in the doorway. "Don't move your hands," he insists. "No matter what."

I nod as he drops to his knees.

He studies the thong then touches a piece of candy. "One." He touches another and says, "Two." He quickly moves his finger across more candy, counting. "Eight pieces of candy in my way to the sweet spot."

"One," he says taking the first piece of candy in his teeth

and biting it off.

"Two," he says, eating another piece as he caresses the backs of my thighs.

He cups my ass with both hands. "Three."

I push my hands harder into the doorway, wondering how I'm going to make it to eight.

His tongue flicks across me as he says, "Four."

He removes one hand from my ass and places his finger through the little hole he's created, touching the very upper part of what he's aiming for.

Ohmigawd. Down just a bit further, I want to beg, as he says, "Five," and flicks his tongue where his finger just was.

"Oh," I say, dropping my hands and running them through his hair.

He moves his tongue under the candy that's blocking his way and gives me a little tease of what's to come.

Then he stops and stands up, grabbing my hands and pressing them against the door casing. "I thought I told you not to move your hands."

"Uh . . ." I say breathlessly.

"Do you want me to get to number eight?"

"Yes." I'm so full of desire and lust that I can barely speak. Plus, his eyes. They have that dark, hungry look that practically hypnotizes me.

"Good," he says, pausing to suck on my breasts before he moves back to bite off number six.

"Seven," he says, biting off another piece while sliding a finger inside of me.

I suck in my breath and hold it as he discovers just how turned on I am.

He quickly says, "Eight," and then delves his tongue into the spot where his finger was.

"Holy shit," I think I say, as I push my hands harder into the doorway for support.

He uses some magical combination of his fingers and tongue on me.

I'm breathing hard and saying *ohmigawd* over and over until my legs are weak and the only thing still keeping me standing is my arms, barricaded across the door frame.

When he feels my knees start to give away, he picks me up and pulls me on top of him on the chaise. I push his boxers down and glide myself across the Titan.

Aiden rhythmically moves my hips against him.

"Aiden, I want to . . ."

"Not tonight," he says, kissing me, but still guiding my motions.

The friction alone causes me to moan and that's when his grip tightens and he loses control.

"God, you're sweet," he says into my ear.

A LITTLE LATER, we're lying in bed and I'm softly trailing my fingers across his chest.

"You know, I was thinking . . ."

"Sounds dangerous," he teases.

"You might not be able to come to France with me. What's your grade in French?"

"Does it matter? I have my dirty French book. That's all I'll need."

"You can cuss and get laid." I roll my eyes.

"So, I'll get laid?"

"Uh, what?"

There's a smirk playing on his face. "Are you saying we're going to do it there?"

"I wanted to do it just now. And I, um . . . I guess that depends on how convincing your French is," I say, teasing him, even though my thoughts are elsewhere.

I just realized my worlds don't have clear-cut lines of separation anymore.

Brooklyn = Malibu. Waves. France. Europe. The beach. Sunrise.

Aiden = Connecticut. Eastbrooke. New York. The loft. Sunset.

I hadn't realized it, but Aiden has been invading what should be Brooklyn territory ever since we were in St. Croix. The surf. The sand.

And, now, he's about to invade France.

The place B came to be with me. Dropped everything. Got on a plane. For me. In the hammock is where we confessed our love for each other. It wasn't long after that we shared our first time. Our summer of waves.

Before my birthday party, I hoped my worlds would come together.

Until they were standing there in front of me.

Sander. Cush. Brooklyn.

Each one representing a different choice. A different life. A different me.

But I didn't need my worlds to come together.

I needed myself to come together.

Aiden kisses my temple. "You have that faraway look in your eye. What are you thinking?"

"That I've changed a lot since the last time I was there."

I stare into the green eyes of the boy who has helped me realize that I don't need separate lives but, rather, should find someone who fits comfortably into them all.

I run the back of my hand down the scruff on his sweet face. "I love you, Aiden."

Never in my life will I forget the way he looks in this moment. The surprise in his eyes. The emotions crossing his face. His lips forming a smile. His big hands holding my cheeks firmly in place as he looks into my eyes and says, "I love you too, Boots."

Thursday, December 22nd

THEY'RE LUCKY.
6PM

AFTER FILMING ALL day, Cooper drives Aiden and me to the airport where we board the Moran Films jet. Everyone else is supposed to be here shortly, in preparation for a seven o'clock departure.

After a few minutes, though, two of my favorite—but unexpected—faces walk through the door.

"Grandma and Grandpa!" I almost yell. "Tommy didn't tell me you were coming!"

I quickly launch myself into Grandpa's arms for a hug.

"Grandma," I say. "How did you talk him into coming?" My grandpa hates to fly because he isn't in control of the plane.

"I told him either he got his ass on the jet, or I was leaving without him. Seeing as he can't cook for himself, he figured coming to France would be better than starving."

Grandpa laughs and walks to the front of the plane, opens the lavatory door, and nods. "Plus, now I can tell Jose and the boys at the ranch that I got to shit on a private jet. They're always singing some rap song about that. I'll be the only one to ever have done it. I keep telling Ma she's gonna have to take a picture of me to prove it."

Grandma makes a hmmppff sound. "I am not photographing you on the toilet." She turns her attention away from Grandpa and smiles at Aiden and Cooper. "And who are these fine-looking young men?"

"This is Cooper," I introduce. "He's sorta my bodyguard."

"When she lets me be," Cooper responds as he takes Grandma's hand in greeting.

Grandma pats his hand. "Well, you must be good at your job. We appreciate you keeping her safe."

He says thank you and then shakes Grandpa's hand, since he's decided to stop exploring the bathroom.

I move toward Aiden and proudly introduce him.

"I'm a big fan of those boots you sent her," Aiden says to Grandpa.

Grandpa puts his big hand on Aiden's shoulder. "Why's that, son?"

"Because they're lucky," he says.

We're interrupted when everyone else joins us. Tommy and Bad Kiki, who barrels over to me, jumps up, and kisses me right on the lips before I can react.

I giggle, scratch behind her ears, and tell her she needs to behave herself.

Matt, Marisa, and little Stormy Moran, Damian and Peyton, Mr. And Mrs. Arrington, Millie and Deron, and Grandma Stevens all join us on the plane.

I'm giving everyone hugs, including Cooper, who is leaving to go spend the holiday with his family, when Tommy asks them to take a seat.

"I have a few surprises. First, we've had a change of destination. We'll be heading to France instead of St. Croix.

With everything that's going on in our personal lives, Abby and I decided to throw a party. In France, on the third Thursday in November, they celebrate the uncorking of the Beaujolais Nouveau wine. This wine is young—only aged for six weeks—and is supposed to be drunk by Christmastime. Many towns in France have entire weekend celebrations with fireworks and festivals. We're a little late, but we'll be doing the same. Everyone up for drinking a few barrels of wine and celebrating the holiday together?"

Matt gives Tommy a one-armed hug as the flight attendant hands out champagne.

Matt holds his glass up.

We all follow suit as he toasts, "A little adventure is good for the soul."

Friday, December 23rd

MIGHT FREAKING EXPLODE.
SOMETIME IN THE MORNING.

WE ARRIVE AT Nice in the morning, head to the house, and are greeted with screams from the girls.

Sadly, they are more excited to meet Aiden and see Bad Kiki than they are to see me. I get a quick hug before they all barrel outside with the dog.

Mom gives me a hug. One that's longer than usual.

"I missed you so much," I tell her.

She strokes the back of my hair. "I missed you more." Then she whispers, "That *has* to be the hottie god."

We reluctantly stop hugging so I can introduce her.

"Mom, I'd like you to meet Aiden, his sister, Peyton, and his parents, Aubrey and Lane Arrington."

Mom doesn't waste any time getting to know them. She pulls them all into hugs like she's known them forever. I study Mom more closely. She's glowing and doesn't look as skinny as before.

The move here has been good for her.

After introductions and hugs, everyone is shown to their guest rooms, instructed to nap, freshen up, and then meet for lunch on the patio at one.

Aiden and I talked almost the whole flight, about everything and nothing, so I'm very ready for a nap. We snuggle up and quickly fall asleep.

WHEN I WAKE up, Aiden isn't in bed, so I take a long shower, dry my hair, and am putting on a dress when there's a soft knock on my door.

I open it to find Kym, who quickly shoves her way into my room, then puts her back on the door and shuts it.

"Whew, I didn't know if I'd make it."

"Make what?" I ask, eyeing the hanging garment bag she's carrying.

"I wanted you to see your dress for later today. I'm dying to show someone something. So humor me."

"I can't wait to see it," I tell her.

"They're almost set up for the *party*. With my subtle guidance, your mom decided on an over-the-top garden fairy fantasy look for the decor. You have no idea the favors I had to call in to get this wedding outfitted on such short notice. I've been sending her overnight deliveries every day. I'm surprised she hasn't suspected something."

"What did you tell her the deliveries were?"

"Dresses. That since her movie came out, every designer assumes she's going to win an Oscar and wants her to wear their design."

"Did she ask to look at them?"

"Of course she did, but I told her not to open them because I had more coming and that we'd make a day of trying them all on for Tommy after Christmas."

"She likes getting Tommy's opinion."

"Exactly. Now, please say a prayer that your mom doesn't freak over this."

"She'll be thrilled."

"I think she will be too. I'm so excited I'm about to burst," she says, unzipping the bag holding my dress.

It's an adorable Sherri Hill dress with a high-low ruffled bottom in a soft peachy-pink.

"I'll be right back," she says. "I have to show you what I got to go with it. And you should see the girls' dresses. Pale green silk, organza tulle skirts in subtle pastels, purple silk sashes. And they'll be wearing wings and carrying floral fairy wands."

I go back to getting ready, putting on some eye shadow, when I hear the door open again.

I was expecting Kym but it's Aiden who walks into the bathroom, grabs me around the waist, and kisses my neck.

"Sleeping Beauty finally wake up?"

"Didn't you take a nap?"

"Not for long. I couldn't sleep. But that's okay. There is a whole lot going on here. I know I've never been to a Hollywood party, but I was walking with Tommy and your Grandpa and looking at the set up. It looks more like a wedding to me."

"Does it look pretty?"

"It's gorgeous. Flowers. A tent. Tables. A stage and dance floor set up in the barn. Just seems really extravagant for such a small group."

"What did Tommy think of it?"

Aiden turns me around to face him. "Tommy thought it wasn't enough and ordered more flowers."

"He's excited everyone's here. It's gonna be a good party."

"Are there more people coming?"

"Uh, no. Just us."

He kisses me, using his tongue in a way that makes me

forget who I am.

After a very thorough kissing, he pulls out my bottom lip out with his teeth. "You're lying."

"You heard what Tommy said about the wine. Parties like this went on all over France in November. They're just more extravagant here. Haven't you ever seen Versailles?"

He moves his lips slowly down my neck.

"I have, but there's also a gazebo fully decorated in grapevines, thousands of pastel flowers, and little butterflies. If I didn't know better, I'd think I was going to a wedding."

"Fine. There maybe is something going on. But it's something that no one is supposed to know about. You absolutely should not say the word wedding in front of anyone. Especially any of the people who are setting up."

His lips move lower, his tongue grazing my cleavage.

He stops kissing me and pops his head up. "They're getting married, aren't they? That's why we didn't go to St. Croix. And didn't you promise never to lie to me again?"

"I'm pretty sure I never promised that. Besides, they aren't even engaged. Mom just likes to plan fun parties."

"Did she plan her own wedding and not know it?"

He doesn't let me answer, giving me a rough, hot kiss instead.

When he stops kissing me, he gives me a grin. It's like his grin contains truth serum.

It flows through the air and collects in my bloodstream.

I hate him.

Okay, well, not really. I just wish I had some powers of my own.

Maybe I do. Maybe I can distract him.

I give him a good long kiss, then kiss down his neck. Suck on it a little.

"If you're trying to distract me, it's not going to work."

Well, shit.

"Do you remember that day in French when I was writing out *Will you marry me?*"

"Yeah, you were doodling words in French and English."

"Maybe I was brainstorming."

It takes a second for that to sink in.

"Are you telling me that Tommy is going to propose today? And this is really an engagement party?"

"Uh, not exactly."

I can see the wheels turning in his brain. Finally, he says, "She *thinks* she's planning a party, but really she's planning her own wedding and he's going to propose and they will get married all in the same day?"

"You are one smart cookie."

"Why are they doing it so fast? All in one day?"

"For a few reasons, one being that we're all together."

Aiden's beautiful mouth forms a little frown.

I don't want to think about Vincent at all today, so I add, "And because they're Abby Johnston and Tommy Stevens. If anyone had even an inkling of an idea that this is more than a party, then, trust me, somehow the paparazzi would have helicopters flying above it, trying to get photos. It's a party. That's it. Do you understand?"

He smiles. "Yeah, I think I do. Really, it's kind of romantic."

"Tommy is amazing to Mom. And, yeah, this party should be *very* romantic."

"When's it going to happen?"

"Tommy asked everyone to meet for lunch on the patio for a reason."

"Would you want to do something like that?"

"Would I want to get engaged and married on the same

day? Would I want someone else to plan it. Hell, no. Definitely not. I've been dreaming of my wedding since I was old enough to hold a Barbie bride in my hands. Of course, back then, I wanted to marry Ken."

Aiden laughs. "Will your mom be disappointed?"

"I don't think so. She had the big wedding when she married my dad. She and Tommy have four kids. This is the perfect thing to do."

"You're right, as usual."

"Oh, gosh. You've been talking to Grandpa."

"What makes you say that?"

"He says that to Grandma when he's letting her have her way."

Aiden laughs. "He told me it's the phrase that keeps a woman happy."

I laugh too. "He cracks me up."

"He's funny. Very straightforward. Asked me a lot of questions."

"Like what?"

"How you've been doing with all this."

"What did you tell him?"

"That you're amazing."

"So, you lied to my grandpa?"

He tickles me, but the tickling turns to kissing, which turns to him pushing me up onto the vanity, the room quickly heating up. It doesn't take much, a gentle touch and my body does the rest.

Sometimes I feel like if we don't do it, I might freaking explode.

"All right, I've got the flower girl dresses to show you," Kym says, walking into the bathroom and totally ruining what I had hoped might happen next. "Oh, sorry," she says, then she looks at Aiden and goes, "Um . . . Shit."

"It's okay," I say, as Aiden backs up, letting me slide off the counter. "He figured it out."

"He *what*?! How?! Do you think your mom knows?"

"He guessed. Tommy added more flowers?"

"That's how you figured it out?" she asks Aiden, looking a little scary. I hope he tells her the truth.

"I just thought there were a lot of flowers for a party, you know?" he says.

"Then he was asking me questions. And he had seen something I wrote when I was thinking up proposal ideas for Tommy."

Her eyes get big again. "Do you know how he's going to ask?"

"Um, yeah. Don't you?"

"No. Asshole wouldn't tell me."

"Everything will be set up by one, right? Before lunch."

"Yes."

"So relax and enjoy a quiet afternoon before things get crazy."

"Things are already crazy. The butterflies on the gazebo look like they belong at a child's birthday party. Hair and makeup will be here at two, but Tommy says he can't say exactly what time the proposal will be, so they will be twiddling their thumbs, wondering what's going on. The barrels of wine that Tommy ordered haven't arrived. And the band's singer has laryngitis."

"I'll go look at the butterflies. There is plenty of wine in the cellar. And, hello, Damian is here."

"That's true." She takes a deep breath.

"Can we see the girls' dresses?" Aiden asks, the question seemingly having a calming effect on Kym.

"Oh, yes. And, here, you will love this." She hands me a box.

I take the lid off to find a pair of boots. They are distressed brown leather with pale pink flowers embroidered up the sides.

"With the way the front of the dress is short, I thought the boots would be perfect. And I know how you love your boots."

I give her a hug. "I do!"

"Me too," Aiden says with big grin. "Me too."

ANYTHING IS POSSIBLE.
NOON

AIDEN AND I walk down to the gazebo to check out the butterfly crisis. The girls are out in the yard, playing, so they follow us down to the pond.

"Where you going, Aye-den?" Gracie asks.

"For a walk. Where are you going, Gracie?"

"With you!" she screams, running ahead of us.

Avery and Ivery grab ahold of my hands, and Emery takes one of Aiden's.

He glances at me and gives me a wink.

I close my eyes and tuck away the memory. The perfect crisp weather that feels more like fall than winter. The bright sun shining on my head. My sisters being silly. Aiden sliding his free arm around my shoulder.

Perfect blissful happiness.

"Watch!" Gracie demands as she drops to the ground and does an off-balance somersault.

"We can do cartwheels and backbends!" Avery tells me.

All the girls rush ahead of us to show off their gymnastic skills.

"You do a cartwheel, too, Kiki!" Ivery says.

I smile, run across the field, do a cartwheel, and then a roundoff. The girls screech and clap like I just did an Olympic-medal-worthy routine.

"Aye-den, you too!"

"I can't do a cartwheel," he says. "But I can do this."

He does a perfect handstand, shows off by doing a couple of handstand pushups, then walks on his hands, before falling over in the grass.

"Get him!" I yell, picking Gracie up and running to where Aiden is lying. We both leap on him and start tickling him, the triplets quickly joining in.

Aiden laughs and almost screams, which makes us tickle him more.

He playfully tosses the girls off him.

They take off, skipping, doing cartwheels, and laughing.

He rolls on top of me, pushes the hair off my face, and looks deeply into my eyes.

We stare at each other for a few moments, his soul speaking to mine in a language I finally understand.

"I love you, Keatyn Elizabeth Douglas," he says.

"I love you too, Aiden I-dont-know-your-middle-name Arrington."

"It's Asher," he says as our lips touch in a very G-rated kiss.

Just like the very first time he kissed me on the Ferris wheel.

It's a slow, perfect, time-stood-still, fireworks-in-my-eyes kind of kiss.

No open mouths, no tongues; just a kiss.

A little teeny kiss.

That means so much more.

Everything with Aiden has always been so much more.

Avery yells, "Look! They're kissing!"

The girls giggle as he slips his hand into mine and pulls me to my feet.

I have the same reaction I did back then.

My hand belongs in his.

Forever.

It's a scary thought. *Forever.*

But being here with my family, sharing them with Aiden, makes it seem not as scary.

Because, right here, I can't see the guards.

I don't feel afraid.

I feel like anything is possible.

Anything and everything.

Which makes me even more determined. I need my life back.

Now.

As we continue our walk to the gazebo, Emery says, "I wanna kiss Michael."

"Who's Michael?" I ask.

She sighs dreamily. "You know, Michael on *The Princess Diaries.*"

"Oh, he is cute. He's a little old for you, though, don't you think?"

"When I grow up, he won't be too old," she tells me very seriously.

"I wanna kiss Prince Eric," Avery says.

"From *The Little Mermaid?*"

"Yeah, he's cute and he has a castle by the ocean. I love the ocean."

"Me too." I lift her up and give her a hug.

She looks at me and Aiden. "You were kissing Aye-den. You love him."

I glance at Aiden, who's grinning like a maniac.

"Are you gonna get mare-weed?" Gracie asks.

"No. You don't have to get married when you're in love," Ivery says with a sigh, like they've had this discussion before. "Momma and Daddy aren't married."

"Would you like it if they got married?" I ask them.

They scream, "Yes!!!"

"If they ever did, you would have to be very well-behaved. No tantrums, Gracie. No screaming. Good little ladies."

"Momma says we will get to carry flowers. But not 'til we're older," Ivery says.

"Yeah, not 'til we are older," Avery confirms.

"What do you think of the pretty flowers on the gaze-bo?" I ask them.

They run around it, through the middle of it, and back to us.

"Look at all the butterflies!" they squeal.

"What do you think of the butterflies?" Aiden asks me.

I take in the octagonal gazebo covered with grapevines, a riot of pale flowers, ribbons, and little butterflies.

"I love them. I can see why Kym was freaking out though. They're a little tacky up close, but when we were farther back the effect was beautiful."

I walk to the backside of the gazebo and decide to pluck off a few butterflies for the girls.

"Come here, girls!"

The four of them tear around the corner.

"What!?" Avery asks.

"Would you each like to choose a butterfly to take back to the house?"

They jump up and down with excitement and yell, "Yes!"

"I want that pretty blue one," Ivery says, pointing to one

clear at the top.

"I don't know if I can reach that one. Hey, Aiden, we need you."

Aiden rounds the corner and, gosh, he is so the God of all Hotties.

His dark blond hair is messily pushed back off his forehead, a few random pieces falling over one beautiful green eye and drawing attention to the sexy freckle underneath. He has a piece of hay in his mouth, a grin on his face, and cowboy boots on his feet.

But it's the hay in his mouth that causes me to realize that Aiden reminds me of my dad. Perfect blond hair, amazing eyes, a beautiful wide smile, and an easy-going demeanor.

When he stands on his tiptoes, reaching up to retrieve the butterfly, his muscular forearm flexes.

It's hot.

And makes me want him.

All of him.

Like, now.

The girls are shouting out orders of which butterfly they want.

Gracie wants to examine all the butterflies up close, so he lifts her high in the air. After she chooses one, he sets her down and takes the butterfly off its flower perch. Then he crouches down to her level and places the pale pink one she chose gently in her open palm.

The exact way he placed a perfect four-leaf clover in mine.

My own stomach fills with butterflies.

"Why don't you girls run back to the house and show your butterflies to everyone," he says.

As they race away, he pulls me into his arms. "You

better always need me." Then he gives me the kind of kiss that sends my butterflies somewhere lower. A hot, powerful tongue kiss.

It's official. I am obsessed with his tongue. With his lips. With him.

Our kiss is interrupted by Gracie coming back and pulling on his sleeve.

"Gracie tired. I need piggy," she says, although she doesn't look the least bit tired.

Avery, who has run back to check on Gracie says, "Gracie is a baby."

"NO! NO! Gracie is NOT a baby! I big girl! Gracie no more wear pull-ups. Mama says I big girl!"

Aiden's chuckling as he crouches down to her level.

"You are a big girl, Gracie. Good job," I tell her, picking her up and putting her on Aiden's back.

"Hang on tight!" Aiden tells her, then he rears up like a bucking bronco and gallops toward the house.

A happy memory rushes to the front of my brain. Me jumping off bales of hay onto my dad's back. Him rearing back and pretending to try to buck me off even though he had a firm grip on my legs. Me telling him to *Giddy-up, horsey* because Grandma had dinner ready.

After he drops Gracie off at the house, I tell him, "You're going to be a good dad someday."

"And you're going to be an amazing mom. You're great with the girls. When do you want to have kids?"

"I'm not sure," I say, putting my head down as reality slaps me in the face.

Aiden cocks his head and reads my mind. "I'm sorry. I won't talk about the future anymore. I understand now why the word forever freaks you out."

A SPECIAL ROCK.
2PM

LUNCH IS LONG and practically an event in and of itself.

The sun is shining and everyone is out on the lawn. The kids are blowing bubbles and running around like maniacs.

Damian, Peyton, and Grandpa are playing croquet. The other guys—Tommy, Matt, Deron, Aiden, and his dad—are tossing around a football. The rest of us are sitting around a large, weathered wooden table, drinking wine and picking cheese and fruit off a big wooden board.

I notice Aiden take out his phone and point it toward Tommy, who just pulled a rock out of his pocket and gave it to Emery.

Oh my gosh. It's time!

Emery comes running up to Mom.

"Look, Mommy! Look what I found!! It's a special rock."

Mom is used to getting *special* rocks. The girls think every plain old rock they find is special.

Mom leans down toward her and says, "What's so special about it, Em?"

"It has a word on it! And I can read it!"

"Oh? What does it say?"

She puts it on the table and yells, "Me!"

"Oh, that is special. Where did you find it?"

"I don't know," she says and happily skips away.

Pretty soon, Ivery prances up. "I found a special rock too, Momma. Look. What does this one say?" She sets it in front of my mom.

"Oh, honey, that one says YOU."

Ivery says, "Me and you." She runs off singing, "Me and you, you and me, we live together in a tree, me and you, you

93

and me, don't get stung by a bee." She's really quite creative.

About five minutes—and a full glass of wine for me—later, Avery marches up, all business.

I'm starting to get nervous.

"Abby, I found a special rock, too." She's decided she's too mature to call Mom and Tommy Mommy and Daddy. "And this one has your name on it."

"It does. ABBY. Good job," Mom says.

When she runs back out to play, Mom turns to me. "What's going on?"

"I have no idea," I lie.

She turns her attention toward Tommy, who is swinging the girls in circles and then laughing when they walk around dizzy and fall down.

A few minutes later, she grabs my arm, almost spilling my wine. "Look, look at Tommy. What is he doing?"

All the ladies turn their attention toward Tommy. He's bent down on one knee next to Gracie, whispering to her.

Gracie starts laughing and running away from him. He chases her.

"They're playing?" I say, like, *Duh, Mom.* "Hey, why aren't you drinking wine today?" I ask, noticing she isn't drinking any, and that is unusual. I mean, this is a party.

"Oh, I was feeling a little dehydrated, so I'm sticking to water this afternoon."

"Oh," I say.

Millie and Peyton are discussing Deron's abs and how dreamy Damian's voice is.

Millie says to Mom, "Abby, did you see Tommy? He just took something out of his pocket and handed it to Gracie. Now, he's whispering to her again. What is he up to?"

Mom smiles and shakes her head. "I have no clue."

"I probably shouldn't tell you this," Grandma Stevens says, and I'm thinking, *&*%!!!!! Don't tell her!*

Mom leans towards her conspiratorially. "What?! Tell me!"

"Well, Tommy told us the girls have a special surprise for you, and we were all supposed to be out here to see it. What do you think it could be?"

I let out a big sigh of relief.

All the ladies start speculating about what the surprise could be.

Mrs. Arrington mentions that it is Christmas. Grandma Douglas suggests that sneaky is synonymous with man.

But Mom shakes her head. "No, he's been working on some deal. He won't tell me what it is yet, but he did say it will be good for all of us."

"I heard him and Matt talking about some new script," Marisa suggests.

"I agree with Aiden's mom. It's Christmas," I say, stating what should be the obvious reason for sneaking around this time of year.

"Looks like you're about to find out," Grandma Stevens says, as Gracie starts barreling in our direction, screaming, "Momma, Momma, MOMMMAA!!! Gracie has special rock too! Read it to me!"

Mom sets it down on the table with the others. "Well, honey, it says WILL."

"YOU, ME, ABBY, WILL? Who's *WILL*?" I ask Mom.

Peyton says, "Oh, maybe it's Prince William. No, wait, he's already taken."

Millie says, "Will. I. Am? Do you know him?"

"Uh, no," Mom says, looking confused.

"I know!" Marisa says, "What about Will Smith? Are you going to do a movie with him?"

"Not that I know of."

"How about William Tell?" I offer, trying to keep them off track. What is with their one-track movie minds? "Or William Shakespeare, or Will Ferrell or—"

Mom interrupts me. "Why does Tommy look so suspicious? Like, more suspicious than usual."

"He's a man," Grandma Douglas says with a laugh.

"Tommy, get your ass over here," Mom yells.

Tommy saunters over, looking way too cool for a guy who has planned a surprise wedding and is about to propose.

"What's up with all the rocks?" she demands.

He stands in front of the table, leans across to kiss her, and then studies the rocks. "Hmmm, well, first off, you have them in the wrong order."

"I do?"

"Yeah, here." He rearranges them so they read, *WILL YOU ME ABBY*.

"Will. You. Me. Abby? That still makes no sense."

Tommy flashes his trademark naughty grin, leans against the pergola post, and says casually. "That's because you're still missing one." He reaches into his pocket, fishes out another rock, and tosses it to me. "Fix that for your mom, will ya, baby?"

I catch the rock, walk to the front of the table, and pretend to study the rocks.

I slide apart the YOU and ME rocks, making space for the important one I'm about to put down.

I slowly lay down the MARRY rock, so the message is clear.

WILL YOU MARRY ME, ABBY.

Peyton, Marisa, Kym, and the grandmas gasp audibly. Millie screams in delight.

Mom's expression is priceless, and you can see a full spectrum of emotions cross her expressive face. From utter shock to understanding, back to utter shock, then to realization, causing happy tears to spring to her eyes.

Then, she does it.

Her mouth turns up at the corners, then her small smile turns into a full-on beaming grin.

She turns toward Tommy, who is now on one knee beside her, showing off a very different kind of rock in a velvet box.

"So? Will you marry me, Abby?" he asks.

She leaps out of her chair and dives on him with such force that she knocks him to the ground.

Now, she's lying on top of him in the grass, kissing him.

And . . . still kissing him.

"Um, hello," I cough. "There are children present."

Mom gives Tommy one more deep kiss.

Then she leans up and says breathlessly, "I would love to marry you, Tommy, my love."

Everyone has gathered around to watch the spectacle.

We all clap and cheer.

When Mom gets up, Emery asks, "Why did you knock Daddy over, Momma? I get in trouble when I jump on sissy like that."

"Mommy is really happy. Daddy asked Mommy to marry him."

Avery jumps up and down with excitement and asks, "When, Mommy?"

Mom looks at Tommy adoringly and replies, "As soon as possible."

Tommy gets himself off the ground, puts the ring on her finger, and gives her another devious grin. "I was hoping you would say that." Then he turns to everyone and announces, "Wedding in ten minutes."

Mom's in shock.

"I think we'll need just a little more time than that," I say.

"So this wasn't really about the wine?" Millie asks.

Tommy grins and shakes his head. "That was just the excuse to get you all here but, trust me, there will be lots of celebrating."

"Okay, so wedding in one hour," I announce. "Everyone meet under the trees behind the barn. If you get ready early, there are cocktails waiting."

Mom is still in shock.

"But I don't have a dress!"

"Actually, you have a bunch to choose from," Kym informs her. "Now, let's go get you ready."

We go into the house and head up to Mom's bathroom, which I know has been transformed into a mini-salon.

Mom's still gushing. "I can't believe he planned all this. The rocks were adorable and to have you girls in on it was so special. How did he come up with it?"

"We've been kicking around engagement ideas for the past month. You should hear some of the crazy ideas we came up with. He told me when I started school that he wanted to ask you. He was having rings designed. When he got sketches back, we picked one and, while they were making it, we starting brainstorming for ways to surprise you. I thought the idea of doing it all in the same day was smart. You remember what a mess planning Millie's wedding was—all the speculation, the drama, the following her around. Tommy wanted this very private. But he had some good proposal ideas. We talked about doing shells on the beach, he thought about taking you skydiving, to the top of a mountain, in a helicopter, on a yacht. You name it. He's really quite creative."

Mom smiles dreamily.

"Have you had a chance to look closely at the ring?"

"No, but it's dazzling."

"Look closer. Around the big stone, there are seven smaller stones. One for each of us. Our family."

Mom looks like she's gonna start crying again.

And . . . she does.

"That is *so* sweet." She hugs me and whispers, "I have a secret."

My eyes get big. The last time Mom had a secret she was pregnant with Gracie. "Really?!"

She grins big.

"Does Tommy know yet?"

"No. I just did the pregnancy test yesterday. About fell off the toilet when I watched it turn pink."

"Pink is probably the right color with all of us girls. Tommy is a brave man."

"Tommy is a good man. We got lucky, blessed, when he came into our lives."

I get tears in my eyes too. "Yeah, we did."

"Aiden seems like a good man."

"He is."

As we approach her room, Kym is waiting by the door. She says quietly, "The hair and makeup team believe they are preparing you for a party."

Mom and I nod in understanding.

ONCE MOM'S HAIR is curled and braided into a pretty updo, Kym has James escort the hair and makeup crew out while we go into Kym's room to choose her wedding dress.

She tries on four dresses. All of them are pretty, but not really what I pictured her wearing.

"I saved the best for last," Kym says, sliding the perfect dress on her.

WORDS THAT FILL MY PAGES.
11PM

IT'S LATE. THE vows have been said, the toasts have been raised, the food has been eaten, the wine's being drunk, and the little kids are tucked into bed. I'm sitting at a table with Tommy and Grandpa, watching Mom dance in a circle with Millie and Kym.

They are being a little wild.

Aiden, who just finished dancing with his mom, kisses my cheek and sits down next to me.

Grandpa watches them dance, then leans toward me. "Your mom's a handful." He nods at Tommy.

Tommy nods. "You've got that right. Of course, that might be what I like best about her."

Grandpa motions toward me.

I put my hand up to my chest. "What? You think I'm a handful, too?"

Tommy and Aiden both laugh. They seem to think that's quite funny.

Tommy says to me, "Uh, yeah." Then he turns to Aiden. "You up for that?"

Aiden grins. "Yeah. I think I am."

"On that note," I say, getting up, "I think I'll go dance with the other handfuls."

Damian intercepts me. "Remember the song we worked on in St. Croix?"

"The *sorta like fate* one?"

"Yeah. I'm going up on stage to sing it for her." He looks nervous. "Tell me I'm not nuts. Tell me it's okay that I'm crazy in love with her when I've only known her a month."

"You're not nuts, Damian. You should trust your feelings."

He shakes his head. "I can't believe I'm going to do this. This song, it's telling her—and the world—exactly how I feel. I've never put myself out there like this before."

"Now who's being dramatic?" I tease. "Your family and friends are going to hear it, not exactly the world."

He looks around the room. "No, but they're my world. The people who I care about most."

"And the people who will both tease you mercilessly and be happy for you. Is she worth a little teasing?"

He glances at her out on the dance floor, his eyes filling with emotion. "I keep picturing our own wedding. I want to marry her, Keats. I'd do it today if I could. I know we're young. I know it's crazy. But I would. My dad would freak if I told him that."

I give him a hug. "You're an adult, Damian. You have to make decisions about your life. Well, almost. A few more weeks and my froggy becomes a man," I say with a laugh.

"Peyton wants to plan something for me. Should I let her, or should we stick with tradition?"

"We've been going bowling and then out for hot wings on your birthday for a long time. Why don't you let me help her plan something and we'll surprise you."

"Sounds good." He nods and takes a deep breath. "Okay, I'm doing this."

He goes onstage, slings his guitar around him, and addresses us.

"I think we all know the story about when Tommy and

Abby met. How people in the room *swore* they could see the sparks fly. Or, so my dad says." He laughs. "No offense, but I always kinda thought it was bullshit. A fairy tale made up to sell more movies. But then it happened to me. I've been working on this song since the moment I met her. The melody kept playing in my head. And as soon as Keats told me the French word for fate is *sort*, the rest of the lyrics flowed. This song is called 'Sorta like Fate.'"

Aiden joins me on the dance floor and wraps his arms around me. "Sorta like fate? I told you that, didn't I?"

"Yeah, you did."

Damian gently plays a few chords on his guitar and starts singing beautifully.

"You're my faith and inspiration,
You're the ink in my tattoo.
You're the water in my desert,
All I think about is you.

You're the sun in all my sunsets,
You're the wind in every breeze.
You're the moon on my horizon,
You're the one that makes me breathe.

It's sorta like fate that we're together,
It's sorta like fate that we're both here,
It's sorta like you and me forever.
My destiny is near.
It's sorta like you and me against everything,
It's sorta like fate . . .
It's sorta like fate . . .

You're the joy in all my madness,
You're the fire in my flame.
You're the smile from across the room,
You're the thought I can't erase.

You're my happy ever after,
You're the beating of my heart.
You're the words that fill my pages,
You're the light in all my dark.

It's sorta like fate that we're together,
It's sorta like fate that we're both here,
It's sorta like you and me forever.
My destiny's so clear.
It's sorta like everything that I ever need,
It's sorta like fate . . .

The spark to all my passion,
My future standing there.
Yeah, yeah, yeah.
You're everything I've ever wanted,
So, baby, don't be scared.

It's sorta like fate that we're together,
It's sorta like fate that we're both here,
It's sorta like you and me forever.
I'm your destiny, my dear.
It's sorta like you and me against everything,
It's sorta like fate . . .
It's sorta like fate . . .
It's sorta like fate . . .
It's sorta like fate.

You pull on me like gravity,
I wanna get down on one knee.
The world can spin around us,
Cuz, baby, now it's you and me."

"Wow," I whisper. "That was beautiful."

Aiden spins me around to face him. "Did you help him write that?"

"Not really. I just helped with the chorus."

"Is the song about us?"

"No, he wrote it for your sister."

"But you helped with the lyrics?"

"A little, when we were in St. Croix. I couldn't sleep and heard him working on it. So I went down to the beach and we just had a conversation about love at first sight and what it feels like."

"And you were thinking about me?"

I don't answer his question but, rather, ask one of my own. It's something I've been wondering about. "Do you really think we're sorta like fate, Aiden? Or was that just the player in you talking?"

Aiden takes my chin in his hand and looks deep into my eyes. "Player Aiden *never* talked about things like love, fate, or marriage. Just like the stars, all that is only for you. Want to know my favorite part of the song?"

I nod.

"*The world can spin around us because, baby, now it's you and me.*"

"Why is that part your favorite?"

"Because that's what I want more than anything. To only have to worry about us."

"And not all the stalker and Brooklyn stuff?"

"Exactly. I love you. I wish that's all that mattered."

I give him a kiss and say, "I love you too."

"Damian's in love with my sister, isn't he?"

"I think that's pretty obvious. In fact, I'd say he's woo-ing her."

Aiden grins. "You really should always listen to me. I'm smart."

"I don't know about that, but you definitely were right about the wooing. Wanna hear something funny?"

"Of course."

"When Dawson wanted us to get back together, I told him he'd have to woo me. He sent a text where he mis-spelled *wooed*. Forgot the e. So it just said he wanted to wood me. I got all mad at him, but it was kinda funny."

"So can I woo you with my wood?" Aiden asks adorably.

"I think it's the only kind of wooing you haven't done yet." I take his hand in mine. "Come on, let's go congratu-late Damian on his beautiful song."

We wander over to the stage. Damian's arm is wrapped around Peyton, whose dazzling grin is just like her brother's. Definitely song-worthy.

"You helped me," Damian says. "I was leaning toward this before our talk. There she was, just sitting on the beach."

He points to me, so I sing, "Singing du wa ditty ditty dumb ditty do."

He smiles. "Flipping her hair like she didn't have a care."

We all laugh.

He's like, "I think maybe I should stop while I'm ahead."

Mom and Tommy join us.

"Damn, you must have read my mind. I think all those things about my *wife*," Tommy says.

Mom gushes, "I didn't think it was a big deal we weren't married, but I'll admit: I like hearing you say that. And, Damian, you better record that song quick. You've got a hit on your hands."

GLIMPSE OF THE FUTURE.
12:30AM

AIDEN PULLS ME off the dance floor and says, "Let's go for a walk."

I take his hand and follow him. He seems to be wandering aimlessly, but I get the feeling I'm being led somewhere.

"Isn't it a gorgeous night?" he asks.

"It's been the perfect night. Mom was so surprised he proposed, and everyone was so surprised by the wedding." I spin around in the grass. "I'm so happy I got to be here with my family. And be with you."

"I like your family. Your grandpa is a character."

"Yeah, he is. I love him. So, where are we going?"

"For a walk," he says cryptically.

A few minutes later, we're standing in the gazebo where Mom and Tommy got married. Aiden flicks a switch and the ceiling lights up with hundreds of twinkle lights.

"Did you do this? The lights? They weren't on here this afternoon."

"I thought we could dance in private. It's a lot prettier than my dorm."

"I love your room. And the twinkle lights."

"Before we dance, I have a present for you. Do you want it now?"

"I do."

He stops and grins at me.

"What?"

"You just said *I do*. In a wedding gazebo. It gave me a glimpse of the future. Of our wedding."

"Does the future ever scare you?" I ask him.

"Not as long as you're in it with me."

Knowing my future is uncertain, I don't reply, but rather focus on the present, untying the ribbon and letting him open the lid.

Nestled in a little black velvet box is a beautiful ring. In the center is a green stone, surrounded by teeny diamonds. Radiating out from it are four silver filigree hearts forming a four-leaf clover, each leaf set with a marquis-shaped green stone. Around the edges of the hearts are more of the little diamonds and behind the clover is more silver, making it look like two clovers sitting on top of each other.

"It's gorgeous," I manage to mutter, overwhelmed by its delicate beauty. "I've never seen anything like it before."

"It's vintage," he says, grinning.

"I love it," I say as he slides it on my left ring finger.

"This isn't your Christmas present. It's a ring from me to you. I love you, Keatyn. I know the future scares you. I know that you can't commit to anything, so I'm not asking you to. I just want you to always know, wherever you are, wherever we are, that I love you. And I want you to carry our luck with you."

My eyes dart above me.

"What are you looking for?"

"I'm waiting for fireworks to go off, doves to flutter around us, or a romantic score to start playing."

"Why?"

"Because this seems too perfect to be real."

"Dance with me?"

"There's no music," I tease.

He pulls me into his arms. "There doesn't have to be."

I look into his eyes. "I love you, Aiden."

"I love you too," he says, as our lips meet.

We share a sweet kiss, then he says, "Did you really think I wouldn't bring music?"

I laugh as he pulls his phone from his suit pocket. Kym hit the swag closet and dressed Aiden to perfection. He's wearing a beautiful tan suit with a light brown pinstripe. A chocolate brown shirt. No tie. His own deep brown Armani lace-up dress shoes.

The song that plays from his phone is a dance remix of my current favorite sexy love song.

He pulls me back into his arms, moves his leg between mine, and kisses me.

Our kissing starts out slow, sexy, and sweet, mimicking our dancing.

But as the song's beat picks up, so do we.

Our kissing changes from sweet to passionate, then to almost frantic.

I feel volatile, like I could explode, combust, or ignite.

His hands are in my hair, my tongue is swirling against his, and my head totally filled with cotton candy. I can't think.

I can only feel.

The fire that is Aiden.

When his lips touch my neck with hard, sucking kisses, I can't help it, I push my hips into his.

Which must have been all he could take, because he picks me up, wraps my legs around his waist, and pushes me against the gazebo's ledge.

My hands immediately move to his pants. Unzipping them.

My mind is spinning.

His love potion is stronger than ever, seeping into my every pore and filling me with uncontrollable desire.

Very quickly, he pushes my skirt up, slides my panties over, and fills me completely. Like he was made to fit me.

And I'm pretty sure he was.

He rocks my body against the gazebo.

It's rough.

Hot.

Hard.

I don't know how long it lasts. Whether it's three minutes or three hours.

Doesn't matter.

It's all it took.

It's like he's the wind and I'm the ocean.

My body moves like a tidal wave in response to every thrust and motion.

It's the most intense, hot, crazy experience of my life.

The Titan owns me, proving it knows what my body wants more than I know myself.

I really thought when we finally did it, I'd be describing it with words like *a joining of the mind, body, and soul.*

But this is pure godly need.

Pent up desire—filling me up, hard and hot.

It's like when he pushed me on his desk and kissed me with his tongue.

I thought then that a god's full power was unleashed on me.

I was very wrong.

This is when he's most powerful.

When he's on the brink of losing control.

It's like all his godly powers—that are usually so well-honed—are in their purest and rawest form.

I think of my scripts.

Making love on a bed of rose petals in a meadow under a rainbow.

Just like the script I wadded up and threw in the trash before I kicked the soccer ball at him, Aiden just took my first-time script and burnt it.

Probably with his hotness.

No more fairy-tale bullshit.

Fuck that.

I rewrite every script I've ever written to this.

This exact, crazy moment.

White heat and electricity sizzling in the air.

Lightning ready to strike inside of me.

Then it's bolts of pleasure, flashes of desire, and burning heat.

Now I understand why mere mortals always succumbed to Aphrodite.

Making love to a god is like nothing on earth.

"Holy shit," he says, his voice deeper and sexier than I've ever heard. "That was . . ."

"Fucking amazing," I finish.

He gives me one more hug, whispers *I love you* into my ear, and then moves away from me.

"Uh, when did you put on a condom?"

"Sometime between when you unzipped my pants and when we did it."

"I swear, you never took your hands off me. Are you sure you're not magical?"

"Yes, I'm sure," he says, laughing and kissing me again. "Take me back to your room, Boots. I'm so not even close to being done with you tonight."

WHEN WE GET back to my room, we lock the door, turn on

some soft music, and dim the lights.

The night is a swirl of kissing, hotness, positions, amazingness, sexiness, and love.

All hot, sweet, and unbelievably, perfectly unscripted.

I never knew sex could be so utterly, breathtakingly beautiful.

I am so in love with Aiden.

And, more importantly, I absolutely know he loves me.

I look at the ring he placed on my left hand and know that's all the commitment I'll ever need.

A few months ago, when B was leaving, I needed more. I practically begged for it.

I understand now why I needed it. I needed emotional reassurance and thought that a label could make our relationship *be* a relationship. I was being clingy, hoping to revive what had fallen apart while we were in Europe. What I was afraid to let go of.

I feel kind of bad. B was right when he patted my chest and told me I should've known it in my heart.

I should have felt it, but I know why I didn't.

Because it wasn't flowing out of him. He hadn't given me his heart. Not in the way I deserved.

Not in the way Aiden has. His love for me shines through his every action.

"I still can't believe you let me lie to you."

"Sometimes I wanted to shake you and tell you I knew. That you could trust me."

"I trust you more than anyone I've ever known."

"And I love you more than I even knew was possible."

I smile at him.

For a long time, I was convinced that love potion resided in his mouth. On his tongue.

But I was wrong. The source of his power is the Titan.

It's practically a godly entity of its own when it's awakened.

Every time I think my sexual credit card is maxed out, he touches me and I'm ready to go shopping again.

And we all know how much I love to shop.

Saturday, December 24th

COOKIES FOR SANTA.
12:30PM

"KIKI! KIKI! GRACIE wants presents!" I wake up to the sound of Gracie screaming outside my door.

I crack one eye open, hoping she will stop so I can go back to sleep. I look at Aiden. He's out. I smile smugly, loving the knowledge that it was me who made him so tired.

Gracie lets out a high-pitched scream, similar to the sound I think someone would make had they just been stabbed.

Aiden jumps up. "What's wrong?"

I grab a robe, quickly wrap it around me, and throw open the door. "Gracie! Are you okay?"

She's sitting calmly on the floor, staring up at me with an angelic smile. "Gracie needs presents. And cookies for Santa."

I scoop her up and carry her into my room, noticing Aiden isn't in bed anymore. "Gracie, when you screamed like that, I thought you were hurt. You need to use your inside voice."

She puts her hand on her hip. "Gracie *did* use her inside

voice but Kiki no answer. I scream because I need Kiki now!"

"What do you need?" I ask again, as I hear the shower running in my bathroom.

Dang. I want to be in there with him.

Gracie must see me looking longingly at the bathroom door because she stands on the bed and grabs my face with her chubby little hands and forces me to look at her.

"Gracie need cookies for Santa."

"You can't put cookies out for Santa until tonight, before you go to bed."

Her face starts turning red, a sure sign she's ready to have a meltdown. I glance at the clock, surprised to see it's just past noon. The last time Aiden used my credit card was around six this morning.

Is it bad that I can't wait to get him back into bed with me?

But it's Christmas Eve and I'm here with my family, so I pull Gracie off my bed and carry her to my closet. "Why don't you pick me out something to wear, and then we'll go make some cookies. How does that sound?"

She gives me a broad smile, wraps her arms around my neck, and lays her head on my shoulder. I automatically pat her back gently and sway with her in front of the closet. "Are you tired, Gracie?"

"No!" she says, leaving her head on my shoulder.

I wrap my arm around her tighter, close my eyes, and keep swaying.

She smells so good. A mixture of baby shampoo and sweetness.

I'm so glad I got to come here. To watch Tommy and Mom finally say *I do*. To hear Damian profess his love for Peyton in front of everyone. To experience what Aiden and I shared last night. To hold my sister in my arms while she falls asleep.

I pray it's not the last time. That I get to hold her like this until she gets too big. That I'm part of her life for a long, long time. That I'll see her experience all the things she wants. That I'll give her advice about friends and boys, so she won't make all the stupid mistakes I did.

Aiden clears his throat. When I turn around to face him, I realize I'm in tears.

"Are you okay?" he asks softly.

I nod.

"You really think you might not survive this, don't you?"

I nod again as he very slowly sits on the bed, my reality finally hitting him full force.

He sits there for a minute, processing it. Then he stands up and wraps both Gracie and me in a hug.

"You always know how to make me feel better," I whisper.

"I love you, Keatyn," he says, kissing my forehead.

"Gracie love Kiki too," Gracie whispers.

MISTY TOES.
2PM

WHEN WE'RE IN the kitchen making cookies with the girls, Aiden asks me, "So what are your Christmas traditions? Do you open presents Christmas Eve or Christmas Day?"

"We have dinner, take pictures, then open all our presents from each other. On Christmas morning, we open our stockings, eat homemade cinnamon rolls, and open our gifts from Santa."

Aiden smiles. "That sounds fun. I bet the girls will be up really early."

"Usually around six. When the kids get up, we all have to get up."

"Those are Grandpa's rules," Grandma Douglas says, adding a dollop of frosting to a cookie.

"Well, Christmas is for kids," Grandma Stevens agrees, putting the finishing touches on a gingerbread man.

LATER, I TAKE a plate of cookies to the guys, who are in the library, drinking scotch and bullshitting.

Aiden and I go into the living room to sit down and relax.

"So, I get to give you your presents tonight, right?"

"You already got me a beautiful ring, Aiden. I don't need anything else."

He arches an eyebrow. "Too bad. Already bought them."

The triplets come tearing into the room and about hit me in the face with a green leaf.

Thank goodness I duck fast.

"Slow down. What are you doing?"

"We have misty toes!" they yell, all of them shoving sad, fake pieces of mistletoe above my head.

"Aye-den, you have to kiss her!" Avery yells.

"Yeah," I say. "Or someone else might."

"Who else is going to kiss you?" Ivery asks seriously.

"Me," Damian says, swooping in, giving me a kiss on the cheek, and stealing their mistletoe. He holds it above Avery and Ivery's heads, picks them both up, and kisses their cheeks.

Then he says, "Let's go find Peyton! She needs mistletoe

over her so we can kiss!"

As he rushes out of the room with the girls, he tosses a green leaf back at us.

Aiden raises his eyebrows at me. "I need more than a kiss. Any chance we could sneak away, now that the cookies are done?"

I look around. Grandpa is napping in the library. Tommy and Matt are in there, too, drinking scotch and deciding which cigars they want to take outside to smoke. Most of the ladies are still in the kitchen frosting cookies and making gingerbread houses.

"Absolutely," I say, as he grabs the mistletoe.

WHEN WE'RE SAFELY locked in my room, Aiden thrusts out his hips and dangles the mistletoe over the Titan.

"I'm surprised he's not tired," I tease.

"Never. Ever. Will he be tired of you."

I bend down and place a little kiss on the outside of his pants.

"Hmm. I'm not sure that's what he had in mind," Aiden says.

I push him backwards onto my chaise—which, after last night, may have to be burned before anyone else can stay in this room—unzip his pants, push my panties to the side and slide onto his lap, causing my naked parts to touch his.

"This or that?" I whisper, as I bite his neck and grind myself into him.

"This. Now," he says raggedly, his voice filled with desire.

He picks me up by the hips and guides me on top of him in one fluid motion.

"God, you're hot," he says, his lips finding my shoulder as he tries to go slow.

But I don't want slow.
I want him out of control.
And I'm learning a few tricks of my own.
One of which is letting myself go.
No insecurities about how I look. No trying to script.
Just raw, uncontrollable need.
For him.

THE DAUGHTER IN ME.
8PM

AFTER CHRISTMAS EVE dinner, which is a formal, sit-down affair in the dining room, we move to the large family room for opening gifts. Because we have multiple families in attendance, the present-opening seems like a bit of a free-for-all. But it's really fun. I help the girls open the puppet theater I bought them and the trunk full of crazy puppets. They stop opening presents for a bit and do a few shows, oblivious to everything. I watch Tommy open the Panerai Ferrari California Chronograph watch I splurged on. I got a little happy dance and a huge kiss on the cheek for the custom guitar I had made for Damian with pieces of his first album cover airbrushed on it.

When Mom opens the gorgeous diamond Chopard cuff I gave her, she says, "Keatyn, this is beautiful. How did you—" She stops and puts her face in her hand. When she looks up, her eyes are full of tears. She motions with her head for me to come to her.

I drop to my knees on the floor in front of the ottoman she's perched on, take the bracelet out of the box, and put it on her wrist. "I knew it would fit you perfectly."

"Your gifts are very extravagant this year."

I nod, tears filling my own eyes. "I bought the girls each a pair of earrings that match your bracelet. Sam, my financial guy, has them. You know, just in case, like, something would happen. They're a bit extravagant, too, but let them wear them, okay?"

Mom nods, pulling me into a hug. "With all of us here—with the wedding—I almost forgot about it, you know?"

"Me too. It's been an amazing few days. I'm so glad I got to be here."

"Your grandfather told me not to worry, but I overheard him telling Garrett that he *is* worried."

"They weren't talking about me, Mom. I'm going to be fine. I promise," I lie. "The gifts for the girls aren't because of Vincent. I just realized life is short. And, if anything happens to me between now and their sixteenth birthdays, I just wanted things to be in order. Grandpa gave me a big trust and I needed to be certain it would all go to them someday. But I hope that I can give them the gifts myself."

"The mom in me says I should make you take this back."

"And the daughter in me will be crushed if you do."

She hugs me again tightly. "I love you, Keatyn."

"I love you too, Mom. I hope you know that. I know this has been hard on us—that it's driven us apart. But it doesn't matter. Nothing will ever keep me from loving you."

"I'm so sorry I haven't talked to you more. I was just trying to protect you."

"I know, Mom. I was, too. Garrett says we're a lot alike."

She laughs. "We are, but you have your father's stubbornness."

"And his eyes," Grandma Douglas adds, joining our hug. "You both need to take care of yourselves. You understand me?"

I SIT BACK down next to Aiden. We've exchanged gifts like clothes and shoes, but I bought him something special too. Something to remember me by. I grab his hand and lead him into the library and shut the doors behind us.

"I have something else that I bought you. It's a bit extravagant. I went a little crazy on Christmas this year. I guess now, at least, you understand why I did."

"Because you're afraid you won't be here for another one?"

"When I bought the gifts, yes, I was worried about that. But I'm not anymore."

"Why not?"

I give him my best smile and lie through my teeth. "Because Grandpa thinks the takeover will go through. And once that's complete, he won't own the rights to the movie anymore. Which means his whole dream of making it goes away."

"And if he can't make the movie, he won't want you?"

"Exactly. Okay, so, here." I shove the present into his hands.

He sits down and opens the beautiful Van Cleef & Arpels watch with a black alligator strap, white lacquer dial, and a bezel set with diamonds.

"This is incredible, Boots."

"I got this brand of watch because throughout history their jewelry designs place a special emphasis on luck. In fact, Jacques Arpels liked to say, *To be lucky, you have to believe in luck.*" He places the watch on his wrist. "It looks good on you. I knew it would."

"I love it."

"I love you," I say.

"And, so you know, I don't just believe in luck. I believe in *our* luck," he says, giving me a sweet kiss. "We're lucky together."

AS WE REJOIN everyone in the family room, Mom is telling Gracie that she needs to change out of her red tutu and into her pajamas.

Gracie throws herself on the floor and screams.

When no one pays attention to her, she calms herself down.

I figure I'll give it a shot. "Okay, you munchkins have to get to bed. Otherwise, Santa won't come."

Gracie folds her little arms across her chest. "NO! NO BED! Gracie not tired!"

The triplets all roll their eyes. They're used to her tantrums.

"Why don't I give you a piggyback ride?" Aiden says, dazzling her with his smile.

She smiles back at him, says, "O-tay," and jumps on his back.

I never did do research to find out how other girls react to his smile, but I could obviously add Gracie to the affected list.

Mom is standing there watching Aiden with big eyes as Gracie bosses him about which way to go.

"Can we keep him?" she says to me.

I laugh.

"Are you keeping him?" she asks pointedly.

I frown at her.

"What's the face for? Don't you want to keep him?"

"It's complicated, Mom. That's all."

"Love isn't supposed to be complicated."

"Well, I didn't think so either. Kinda like I thought you and Tommy went to the ballet and lived happily ever after."

She scrunches up her face. "Okay, fine. Love isn't supposed to be complicated, but it always is."

"Mom, can I ask you a question?"

"You just did," she teases.

"Did you like B? Did you like us together?"

Mom rubs her fingers across her eyebrow. I do the exact same thing when I'm stressed.

"I think that's complicated."

"Tell me."

"Keatyn, all I'll ever want is for you to be happy."

"I know, but . . ."

"When you and Brook started dating, you seemed deliriously happy. I was happy for you. But when you came back from Europe, it seemed like you weren't as happy."

"I wanted a relationship and he didn't. In retrospect, I understand why he didn't. He didn't think we needed to label our love. I should have known better. You and Tommy didn't need labels."

"That's not true at all. We have been in an exclusive and committed relationship since a few months after we met. But it was kept between us. Not something we needed to shout out to the world, because it didn't matter to us what anyone else thought. All that mattered is what we felt."

"B got us matching tattoos because he thought we'd be together forever. That was his big commitment. I was just too immature to see it. I thought if I couldn't scream it from my social media that it wasn't real."

"And now?"

"I know better. And I love Aiden, but B . . ." My hand immediately goes to my chest.

"Is still in your heart?"

"Yes. And I don't know what that means."

Mom pats my hand. "You'll figure it out, honey."

"Are you serious? That's your advice? Can't you use the wisdom you've gained from being alive for almost forty years to tell me what it means?"

"I'll give you the advice Grandpa Douglas gave me when I was struggling with my own feelings."

"What did he say?"

"He told me to follow my heart because it would always lead me home."

"When were you struggling with your own feelings? When you met Tommy?"

"Yes. I felt like falling in love with him was a betrayal to your father. To your grandparents. I lost my own parents at a young age and they had become my family. I was afraid they wouldn't understand."

"But they did."

"Yeah, they did. They lost their only son when your dad died. Having Tommy and the girls in their lives has helped them heal too."

"I want to go home," I say quietly.

"Then follow your heart," Mom replies.

Sunday, December 25th

ONE OF HER STEPS.
3PM

I'M PUTTING OUR gifts from Santa in my room when my phone rings. I look down and see that it's B. I had texted him, along with all my other friends, last night, wishing them a Merry Christmas, but he was the only one I hadn't heard back from.

"Hey, B!" I say. "Merry Christmas!"

"Keats, um . . . shit."

"Brooklyn, what's wrong? Are you crying? Are you okay?"

"Not really. My mom just called me."

"Your *mom*? But it's been . . ."

"Eleven years."

"What did she say?"

"That she was sorry. She's apparently going through rehab and trying to get her life together. I'm one of her steps."

"Do you know why she left?"

"She says she left because my dad was too controlling and she was tired of him telling her what to do."

"That might be a good excuse for why she left him. It doesn't explain why she left you."

"I always thought it was because I got in trouble for not paying attention at school."

"Is that what you've thought all these years?"

"I did when I was younger. Now, I know that's not why you leave someone. She wants to see me."

"Are you going to?"

"My dad will be pissed."

"Brooklyn, you're twenty years old. You're in charge of your life."

He sighs. "I'm not in control of anything, Keats. My dad controls my career. Fucking security controls everything else. I'm sick of everyone telling me what to do and people getting mad at me for what I can't do."

"I'm trying to get our lives back."

"I'm sorry I bailed on you."

"I understand why you did it. I just don't understand why you didn't tell me yourself."

"It's not just my dad. It's her."

"The girl you're seeing?"

"Yeah. What I said about you when I won hurt her. She didn't know about you. About us."

"What did you tell her?"

"That you're the only girl I've ever loved, but that we couldn't see each other."

"Did she want to know why?"

"I told her your parents don't like me."

"We tell similar lies, B. That's what I came up with too."

"Do you feel bad lying?"

"I did, yes. Aiden knows the truth now. I had told him a lot about you, but when Damian put you on speakerphone, he was there. He heard."

"How did he take it?"

"He was upset."

"He's in love with you?"

"Yes."

"This is hard. Us. I need to see you. Figure my life out."

"What do you need to figure out?"

"Our lives. My career. Everything just feels out of control. I hate it."

"Life is divine chaos, isn't that what you told me?"

"Yeah, but mine doesn't feel very divine right now."

"So decide what you want to do and do it."

"I need to see my mom, Keats. I was sort of hoping maybe you'd go with me."

"Where is she?"

"Malibu."

"Oh, B. I'm not sure being in Malibu is a good idea for either of us right now."

"I heard you went back and danced at that club."

"How did you hear that?"

"Garrett's security guys were talking about it. About how stupid it was."

"It was well-planned. I was in and out of there fast."

"So, in theory, if we planned it well, you could come, right? And it would give us a little time together. We need it, Keats."

"Where are you now?"

"Hawaii. The first three stops next year are in Australia, so my dad has us booked to be there until the tour starts back up in March."

"So, the tour is over for the year?"

"Yeah. When did you think it would be over?"

"I don't know. You talked about going away for a year. I

guess that's what was in my head."

"We said we'd give it a year and see how I did. If I could get sponsors. I won one event, but I didn't do all that well in the others, so my dad will be picking up most of the tab for next season."

"Which means you'll still have to listen to him?"

"Yeah," he says somberly.

"If you didn't have to listen to him, what would you do differently?"

"I'd focus on surfing. Nothing else."

"Isn't that what your dad wants?"

"He's more focused on the business side of it. The social media. He thinks I'm going to get sponsors, commercials, and deals because of his business savvy. That I don't have to be that good to be famous. That I have a marketable look."

"Did something happen between you and your dad? You've always gotten along."

He's quiet for a second. Then he sighs. "He lied to me."

"How?"

"All this time, he's known where she was. He purposely kept us apart."

"Why?"

"I'm not sure what to believe. She said that he wouldn't let her see me."

"B, your dad loves you. There has to be a good reason."

"We got into a fight. Today. On Christmas. I wanted answers. He said she was mentally unstable. Didn't want to talk about it. I kept pushing. I asked how I could trust him when all this time he'd been lying to me. You should've seen the look on his face when he walked out the door. It killed me."

I picture the look on Aiden's face when he walked out of the dance.

"You need to find him and apologize."

"How do I trust him?"

"Sometimes you have to lie to protect the people you love."

"I want to see my Mom. I need to see her. I need to understand."

"Then see her. But listen to your dad's story before you decide he's lied to you about everything. Maybe he only lied to you about one thing. When are you supposed to see her?"

"What's taking you so long?" Aiden says as he walks through the door.

I hold a finger up, asking him to give me a minute. He narrows his eyes at me, trying to assess the situation.

"On January third," Brooklyn says.

"I'll go with you, B."

"Really?"

"Yeah, really."

"I can't believe I'm going to see her. After all this time." He starts crying, and then so do I. I wish I could reach through the phone and hug him.

"It'll be okay. B?"

"Yeah?"

"I didn't send you a Christmas gift because you're supposed to be with that girl."

"I didn't send you anything either."

"I want to sponsor you next season. No strings attached. Just text me what you need. It's my Christmas gift to you."

"Keats, I can't let you do that."

"I went crazy on Christmas this year."

"In case it's your last one?"

"Yeah . . ."

"Don't fucking say that."

"I'm saying it, B, because it's true. Now, go find your

dad and let him tell you his side of the story."

"Fine. I will. Merry Christmas, Keats."

"Merry Christmas, B."

Aiden looks at me expectantly.

"Um, I need just a minute." I put my face into my hands, take a few deep breaths, and try to process everything that just happened.

After a few minutes, Aiden sits on the bed next to me, wraps his arm around me, and kisses the side of my face.

"You okay?"

I nod.

"Wanna talk about it?"

"Not really, Aiden," I say, but then I see his eyes and remember what he said at Stockton's about his imagination. "It was B, as you heard. He was upset."

"Where are you going with him?"

"To visit his mom. He hasn't seen or heard from her since she left over ten years ago. Until today. And, to top it off, he found out that his dad has been lying about her all this time. He told B he didn't know where she was, but he just didn't want him to see her."

"Why?"

"His dad says she was mentally unstable. They got into a fight about it. He was upset."

"Why were you crying?"

"Because he started crying when I said I'd go with him."

Aiden is quiet and seems to be choosing his words carefully. "Will you be gone for long?"

"He wants . . ."

"You?"

"He wants to see how we feel. When we're together."

Aiden looks up at the ceiling, closes his eyes, and goes, "Boom."

And that sets me off.

"You're right. I'm in no position to be saying I love someone or sleeping with them when my life is such a mess. It's not fair to you. It's just, you made me feel—never mind. I have to go." I'm ready to start crying, and I'm tired of letting him see me cry. "Uh, I'll see you later," I say as I rush out the door.

"Keatyn. Wait."

I don't wait. I run outside, down the long drive, and to the gate. I see the guards and feel trapped.

Caged.

Like an animal in the zoo.

I have to get out of here, so I walk to the gate and open it.

"You can't leave," one of the guards says to me in French, another guard quickly repeating the same phrase in English.

I drop to my knees, bang my head against the gate, and start bawling.

A FEW MINUTES later, I hear Grandpa's voice.

"What's all this ruckus about?"

I wipe my eyes and turn to look at him.

He hands me a to-go cup.

"What's this?"

Grandpa smiles. "My special lemonade, of course."

"I need to go for a walk," I tell him.

"Then let's go," he says. "Boys, open the gate."

Surprisingly, the guards listen to Grandpa.

As we walk out onto the road, he turns back and instructs them not to follow us.

I take a deep, cleansing breath, pulling as much air into my lungs as I can before exhaling it.

"Talk," Grandpa commands.

"I'm hurting people that I love."

Grandpa studies me for a moment. "Sam told me you picked out a resting place."

"I thought our dealings were supposed to be privileged."

"They are," he laughs. "From everyone but me."

"So you know everything I put in my will?"

"Yes. You're a smart and caring young woman. I'm very proud of how you've changed. You're not the same girl you were when you visited me last summer."

"Having your life in danger makes the things that should be important more clear."

"Like what?"

"Love, mostly."

He nods, agreeing. "In the grand scheme of life, that's all that really matters. The people who you love."

"I need a plan, Grandpa. Mine is a mess. And, between filming and the wedding, I haven't had time to think about what's next."

"Then start with what's first. What will you do when you take over the company? How will you handle it?"

"Mostly, I want Vincent to know it was me. I want to personally fire him. I want to tell him I'll be remaking *A Day at the Lake.* Then I want him escorted out of his building."

"So do it."

"Do you think it will actually happen?"

"Do you doubt your Grandpa?"

I smile. "No."

"I won't let you confront him in person. But if you want to see him, I'll agree to a video conference."

"Put me on a big screen, huh? Hell, that's even better. Honestly, if I really wanted to piss him off, I'd wear Mom's bikini from the movie and scream."

"That's brutal," he says, slapping me on the back. "I love it. Then what will you do?"

"The movie is cast except for three characters. I'm going to do a press release. And then I'm going to cast the parts. I'll go back to New York City. I'll go to Malibu. Be seen around."

Grandpa shakes his head.

"It will be okay. We'll have Mom's publicist set it all up. He'll only see pictures of where I was last night, not where I am now."

"I had a chat with Garrett. He thinks pushing Vincent is a bad idea."

"I think it's a bad idea too, but it's my only option."

"Your Cooper is very loyal to you, isn't he?"

"Yes. He's become more than a bodyguard to me. He's more like a friend. His sister was killed by a stalker."

"No wonder he's on your side."

"If something doesn't happen quickly, I may have to deal with Vincent face-to-face."

"Hotshot, there's bravery and there's stupidity. It's a fine line."

"I hope to be on the smart side of stupid."

Grandpa breaks out laughing. "Now tell me the real reason why you were crying."

"It's Aiden."

"You love him. It's pretty obvious."

"I do, but I shouldn't."

"Why not?"

"Because he makes my life feel like a fairy tale when it's not. I'm setting us both up for heartbreak. I told him I loved him. I shouldn't have."

"Did you mean it?"

"With everything I am."

Grandpa's face changes.

"What?" I ask.

"Grandma had a bit of a scare this week."

"What kind of scare?"

"A man followed her from the grocery store and tried to run her off the road."

"What did she do?!"

"Your grandmother is one smart cookie. She turned onto one of the dirt roads that lead through the fields. He didn't follow her."

"Do you know why?"

"We put the hostile takeover together fast. The owner-ship of one of the shell corporations wasn't as tight as it should have been. My name was on it. Since our last names are the same, it probably didn't take Vincent long to figure out who's behind the takeover. This trip came at a good time."

"Stay here. Until this is over."

"Your grandmother is."

"You too, Grandpa. You can help from here."

"I can handle myself."

"I know you can, but you're not getting any younger."

"Cunning beats youth any day."

"Except in a fight."

"We're in a fight right now. This takeover is part of the beat down. You want Vincent humiliated. You want him too hurt to fight back. The only problem is that when a man has nothing to lose, he becomes desperate."

"That's exactly what I want. For him to be so desperate he won't be able to think or plan. Up until now—following people, breaking into rehab, maybe even the killings—were probably jobs he paid someone to do. I need him so beat down that he won't be able to think straight. I want him so mad he'll do things himself. I want him to feel trapped. Caged. To feel like everything he loves is lost. I want him to feel like I do."

"Cooper told Garrett he's afraid you're going to let yourself get kidnapped."

"There's really no other way. And, once we take over the company, it's got to happen quickly. Because no one I love will be safe. It would also make me feel better if you were here. Those highly-trained guards of Garrett's just let target number one walk out the front door simply because you have an authoritative voice. Vincent is a good actor and a good liar. I'd feel better with you here."

"Good point," he says with a nod. "If I agree to stay, will you agree to discuss your plans with me first?"

I consider lying to him, but I can't. "I'll try to. I value your opinion, Grandpa."

"That's good enough for me," he says as a black car pulls up next to us. "Looks like our walk is over."

Garrett gets out of the car and motions for us to get in.

On the short ride back to the house, he starts to chew me out, but Grandpa quickly intervenes.

"You should be chewing out your boys at the gate. They're the ones who let me walk out with her."

"You're a guest," Garrett counters.

"Shouldn't matter. It's a weakness."

Garrett thinks about that for a second then says, "You're right."

AIDEN MEETS ME at the front door.

Before I have a chance to speak, Grandpa says, "Aiden, my boy, why don't you and I go have a chat in the library while Keatyn helps her grandma in the kitchen."

Aiden glances at me, those tractor beam eyes holding

mine, speaking to me.

I sigh. Because now that I know what they're saying, they make me want to start crying again.

I do what I'm told and head to the kitchen, where the ladies are pitching in to make Christmas dinner. Grandma is sitting at the kitchen table, so I join her.

"Grandpa and Aiden are having a *chat*. What does that mean?"

"You'll know soon enough," she says with a chuckle.

"How?"

"If he doesn't come back bleeding, Grandpa thinks he's a keeper."

I hang my head. "I can't have a keeper right now, Grandma. I heard about the man who tried to run you off the road. Grandpa agreed that the two of you will stay here in France for a while. Until this hostile takeover stuff gets settled."

"I've always wanted a vacation in France. And any extended time with my granddaughters is welcomed."

"They're a handful."

She studies my face. "For years after your father died, I couldn't look you in the eyes. They are so much like his."

"Are you okay with Mom and Tommy getting married?"

"We can't control who we love. Just like we can't control when someone we love is taken from us. I'm very lucky that there's still a piece of your dad in you. And when you have kids someday, he will live on in them."

"Inga read my palm."

"She read mine years ago. Thought she was nuts at the time, but the woman was spot on. How many kids did she say you would have?"

"Four. But I don't think that will happen."

"Why not?"

"When she read it again, she said that death is coming for me."

"Death comes for everyone, eventually."

"Yeah, I guess you're right," I say, dropping the subject so Grandma won't have to think about losing someone else she loves.

"I like Aiden."

"I like him too."

"Is he the reason for all your cryptic questions about love?"

"I love him. But part of me still loves Brooklyn. And until I'm with him again—until I can see him again—I can't give Aiden my full heart."

I see Grandma glance behind me.

"He's not bleeding," she says. "Whoever you choose deserves your full heart."

"I know."

"Keatyn," Aiden says. "Wanna go for a walk?"

Grandma winks at me.

"Yeah, sure," I tell him.

I join him in the hall. He takes my hand and leads me up the stairs and into my room.

"I thought you wanted to go for a walk?"

"I just want to talk to you."

"You're not bleeding," I say.

"Why would I be bleeding?"

"Grandma said if you weren't, it meant you and my grandpa had a good talk."

"We did." He pulls me into his arms. "I love you."

I smile at him, but I don't say it back.

I can't.

I shouldn't.

Aiden lets go of me and starts pacing, much like he did on the beach.

"I believe in us," he says. "If you need to go see him—if you need to meet his mom—you have my full support. But I'm really concerned about you going back to Malibu. Is there a way you could get him to change the location?"

"I appreciate your support, Aiden, but I think it would be best if I wasn't with anyone right now."

He moves closer to me, pressing his chest tightly against mine and talking on my neck. "What does your heart want, right now?" he whispers.

"You," I whisper back. "It wants you."

Aiden kisses me, a kiss so powerful it makes me cry guilty tears.

"What's wrong, baby?" he asks gently.

"You know my life is a mess."

"Your grandpa just gave me some good advice about life."

"What'd he say?"

"That if you follow your heart, it will always lead you home."

I shut my eyes tightly, knowing he gave the same advice to my mom once.

"Do you believe him?" I ask, hoping with all my heart that the answer is yes.

"I think the more important question is, do you? I know what you're thinking. That it's good advice for everyone *but* you. Right?"

"Kinda."

"To answer your question, I believe that if you follow your heart, anything and everything is possible." He places his hand across my chest. "I love you, and I understand what you need to do. I'm going to help you in any way you will let me, but your grandpa told me this is your battle to fight and that I need to respect that."

"He's smart."

"Remember when I asked you to promise me tomorrow? I didn't fully understand your situation then."

"You don't want my tomorrows anymore?"

"I want you forever, but I understand now why forever scares you. It's your situation, not me."

"I lied to you earlier. I don't think he'll forget about me once I take over his company. I think it's going to make him very mad. Very soon, I'm going to have to face him. No matter how much I try to plan for it, I can't control it. And the reality is that I might not survive."

Aiden holds me tightly and whispers in my ear, "Follow your heart, baby. That's all I ask."

I promise myself, then and there, that no matter what happens, to do just that.

Keep following my heart. Keep doing what feels right.

"I wasn't going to tell you again. But I love you, Aiden. I really, really do," I say, tears flowing freely down my face.

"I love you too," he says, gently wiping them away.

Tuesday, December 27th

EVEN WHEN YOU FEEL LOST.
4PM

AFTER GETTING HUGS and kisses from everyone, Peyton, Damian, Aiden and I left for the airport. We boarded our plane and slept the entire flight.

Cooper meets us upon arrival and takes us to my loft.

As much as I loved being with my family, it feels surprisingly good to be home.

Damian checks the place out, helps himself to an energy drink, and then plops down at the kitchen island and starts making calls about the music video production.

Peyton gets her bags situated in their room, kisses Damian, and says she's going to take a bath. I think she's worn out from all the wonderful wedding and Christmas chaos.

Aiden pokes around the kitchen, looking for something to snack on, while I take Cooper upstairs.

I need to give him his Christmas present.

He opens the Tiffany gift box to find a round silver container with the date of his sister's birth engraved on the top. He opens the container, sees what's inside, and looks up at me. "A compass?"

"I know helping me has been hard for you. I just want you to know that I appreciate it. And I know that she'd want you to know that even when you feel lost, you'll never be alone. She's always with you, Cooper."

"You put her birthdate on the top."

"I think you should start celebrating her life, not re-membering her death."

His eyes get watery as he looks up at the ceiling and nods. Then he looks down at the compass, shuts the lid, and runs his fingers across her birthdate. "You're right. Thank you. That is what she'd want."

"You have to stop blaming yourself. You were too young to do anything about it. I also want you to know that it's okay to tell me no. I may not always take your advice, but, regarding my safety, I value your opinion more than anyone's."

He smiles at me. "I'm going to hold you to that."

My nose perks up at the smell of garlic wafting through the air.

"Aiden's cooking," Cooper says. "We should get down there."

As we're going downstairs, the intercom buzzes. I glance at the monitor by the door and see Riley grinning into the camera. I hit the button to buzz him in, then walk out into the hall to greet him.

"I missed you!" I tell him, throwing my arms around him in a hug. "Did you have a good Christmas?"

"Of course. With all the Johnsons around, you know it's going to be a good time." He lifts his nose to the air. "What are you cooking?"

"I'm not sure. Aiden's sautéing garlic for something he's creating."

"Smells good. I'm suddenly starved."

We all gather around the table and eat the pasta Aiden made while we talk through the plan for tomorrow. Riley says, "All the sets from school were delivered yesterday. My family worked on the surfboards, which turned out to be a lot harder to make than we anticipated."

"Why?" I ask. "I thought you were just going to put them on a spring."

"That was the plan, but the springs we tried were either too flimsy and wouldn't support the weight of a person, or they would support the weight but wouldn't hardly move."

"What'd you do?" Damian asks.

"Let's just say my uncle has a Porsche 911 in our garage that may or may not be missing its MacPherson struts."

"That's brilliant," Aiden says with a laugh.

"We thought so, too," Riley says, his phone buzzing in his hand. He pops up from his chair. "Ariela is here! I haven't seen her since the dance."

"Why don't you go let her in?" I say.

ABOUT TWENTY MINUTES later they join us in the kitchen, both looking a bit disheveled.

"Must have been quite a reunion," Damian says under his breath, looking a little jealous.

Riley giggles.

Yes, he giggles.

What the hell were they doing in my hallway?

I get up and give Ariela a welcoming hug and offer her some of Aiden's pasta.

"She's not hungry," Riley says a little too quickly.

She folds her hands over her flat stomach. "I swear, I won't be hungry for a week. I ate so much over Christmas."

"And we've got to get up early tomorrow. Probably

should all be getting to bed," Riley suggests, as he places his hand over Ariela's ass. You can practically feel the sexual tension in the air.

"Yeah, we should," Damian says, dropping his fork and agreeing the second he sees Peyton wander into the kitchen in a silky bathrobe.

Cooper stands up and starts clearing the table and stacking dishes in the sink. "How about I clean up, since Aiden cooked?" he offers.

I smile at him. "That'd be nice. I have serious jet lag."

"Me too," Aiden says, throwing Cooper a dishtowel. "Thanks, Cooper." Then he turns to everyone and says, "See you all bright and early."

"Not that early," I say. "We're planning to leave at nine, right, Damian?"

"The band is on the red-eye from LA tonight, so let's plan on ten."

I BRUSH MY teeth and slide into a silky black cami set that Kym gave me for Christmas.

I make a sexy entrance, only to find Aiden completely crashed out, lying diagonally across my bed.

I slide in next to him and go to sleep.

Wednesday, December 28th

COTTON CANDY. FERRIS WHEEL.
10:30AM

WE MEET THE band at the video shoot location. Troy gives me a big hug, as do Ethan and Billy, and I introduce them to everyone.

Very quickly, Riley gets down to business. He's even more prepared than I expected, with little drawings of each scene he wants to shoot.

Lying on our stomachs in front of the beach backdrop, facing each other.

"You'll need beach towels," Ariela chimes in. "And sand."

"Sand is being delivered shortly. Can you make a list of what we still need?" he asks her sweetly.

Running through the sand, laughing and holding hands.

"What are you going to wear?" Peyton asks me.

"I brought a couple of bikinis and some little dresses, but I wasn't sure what you wanted, Riley."

"We'll look at the costumes later. Let's make sure the scenes are what the band wants, first."

He continues showing more boards.

On surfboards, in front of the ocean backdrop. Big, corrugated cardboard waves in front.

Eating ice cream together.

Riding on the back of a scooter, my hair blowing behind me.

The band, all in Ray-Bans.

In front of the amusement park backdrop, me feeding Damian cotton candy.

Riding a Ferris wheel.

"That's going to be a tough one," Riley admits. "I don't know how we can recreate a Ferris wheel."

"You don't need the whole wheel, just a seat from one," Aiden says. "Surely, we could find one somewhere."

"I'll put you in charge of that," Riley tells him.

Sitting around a bonfire, Damian and the rest of the band performing the song.

In the moonlight on the shore. The big moon backdrop behind us.

Kissing.

Looking in love.

"So those are the date scenes that we'll intersperse into the video. We'll also shoot the band playing the song in front of all the backdrops," Riley says. "I thought we'd start with those shots while the girls get together the other props and wardrobe. What do you think?"

Troy slaps Riley on the back. "I think it looks like a whole hell of a lot more fun than the video they wanted us to shoot."

"I agree," Ethan says, grabbing his guitar case. "I'm ready to get started."

The band gets set up on the sound stage. A few of the crew members from the *Retribution* set show up, ready to get going, and I take Ariela, Aiden, and Peyton to my dressing room.

"So, we need two beach towels, cotton candy, a big sparkly heart, five pairs of Ray-Bans, and clothes for Damian and Keatyn," Ariela says.

"And a Ferris wheel seat," Aiden adds.

"Let's split up. Peyton, you make the heart. Aiden, you find the Ferris wheel seat. I'll get cotton candy, sunglasses, and beach towels. Let's see what you brought for clothes, Keatyn."

I try on the bikinis I threw in my bag this morning and model them.

When I'm in the last one, Aiden says enthusiastically, "That one. Definitely."

"Are you sure? I thought I looked better in the blue one."

He cocks an eyebrow at me. "Why don't you show those two to Riley and the band and see what they think?"

"Uh, okay." I put the blue one back on and sneak into the sound stage.

When Riley says, "Cut," at the end of the song, I run up, model this selection, and ask them to wait for me to try the other one on.

I change quickly and come out in Aiden's choice. A skimpy, sparkly, zigzag-printed triangle top and teeny bottoms.

"That one," Troy says, the rest of them unanimously agreeing.

"You don't like the blue one better? It looks like the ocean."

"You're the eye candy, Keats."

"Me? No. I'm just the background girl who's going to help bring the story to life."

Riley starts laughing. He wraps an arm around me and leads me off the set. "Definitely that bikini. And, for the date scenes, I want the bikini top with a very skimpy pair of jean shorts. Then one of your flirty little short dresses and heels for the amusement park and the moonlight scenes."

"Okay. I like how you're taking control, Riley," I tell him as I dash offstage.

WHILE EVERYONE LEAVES to get their props, I play around with some makeup, then get bored and go in to watch the band perform the song a few hundred times.

"Put the bikini, shorts, and some heels on," Riley instructs me a few hours later. "I want you to dance around while they're playing. Kind of like you did with me and Dallas in the video we made on the plane."

I change quick, come back out, and have fun dancing. Shimmying against Damian and Ethan as they play their guitars. Sitting on Troy's lap playing the drums. Pretending to let Billy teach me to play the keyboard.

"Do that thing you do, with your hair," Riley instructs, running his hand through his own hair and shaking his ass.

I burst out laughing and dramatically cover my eyes.

Damian says, "The way she just covered her eyes was adorable."

"Keep singing," Riley says. "Keatyn, go."

I close my eyes and move my body like I did for Aiden on the pool table, slow and sexy, while pushing my hair back off my face.

"Perfect," Riley says. "Now, open your eyes and lick your lips."

I try to lick my lips in a sexy way, but just end up laughing. I know I look like a total dork.

"You need some motivation," Riley says. "Where's Aiden?"

"Just got back," Aiden says from behind the cameras. "I found a Ferris wheel seat. It's being delivered later today. We may have to paint it, though. I think it's in pretty rough shape."

"We'll worry about that later. Come stand here," Riley says, positioning him just off camera.

"All right, Keatyn. It's just you and Aiden."

My eyes brighten immediately and a smile plays on my face. As he smiles back at me, I break out into a broad grin. I can't help it.

Aiden shoots me a kiss, so I kiss my fingertips and blow one back to him. Then I just stare at him and lick my lips, not even thinking that's what I'm supposed to do. I'm just reacting to how he makes me feel. Hungry.

"Perfect," Riley says. "Okay, cut. Let's take a break. I'm starved."

"I had craft service bring us in some food," Damian says. "Let's eat."

AFTER A LATE lunch, we film Damian and me in the scenes in front of the backdrops.

First, the carnival scenes, with me trying to shove a large puff of pink cotton candy swirled on a stick in Damian's face.

Peyton combined silver and hot pink glitter with bugle beads to make a heart to hang over our heads during the *Crazy love is what I feel* scene.

We film all the scenes except for the Ferris wheel and the surfing scenes.

When Riley decides he has enough takes, we quit for the day.

"I need to upload all of today's video, see where we're at, and then we'll shoot more tomorrow. Great job, everyone. Let's meet back here at the same time."

He grabs Ariela and pulls her into his arms. "Thank you for getting all the props."

"I loved tracking things down and helping you with the details," she says sweetly. "We're a good team."

I hear him whisper, "I love you, kitty," to her. Then he says, "We're going to LA when we graduate to do this together. Full time."

"That sounds really fun," she agrees.

WE ALL HOP in a car and head back to my loft. "So, you ready for some more acting?" I ask Damian. "Tonight's the big public date, right?"

"Yeah, it is," he says, grabbing Peyton's hand. "My publicist set it all up with those reporters. We deleted all of Peyton's social media while we were in France and followed your advice for preparing a written statement about her. We didn't bother to include her last name. Just some basic facts, like her name—but we're spelling it Payton—and how we met in Napa Valley at a party. How it's new."

"That's perfect," I say, as the driver drops them off at Damian's dad's building. Cooper was afraid to let him come back to the loft tonight after their date, for fear he might be followed.

"They don't need to know everything. We'll fulfill your bargain by giving them a few photos. I still don't want them to get any really clean shots of her face, though. I want to protect her for a little while longer," Damian says.

"That's sweet. And smart," I tell him.

A SHORT RIDE later, we're at my loft.

"I'll be working late," Riley says. "Ariela, is it okay if we order in?"

I'm about to agree that it sounds nice when my phone buzzes with a text.

> **Knox:** You back in town? Should we make our first public appearance? Hit the club? Do a sloppy drunken exit? Or are you wanting a good girl image?
>
> **Me:** I am back in town. The club sounds fun. And as far as my image goes, I'd like to be somewhere between good and not-so-good.
>
> **Knox:** I can help with the not-so-good. Meet me around 11? Or should I wine and dine you first?
>
> **Me:** There's some stuff I need to tell you. Let's do dinner, privately.
>
> **Knox:** Oh, baby, I thought you'd never ask.
>
> **Me:** Very funny. I'll meet you at your hotel at 10.
>
> **Knox:** This probably goes without saying, but dress hot.

"You're going to have dinner with Knox? Alone. In his hotel room?" Aiden asks me, reading over my shoulder.

"Yeah, I feel like I need to tell him what's going on with Vincent before he's photographed with me. I want him to know that it could put him in danger."

"I don't think he'll care. He's a publicity hound."

"A very calculating publicity hound, from what I can tell. And this is just the first step of my plan. I want to be photographed. I want Vincent to start seeing pictures of me. Going clubbing with Knox practically assures that I will. And, hopefully, it will draw some of the attention away from Damian and Peyton. I'm gonna go get ready."

"I'm not sure I like this," Aiden says as I walk away.

I hear Cooper say to him, "Don't like what?"

I PULL ON a slinky dress. I'm sitting on my chaise, putting on a pair of platform heels when both Cooper and Aiden join me in the closet.

"What's up?" I ask them.

"We're coming with you," Aiden says.

"No, you're not," I reply adamantly.

"Didn't you just tell me a few days ago that you'd listen to me?" Cooper says.

"Yes, Cooper, I will consider letting you come with. I will not consider letting Aiden."

Aiden taps his foot and purses his lips.

"Aiden," I say. "You promised."

He runs his hand through his hair, frustrated. "Yeah, I did."

"Tell me your plan," Cooper says.

"I'm sure Aiden already told you, but I'm meeting Knox at his hotel. While we have dinner, I will tell him the risks of being seen with me. Then, depending on his reaction, I may go to a club with him. And, hopefully, we'll be photographed together. It's all part of my plan, Cooper. Is Vincent in California right now?"

"Yes."

"Then there's nothing to worry about."

"There's a lot to worry about, but you're right that I don't think we have to worry about Vincent in this situation."

"Awesome," I say, grabbing a Fendi baguette. "Don't wait up."

I walk to my front door as Aiden says, "How are you getting there?"

"His driver should be here to pick me up in a few minutes."

Aiden pushes me against the door and kisses me hard. "You better be careful."

"I know you worry about me, Aiden. But I'll be fine. It's not really any different than being on set together. It's just for the cameras."

"I'm not worried about you and Knox. I'm worried about your safety. You keep talking about a showdown. About how you might not make it."

"We're not to that point yet. This is just a little prequel. Something for him to think about while we take over his company."

He kisses my nose. "I love you."

"I love you too. I'll text you."

"That would make me feel better."

I kiss his nose. "Good."

"Using my own tricks against me, huh?"

I give him a smile as I walk out the door.

MAKE SOME NOISE.
10PM

KNOX GREETS ME with cheek kisses, escorts me in, and gives me the grand tour of his hotel residence. It's gorgeous. Dark wood, modern furniture, lots of glass, steel, and marble. Big, fluffy bed, dining table set with candles.

"Champagne?" he asks.

"I'd love some."

"Sit," he says, gesturing to a pair of chairs set in front of an expanse of glass looking out at a beautiful view of the

Manhattan skyline.

We take a seat as a butler serves the champagne.

"You have a gorgeous view."

He clinks my glass. "Here's to sharing something special."

I lean toward Knox, knowing full well the butler will hear my whining. "Knox, baby, I thought we were going to be *alone* tonight."

Knox touches my face and stares into my eyes, much like he did the other day when we ran through some new lines. "Your wish is my command."

He waves a finger at his bodyguard. "Make yourselves scarce."

The bodyguard nods and leaves, taking the butler with him.

I'm about to spill my guts when the doorbell rings.

Knox rolls his eyes and goes to the door.

"Our food is here," he says, looking irritated at the waiter for intruding. "Just set it up on the dining room table."

The food is set up painstakingly slowly; Knox signs the bill and puts the Do Not Disturb sign on the door.

"No more interruptions," he says, politely holding my chair out for me.

"That's good. Shall we eat first? The food looks amazing."

"It is. One of the reasons I'm staying here. So, what's the deal with you and Aiden? I noticed your new ring."

I glance at the beautiful ring Aiden gave me in the gazebo. "He just gave it to me."

"Is that what you wanted to talk to me about?"

"No. I wanted you to know about my situation before we're seen together."

"Your situation?"

"I have a stalker."

"Don't we all? The one here almost had someone at the front desk convinced she was my sister, that I was in danger, and she needed to check on me. I think she's pitched a tent outside, so she'll know if I leave."

"Mine is a little more than that. His name is Vincent Sharpe."

"I know that name. He does, um—movie futures, right? And, oh, I know, he was doing that nationwide search for the next Abby Johnston." He pauses and stares at me. "That's a weird coincidence."

I take a big drink of champagne. "Knox, I don't know you very well yet. And I want to trust you. Can I trust you?"

"I'm not my image. You know that."

I nod and keep going. "Vincent is a long-time fan of my mom's, although Mom never knew who he was. He was just someone who sent her sweet stuff over the years, starting not long after *A Day at the Lake* released. He had a rough childhood, but was taken in as a young teen by his grandmother, a former film star, and sent to the finest schools. He inherited money when his mom and her—I think—sixth husband were killed. He took that money and invested it in a small production company. One that owned the rights to *A Day at the Lake*. Since then, he's built up the company and become known as a movie futures golden boy. This past spring, we believe, he got into my mom's trailer on set and left her a gift. We also believe he took a photo of me and Mom from a Hawaiian vacation. We were on the beach, both in bikinis. The theory is that he saw the Abby he fell in love with in that photo. Me. After that, I met him. He told me he wanted to make a movie with me. We became friends, sort of. I had dinner with him. Invited him to my birthday party. Where he tried to kidnap me."

"Kidnap you? Why isn't he in jail?"

"It was my birthday party. I'd been drinking. He's rich and good-looking. He said it was just a mistake. That he'd been trying to help me. The police didn't have enough evidence to charge him. But he had a van out back with drugs and restraints. He told me we were going to make the movie together. Even after it all happened, part of me still didn't believe it. Like, did I make a mistake? Mom had just finished filming *To Maddie, with Love,* and we think those sex scenes set him off. He started calling her a whore. He put a threatening note in my little sister's backpack. And his grandmother, who he idolized, passed away. Hell, I even helped him spread her ashes on the beach. But that same night—the night of my party—after I was back home, he broke into my boyfriend's house, took one of my bikinis, and left a packet of pictures for my mom."

"Your mom was smoking hot in that film. I loved it. So, what were the pictures of?"

"Me. He'd been following me and taking photos for months. I had no idea. Everyone freaked out. They thought about putting me in a witness protection program but ended up sending me to boarding school. They made me leave my friends without telling them a word. Set me up with a different name. I had to lie about who I was. They said he'd forget about me. But he hasn't. He broke into rehabs trying to find me. He messaged me on my old Facebook profile. He showed up at my ex's surf tournament. He followed my mom shopping in New York City and accidentally found me. I was lucky to have gotten away. He almost got me in Miami when I saw Damian. He sent photoshopped pictures to my mom where Tommy's head gets blown off. After my ex won his first pro surf tournament and dedicated it to me, he got the same type of photo. And the nationwide search . . ."

"He was trying to find you."

"Yeah. And it almost worked. Both my drama teacher and a friend offered to nominate me. But that's not the worst of it. The guy who did my tattoo was murdered after Vincent got a matching one. I went to the club where he always goes looking for me and danced in a cage to piss him off. The next week, a girl from the club was murdered, her body stabbed with scissors. After the New York incident, he sent a photo of me to my mom. The photo was stabbed with scissors. Going back to the club in LA was the start of me fighting back. I'm also trying to do a hostile takeover of his company. If that works out, I'll own the rights to the movie he so desperately wants us to make. And when that happens . . ."

"He'll really be pissed?"

"Yes. And anyone close to me will be in danger. That's why I needed to talk to you in private. I want to make sure you understand the risks of being photographed with me."

"You want to be photographed, though?"

"Yeah. It's part of my plan. I'm hoping to take his attention off the people I care about by allowing him to focus on me. Up until now, he's been meticulous in his planning. I want him desperate, so he'll start making mistakes. Then maybe we can get the proof to have him arrested."

"Do you want him to find you?"

"For now, I just want him to see photos of me from the night before."

"So a different club every night?"

"Different club. Different cities. Different guys, even."

"Basically, my plan, only with higher stakes."

"Yeah."

Knox grins at me and cuts a piece of his steak. "Eat up. Our food is getting cold."

I take a bite of the lemon chicken pasta he ordered me. "This is really good. What are you thinking?"

"I'm letting it all soak in first."

"Okay."

We eat in silence for a few minutes. Then he asks, "So, what about Aiden?"

"I don't want him to find out about Aiden."

"So you won't be photographed with him?"

"No."

"So you need me?"

"Not exactly. You would just up the stakes a little."

"How so?"

"I'm shooting a music video with *Twisted Dreams* this week."

"That's Matt Moran's son, right?"

"Yes. Damian is my best friend. The video will premiere on New Year's Eve. I'll be Keatyn Douglas again."

"Do you act slutty in the video?"

"I'm in a bikini for most of it because it's set at the beach. There are a lot of similarities between the video, my real life, and *A Day at the Lake*."

"Nice. I'm in, by the way. We'll be careful. Make some noise. See what happens."

"Are you sure?"

"Hell yeah. You're practically Hollywood royalty, sugar. I'd be stupid not to have a fake affair with you. Besides, the more press we get together, the more people will want to see our movie."

"Unless you end up dead."

"I have a bodyguard. You have a bodyguard. Surely, they can keep us safe."

"The paparazzi know where you live."

"It will be fine. Finish your food. Drink up. Then we're gonna party Knox-style."

I drink the rest of my champagne then laugh. "You have your own style?"

"Yep. Be prepared."

"You better like to dance."

"I love to dance. By the way, what does Aiden think of this? Is he going to be pissed at me?"

"He understands what I have to do to get my life back. But he really doesn't like it."

"I'm surprised he didn't want to come with. Even just to watch out for you."

"Oh, he did."

"But you're stubborn, aren't you?"

"Yeah. He knows if he pushes me, I'll be gone and he won't see me until this is over."

"Do you like the champagne?" he asks, filling up my glass.

"It's good champagne," I reply.

"If you had your choice, would you drink it at the club?"

"I don't usually sip champagne in the VIP section, if that's what you're asking."

He looks at his watch. "Thank god. I'll only deal with girls like that if I'm gonna get laid."

While he grabs his wallet, I text Aiden, who I know will relay the information to Cooper.

Me: *He's in. Headed to a club. ifly.*
Hottie God: *Be careful. ifly2.*

"I just realized something," I tell Knox as we're being driven to the club.

"You've fallen madly in love with me?" he says with a mischievous grin.

"Afraid not. It just hit me that all my life I've been taught to avoid the cameras and the places paparazzi hang out. How do you know where to go? What if we go and they aren't there? This will be a waste of time."

"You will never again say time spent with Knox Daniels is a waste. You will ruin my well-honed reputation." He pats my hand. "You have a lot to learn. It's cute. Tonight you will watch and learn from the master."

"But how do you know they'll be there?"

"My assistant tips them off. They all think I'm a horrible boss and she's on the take."

"So, she tells them where you're going to be?"

"When I want them to know, yes. The first club we're going to allows them inside. Photos will be taken of us when we arrive and when we're on the dance floor. They usually don't allow them in the VIP section, but the staff talks to them. So, if you want people to think we're together, you'll need to act like it the whole time."

"*Sources at the club say the couple were dancing closely and seen canoodling in the VIP lounge. They barely looked at me when I took their order, a waitress says. They only had eyes for each other.*"

"Exactly," Knox says with a laugh. "After we are seen canoodling, we'll go to another club. We'll let it slip that we're headed there next, but it's much more private. We can just have fun. It's when we leave there that will matter."

"What do you mean?"

"Are we drunk? Are we kissing? Do we look high? Are we in a fight? Am I taking you home? Are we going back to my place?"

"I clearly didn't think far enough ahead."

The car pulls to a stop. "You ready for this? I'll get out of the car, put my hand inside to help you out, being the gentleman that I am. Come out slowly. Let them get a glimpse of those luscious, long legs first. Then gracefully get out of the car."

THE PHOTOGRAPHERS ARE there, just like Knox said, and we do exactly as we planned.

Sort of.

Once I'm out of the car, the reporters yell, "Who's your date tonight, Knox?"

Knox slides his hand down the side of my face and under my chin, gently raising it upward as the cameras flash.

"All I'll say is she looks a whole lot like her mother."

I decide to give Knox and the cameras the works, moving the corners of my mouth upward, curling my lips into a little smirk, and then giving them the full smile that people say is just like my mom's.

He shakes his head at me, leans in, and whispers loudly, "Beautiful."

I toss my head back just a little and laugh, like he said something funny, as he grabs my hand and pulls me into the club, his bodyguard leading the way.

Even though I know Vincent is in California, I still find myself on edge, searching faces for one that looks like his. Looking for someone who might be watching me a little too closely.

A guy in a suit leads us to the VIP area that rings the dance floor and is very visible from the rest of the club. Our section will seat a party of twenty, even though it's only the two of us. There's a chilled bottle of Don Julio waiting for us along with a full bottle service set up.

We haven't even sat down before a group of girls bounce

over, calling out Knox's name. The VIP bouncer stops them by putting up his thick hand. "I'm sorry, ladies. You'll have to leave."

"But we partied with him last week," a pretty brunette pouts. "Knox!" she says again. "It's Marcy, *remember?*"

Knox surprises me when he leaves my side and joins her.

"Marcy," he says, giving her air kisses. "Of course I remember. Have you ever met Keatyn?"

The girls don't look thrilled, but are polite as he grabs me, kisses me square on the lips, and then drags me over to meet them.

"Ladies, this is Keatyn Douglas. Bet you can't guess who her mom is."

It's then when I realize why he talked to Marcy.

And that I should play along.

I lay my hand on his chest, pushing away from him just like my mom does to Tommy. It's adorable because she never leaves his arms. Then I use her voice. Older, more mature, with a slight southern twang to it. "These girls don't care who my momma is."

Marcy's smile fades. "Oh. My. God. You sound just like Abby Johnston."

I roll my eyes at Knox like I'm irritated he spilled the beans then give him my pout. "Knox, baby, I thought it was going to be just us tonight."

He hugs me tighter, kisses my neck, and says sexily, "Oh, it most definitely is," as his bodyguard stands shoulder to shoulder with the VIP bouncer and says, "Sorry, ladies."

Knox sits down and pulls me onto his lap, snuggling with me. "Am I good or what?"

"You're devious, that's what you are."

"Shots, then dancing?"

"Absolutely."

He raises a finger and a waiter rushes into our section. "We'll have some tequila shooters."

"Yes, sir, Mr. Daniels," the waiter replies, pouring shots and lining them up in front of us.

Knox clinks my glass with his and we down the first shot, then the second.

"Let's dance."

He leads me out to the dance floor and pulls me into his arms.

It's at this point I realize that sometimes I'm not very good at pretending.

Because sometimes my real life gets in the way.

And it's because I'm not dancing with Aiden.

As much as I want to pretend that I'm into dancing with Knox, I'm just not.

This is going to be harder than I thought.

I close my eyes and try to pretend I'm dancing with Aiden. But Knox doesn't move the way Aiden does. His leg doesn't fit between mine like it should. His hands don't grip my hips like he owns them.

"Uh, I need to pee," I say, suddenly coming up with a way to get off the dance floor and quickly fleeing.

I don't even think about my safety or Vincent until I'm rushing out of the bathroom and a brick wall of a man is standing in front of me, blocking my way.

"Where's a pretty little thing like you going in such a big hurry?" he says, taking a step toward me.

I back up as warning bells go off in my brain, the hair on the back of my neck stands on end, and my stomach feels sick. This man is dangerous, and I'm not sure even with all of Cooper's training that I'd stand a chance against him.

I look behind him, hoping someone else will need to use the bathroom, but there's no one coming. He takes another step toward me, but this time I don't step back. Instead, I move toward him, letting my shoulder bump into his and say, "Excuse me."

He doesn't move, so I speak louder. "I said, excuse me!"

He grips my shoulder tightly and pushes me against the wall, setting off visions of being raped in the bathroom.

"I'm going to say it one more time. *Excuse me.*"

The guy laughs at me, so I do what I've practiced over and over. I curl my fist, punch him in the throat, sweep kick his kneecap with my heel, and then stand back up quickly, using my leg strength for leverage as I thrust my elbow up under his chin.

He groans and falls to the floor, clutching his knee. I step over him and run back to the VIP section in tears.

Knox is out dancing, surrounded by women, but his bodyguard rushes toward me. "What's wrong?"

"What's wrong is you suck as a bodyguard. I was attacked by a huge man coming out of the bathroom and you were nowhere to be found. Tell Knox I said goodnight."

I pick my handbag off the couch and storm out the door, completely forgetting about the cameras until they start flashing.

"Keatyn! Where's Knox?"

"Why are you crying?"

"He's a cad, isn't he?" a girl without a camera says. She has a wild look on her face, and I'm sure she's the stalker he spoke of.

I cover my face with my hand, turn around, and run straight into Knox, who wraps me in a hug.

"I'm sorry," he says as the cameras flash around us.

He pulls me back into the club as the valet waves our driver forward. It's then that Knox's bodyguard finally does something worthwhile, working with the club's bouncers to shield us as we get into the car.

"Tell me what happened," Knox says, still holding me protectively.

I shake my head. "I just want to go home."

"They're following us," his driver says.

"Then take us back to my place."

ONCE WE'RE SAFELY back in his hotel, I take out my phone and call Cooper. "I need you to come get me, but there's paparazzi everywhere."

"They'll be out there until morning," Knox says. "Waiting to get the morning after photos. So they can say you spent the night. They can see if I walk you to the car. If it's a walk of shame or if we get coffee together."

"What happened?" Cooper says in my ear. "You sound upset."

"We'll talk about it later. It sounds like I'm stuck here."

"Aiden wants to talk to you."

"'Boots, are you okay?" Aiden's silky voice comes over the phone, which makes me start crying.

"No."

"I'm coming there."

"You can't."

"Keatyn, no one knows me. I'll look like any other guest checking in." I hear Cooper talking in the background. "Cooper says he'll bring your wig and some clothes."

I take a deep breath. "I need a minute to think about what I want to do. I'll call you back when I figure it out."

"You just told me you weren't okay."

"I wasn't. But now I am."

"What changed?"

"I talked to you."

I swear I can feel him smiling through the phone.

"Okay. Call me back."

I end the call and set my phone down.

Knox sits down and hands me a bottle of water. "I'm sorry. I didn't tell Hugo to watch you. He doesn't normally watch out for the girls I'm with."

"It's okay. I handled it."

"The bouncer said you took some big guy down. Wiped out his knee."

"When I came out of the bathroom, he wouldn't let me by. I asked nice twice. Then he grabbed me by the shoulder and tried to force me into the bathroom. I don't even want to think about what he wanted to do to me in there."

"So you punched him?"

"Yeah. Jab to the throat. Heel to the knee. Elbow to the chin. Cooper taught me well."

"What do you want to do? We're in this far. If you really want to play it through, you let me kiss you and put you in a car in the morning."

"I have to finish shooting a music video tomorrow at the studio. Why don't you come with me?"

"Sounds like a plan. Do you want to watch a movie?"

"I'd really just like to go to sleep, Knox."

"Come on then, I'll show you to your room."

I TELL KNOX goodnight, wash my face, lie in bed, and call Aiden.

"Can you put me on speakerphone for this part, so Cooper can hear?"

"Uh, sure."

"So, I'm going to spend the night here. I was wrong not to bring you with, Cooper. He told me his bodyguard was the best, but he was wrong. I sort of almost got attacked by a huge guy at the club."

"What do you mean, almost attacked?" Riley says.

"I didn't know you were on too, Riley. How's the video coming?"

"It's coming fine," Aiden says. "Tell us what happened."

I tell them what the guy did, what I did, how we left, and how the photographers followed us here. "So, my plan is to just go with it. I mean, I went through all of that to make people think we're together, I might as well let them think I spent the night. I can't come home. I don't want to risk it. We'll both come to the studio tomorrow, as if he's filming. Then, later, he can go home without me, and I'll go home with you guys."

"It's good to know you can handle yourself under pressure," Cooper says. "But you shouldn't have had to."

"I know. I'm sorry. I'll see you all in the morning."

"I'm taking you off speaker and going in the bedroom," Aiden says sternly. "We aren't done talking."

"Good," I say. "Because I'm not finished talking to you."

"Where are you right now?"

"Lying in bed, wishing I were with you."

"I'm kind of mad at you."

"I know. Aiden?"

"What, baby?"

"I'm not that good of an actress."

"What makes you say that?"

"I was fine pretending to be into him when we got out of the car at the club. He even kissed me on the lips for the cameras. Didn't faze me. I was just playing my role. Inside the club, I pretended some more. Until he took me out to dance."

"And then what?"

"I couldn't pretend anymore. Dancing with him felt

so—wrong. So foreign. Not the way it feels with you."

"How does it feel with me?"

"Don't you know?"

"Of course, I know. We fit together perfectly. And not just when we're dancing. In every single way. I told you: BK. Before Keatyn. You've ruined me."

I smile, thinking about all the ways Aiden has ruined me. With his lips. His tongue. And even some other parts. But it's not just physical. It's not just the way we fit together on the dance floor. Or the way our bodies mold to each other when we're in bed. It's the way he talks to me when he's upset. His unwavering faith in us. In me.

"I'm sorry I have to play these games, Aiden. Don't lose faith in me, okay?"

"Am I going to see a picture of you kissing Knox in the papers tomorrow?"

"Hopefully."

"And you think that will help your situation?"

"Hopefully. I'm tired, Aiden," I say. Not just because I'm sleepy, but because this whole ordeal is wearing on me.

"I'm tired too. Night, Boots. I love you."

"I love you too, Aiden."

Thursday, December 29th

SO HAPPY ABOUT IT.
7AM

"RISE AND SHINE," Knox says, bouncing on my bed early in the morning.

I open one eye. "What time is it?"

"Seven."

"Why are you up so early? And so happy about it?"

He pats his firm stomach and flexes a bicep. "You don't think I look like this naturally, do you? I work hard for it."

"At seven in the morning?"

"Yes, ma'am. Wanna go work out with me? Show me some of those moves you used on that guy last night?"

"I don't have any workout clothes. And I'm not really awake."

"I ordered some clothes for you to wear. They're being sent up when the store downstairs opens up at nine."

"Really? That was sweet of you."

"If I'm right about things, we're going to be starring in a lot of future movies together. I need to protect your reputation."

"Protect it? It was your idea that I *spend the night*."

"Yeah, but if you leave in last night's dress, it looks like a one-night stand. If you leave in something else, it looks planned. Subtle difference, but still."

"Yeah, I suppose you're right."

"And maybe I'm trying to be nice to you."

"Why?"

He pulls a newspaper out from behind his back and tosses it on the bed. "Page six."

I flip the paper open.

Knox Daniels and Keatyn Douglas—Hollywood's New Couple?

Rumors are flying this morning after resident playboy, Knox Daniels, and the daughter of Abby Johnston, Keatyn Douglas, shared a night out. Onlookers at the club say the couple kept to themselves in a large VIP section, snuggling and kissing when they weren't glued to each other on the dance floor. "She pouted and called him baby when a group of girls tried to crash their party," a waiter said. Knox, who is a regular at the club, usually keeps the section filled with gorgeous women. "He only had eyes for her," a club goer tells us. Friends of the couple say the two met when Keatyn visited her mom's long-time beau, Tommy Stevens, on the Trinity: Retribution *set before the holiday. Although, if these photos are any indication of the volatility of their relationship, we'd say this pair is in for a bumpy ride.*

The accompanying photos are of Knox and me, looking perfect upon arrival at the club. He's holding my chin and giving me an adorable kiss. There are two grainy photos of us in the club, one of us in the VIP section and the other on the dance floor. But then there's a photo of me from when I rushed out of the club in tears.

"I look horrid!" I screech.

"You don't look horrid. I mean, it's not the most flattering angle, and you do have mascara running down your face, but you look pretty in all the other ones."

"Oh, and look at the caption under the photo of you hugging me and helping me into the car. *Knox knows how to make up.*" I roll my eyes until I see a smaller photo of Damian and Peyton below this article. Peyton's face is partially obscured by Damian's arm as he leans in to kiss her. There's a little story about the normal girl from Napa Valley who caught the rocker's attention. I decide that one bad picture of me is worth burying the story of their date.

"So, all in all, it was a good night. We planted our relationship seed."

"Are we having a relationship? I thought you were into one-night stands."

"Normally, I am. But I can see the value of this. For us. Long term."

"Knox, when things go down with the stalker, I'm not sure if I'll survive it."

"Even better. I can be in mourning. Imagine the sympathy sex I'd get."

My eyes get huge. "Knox!"

He pats my shoulder and smiles. "I'm just joking. You can untwist your panties now."

"You're horrible."

He laughs. "Now that you're awake, do you wanna go for a run?"

"A run? But you said the reporters will still be—"

"Exactly." He points to a little pile of running clothes. "Before you go off on me, these are my sister's. She visits a lot and keeps stuff here so she never has to check a bag."

"Does your bodyguard run with you?"

"Does he look like he can run? No, I go by myself. Part of *why* I run. Gotta be fast enough to get away from the hordes of women who chase me."

"I'm calling Cooper and having him meet us."

"Cooper looks like he's in pretty good shape. Sucks at poker, but could probably kick my ass." He sizes me up. "Although, from the sound of it, you probably could too. Do you think he'd teach me to fight?"

"Maybe." I grab my phone off the nightstand and see some texts from Aiden.

> **Hottie God:** *Good morning, beautiful. I miss sleeping with you.*
>
> **Hottie God:** *And waking up with you.*
>
> **Hottie God:** *I just miss you.*
>
> **Me:** *I miss you more.*

I'm smiling as I call Cooper. "Hey, Knox and I are going running in the park. I'd like you to join us. Just come over to his place and we'll meet you in the lobby."

"Does Knox go for a jog in the park every morning?"

"Um, I don't know. Let me ask. Knox, do you go for a run in the park every morning?"

"No. I usually run on the treadmill. Especially in the winter."

"Did you hear that?" I say to Cooper.

"You're in the paper this morning. We don't want to do anything routine. Make sense?"

"Yes, it does."

"But it is a beautiful morning. I'm assuming there are photographers who will see this run?"

"That's the plan."

"I'll be right over," he says before hanging up.

THE THREE OF us go on a run, are successfully photographed together, and then head to the studio to finish the video.

The second I arrive, Aiden grabs my hand, pulls me into my dressing room, and kisses me furiously.

I'm instantly hot.

I push him against the door, lock it, and unzip his pants, wanting nothing more than for him to take me.

"Do we have time?" he says breathlessly, as he strips my panties off then picks me up and moves us to the couch.

"We should always have enough time for this," I say as he kisses my neck.

I arch my hips, push his jeans down with my feet, and guide him into me.

He slams his mouth down on mine, kissing me like we've been apart for months, not just one night.

Desperate.

Aching.

Needing.

Each other.

His tongue delves deeply into my mouth.

I match his intensity, grabbing his ass and pushing him to go faster.

"Oh, god," he says, moving even more quickly as his body complies with my hands' request.

A burst of fervent energy.

Then, suddenly motionless.

His face buried in my hair.

His lips finding my neck, then my cheek, then my ear. "I maybe kinda missed you," he says adorably.

"I may spend the night with Knox more often."

"I don't think so, Boots," he chuckles.

I give him a kiss. "I better get cleaned up and get my

bikini on."

"That's the only bad thing about a quickie. It's over way too quick," he says, letting me up and smacking my butt as I walk away.

"CUT!" RILEY YELLS for the fourth time. "Damian, you look constipated and Keatyn, you're supposed to be looking at Damian. It looks stupid."

"That's because we're about to fall off the boards!"

"It's not just that," Ariela says. "It looks fake because they're not wet enough."

"We spritzed them down," Peyton says.

"Yeah, but you can't really see the water. If they're in the sun and wet, they should sort of shimmer," Ariela counters. "Wait! I know!" she says, running off set. She comes back with the water spritzer and a bottle of body oil. "Let's try mixing them."

"Water and oil don't mix," Aiden says, stating the obvious.

"I know, that's the point!" Ariela replies. She rubs both Damian and me down with oil, then spritzes us with water again. This time, the water beads and slides down our bodies.

"See!" she says to Riley.

Riley grabs her and kisses her. "You're a genius."

"Is there any way we could put a second spring under the surfboards, so they're a little more stable?" I ask Riley. "If we weren't constantly worried about falling off, it'd be easier to look like we're having fun."

"We don't really have enough time to do that."

"Come here and help me," I tell him, "while I figure this out."

He stands next to me as I get back on the board, putting

my hand on his shoulder for balance.

After trying a few different foot positions, I find one that feels comfortable and even lets me move the board.

"That's it! Damian, put your feet like this, right over the spring. I think that's why we were struggling. We were doing what's natural on a surfboard, but it doesn't work for this because of the middle support."

Damian quickly gets the hang of it and Riley checks out how we look on camera.

"You look much better," he says. "You're smiling."

"I think we should do some shots of us just sitting and floating together. We do that all the time."

"Yeah, let's do that. We could probably lie down on our boards and pretend to paddle, too," Damian agrees.

"Let's try it," Riley says. "And remember to look like you're having fun."

We get some successful shots of us lying on our boards and paddling with our arms, then floating on the boards, holding hands.

"Do you think you could do a handstand. Act like you're showing off?" Damian asks me.

"It's usually the guy who shows off," I tease, laughing.

"I love the laughing," Riley says. "Do more of that."

I glance at Damian. He gives me a nod, encouraging me to try doing a handstand. I can do one in the water, but I'm not sure if it will work here.

I pop up on the board, place my hands directly over the spring, and flip my feet up into the air.

"Ah!" I yell as my body leans dangerously toward Damian, finally hitting the tipping point and falling onto him.

He laughs, catches me, and pulls me over onto his board, somehow, without knocking us both off.

"That was adorable!" Ariela shrieks, jumping up and

down and clapping.

"Can you both stand up on that board?" Riley asks.

"You go first," Damian says.

I stand up. Once I'm set, I feel Damian standing up behind me. But then he grabs my waist and we both go flying off the board into the fake waves and, thankfully, onto the stunt mats Aiden thought to put below.

"One more time with both of you up on your own boards, smiling this time, and we should have enough for this part."

THE REMAINDER OF the day is spent shooting more of the date scenes. We order in food and sit back, watching as Riley works his video magic.

Friday, December 30th

SEXY AND SKANKY.
1PM

RILEY IS STILL putting the finishing touches on the video when I get a call from Kym. She's in town dressing other stars for their New Year's Eve appearances and wants us to meet her.

"Are you sure you don't need anything else?" I ask Riley, who mutters something unintelligible to me and nods his head.

I wrap my arms around Aiden's neck. He and Damian are sitting on either side of Riley's workspace, which consists of multiple computer monitors, each playing different footage.

"Do you want to come with us?"

"Naw, you girls have fun. I've got a couple new suits at the loft. I'm sure one of them will work."

"I think Kym wants to dress you. So we kinda match. But she knows your size. If I think you'll like it, I'll bring it home."

He kisses my arm then turns around and kisses me goodbye.

COOPER ESCORTS PEYTON, Ariela, and me to Kym's new digs. Her lab, as she calls it. She thinks of herself as a mad scientist of fashion. Mixing and matching things together and giving each of her clients a different look. When we arrive, she greets Cooper with great enthusiasm, running her hands across his broad shoulders and telling him how fantastic he'd look after she was done with him.

She greets the girls with air kisses, leads us into a show-room space, and directs us to a buffet of snacks and drinks.

"Are the guys not coming?" she asks, pulling me aside.

"No, they're still working on the video, so we're just supposed to bring everything back to the studio with us. And I sent you my friend Riley's measurements and photos."

"I got them and should have everything pretty well set. Let me go grab your rack of clothes and you can start trying on while I get Mr. Sexy's measurements," she says with a sly grin.

"Just what all are you planning to measure, Miss Cougar?"

"How old is he, anyway? Tell me he's at least twenty-five."

"Uh, not quite. He acts way mature, though, if that's any consolation."

"At least he's legal." She sighs, glancing in his direction then giving me the eye. "He's been guarding your body."

I smirk. "Yes, he has. And teaching me self-defense. I will admit, he's quite powerful. And it's kinda fun when he throws you on the floor. Even if it hurts a little."

"Oh, my god. I want to be manhandled."

"You know, I always thought you and James might get together."

She rolls her eyes. "We've gotten together."

"Really?! And?"

"And nothing. We're friends. We get lonely sometimes. We have a little fun. I want something more serious. I'm still waiting for a guy to whisk me off to a Russian ballet."

"Aren't we all."

"Oh, give me a break. At the wedding, Peyton was telling us all the things that Aiden's done to woo you."

My face breaks out in a wide smile. I can't help it. Aiden makes me smile. "He's pretty dreamy. Really, he's kind of my dream guy in many ways."

"What ways is he not?"

"He's not B."

She sighs. "He didn't dance with you at your birthday party, Keatyn."

"No, but he came to it. He even dressed up. I've realized a lot, Kym. I know I complained about him sometimes. But, looking back, I probably wasn't the easiest person to love."

"Bullshit. You are very lovable."

"I wasn't then. Don't I seem different to you than I did last summer?"

She gets tears in her eyes. "I'm lucky your mom took a chance on me all those years ago and I've gotten to be part of your life. I'm proud to say I've helped dress you for nearly every important occasion in your life."

"You have. I'll never forget the dress from Mom and Tommy's first date. It's still in my closet. I'm hoping to have a little girl who can wear it someday."

"You have a great style. You never look like you try too hard but you always look put together. It's a look young girls will want to emulate once this movie comes out. You need to remember that when you choose your outfits."

"Nothing too skanky?"

"There's a big difference between sexy and skanky."

"Does that mean you picked me out something sexy?"

"Sparkly and sexy. That's what the perfect New Year's Eve dress should always be. Remember when I told you to have an intervention if you ever saw me cooking for a man?"

"Yeah."

"That Cooper makes me want to put on an apron and bake a cake."

"You're bad!"

She giggles. "I know!"

SHE ROLLS RACKS of clothing into the showroom, shows the girls their selections, and sends them behind the curtain to start trying on.

"Okay, Keatyn," she says. "Let's look at yours. Notice, you don't have as many options."

"Why's that?"

"Well, I know you better, for one. I know all these will look great on you, but I want to talk you through them."

I nod at her, so she holds up the first dress.

"This sparkly, silver sequined dress. What do you think of it?"

"It's really pretty. I love the plunging neckline. The sequins are mixed with spangles, which makes it a little different. The cut is pretty, but it's a little—um, predictable, maybe?"

"Exactly. Very good. Okay," she says, holding out the second option. "What about this?"

I examine the dress. "This one has great lines for me. I look good in a tank style dress and I love how it's covered in black sequins that are more matte than shiny. And the bottom, how it flares out and is covered in shiny black feathers, it's so cute! I really like it."

I run my hand across the soft feathers, remembering when Aiden stole my feather earrings after our tutoring with food date.

"You seem like you want to add a but."

"I'm a little worried how the feathers will hold up to a night of dancing."

"You going to be grinding on Aiden?"

"Absolutely."

"Tell me what you think of the dress itself. What message would it send?"

"This dress has a little edge. The combination of the tank style and the matte sequins pair unexpectedly with the feathers on the bottom. You know I like mixing things that seem like they shouldn't go together. And with a great pair of shoes, I think it'd be a good option."

"Tell me what you think of this last dress," she says, pulling it out.

"Oh, wow. I love this one. It's a little more mature than the others. No, that's not it. It's like rocker chic. It has an edge that I love, but still has an elegance about it."

"Tell me about how you're dressed in the video."

"My wardrobe consisted of a bikini, a bikini and shorts, and a cute little mini-dress."

"So, it's sexy?"

"They did choose the skimpiest bikini I had, so, yeah. But it's how any girl looks on the beach."

"Except you have a ridiculously good body and you're gorgeous. My point is, in the video you will look like a model, not an actress. If that was all you wanted to be, I'd put you in the silver dress. If you were a model wanting to be an actress, I'd put you in the feathered dress. But you are Hollywood royalty and this televised New Year's Eve party is your coming out. Not as Abby Johnston's daughter, but as Keatyn Douglas, future movie star. *This* dress will scream it to everyone who's watching."

I get tears in my eyes looking at the dress. It's like I'm standing in a doorway, looking out at my hopes and dreams. All of them there, waiting for me. Acting. A career that I'll love. Movie premieres. Award shows. Red carpets. Magazine covers. My scripts becoming box office hits. It's everything I've ever dared to dream.

"Can I try it on now?" I ask.

She gives me the dress, but not before giving me a hug.

Saturday, December 31st

THAT MANY TIMES.
11:55PM

TWISTED DREAMS AND I are on stage. We just finished an interview and now the world premiere of the "Meet Me at the Beach" music video is being shown.

While the video plays, they ask Damian and me to stay on stage for the countdown to midnight.

A makeup artist runs powder across our faces and a producer says, "You'll be on screen for the midnight kiss."

"But, uh . . ." Damian says.

"We don't have time to discuss. And watch what you say. Your microphones will be live," she tells us. "And, we're back in three, two . . ."

The New Year's countdown starts, the ball drops, and Damian looks into my eyes. If they flash back to us, we'll probably look like we're in love.

"3! 2! 1! Happy New Year!" we yell as confetti and glitter drop from the ceiling.

Damian grabs me around the waist, goes *Ribbit* into my ear, and then dips me dramatically and kisses me.

I come up hugging him and laughing.

We get the okay to leave the stage and I immediately find Aiden.

"I need a New Year's countdown redo," I say, slipping into his arms.

"You looked like you liked it," Aiden says, referring to my kiss with Damian.

"It was supposed to look that way. The dip was dramatic so people wouldn't notice he didn't fully kiss my lips. Kissing Damian is like you kissing your sister."

Aiden cups my face with his hands. "Sounds like you need your lips fixed."

A big grin forms on my face. "That's exactly what I need."

People are still kissing and cheering. There are more shouts of *Happy New Year*. Confetti is still swirling through the air. But when Aiden's face is close to mine and he slowly starts counting down from ten, it's like the world disappears and there's only us.

"9 . . . 8 . . . 7 . . . 6 . . . 5 . . . 4 . . . 3 . . . 2 . . . 1."

The second our lips touch, mine are fixed.

"Happy New Year, Boots."

"Happy New Year, Aiden."

"Next year, and from now on, I don't care what's going on in your life. I'm going to be the one kissing you at midnight. We'll run away if we need to keep you safe, but those lips are mine from now on. No more pretending, unless you're on a movie set. Promise me."

"Uh . . ."

Aiden frowns but says, "Fine. Promise me that if we are together next year, I'll be the only one you kiss at midnight."

God, he is so amazing.

"I promise. Speaking of that, who did you kiss at midnight?"

"I kissed my sister on the cheek and then Riley kissed both of us. I really want to get you home."

"Why's that?" I flirt.

His hands move very inappropriately to my ass, giving it a squeeze. "I think you know exactly what I have in mind."

"Maybe I want you to tell me."

"We still haven't used the feather from your Naughty Santa."

"Oh, gosh. We better get going."

THE CAMERA LOVES YOU.
3:20AM

OF COURSE, WE couldn't leave right then, so it's already past three by the time we're all in the limo heading home from the party.

Aiden's arm is wrapped around me, and I'm still thinking about the feather when I feel my phone vibrate inside my clutch.

Other than a few selfies with everyone at the party tonight, I really haven't looked at my phone. Cooper told me he'd handle everything. That we should relax and enjoy our night.

I pull my phone out to check it.

There are some Happy New Year group texts, but one catches my eye.

B: Had I known you were partying with Damian tonight, I would have joined the fun. Loved the video.

I reply.

Me: Happy New Year, B!! I'm glad you liked the video. We

had a lot of fun making it.

B: *You know, the camera loves you. But, then, I always said you have a very expressive face.*

I drop my phone in a panic, instantly knowing that I'm talking to Vincent and not B.

Aiden sees the look on my face. "What's wrong?"

Damian picks up my phone. "That doesn't sound like something Brook would say."

I bury my hands in my palms, trying to drown out their voices so I can think straight.

"You're right, he wouldn't say that. I think Vincent has his phone." I turn toward Cooper. "Will you please call Garrett and find out who is on B's security detail tonight and where the hell he is?"

Cooper starts dialing.

Aiden touches my arm sweetly, but I pull away, my hands shaking. "I. Need. My. Phone."

"You're not thinking of replying, are you?" Damian asks.

I try to grab my phone from him, but he puts it behind his back.

"Damian, don't mess with me!"

"Keatyn, you need to think this through. Couldn't he track you?"

"I have a number with a Georgia area code and billing address. I'm in a moving car. He already knows I'm in New York. Give me my phone. Now!"

"Give her the phone," Aiden says to Damian in a commanding tone, causing Damian to immediately comply.

Me: *What's up, Vincent?*

B: *What are you talking about? This is Brooklyn Wright's phone. By the way, I wanted to wish you a Happy New*

Year. This is our year.

I look at Aiden, who I know is reading along with me. "Sick," he says. Then he reads the text out loud.

"What are you going to say back?" Riley asks.

I notice a grim look on Cooper's face as he says, "I'll put her on speaker."

"Garrett!? Where is he?" I yell.

"He's in Malibu," Garrett replies through the speaker. "He had a New Year's Eve party at his house. Refused security."

"But, Garrett! I told you . . ."

"Let me finish. After the rose incident, you expressly told me not to listen to either Brooklyn or his dad regarding their security, so I had a team outside the home."

"Front or back?"

"Front. That's where everyone entered the party."

"Fuck," I mutter. "Call them, Garrett. Tell them to enter the house—by force, if necessary—and find Brooklyn! What about Vincent? Aren't there supposed to be two teams on him?"

"He went to a New Year's Eve party at a mansion in Bel-Air. They couldn't follow him through the gates, so they are waiting for his car to come back out."

"So, in other words, you have no idea where either of them are?!" I look up at Cooper. "Tell the driver to stop the car. I have to get out."

I feel trapped.

Claustrophobic.

Sick.

When the car stops, I quickly get out.

Please let Brooklyn be okay.

Maybe he dropped his phone earlier today.

Maybe he left it on the beach when he surfed. He always

does that.

I start walking up the sidewalk randomly, but then see a cute brownstone.

One with steps that I plop down on.

I have to calm down and focus. Focus on getting information from Vincent.

Me: *Why do you have Brooklyn's phone?*

B: *I keep telling you. This is your beloved B, who has a lovely home that is perfect for a party. It was the perfect place to watch your video. I wasn't thrilled with all the comments my friends were making about you, but I guess that comes with the territory of dating someone famous.*

Me: *We aren't dating anymore. If you were really B, you'd know that. We've been over for a long time.*

B: *You're just playing hard to get. But know this. I want you back. And no one you love will be safe until we're together. By the way, how's Grandma?*

Cooper sits down next to me. "Garrett just called back. Keep in mind, it's just past midnight in California, but they couldn't find Brooklyn anywhere in the house and no one seemed to know where he is. His father apparently isn't in town."

"Do you know about what happened to my grandma?"

"Yes."

I hand him my phone. "Read the texts. Screen shot them. Text them to Garrett. See if there's anything he can do, legally."

"There isn't, Keatyn. He keeps saying he's B. You aren't going to be able to prove otherwise."

"B would never threaten me."

"If he were the jealous boyfriend, he might."

"That makes no sense, but whatever. I need to talk to Damian."

I peek my head in the limo door. "Damian, start calling and texting all our friends. All the surfers. Girls they hang out with. Anyone and everyone who's numbers you have that could possibly have been invited to his New Year's Eve party."

"Do a mass text to everyone you know," Riley instructs Damian. "Include our numbers on it and we'll start calling each one."

"And pray someone knows," Aiden adds. His voice is like a shock to my heart.

I look at him, at Damian, at Peyton, at Riley, and at Ariela.

My friends.

I become instantly worried.

About location services.

Phone tracking.

Hacking.

My plan is supposed to revolve around Vincent knowing where I *was,* not where I am now.

I quickly get out of the car and grab my phone out of Cooper's hand.

"Do you have a pocketknife?"

Cooper reaches in his pocket and pulls out something that is much more than a pocketknife.

When my eyes get big at its size, he shrugs. "It's ceramic, passed through the metal detectors at the party tonight."

"I think we need to take out my SIM card. I don't want him to be able to track me. Even if it's only a remote possibility."

Cooper gets up, opens the passenger door in the front of the limo, and asks the driver if he has a paperclip. He leans out of the door shaking his head then asks everyone in the back.

"Keatyn, do you still have the envelope that the tickets were in?" Aiden asks.

"Uh, I think so?"

He picks up my baguette, flips open the clasp, grabs the envelope, digs inside, and pulls out a shiny paperclip.

"You're brilliant," I tell him, quickly using it to pop the SIM card out of my phone.

I hand it to Cooper, who throws it in a trash bin. "Let's get the hell out of here."

ONCE WE'RE ALL back in the car and moving, Cooper whispers to me, "I don't want this driver to take us to your loft. New plan for getting home, don't you agree?"

"Yes. We could be being followed right now."

"We'll never get a hotel room on New Year's Eve."

"Let's go to Damian's. Get dropped off. Go in the building. In the elevators. It's controlled access, so no one could follow us. If they break in later, no one will be there because they're all still in France." I notice that Damian has stopped making phone calls and is looking at me. "Any word?"

"No. I just heard you say my name."

I lean over and whisper to him. "If we got dropped off at your dad's building, could you run up and get the keys so that we could use his car?"

"I wouldn't even have to go upstairs," he whispers back. "It's got an access code on the door handle. The keys are always in it."

"Perfect."

EVEN AFTER SHAKING any tail we may have had and getting back to my loft, we still haven't heard from anyone who knows where Brooklyn is.

"Go ahead and get some sleep," I tell everyone. "It's long past midnight there now, so everyone has probably headed home."

I go in my room with Aiden, walk into my closet, and am stripping off my party dress when one of Aiden's Eastbrooke sweatshirts catches my attention.

A scenario flashes through my brain. Vincent finding out where I live. Searching the loft for clues. I grab Aiden's sweatshirt and toss it on the floor. Now I'm crying, as I frantically whip through his clothes, searching for more.

"What are you doing?" Aiden asks as he comes into the closet.

"You can't have this stuff here! You have to get it out!" I yell.

"My clothes? But you said . . ."

"Anything Eastbrooke. Help me. I have to make sure . . . Because if anyone . . . And I don't want . . ."

I collapse, falling to the floor in a puddle of emotions.

Aiden drops to the floor next me, pulls me into his arms, and lets me cry.

After a few minutes, he kisses the top of my head and says, "Shhhh. Calm down, baby. Listen to your heart. What does it say?"

I look up at him. "What do you mean?"

"Your gut. Your interaction with Vincent. Do you think he has Brooklyn?"

I squint at him, taking a deep breath and clearing my mind as he wraps a cashmere robe around me.

"You're shaking your head," he says, pulling me out of my reverie.

"I am?"

"Yes."

"I don't think he has him."

"Why do you think that?"

"Because Vincent was still threatening me. Still trying to scare me. If he had Brooklyn, he wouldn't have to try. He wouldn't have brought up my grandma. He would have hinted that he was with Brooklyn or something. I think he just wanted me to know that he was close. Too close."

"Are you sure?"

"Not at all. My brain is panicked and on overload. But my heart isn't . . . as panicked."

Aiden gets up, pulls me up with him, and kisses me. "We didn't get breakfast. Why don't I cook and you man the phones? I know you won't be able to sleep until you know for sure."

I want to start crying again because of Aiden's unwavering support. He flicks my bottom lip and says with a laugh, "You don't have to give me the pout. I'll make bacon."

I let out a laugh.

Then I grab him, hug him tightly, and whisper, "I want bacon," even though I mean something else entirely.

Sunday, January 1st
BEING REALLY LOUD.
1PM

WE GOT NUMEROUS call backs this morning.

But no one has the information we need.

No one knows where Brooklyn is.

They all assume he's at his house.

They remember watching the music video with him. Watching the ball drop in New York.

Doing shots.

I'm still pacing.

It's what I've been doing since we got home.

I'm really worried.

And the longer I don't hear from him the more worried I get.

I'm currently seriously contemplating stealing Damian's phone, running off with Cooper, and getting to a location where I can call B's cell.

MY PHONE RINGS with a call from Mark at 1:26.

At this point, I'm not holding out much hope that he'll tell me anything different.

In fact, knowing him, he's probably going to give me shit for calling so many times while he's trying to sleep off New Year's Eve.

"Hey, Mark," I answer.

"Keats?" B's groggy voice asks.

"Brooklyn?! Where the hell are you?! Are you okay?!"

"I'm at Mark's. I'm pretty hung over and you're being really loud."

That sets me off. "What the hell were you thinking? You had a party at your house? Did you know that Vincent was there?"

"What are you talking about?"

"Where's your phone, B? Why aren't you calling from it?"

"I couldn't find it last night. I'm sure I just set it down somewhere."

"Vincent texted me from it last night. He was there. In your house. Said he watched the music video there. Said your friends were saying things about me."

"They were. I didn't like it."

"You didn't like the video?"

"No, Keats. They were all slapping me on the back, making sexual comments. It upset me."

"Why?"

"Why? Because they shouldn't be talking about my girl like that."

"Your girl?"

"You know what I mean. They all think we're still together. Most of them were watching the live footage when I won."

"I want you out of Malibu. Now."

"I can't. I'm meeting my mom on Tuesday, remember?"

"You need to cancel it. Or at least meet her somewhere else."

"I'm not canceling. I already told her to meet me at Buddy's at six. There will be lots of people there. Plenty safe. Are you still coming?"

"You seriously won't change it?"

"I can't. I promised."

I let out a sigh to calm myself down. "Fine. I'll be there. Let's meet a few minutes early. We need to talk."

"We need more than a few minutes, Keats. Why don't you come in the night before. We can surf in the morning. Hang out. Chill. We need some time together."

"Are you still drunk? Don't you understand that Vincent got close enough to you last night that he was able to steal your phone? He. Was. In. Your. House. That should be freaking you the fuck out."

"I don't know, maybe. You're right. I didn't really think it through. I just know I have to see her."

I close my eyes shut tight. "Tell you what. I'll come in a little early and we'll work out a plan that will keep us both safe."

"Okay, Keats."

"Go back to bed, B. I'll talk to you later."

I HANG UP the phone, cover my mouth with my hand, and scream into it.

"A little frustrated?" Cooper asks.

"Is that how you feel when you think I'm doing something stupid?"

Cooper just smiles and laughs at me.

I'm about to collapse in bed when Tommy calls my house phone.

"You weren't answering your cell," he says.

"It's broken. Sorry. Hope I didn't worry you."

"I immediately called this phone, so I wasn't worried

yet. Hey, I have a big favor. Could you and Damian run over to Matt's house and take Bad Kiki for a quick walk? The dog sitter just called and said she's sick. Probably hung over."

"Are you back in town?"

"Yeah, Moffett called and requested a meeting with Matt and me."

"But it's New Year's Day."

"I know, but he's flying back to LA tonight and didn't want to miss us. And, when the head of the studio requests your presence . . ."

"You get on a plane."

"Yep. We left Nice at seven am. It's going to be a long day."

"We'll be happy to walk the dog, Tommy."

"Thank you."

DAMIAN AND I pick up Kiki and take her to Central Park, with Cooper in tow.

Aiden offered to go with Damian, but I'm even more nervous about having him anywhere near either of us in public.

"I haven't had a chance to check online with all the B stuff that went on, but have you heard anything about the video? Do people like it? Like the song?"

"Yeah, they do. We've gotten hundreds of thousands of hits already. It's going to be huge." He smirks at me. "I think a lot of the views are guys watching you over and over. Probably touching themselves."

I smack him on the back. "Gross, Damian. They are not."

He shrugs.

"More like all the little teeny boppers are watching it a

million times and wishing they were me. Listening to your dreamy voice. Pretending to be the girl you take on the perfect date."

"I don't care who watches it or what they're dreaming about. I think this song is going to be a big deal for us."

"It's going to be huge for Riley too. I can't believe how he can take all those pieces and put them together to tell a story."

"It's very fresh and fun. The band is pumped. Did you have fun last night—at the party?"

"Yeah, it was a lot of fun. Aiden made me promise to kiss him at midnight next year, though."

"Peyton said the same thing. It was probably a good lesson for us. Never to get so wrapped up in our public personalities that we forget the moments that matter with the people we care about."

"If it weren't for Vincent, I would have said yes but made sure our dates were close by so we could have kissed them."

"Yeah, I thought about that too."

"So, we're not really stupid. I'm hoping between the video being kinda sexy, being seen out with Knox last week, and then being seen kissing you on New Year's Eve that Vincent is starting to hate me."

"He didn't seem mad when he texted you. You said he's smart. I think he knows you're playing him."

"I just need for him to be distracted trying to find me and not messing with people like B."

"Do you really think B was in danger? Sounds like maybe Vincent just wanted to talk to you."

"He tried to have my grandma run off the road."

"I know. I just wondered if he meant to scare her or if he really wanted to hurt her."

"For now, I think he's trying to scare me."

"Is it working?"

"Yeah, it is. Damian, once I take over his company, I'm going back home to face him."

Cooper, who's been quiet for most of our walk, chimes in. "No, you're not."

"I'd have to agree with Cooper," Damian says.

"On that note, let's head back."

We take Kiki back to the Moran apartment and then carefully work our way back to the loft.

I'M JUST GETTING ready to take a nap when Tommy calls again.

"So, the meeting with Moffett went well. He saw the article about you and Knox, the music video, and the number of hits it's gotten. He wants to strike while the iron is hot and officially announce your role in the movie. He's having a press release drafted for tomorrow. Are you ready for that?"

"Yeah, I am."

"What do Garrett and Cooper think?"

"They're on board," I say, although I highly doubt they are. I don't want to lie to Tommy, so I add, "And there isn't much we can do about it if they're not."

"Unless you want to rethink the role. It's not too late to back out, Keatyn. You haven't even signed the contract yet."

"No, but we verbally agreed to the terms. I'm not going to renege on that. I'd never get another job."

"I'm more worried about your safety."

"I'd rather try to stay safe being in the public eye than in hiding. I'm not doing it anymore. I told you that. We'll just have to leave it to the experts. Plus, if he's focused on me instead of trying to get me to come out of hiding, I'm hoping it will mean everyone around me will be safer. Does that make sense?"

"It's sort of the opposite of what Garrett originally told us."

"It is. But that's not his fault. He did what he thought was right at the time. And I agree that it was. It just isn't now."

"So, forgetting about all the Vincent stuff, this is still a big deal. You're creating the perfect publicity storm. The studio is thrilled. Moffett himself wants to talk to you and Knox about continuing the franchise."

"Really? That's awesome! Knox said he thought that might happen, but I sort of thought it was just wishful thinking."

"No way, baby. You're going to be a star, just like your mom."

"Tommy, I can only hope to be half as successful as Mom."

"I thought you were going to say you don't want to be like her."

"I probably would have a few months ago. I didn't want to be compared to her. I didn't think I could handle the comparison. But, now, I hope I can. I'm gonna let you go. I need some sleep."

I WAKE UP to the loft's phone ringing again.

"Hello?" I answer groggily.

"Guess what, Hotshot?" Grandpa says.

"What?"

"We did it. The last investor called. Apparently, he had lunch with Vincent today and wasn't happy with the way things went. He didn't elaborate. Just asked if our offer still stood. I should have lowballed him at that point, but I didn't. The company is yours. Shall we schedule a meeting for tomorrow morning, so that Mr. Sharpe can get fired by the new owner?"

"Yes, we should. How about nine o'clock his time?"

"I'll make it happen. I'll also be sending you an email with some talking points along with the instructions for logging into the video conference."

"Thank you, Grandpa."

"You're welcome. Just promise me you'll stay out of California for a while. I suspect Vincent isn't going to be very happy."

As Grandpa ends the call, I lean back, throw my arms up in victory, and scream with delight. "Aaaahhhh!!!"

Aiden and Cooper barrel through my bedroom door at the same time. "What's wrong?"

I laugh, almost hysterically. I'm so damn happy. "Nothing. Everything is going perfectly."

LATER, I TEXT Knox.

> **Me:** The takeover of Vincent's company went through. I have an online meeting tomorrow to personally tell him the good news. Then I'd like to be seen. You wanna have lunch with the new chairman of the board?
>
> **Knox:** I'd be honored. I assume you want this lunch to be photographed?
>
> **Me:** Yes, I do.
>
> **Knox:** You're a girl after my heart, Keatyn. I'll let my assistant know where we'll be.
>
> **Me:** Thank you. Cooper and I will pick you up at noon. I'm going shopping at Bergdorf's after. Maybe we could go somewhere close?
>
> **Knox:** Do we get to shop together? That would be romantic.
>
> **Me:** Romantic looking, you mean?
>
> **Knox:** Of course, sugar. Whatever you say.
>
> **Me:** There's hope for you yet. See you tomorrow.

Monday, January 2nd

NO NEED FOR THREATS.
10:30AM

I WAKE UP to Aiden sprinkling little kisses across my shoulder.

"You were naughty last night," he whispers, referring to the party I threw for myself. Riley and Ariela left for home yesterday to get ready to go back to Eastbrooke. When I took my nap, I went to sleep feeling a little sad. Sad that they're all going back without me.

But that sadness was quickly replaced with joy when Grandpa called and told me about the takeover. I immediately decided to throw a party.

It was a small party. Just Peyton, Damian, Aiden, Cooper, and me. But still, it was fun.

Especially after a few shots.

And even more so when I dragged Aiden into my room and used the feather on him.

Let's just say there is still a smile plastered on my face.

"I think you like it when I'm naughty," I reply, sliding my hand down his chest and stopping to rest on his boxers.

He grins at me, removes his boxers, and kisses me. "Yes,

I do."

AFTER SOME MORE naughtiness, I get up and spend a lot of time getting myself ready for the video conference. I want to look like my mom did in the movie, so I blow my hair out and finish it with a straightener.

Then I stand in the middle of my closet and look at my clothes. If it was just Vincent and me, I would wear a bikini. But I'll be speaking to the entire board of directors.

I need to look as professional as possible, so I chose the suit I begged Kym for when I saw it at her studio last week. It's a violet Oscar de la Renta asymmetrical sheath dress with a matching belted peplum moto jacket. It's the perfect combination of fashion forward and understated elegance.

I study myself in the mirror, deciding the bold collar and my hair are competing, so I pull it back into a chic bun and add the glossy black enamel flower earrings that Kym paired with it.

Glancing at the clock and knowing it's almost time, I grab a pair of black suede Alaïa stiletto booties with white dots. I don't know if they really match, but they make me feel fierce, and I'm going to need that.

"So, what do you think?" I ask Aiden when I walk out to the kitchen.

"You look older. Professional." He glances down. "Not sure about the little boot things with it, though."

"I like them."

"That's all that matters, then," he says, giving me a steamy kiss. "Are you ready for this? To face him? To fire him? To speak to a freaking board of directors?"

"Yeah, I'm ready. I'm going to get set up in the dining room. The rest of you cannot make a peep."

"Can we watch? Listen?" Cooper asks.

"Yeah, you can. Grandpa will be conferenced in, too. I'll give you the link, but you have to go upstairs."

"Are you sure?" Aiden asks. "I don't really need to watch. I can stay down here with you."

"I appreciate that. But I need to focus. Concentrate like I would on a movie set. I've memorized the key points Grandpa sent me and I know what I'm going to say."

"Well, good luck, then," he says, first kissing his clover tattoo and then kissing mine. "I love you."

"I love you too, Aiden. Now, get upstairs."

I GET THE computer set up so that I can stand in front of it, rather than sitting down. Grandpa said it will make me look stronger. More dominant.

Part of me wants to laugh. I mean, I'm freaking seventeen and I'm taking over a company? I might be as nuts as Vincent.

I watch the scene in the boardroom start to play out on my computer.

The board members are gathered in the room, greeting each other and chatting.

When Vincent walks in, they all take their seats. I can tell by the way he narrows his eyes that he's noticed a new face in the room, but he doesn't comment, just takes his spot at the head of the table.

Once everyone is seated, the vice-chairman of the board, who happens to be the investor who sold us his stock yesterday, stands up.

"Mr. Chairman," he says, addressing Vincent. "We need to discuss the new ownership of this company."

Vincent looks confused. "What the hell are you talking about, Mac?"

"Why don't I direct your attention to the screen at the

back of the room. I'll let the new owner speak for herself."

This is my cue. I press record on the remote in my hand and stand up straight and proud.

Time to roll the dice.

"Hello, everyone. My name is Keatyn Douglas and I'm the new majority owner of A Breath Behind You Films."

I glance at the computer screen, which is showing me Vincent's reaction. Right now, he doesn't look pissed. He's looking at me curiously. His head tilted slightly. His eyes focused. He really just looks intrigued.

So I continue. "The board of directors met in executive session last night and determined that it's time for a change in leadership. They named me the chairman of the board. Effective immediately."

"What the fuck?" Vincent says, looking around. "Is this a joke? You bring in Abby Johnston's daughter as some little prank?"

The vice-chairman shakes his head. "I'm afraid not, Vincent. We've had a good run, but . . ."

I keep going, "My first order of business is to introduce the new CEO and president of the firm, Chance O'Daniels. Many of you know him as the former CEO of Douglas Oil and Gas."

Vincent stands up. "You can't fire me. This is my company. My company, do you understand me?"

"It was until you decided to leverage everything to make the movie you have become obsessed with, Vincent," one of the board members who didn't sell to us says. "You left us wide open for a takeover. And now we have a teenager running the company?"

"I may be young, but I'm saving this company from its downward spiral, one which would have taken your investments with it. I didn't just buy it on a whim. I'm very serious about building this company for the future. For my future. And although Mr. O'Daniels doesn't know the business yet, he does know what makes a company successful. Please welcome him."

"This is bullshit. Preposterous. I won't stand for it," Vincent says loudly. "I'll fight this." He turns to the vice chairman. "When did you sell? Right after our lunch yesterday? Where you promised to stay on my team?" He gets in the man's face. "You backstabbing son of a bitch."

"You better back off, Vincent," the man replies. "Or we'll have security escort you out."

"Escort me out of my *own* building?"

"It's not your building anymore, Vincent," I say, causing him to walk up to the screen and stare directly at me.

"You think you're so smart. This will all blow up in your face. Trust me."

I give him a smile just like my mother's. "Oh, there's no need for threats, Vincey. I'm going to honor what you started and make the movie you're so passionate about. The company has too much invested not to." I blow him a kiss like my mom did on the movie poster. "What do you think of me starring in it myself? I mean, that's what you wanted, right? That's why you were doing the nationwide search for me. Well, I'm here now."

"You're playing a very dangerous game, Miss Douglas. Our worlds were always going to collide, but now there's no avoiding it. We're on a collision course. One you can't change," he says, his face bright red but his voice stone cold.

It sends chills up my spine.

"You're just mad because I've written a better script than you. And in my script, Vince will die at the end. *Just* like in the original."

"You little fucking bitch!" he screams at me. "No one

you love is safe, do you understand me? No one!"

Chance O'Daniels comes back on screen with two policemen. "Please escort Mr. Sharpe from the building. We will pack up his personal effects and forward them to his home address."

Vincent gives me a fiery, wild-eyed look. One that leaves me knowing I've succeeded in pushing him over the edge.

But then his face becomes a mask of calmness.

And calm Vincent scares me way more than out-of-control Vincent.

He turns away from me, straightens his suit jacket, and says politely to the policemen, "No escort is necessary. I will leave of my own accord. But if you would be so kind, I'd like you to accompany me to my office first so I can retrieve some personal belongings."

He gets a nod from the policemen and leads them out of the boardroom.

"Well, that went better than I expected," the vice-chairman says. "Let's get on with our meeting."

I listen to the new CEO lay out his plan for restructuring the company and then adjourn the meeting.

The second it's over, my new cell phone rings.

"Well, Hotshot, what'd ya think?" Grandpa asks. "By the way, Garrett Smith and your Cooper are conferenced in on this call."

"I thought it went well," I lie. "What's your take on it, Garrett?"

"He reacted as we suspected he would. Was royally pissed off. Cooper, do you feel that your location is still safe, given all that's been going on this week?"

"Yes," Cooper replies. "We've been very careful. And I've made Keatyn start wearing her tracking necklace at all times, just in case."

"I'm more worried about my family, Garrett. You have to make sure they stay safe."

"We're doing everything we can."

"And you're still following him?"

"Yes."

"Do the people who follow him have to send you reports?"

"Yes."

"May I get copies of those reports? I need to know what he's up to. Where he is at all times."

"I'll have my assistant email you the reports," Garrett agrees.

"Sounds good," I say cheerfully. "Anything else we need to discuss?"

"I don't think so," Garrett says. "We'll take it from here. What he does in the next forty-eight hours should give us a good indication of what's to come."

When he ends the call, I turn around to find Aiden, who pulls me into a hug.

"I shouldn't have done it, Aiden," I confess. "I shouldn't have done it."

"Why do you say that? You said you wanted to push him. To make him mad. It looked to me like you accomplished that."

"I wanted him out of control," I reply as Cooper, Damian, and Peyton join us in the dining room.

"He yelled at you. I thought he was going to punch that guy," Damian says. "Isn't that what you wanted?"

"Yeah, I guess you're right," I lie. "It went well. I'm just worn out. Not thinking straight."

"Why don't we let Cooper and Keatyn talk?" Peyton suggests, herding Damian and Aiden back upstairs.

Cooper sits down and motions for me to do the same.

"He wasn't out of control, was he?"

"Nope."

"The way he was able to go from pissed beyond belief to completely in control was interesting to watch."

"Did Garrett not notice it?"

"I'm sure he did. He's good at what he does."

"So, why didn't he say anything?"

Cooper's cell rings. He looks at it and says, "I think he's about to."

After his conversation with Garrett, he says to me. "He definitely noticed. And he's worried. He's got the house in France on lockdown, which takes care of your mom, sisters, and grandparents. They talked Tommy's mom into staying for a while too."

"That's good."

"Tommy will have another man with him full-time, starting tomorrow."

"Okay."

"That leaves you."

"What does he suggest I do?"

"He wants you to stay here. He would prefer you not leave the loft at all."

"You know that's not part of my plan, Cooper. And I promised B that I'd go to Malibu tomorrow. I know the timing sucks, but we're going to have to do it. Quick. In and out. Just like those nights we visited the club. We'll come back here so I can say goodbye to Aiden before he goes back to school, and then we're going to live on the move. Tomorrow won't be our only trip back home."

"Vincent is right. You're playing a dangerous game."

I GO UPSTAIRS and tell Aiden, Peyton, and Damian goodbye.

"Where are you going?" Aiden asks, following me down the stairs. "I thought we were going bowling?"

"You *are* going. I can't. I just took over his company. I have to be seen out and about. I'm meeting Knox for lunch, going shopping, and then having dinner with Tommy."

"But . . ."

Aiden doesn't look happy with me. I probably shouldn't have just sprung this on him. But, honestly, it's starting to get hard to remember who I've told what to. And as much as I will miss him, I'm glad he has to go back to school. I need to be able to move around quickly. That's hard to do with a group of people. Now, I just need to figure out what I'm going to do with Damian.

"Damian is coming to Connecticut to say goodbye to Peyton. I sort of thought you'd come too."

"He is? How long is he staying?"

"Uh, I'm not sure. He said something about needing to go to Miami. I think he leaves Saturday afternoon, maybe."

"I don't think I will be able to come, Aiden. I wish I could, but I have to keep going. And I'll be honest, I'd rather have you back at Eastbrooke."

"I want to be with you."

"I know you do, but it has to be this way. I'm sorry."

"What if I refuse to go back to school without you?"

"You promised to do what I asked regarding your safety, remember?"

He pushes me against the wall and kisses me hard. It's the kind of kiss that would normally make me do whatever he asked.

"Doesn't mean I have to like it," he says, keeping me pinned with his chest.

"Aiden, please don't make this harder on me than it already is," I beg. "I really can't take much more today."

He pulls me into a hug.

"I knew it was bothering you more than you were letting on."

"Of course it is. But I can't show it. I have to go out and pretend to be on top of the world."

He nods and gives me a kiss. "Be safe, Boots."

JUST PLAYING ME.
NOON

COOPER AND I pick up Knox. He gets in the car, gives me a kiss on the cheek, then fist bumps Cooper. "I fired my bodyguard. Where can I get another one of you?"

"We can put you in touch with the security company that Keatyn uses," Cooper replies.

"Cool. So, how did today go?"

"It went well."

"Did you really fire Vincent Sharpe from his own company?"

"Yeah."

"Amazing. You look amazing, too. I'm digging the suit. And the boots."

"Thanks. It's what I wore for the meeting."

He gives the driver the address of where we're going and, as we hoped, there are a few photographers waiting for us outside.

"Knox! Keatyn! Can you stop and give us a picture?"

Knox pretends to whisper in my ear and I pretend to agree, nodding my head and stopping to pose for a happy couple photo.

After lunch, we walk to Bergdorf's, where I help him

pick out an Alexander McQueen tonal jacquard suit with a skull pattern for an event he's going to this weekend.

"Maybe we should get you a dress so you can join me. Do you have plans this weekend?"

"No. Aiden will be back in school, so I'll probably be back and forth between here and LA for however long it takes."

"However long *what* takes?"

"For something to happen with Vincent. Preferably something that would put him in jail."

"Like what?"

"Attempted kidnapping. Kidnapping. Stalking, maybe. Whatever."

"You get kidnapped in our movie."

"I know. Probably why I'm so good at the role. I barely have to act. Tommy is like my father. I've almost been kidnapped . . ."

"That must be weird."

"It kind of is. But I'm excited, regardless. Oh, and I think you were right."

"About what?"

"Us maybe taking over the franchise. Tommy and Matt had a meeting with Edward Moffett yesterday. He's going to announce my role sometime today."

"He probably saw the video. And the pics of us."

"He did. Wants to strike while the iron is hot."

"You looked hot in the video." He winks at me then gives me a steamy kiss right in the middle of the men's department.

"What the hell was that for?"

"Just playing my part," he says, quietly, still holding me in his arms.

"You don't need to kiss me like that."

He grins at me. "Maybe I just felt like it."

"And maybe you're just playing me."

He grins at me. "I'm pretty sure it goes both ways, sugar."

"I'm going to warn you. I'm celebrating the takeover by purchasing an insane amount of shoes as well as some new handbags. I hope you don't bore easily."

"Why stop there?" he says, egging me on. "Let's find you a dress to wear this weekend."

"What kind of dress would I need?"

"Something long and classy. I liked the dress you wore on New Year's Eve. It was sophisticated but edgy."

"Thanks. I liked it too."

After very little looking, Knox holds up a J. Mendel black strapless gown with a leather bodice and columned skirt. "How about this?"

"I think I need to try that on. It would look perfect with your skull suit."

AFTER SHOPPING, WE drop Knox off at his place and then go meet Tommy for dinner. We've just ordered when Tommy gets a text from his publicity team, letting him know that the press release has been sent out. Tommy hands me his phone so I can read it.

The official joint statement from Moran Films and High Adrenaline Productions:

Keatyn Douglas, daughter of Abby Johnston and the late Mark Douglas, has been officially cast to play the role of Tommy Stevens' daughter, Harper, for the third movie in the Trinity *Trilogy,* Retribution. *Director Matthew Moran said, "We're thrilled to have signed Keatyn. She was always my first choice, but we needed to prove her acting abilities. Because of her great screen*

test with co-star, Knox Daniels, the writers are current-
ly expanding both actors' roles. We expect to see great
things from these two in the future."

"That sounds good," I say. "When do you start filming again?"

"Tomorrow. And we should have your new schedule in the next couple weeks."

"Sounds good," I say again, stifling yet another yawn.

"You had a busy day. I should let you get back home," he says, asking the waiter for our check.

His phone, my phone, and Cooper's phone all buzz at the same time.

"Looks like another version of the press release," Tommy states, glancing at it and then setting his phone down.

But I get a frantic text from Damian.

Damian: *WE HAVE A PROBLEM! DID YOU READ THE ARTI-*
CLE I JUST SENT YOU? AND, MORE IMPORTANTLY, DID YOU
SEE THE PHOTOS??!!
Me: *Uh, no, I didn't. Hang on.*

I open the article up and read a different version.

Keatyn Douglas: Hollywood's Next It Girl?

The official joint statement from Moran
Films and High Adrenaline Productions:
Keatyn Douglas, daughter of Abby Johnston and the
late Mark Douglas, has been officially cast to play the
role of Tommy Stevens' daughter, Harper, for the third
movie in the Trinity *Trilogy,* Retribution. *Director*
Matthew Moran said, "We're thrilled to have signed
Keatyn. She was always my first choice, but we needed
to prove her acting abilities. Because of her great screen

*test with co-star, Knox Daniels, the writers are current-
ly expanding both actors' roles. We expect to see great
things from these two in the future."*

The real story:

*Talk about a good gene pool. If ever there was a girl
made for the spotlight, it's Keatyn Douglas. Our sources
on the* Retribution *set say that Knox and Keatyn are
already a couple. That they were burning up the place
with their chemistry and have become very close. We
know they were goo-goo over each other at a hip NYC
night club last week, but then got in a wicked fight
that saw poor Keatyn leaving the club in tears, only to
be stopped by Knox and whisked off to his penthouse.
The couple shared a special night together, capped it off
with a brisk morning jog through Central Park, and
carpooled to the movie set.*

*But, let's be real. We all saw Keatyn's music video
debut, and no one can deny the chemistry between her
and* Twisted Dreams' *lead rocker, Damian Moran,
the son of director Matthew Moran. Although just days
before, Damian was seen with a leggy blonde, who we
all know he kissed on New Year's Eve. In further
evidence are these photos of the couple's arm-in-arm
stroll through Central Park with their doggie pal and
the entrance to their secret love nest. Add to the equa-
tion professional surfer, Brooklyn Wright, who pledged
his love to Keatyn after winning the Surf City Hawaiian Open just a few months ago and high school
sweetheart, actor Luke Sander, and it looks like our
new it girl knows how to play the field.*

And what a delicious field it is.

*P.S. Vincent Sharpe, if you're reading this, stop the
silly nationwide search and cast Keatyn in the remake*

of A Day at the Lake.

P.P.S. Because, seriously.

Below is a photo of Damian and me at the entrance to my loft. The address numbers clearly visible.

"Fuuuuck," I say loudly, causing the restaurant patrons to give me disapproving glares.

"What's wrong?" Cooper asks.

"The loft has been burned. Somehow, someone must have followed us home from the park when we took Kiki for a walk. We have to get Damian, Peyton, and Aiden out of there. I can't go back. Shit."

Tommy looks panicked. "What are you going to do?"

"Let me think for a minute," I say.

"How did they follow us to your loft? We've been so careful," Cooper says.

"Apparently, not careful enough," I snap. I'm pissed.

Because, not my loft.

It's the only home I have.

I text Damian back.

Me: *Look out the windows. Do you see anyone out front?*
Damian: *Hang on.*
Damian: *No.*
Me: *They would think only you and I are there, right?*
Damian: *So I should be the only one to go out the front?*
Me: *Yes. Press-wise, people have forgotten about Peyton already. They think I'm seeing both you and Knox.*
Damian: *I'd prefer it that way.*
Me: *Me too. So send P & A out the back. Tell them to follow the alley, take the first right, and then get a cab to the Plaza Hotel. Tell them to go to the Food Hall and get some yogurt. Cooper will find them. Tell them if they see Cooper to pretend like they don't know him and to shop around a little. He's going to want to make sure they*

don't have a tail, just in case.

Damian: *Got it.*

Me: *At the same time, you go out the front and catch a cab. Go straight to your dad's apartment. I'll message you when I get all the pieces in place. Text me when you're at your dad's.*

Damian: *Will do. Are you freaking out?*

Me: *A little. I'm good now.*

"Tommy, Cooper and I are going to head out. I have to find somewhere to stay tonight."

"Just come to Matt's apartment," Tommy says.

"Damian is headed there, but I can't send Aiden and Peyton there. The press has already forgotten about Peyton. Damian kind of wants to keep it that way."

"You're very protective of Aiden," Tommy observes.

I nod, then stand up and give Tommy a hug goodbye. "Come on, Cooper."

Cooper gives Tommy a nod, but as we leave he's looking at the floor.

I grab his arm. "It's okay, Cooper. It's not your fault."

"It's absolutely my fault," he replies, marching ahead of me.

"No, it's mine. I'm pushing you. Putting myself in situations that aren't easy to control. I know the risks. It just makes me sad. Not being able to go back there."

"All our stuff is there."

"I have a lot of new shoes in the car," I tease. "You can borrow some."

"Not funny," he says with a little chuckle as we get in the car. "Why don't you let me plan what's next."

"Okay, what are you thinking?"

"I'm going to check us all into a hotel. You can sneak in and I'll go get Aiden and Peyton. Where do you want to stay?"

"Let me call my travel concierge and have her find us a suite."

A FEW MINUTES later, I say, "We're all set up at the Four Seasons. They have a three-bedroom suite that will be perfect for all of us. I'm going to have you drop me off a block from the hotel. I tweaked your plan a little and made myself an appointment at the spa. While I'm there, you go get Peyton and Aiden. Since it's close, you can just walk over, double check they're not being followed, and get them settled. Then you can text me and take me straight up to the room. Does that sound okay?"

"Yes, that sounds fine. I'm sorry I snapped at you earlier."

"It's okay, Cooper. It's been a pretty crazy day. Maybe I'll send you down for a massage once we're all settled."

"Now that sounds like the best idea you've had in a while."

START WITH ME.
9PM

AIDEN SAYS FLATLY, "You went a little crazy shopping today."

I look at my purchases littered across the bedroom floor. "Yeah, I did. I was supposed to be celebrating, having a great day."

"Did you have a great day? I mean, before we had to move."

"Shopping was fun—well, parts of it—but I was sort of

going through the motions."

"That's because you're trying to live a pretend life. There's no joy in it."

He takes the garment bag out of my arms and unzips it to take a look. "Another rainy day dress?"

"Um, no. I'm going to a gala Saturday night."

"With Knox?"

"Yes."

Aiden pushes his hand roughly through his hair. "I don't understand this. Remind me again why it's okay for you to be seen with Knox but not me? I'm okay with the danger too."

"I know you are," I say quietly.

"Tell me why," Aiden says adamantly. I can tell he's pissed.

"Because with Vincent I'm not that good of an actress."

"What do you mean?"

"He followed me for months, Aiden. In that time, I hung out and partied with a ton of guys, the main ones being Sander, Cush, Damian, Troy, and Brooklyn. Vincent took photos of me and Cush together. He saw us at soccer, at the club, at the boardwalk, and at a party. I think I even told him I was in love with Cush."

"But I thought you loved Brooklyn?"

"I did. And Vincent knew it even though I didn't. He's always focused on B."

"What's that got to do with me?"

"There's no way I could hide my feelings for you. Damian says when I'm with you love is written all over my face. If Vincent were to see us together, you'd become target number one."

"I don't care. We'd be together. I could help keep you safe."

"Aiden," I choke out, my eyes filling with tears at the thought of Vincent discovering him. "Please, no."

"So, if you stop seeing Knox publicly, I should worry you've fallen in love with him?" he says, trying to joke about it but failing. I can see the jealously raging behind his eyes. I hate that I'm putting him through this.

"I hate this as much as you do, Aiden. I know you don't understand. I don't even really understand. But it's in my gut. It's something I'm being driven to do. I don't have a choice."

"You always have a choice about how to live your life."

"I agree wholeheartedly. My situation is just different right now. Vincent and I have been on this path for a while. I can't avoid the collision. It's just a question of when and where it will happen."

He walks across the room and reaches into the small bag he brought with him from the loft and pulls out something I cherish.

"Here," he says, handing me my book of Keats poetry. "I knew you'd want this."

I hold it in my hand, staring at it. Thinking about what it means to me. All the feelings I have wrapped up in the pages of an old book. I gently open it, read B's inscription and then turn to the center of the book to see that, thankfully, Aiden's lucky four-leaf clover is still pressed inside.

I cover my mouth, trying to stop myself from crying, but I can't. I just mutter out, "Thank you."

Aiden pulls me into his arms for the first time since I arrived. I know he's mad at me but, even mad, he still did something so incredibly thoughtful. I lay my head on his shoulder and just breathe him in.

"What did you have done at the spa?" he asks.

"A hot stone massage with lavender oil."

"Are you relaxed?"

"Kind of."

"Did you see the size of the bathtub in our room? What do you say we order dessert and take a bath?"

"Is Damian staying at his dad's tonight?"

"Yeah, that's the plan. He and Cooper will figure out how to get him here tomorrow. Cooper seemed stressed."

"He feels responsible for the loft getting photographed."

"Well, it is his job."

"Yeah, but I shouldn't have been out walking the dog in Central Park. I should have let Cooper do it. I wasn't thinking. And I'm *always* thinking."

"You had been up all night worried about Brooklyn."

"We all had been."

"So tonight we're in a gorgeous hotel suite. We should take advantage of it. Everything else you need to do can wait until tomorrow."

I sigh. "Agreed. And you're right. Why don't you order dessert while I run the bath."

"Perfect," he says.

I'M HALF ASLEEP in the tub when Aiden walks in, naked, carrying tiramisu and some kind of sinful-looking chocolate pudding. Both the desserts and his nakedness capture my attention.

"I don't know which I want first. You or the dessert."

He laughs and slides in the tub. "Let's start with me."

Tuesday, January 3rd

CALL ME!
11:30AM

I WAKE UP to a text from Knox along with a link to an article.

Keatyn Douglas Takes Over the World.

Okay, not quite. But rumor has it that none other than our new favorite It Girl, Keatyn Douglas, has become the chairman of the board of A Breath Behind You Films in a hostile takeover from none other than movie futures golden boy, Vincent Sharpe, grandson of the late Viviane Sharpe. Below is a still shot from her video conference with the board. Looks like Keatyn took our advice about starring in the remake of her mom's movie seriously and just bought the whole damn company.

P.S. Just how much do you inherit from an underwear model?

P.P.S. Because, seriously.

P.P.P.S. Love your suit, Keatyn. Oscar?

What do you do after you take over a multi-million-dollar production company?

An intimate celebratory lunch with your hot co-star, Knox Daniels?

Check.

Shopping at Bergdorf's with your hottieguard—I mean, bodyguard—in tow?

Check.

Dinner with your mom's longtime beau, Tommy Stevens?

Check.

We love you Keatyn!

P.S. And your taste in shoes and handbags. Celine, Alaïa, Chanel, Louboutin. Yes, please.

P.P.S. Take us shopping with you!

P.P.P.S. Call me!

Me: She called you hot. That's what you're most excited about, right?

Knox: Ha. Just showing you that I'm a man of my word. You wanted publicity, sugar. You got it.

Me: Unfortunately, a little too much yesterday. They got a photo of my loft, so we had to move to a different location. At least until Aiden and Peyton go back to school.

Knox: Where are you?

Me: Four Seasons.

Knox: I just whistled, in case you couldn't hear me. Can I move in too?

Me: LOL. What would you think of that?

Knox: Wait. Think of what?

Me: If I moved in with you.

Knox: I think that might cramp my style a little.

Me: Not in real life. In fake life.

Knox: You wanna go all the way and get engaged at the

top of the Eiffel Tower or something too?

His text is like a blow to my heart, knocking the wind out of my fake life.

I don't want to have a fake life.

I want to have *my* life.

Me: Um ... I have to go. I'll talk to you later. Thanks for the heads up on the article and hanging out with me yesterday.

Aiden is sleeping on his side, his back to me, so I snuggle under the covers next to him, pressing my chest tightly to his back.

"Morning, beautiful," he says, kissing my arm.

"You have to go back to school tomorrow. I thought we could spend the day doing whatever you want to do."

He flips over quickly, gives me a naughty grin, and trails a finger down my cleavage. "*Whatever* I want to do?"

"I think we did *whatever* quite a few times last night. But, yes, whatever you want."

He looks toward the window. "Is it nice out?"

"It snowed a little last night, so it's cold."

"Perfect. I say we order room service and stay snuggled up in bed all day."

He drags a hand through his messy hair, blinks beautiful green eyes, and then rubs at the scruff on his face. It's something most people do when they wake up, but no one else looks like him doing it. It's the epitome of sexy.

On a scale of one to ten, it's off the charts. Even hotter than the pool table.

Because he's in bed with me.

He's naked.

And he's beautiful.

Every single bit of Aiden is beautiful.

I hate that I have to say this and I hate that I'm hurting him.

"Well, not all day. Remember, I have to go to California late this afternoon."

The smile slides off his face. "Where you and Brooklyn are going to see how you feel?"

"Where we're going to see his mom and then I'm going to convince him to get the hell out of Malibu. As for the how we feel part, I don't know what will happen."

"I don't want you to go, Boots."

"Aiden, I'm sorry. I know this has been rough for you. My spending time with Knox. Fake kissing Damian at midnight. I'm trying so hard to get my life back."

"But at what price?"

"I wish I knew. Just promise me that whatever happens, you won't hate me."

"I could never hate you."

"Depending on how it all ends, Aiden, you might," I say, already envisioning my plan for tonight. If I'm going to have to be in Malibu anyway, I might as well use the trip to piss Vincent off some more.

Aiden shakes his head then kisses me. Kisses my lips. Kisses my neck. Kisses slowly down my body.

My body responds like it always does, but my head— well, my head just isn't into it. My brain is on overdrive. Trying to figure out how to get Damian here safely. Deciding where Cooper and I are going to live. Wondering if I should go with my original plan of renting a yacht and a helicopter.

Aiden pushes his hand between my legs, spreading them apart to allow his mouth access.

Oh, wow.

Wait. What was I thinking about?

As his tongue—that godly tongue—works it's magic on me, my brain ceases to function.

Okay, it's functioning but it's got just one train of thought.

Fuck me.

Make me forget everything.

Run away with me.

Marry me.

Have babies with me.

We can live in a shack on the beach.

I don't care if I ever see my family or friends again.

Just please don't stop.

Ever.

As I'm about to climax, my brain awakens harshly and a memory stops me from thoroughly enjoying myself.

I'm lying in bed with B. We're in France. It's the morning after our first time.

"I've been thinking about not going home. About living here. Or traveling the world."

"You kinda need to finish school first, don't you think?" he says.

"I'll do it like you did. Like, online or something. I don't want to go back home."

"You can't run away from your problems, Keats, because eventually they'll come and find you."

And I know without a doubt that he was right. My problems are coming to find me.

"WE'RE SO GOOD together," he says, gazing into my eyes. "I'm not sure how I'm going to survive without you.

Remember what I told you on the beach? How you have my heart?"

"I remember, Aiden. And I don't know where I'll be exactly, but I'll text you, I promise. Whenever I can."

"You better. It's all that will keep me going. Are you sure you can't come back to school?"

"I accidentally led someone to my loft. I'd die if I led Vincent to Eastbrooke. I don't think he'd care who he hurt in the process of getting to me."

"Do you have any idea how you've changed my life? What you mean to me?" He looks teary. "I'm going to miss you."

"Aiden, I can't do this."

"Do what, baby?"

"This whole goodbye thing."

"I'm sorry. I just want to make sure you know how I feel before you go."

I jump out of bed. I can't take this anymore. It's killing me.

PRETTY SHITTY.
1PM

COOPER AND I are getting ready to head to the airport when I get a call from Tommy.

"Keatyn!" he says frantically. "Where are you?"

"At the hotel, getting ready to leave for the airport."

"You can't go. Kiki was kidnapped. The dog sitter was hit on the head and knocked out. They took her to the hospital. There was a note in her backpack."

"What did it say?"

"It said, *My dearest, K. Lying. Flying. Plane goes down. Boom, splat, on the ground. Woof. Ruff. Dogs do say. Rounds two and three go my way.*"

"Ohmigawd."

"What? I don't get it, do you?"

"I think he had something to do with my dad's death, Tommy."

"Are you serious?"

"Does Mom know? Did she ever suspect that? Was there ever any question?"

"Not that I'm aware of. I just remember hearing there had been some kind of mechanical failure. Holy shit. Do you think his obsession goes that far back?"

"Maybe it does. Maybe Vincent thought he was like Matt and didn't support Mom's dreams."

"Your mom has never mentioned anything about your dad not being supportive."

"His career was going well and he wanted mom to slow down. He thought she should quit for a while so I could have a normal childhood. I remember them fighting about it."

"Wait, are you talking about Matt Moran?"

"No, Matt. Mom's boyfriend in *A Day at the Lake*. He didn't support Lacey's dreams. That's why Vince wanted to kill him."

"This is from the movie?"

"Yes, Vincent is obsessed with it. Reread the last part again."

"Woof. Ruff. Dogs do say. Rounds two and three go my way," he recites. "What do you think rounds two and three are? And why do they go his way?"

"I'm assuming round one was the takeover. I won that round. Round two. He took Kiki."

"So, what's round three?"

"I don't know. Did you look everywhere for Kiki? All over the park?"

"Yeah, both Matt and I went and looked for her everywhere. We called for her. And she walks that path every day, she'd know her way home. I'm actually sitting outside right now hoping she'll show up. I've called Animal Control three times. She has a chip, so they'll contact me if they find her. As much as that dog drives me nuts, I love her. The girls will be so upset."

"Don't tell them yet, Tommy. I'll find her."

I hang up the phone and yell, "Cooper!"

He comes rushing out of his bedroom in just a pair of sweat shorts. "What?!" he says, as Aiden comes running out of our room, both of them on edge.

"I'm going out. I'll be back in a few minutes. I have something I need to do."

"You can't just leave. I'm coming with you," Cooper says.

"Fine," I say, throwing on Aiden's ball cap in an attempt at a partial disguise.

Cooper runs back to his room, returning fully dressed, and says, "Where to?"

"A department store."

We walk at a brisk pace to the nearest large department store, where I go to their customer service area and use their house phone to call B's old cell number collect.

Vincent answers with, "Good to see I have your attention."

"Give me back the dog."

"You took away something I love, I'll take away *everything* you love."

Click.

I slam my head against the wall in frustration.

I'll take away everything you love echoes in my head.

I have to figure out what round three is.

Everything I love.

Everything I love.

My family. Safe.

Tommy. Mostly safe.

Brooklyn.

Shit!

I pull my cell phone out of my pocket and call him.

"B, you absolutely can't go tonight. Move it to tomorrow. Move it to a different location."

"This is going to be a defining moment in my life, Keats. I can't change it. We'll meet my mom at Buddy's and then, later, we'll tell my dad that you're sponsoring me. Then it will be just you and me. We can figure us out. See how we feel. Are you on your way to the airport?"

"Listen to me. I *need* you to reschedule and leave Malibu, now. Go to Australia with your dad."

"I just told you, we're meeting my dad tonight. He's in town for some business meeting. We're going to Australia together later in the week. What happened? Why do you sound so panicked?"

"Bad Kiki was kidnapped by Vincent."

"Are you sure?"

"Yes, B, I'm sure. He left a note in the dog walker's backpack. It's exactly like the note he left in Avery's backpack. It even—um . . ."

"Um, what?"

"Mentioned a plane crash."

"You think he's going to crash my plane to Australia? He's a stalker, Keats, not a terrorist."

"No, I don't think that. I think he had something to do

with my dad's death."

"Oh . . ."

"Yeah. And I just talked to him. He told me he'd take away everything I love."

"So, if he's in New York, wouldn't it be better for you to be here?"

"He's not here. He didn't kidnap the dog himself. I'm sure he hired someone to do it. He's still in LA. I have people keeping an eye on him. He seems to hire people to do most of his dirty work."

"So, same thing. If someone is watching him, they'd know if he came after me, right? I'm fine. I'm going to see her, Keats. I have to. I promised. *You* promised."

"Please, please, reschedule. I went ahead and did the hostile takeover without your help. Yesterday, I fired Vincent from his own company."

"You did all that on your own?"

"My grandpa took care of it, but the end result is the same: I now own the majority of the production company. I'm the chairman of the freaking board."

"That's crazy."

"I know."

"I'm proud of you for fighting back, Keats."

"I want our lives back."

"I want my mom back. That's why I'm doing this with or without you."

"I hate to even suggest this, but what if Vincent found her and got her to contact you? To lure you in? You could be walking into a trap."

"That's a pretty shitty thing for you to suggest."

"Your dad kept you apart all these years for a reason."

"I had this discussion with my dad. I'm not having it with you! I'm going to see her and no one is going to stop me. Not my dad, not you, and certainly not fucking Vincent!"

He hangs up on me.

When I call back, he doesn't answer.

COOPER, WHO'S BEEN standing next to me the whole time, wraps a strong arm around me.

"You need to fill me in on the details of what just happened."

"Vincent is in LA, right? Wouldn't they have called you if he left town?"

"Yes, they would have."

"Tommy called me. Kiki was stolen. The dog sitter got knocked out and a note was left in her backpack." I tell him what it said. "I called B's old cell number collect and Vincent answered. He reiterated the note. Said he's going to take everything I love and hung up on me. Then you heard me call B. He hung up on me too."

"You really decided not to go?"

"I may be crazy, but I'm not stupid."

Cooper smiles. "Good to hear. Keep your head down and let's get back to the hotel."

SORT OF AWKWARD.
11:55PM

WE SPEND THE rest of the day in the hotel suite. Through a bunch of complicated maneuvers, Cooper got Damian here without being followed. Knowing Damian wants to stay in Connecticut with Peyton for a few days before going to Miami, we had a discussion about where he would stay.

Cooper didn't think it made sense for him to check into a hotel like he had planned, in case the hotel staff recognized his name, so he offered a solution. To let Damian stay in his faculty quarters on campus. Since his stuff is all still there, no one will be using it. And it will work out well, provided Peyton can sneak him in. He promised once he got there not to step foot outside, citing that it would give him some quiet time to write. Peyton says she can make sure he's fed and watered, so to speak.

Although I'm a little iffy about their plan, Cooper seems to think it will work and I've come to the realization that I can't control everything.

Kind of like my scripts that no one would follow.

Aiden isn't thrilled about going back to school without me, but he's very relieved that I'm not going home today.

But I feel like I'm letting Brooklyn down. Breaking a promise.

My gut tells me I had to.

But that doesn't make it any easier. Aiden's been trying to take my mind off Kiki and my fight with B by keeping me entertained. We've played cards, listened to music, watched movies, and ordered room service.

As midnight approaches, I'm getting fidgety. I've tried to call Brooklyn every hour since nine, which would have been six, seven, and eight o'clock his time.

"He met with his mom at six. It's been three hours," I say aloud, interrupting the movie we're watching.

Aiden presses pause. "If he hasn't seen his mom in years, they probably have a lot to talk about."

"Plus, he's mad at you," Damian adds. "You know how he gets. He's probably ignoring your calls."

"You're right! You call him!"

"Fine, but if he doesn't answer, I don't want you to

freak out. He's probably still with his mom."

"Just try."

Damian gets out his phone, hits a few buttons, and puts it up to his ear. "Straight to voicemail," he says, hanging up.

"Why don't we order some dessert?" Aiden suggests.

Peyton goes, "That sounds yummy. You know you love chocolate!"

"Chocolate makes everything better," Cooper says, quoting what I usually say.

I'm lucky they're here. I'm a basket case as it is. I can't imagine how I'd be without their wonderful distraction.

"I agree. Let's order dessert."

WE ARE FINISHING up our dessert when my phone rings.

"It's Brooklyn!" I say, supremely relieved to finally hear from him.

"Hey, B! How did it go?"

"Are you not with him?" his dad says. "I thought the two of you were meeting me at the house at 8:30 to talk. Where are you?"

"I'm in New York. Is he not back yet? Wait, you called me from his phone."

"Yes, that's why I called you. I thought you were with him and I couldn't get ahold of him because he left his phone here. Why didn't you go to dinner with him? Does that mean he went alone?"

"I assume so. I tried to talk him out of going. Told him it was too dangerous for us to be together in Malibu."

"He should be home by now. Do you know where they were meeting?"

"They were going to Buddy's. Hang on, let me use my friend's phone and I'll call there."

I grab Cooper's phone, look up the number for Buddy's,

and call it.

"Hey, is Darlene working tonight? Could I speak to her?"

A few minutes later, our usual waitress answers.

"Hey, this is Keatyn. I don't know if you remember me but I always used to come in and get spicy shrimp with Brooklyn."

"I remember you. He was here tonight. Told us all about how he's been off surfing."

"Is he still there?"

"Uh, no. He left quite a while ago. He met with an older woman. It seemed sort of awkward, like he didn't know her well. She didn't stay long. He ordered dinner and had a couple of beers after she left. Seemed upset. Picked at his food. Left around seven."

"That was two hours ago. Did he happen to say where he was going?"

"No, he didn't. Oh, wait. Maybe. He said something about clearing his head with a walk on the beach before he had to go deal with his other parent. Was that lady his mom? Now that I think about it, they did share a resemblance."

As she continues talking about their blonde hair and blue eyes, I whisper, "He left two hours ago."

"How would he have gotten there?" Cooper asks.

"Darlene, did you notice if Brooklyn had his motorcycle helmet with him?"

"Yeah, he did. He even mentioned how good it was to ride it again."

"Okay, thanks for all your help."

"You're welcome. Don't be a stranger."

I hang up and go back to my call with B's dad. "You probably heard part of that. He left a couple hours ago. Is his bike home?"

"His Jeep is in the garage but his bike is gone. Sounds like things didn't go well with his mother. Not that it's a big surprise. I tried to warn him. He's probably riding around, blowing off some steam."

My mind immediately flashes to Vincent's words. I'll take away *everything* you love.

"Remember the hostile takeover Brooklyn wanted to help me with?"

"Yeah?"

"It was announced yesterday. I fired Vincent from his own company. He threatened everyone I love and even had our dog kidnapped. I'm really worried about Brooklyn. Please call me the second he gets home."

"If you ruined everything we've worked so hard for, he'll never forgive you," his dad says coldly.

"Mr. Wright, his surfing career should be the least of your worries right now. You should be more concerned about his life."

"Are we being a little dramatic?" he asks.

My phone buzzes with a notification. I'm trying to control my temper, so I peek at it and see B's name.

"B just messaged me. He's okay."

"What did he say?"

I toggle over to my Skype notification.

Brooklyn: *Skype me now.*

That's weird.

"Um, he wants to video chat with me. Are you sure he's not up in his room?"

"Uh, I don't think so, but maybe I didn't hear him come home. I'll go check."

I run to the bedroom, sit at the desk, and power up my

laptop, thankful that Aiden thought to bring it from the loft.

I bring up the program, see B's smiling face next to the word *Online*, and click to call him.

I'm just so thankful he's okay. He probably snuck in because he didn't want to deal with his dad. He's probably going to tell me he's sorry for hanging up on me and how awkward it was with his mom.

As the screen shows him answering, I smile.

But then my heart stops beating when Vincent's face shows on the screen instead.

He gives me a chilling smile. One that makes my whole body shiver.

"We have the dog. We have Matt," he says. "As soon as we have you, we'll commence filming."

Matt? Lacey's boyfriend in the movie?

Did he cast Brooklyn as Matt?

No. He's probably just trying to freak me out. Probably stole his computer since I destroyed my phone and he needed another way to get in touch with me.

But how did he get Brooklyn's computer?

I imagine the scene at Buddy's.

B's distracted and talking to his mom.

Someone grabs his backpack.

Although, I don't know why he'd take it to dinner.

No, wait. I do. He'd want to show his mom videos of him surfing.

I look Vincent straight in the eye. "Who did you cast as Matt?"

A smirk plays on his face. The first show of emotion I've seen. "Your boyfriend, Brooklyn, of course."

"I don't believe you."

Vincent narrows his eyes at me. The emotional mask returning.

From the corner of my eye, I see Aiden and Cooper come into the bedroom.

I pretend to adjust my laptop screen, but instead I hold my hand out past it, gesturing at them not to come any closer.

My eyes are glued to the screen, Vincent and I locked in an online staring match.

Finally, he blinks and says, "You want to see who I cast? Is that it?"

"Yes, Vincent. I need to know who my co-star is before I'll sign on to the project."

"Very well."

There are blurs across the screen as Vincent moves the laptop away from his face.

I can't make out anything until the movement stops.

Then there is a single image.

Brooklyn. Lying on a mattress motionless.

I quickly take a screenshot.

"Believe me now?" I hear Vincent ask.

"I want to talk to him."

"As you can see, he can't talk right now. He's asleep."

"Asleep or dead?" It's hard to tell. I can't see him breathing.

There are more blurs then Vincent's face. "Come home," he says then ends the call.

Tears stream down my face as I stare at the blank computer screen.

I shake my head.

I expected Vincent to kidnap me at some point.

I was prepared for it.

I didn't expect this.

What am I going to do?

Cooper clears his throat.

I look up at everyone waiting expectantly in the doorway.

"He's got Brooklyn," I say, crying hysterically. "He's got Brooklyn."

WHAT FOLLOWS IS a night of complete chaos.

Fits of anger.

Calls with Garrett.

Pacing with worry.

Calls with my family.

Uncontrollable crying.

A call to B's dad.

As if I wasn't already feeling guilty enough, his dad flat-out blamed me.

Yelled at me.

I tried to explain, but it didn't matter.

And it doesn't.

He's right.

It's all my fault.

BY THREE IN the morning, Damian and Peyton have fallen asleep on the couch, Aiden is pacing across the living room floor, and I'm sitting in a chair across from Cooper trying to convince him that I should do exactly what Vincent wants me to do: go home.

My phone rings with a call from Garrett.

I quickly grab it off the coffee table and answer with, "Did you find him?"

"No, we haven't. I'm sorry," he says.

By this time, I'm done crying. I'm just straight pissed.

"How am I supposed to believe that you'll be able to keep anyone I care about safe?"

"I can only do so much, Keatyn. Brooklyn refused security the whole time he was in Malibu. And, believe me, we tried to talk some sense in him. We even did as you asked and watched the house and followed him wherever he went."

"Were they watching him today?"

"Sort of."

"What the hell does that mean?"

"Brooklyn called the cops on them a few hours before he left for dinner. My men were at the police station getting things sorted out."

"Why would he do that?"

"I don't know. Did the two of you fight?"

"Yes. He was really upset when I told him I wasn't coming there."

"You were planning to?"

"Yeah. He wanted me to go with him to meet his mom. When we found out about Kiki, I called him. Begged him to reschedule. Told him it wasn't safe. He wouldn't listen to me. Then I suggested that it could be a set up. That's when he hung up on me."

"We located his mother and interviewed her."

"So it wasn't a set up?"

"No."

"What did she say?"

"That they talked. That she was so excited to see him but that it was more awkward than she imagined. I think she had grand images of the little boy she left rushing into her arms."

"Do you know the real story?"

"Brooklyn's father said she's bipolar. That, back then, the disease wasn't as widely understood. They diagnosed her with depression but she wouldn't take her medicine. When she didn't, she was all over the place. Crying for days, then, the next, getting dressed up and maniacally shopping. She'd have fits of anger, too. In one of those fits, she pushed B down the stairs. He was fine, just a broken wrist, but that's when his dad knew he had to do something. He had her charged with child abuse, filed for divorce, and got the court to issue a restraining order."

"That's sad. But I can see why his dad just let him think she left. It was easier than trying to explain everything else. We have to find him, Garrett. As soon as I get off the phone, I'm heading to the airport. I'll see you soon."

"No, you won't."

"I won't see you?"

"Keatyn, would you like me to use every resource I have available to search for Brooklyn?"

"Yes."

"Then I need you to go back to Eastbrooke."

"I can't go back there."

"Yes, you can."

"But everyone knows who I am. I'm still the one Vincent wants. I can't put Eastbrooke in that kind of danger. I can't go back!"

"We successfully kept everything off social media. Vincent would've already gone there if he believed you were there. It's safe. That's why we sent you there in the first place. And I can't do my job if I'm worried about you. I need all our manpower focused on finding him."

"But you have the police. I sent you the screenshot."

"Keatyn, the screenshot doesn't really prove anything. You didn't get any photos of Vincent. Had you recorded the call it would be a different situation. We would have some proof. All we have is a photo of a young man lying on a mattress. It doesn't prove he was kidnapped. It doesn't tell us who kidnapped him. It helps that his dad believes you and reported him kidnapped, but since there is no proof of that either—"

"What kind of proof do they need?"

"They interviewed the staff at the restaurant. No one saw a struggle. No one saw anything or anyone remotely suspicious. The police see a young man who is upset with his father and didn't come home. Now, the fact that his motorcycle is still at the club helps us a little, but the police work at their own pace."

"I thought you had guys following Vincent. Where the hell is he?"

"We don't know."

"What the fuck, Garrett? How can you not know?"

"Our men report that Vincent has been in his home since you fired him."

"We know Brooklyn is with Vincent. So, if Vincent's home, someone got Brooklyn and took him to Vincent. They're probably in his house! Go get him!"

"We tried that. I called in a favor with the police. Got them to agree to question Vincent. They went to his home, but Vincent didn't answer."

"So they just left?"

"The police can't search a property without a warrant unless they have just cause. When they looked in the windows, they reported seeing a room trashed in a way that indicated a struggle. They suspected Vincent might be hurt, so they broke the door down and went in."

"What did they find?"

"Nothing."

"Did they search for clues?"

"They didn't. But after they left, one of my guys may have had a look around. He came up empty. There wasn't one shred of evidence that would suggest he was obsessed with you or your mom. No photos. No magazines. Nothing.

Which is a bit unusual in cases like these. Do you remember anything from your video chat? Did you see anything or notice any details that could give us a clue as to where he was. What about sounds? Could you hear a city? The ocean?"

"When he swung the laptop around I saw a blur of colors and images. Pictures, I think, on the walls."

"That would make sense. Wherever he's holding Brooklyn is his base. The place where he keeps his obsession hidden from the outside world."

"Like a secret apartment or something?"

"Yes, and we've got to find it. If we find it, we'll find Brooklyn. We're meeting with a judge in the morning to request a warrant to search all of his properties."

"Technically, I own some of those properties now, right? The business ones?"

"Yes, we've already scoured the county records and have compiled an extensive list of both personal and business real estate holdings."

"You have my okay to search anything owned by the company. He is obsessed with making the movie, so it would make sense that he might do it somewhere there's already a set."

"We'll start searching the company's properties now. On one condition."

"What's that?"

"You go to Eastbrooke while we do."

"And if I don't?"

"I quit and you can let the police handle it."

"You're not serious."

"Oh, yes. I am. And just so you know, if you decide to accept my resignation, even with your family connections, it would be at least twenty-four to forty-eight hours before you could get another firm on board. Do you want to lose that time?"

"No."

"Then here are my terms. You and Cooper are going back to Eastbrooke. You will give me seven days to find Brooklyn before you threaten to come to Malibu. And you promise that during those seven days you will not set foot off campus. No getting your nails done. No pizza dates. Nothing. I will be sending additional guards to the school's entrance. They will be under orders not to let you leave. Am I clear?"

"Seven days is a long time, Garrett! Why don't I just come home? I'll let Vincent find me. Take me to where Brooklyn is. You can rescue us both."

"Keatyn, I can assure you it would not be that easy. A simple case of kidnapping would quickly escalate into a hostage situation."

"Then get some special forces to come in the middle of the night. Kidnap Vincent. Save us."

"I'm wasting precious time right now, Keatyn. You know my terms. Seven days or I quit."

"What if you don't find him in seven days?" I ask, hating that the words even came out of my mouth.

"Then we'll do it your way." He sighs. "Look, Vincent has been planning this for months, maybe even years. I know seven days seems like a long time, but it really isn't in the scheme of things. You said Vincent told you that he has Matt, right?"

"Yes."

"So, in a warped way, Brooklyn has agreed to play the role and signed a contract. Vincent won't hurt him until he has you. That's the main reason I want seven days. If Vincent gets his hands on both of you, his plans will accelerate. And when they do, I can't guarantee that either one of you will survive. If you want to keep Brooklyn alive, you will give me seven days."

I nod, knowing that he's right. Vincent will keep Brooklyn alive until he's able to redo the movie his way.

And he can't do that until he has me.

I let out an audible sigh. "Fine. I agree."

"Thank you. I'll keep you posted every step of the way."

As I hang up, Cooper says, "What did you just agree to?"

"We're going back to Eastbrooke," I say.

Wednesday, January 4th

MY GUILT.
9:30AM

AIDEN WAKES UP when I get out of bed.

"You go back to sleep. I'm going to check in with Garrett."

"I'll get up too. I want to hear if there's any news."

I throw on a robe and go out into the living room, where Cooper is already up, dressed, and on the phone.

"No news," he says as Peyton and Damian wander out in matching robes.

"You know, Cooper. I promised to go back to Eastbrooke, but I never promised to go to class."

"Not go to class?" Aiden asks. "How's that going to work?"

"I'll sneak onto campus, but I won't check in. I'll call the school and say that I'm staying with my family and will be there later or something."

"Will you just sit in your room all day?"

"I'll just sneak in with Damian and stay with Cooper. I can't go to class. I don't even have my uniforms. They're all at my loft and I can't go back."

"You can wear mine," Peyton suggests sweetly. "My parents are meeting us at school with all our stuff."

"It's not just that. I don't want the other students to know I'm back. I can't deal with that right now. I can't deal with homework or teachers. I'll go crazy. Besides, it's silly. I'll be going back to Malibu in six days."

"I thought it was seven?" Cooper asks.

"Seven started yesterday."

"Technically, when you agreed to seven days, it was today."

"Fine. Whatever. It's silly to go to school for even a few days when I know I'm leaving."

"It will give you something to do," Aiden suggests, kissing my nose. "Keep you busy. And it won't be bad. The first two days of classes will be getting back into the swing of things. We won't have homework. There's a basketball game on Friday night and a dance. Saturday we'll hang out and watch football. It will help pass the time."

"Brooklyn is lying on the floor somewhere, helpless, Aiden," I snap. "I'm not going to a damn high school basketball game and pretending I give a shit about it."

Aiden gives me a glare, gets up, and walks out of the room.

Cooper watches him go and says to me, "I'd like you to be enrolled in school. If you want to pretend to be sick, you can."

"Thanks. Um, Cooper, can I talk to you in private?"

"Sure, let's go downstairs to the lobby."

"That's not exactly private."

"Why don't I take my brother and Damian down to the restaurant for breakfast?" Peyton offers.

I give her a hug and say, "Thank you."

"We're all trying our best to help you get through this,"

she says quietly. "Especially Aiden."

Her words just add to my guilt.

And my guilt is piling up higher than the Empire State building.

They clear out and Cooper sits on the edge of a chair. "Shoot."

"I can't do it. I can't wait seven days. We need to come up with a new plan to present to Garrett. Or I just need to go myself. I'm stronger than Vincent thinks I am. I'll attack him when he doesn't expect it, like you taught me to. It worked on the guy in the club. Or I could take a gun, a knife, and some pepper spray."

"Keatyn, he'd check you for weapons. And a wire. And trackers. He's not stupid."

"I think he would be so shocked I showed up that he'd forget."

Cooper just stares at me.

"Okay, he probably wouldn't."

"Wait! I know. What if I Skype him? Garrett said if I could record him confessing that the police could arrest him."

"They can't arrest him if they can't find him."

"I'm a mess, Cooper. And every single time I look at Aiden, I just feel guilty. Like I'm somehow cheating on Brooklyn."

"I don't know all the background on the two of you. So, before you got sent to Eastbrooke, you and Brooklyn were dating?"

"We spent the summer together in Europe. When we got back, he found out that his dad had gotten him a few sponsors and he was going out on tour. He was leaving me. He thought we should date other people."

"You were young. You were going to be apart for long

periods of time. That sounds like the mature thing to do. My high school girlfriend and I did that when we went to different colleges."

"How'd that work out for you?"

"She met someone else. Fell in love. A year later she was pregnant and getting married."

"Do you wish you would have stayed together?"

"I don't think it would have mattered, Keatyn. She fell in love with someone else. If our love was meant to be, she wouldn't have."

"I fell in love with Aiden. Does that mean I'm not meant to be with Brooklyn?"

"Was it the same situation? Were you and Brooklyn dating each other but also free to see other people?"

"We weren't dating each other. I thought we were over."

"What do you think now?"

"I feel like I'm holding a live grenade and if I make the wrong move, everything around me will explode."

"You need to try and be patient. At least for the next few days. Garrett said there are a lot of properties to check and that it's going to take them the majority of the next three days just to do it right. Last night, Garrett told you something that made you agree to wait. What was it?"

"That Vincent won't hurt Brooklyn until he has me. And that seven days in Vincent time isn't that long, considering he's been planning this for months."

"Do you still agree?"

"Yes."

"Then let's get you back to school."

FOUND A BODY.
8PM

THE REST OF the day is spent traveling, moving stuff into our dorms, saying hello to our friends.

Although, really, that's what everyone else is doing. I'm hiding out in Aiden's room.

I don't want to talk to anyone. Not even Damian.

I'm a wreck.

"Why don't I go get us some hot chocolate?" he says.

I lie on his bed and stare up at the twinkle lights while he's gone.

They take me back to that night on the beach. When I made a wish on the moon. When Brooklyn told me I was desirable.

I decide I can't wait any longer.

I call Garrett.

"You told me you'd keep me updated. I haven't heard from you," I say when he answers.

"Sorry, we've been all over. Trying to get search warrants. Searching the production company's properties."

"And?"

"We've been through about a third of the holdings. Have come up empty."

"And the warrants to search Vincent's properties?"

"I'm afraid they were denied."

"How?"

"To get a warrant, you need probable cause. Often, we can get that probable cause based on the word of another person. But the judge has to decide if the person's word is credible. You are a seventeen-year-old living out of state. We also had bad luck and got the same judge who refused both the plea to charge Vincent with attempted kidnapping and our request for a restraining order, back in August. He said that Vincent is an outstanding citizen and community leader who doesn't even have an unpaid parking ticket. Then, off the record, he told us that he didn't want to see us again or he'd charge us with harassment."

"Garrett, you have friends in high places. Can't you get a different judge? Don't you think it's a little odd we keep getting the same judge? Could Vincent have paid him off?"

"It's possible. But, regardless, what's done is done. We can't file for a new warrant unless we come up with something new. Evidence. A witness who saw Vincent and Brooklyn together. Besides searching properties, we're also trying to find the abduction site and combing the area for witnesses."

"So, should I try to Skype him? Get him to admit he kidnapped B? Record it this time?"

"Let's finish the search of the company's property first. If we don't turn up any new evidence or find Brooklyn, I'll consider it."

"How long will that take?"

"We'll discuss it Friday evening. How's that?"

"Okay."

"And, Keatyn, no news is good news," he says as I leap off the bed when Aiden kicks the door open with his foot—scaring the shit out of me—because his hands are full.

"What does that mean?" I ask, trying to calm myself down.

"It means no one has found a body."

I grab my stomach and start to cry. Then a wave of nausea hits me, and I run in the bathroom and throw up my dinner.

Aiden picks me up and carries me to his bed, cradling me in his arms as he sits down.

"What happened?" he asks, running his hand soothingly down my arm.

"Nothing," I say, not wanting to repeat what he said. It's easier to stick to the facts. "There's no word. They've searched about a third of the studio's properties, been scouring the area around Buddy's, and tried to get a search warrant. They've come up empty."

"Why did you throw up?"

I cover my face with my hand, lean against his chest, and start crying again.

He doesn't say anything.

Just holds me tightly.

I can't stop crying. It's like, now that I've finally let it all out, it won't stop.

"Shhh, baby," he says, smoothing down the back of my hair. "Tell me what happened."

I take a breath, shuddering, trying to stop crying.

"Garrett said no news is good news."

"What did he mean by that?"

"That's what I asked him. He said that it meant they . . . they . . . they . . . hadn't found a body yet."

Aiden takes a sharp breath. "That's an awful thing to say."

"I know. It was supposed to make me feel better, but the thought of a body showing up. I don't know why that never really crossed my mind. I just pictured him kidnapped, not dead. You know?"

Aiden pushes my chin up and kisses my forehead. "It's because you've been listening to your heart."

"What do you mean?"

"I'm not sure, but it's like, through all this, you've known, somehow. Were you and Vincent close? Like, before he tried to kidnap you?"

"Part of me wants to say yes. Part of me wants to say

no."

"Tell me about the part that wants to say yes."

"We sort of instantly connected. He looked into my eyes like he knew me. He was nice. He caught me one night when someone pushed me. He noticed things about me that other people didn't."

"Like what?"

"Stuff about me. My posture. My expressions. How I bite my lip when I'm trying to tell a lie. That I have a very expressive face. Granted, I wanted to be an actress, so I loved hearing those things, but it never felt like he was just blowing smoke up my ass or trying to impress me. He seemed sweet and sincere. I mean, he did flirt with me, but it was playful; the kind of things that could have dual meanings."

"Did that bother you?"

"No. I liked it. I liked him. I had little fantasies about what being with a man would be like. And when he took me to dinner to thank me . . ."

"Thank you for what?"

"Oh, one day I came home from school really mad. I was pissed and walking down the beach and ran into him. He was upset. Told me that his grandmother had passed away and he was supposed to spread her ashes on the beach. He was having a hard time doing it. He didn't really have anyone special in his life, I guess. And I was there. And I could relate because I had lost my dad. So I said some things that I hoped gave him comfort. He told me all about his grandmother, who was a famous actress, and her life. How she had met the love of her life on the beach. It was all very romantic—the kind of love I dreamed I would have with B. You know, we met each other on the beach, and it was love at first sight just like hers. He told me about his bad childhood at some point, too. About how his grandmother had taken him in and given him a better life. How he went to an exclusive prep school and how if you told yourself something enough, eventually, you'd believe it."

"Like what?"

"Like being good enough. Being strong. Stuff like that. Anyway, he told me his grandmother would love that he spread her ashes on the beach with me. Because I was special. That he was going to make this amazing movie with me and every man who saw it would fall in love with me. Anyway, I held his hand and said a few words, and then we sprinkled her ashes and tossed the urn into the ocean. He texted me the next day, invited me to dinner. We had fun. Flirted. But he never took it further. Kissed me on the cheek goodbye. Held it way too long, but it was sweet, not at all creepy. We just talked a lot whenever I saw him. I told him things I hadn't dared tell Brooklyn or my friends."

"That's why people tell bartenders their problems, right? Easier to tell a stranger than a friend."

"Yeah, probably. Anyway, we saw each other like that off and on. And every time we did, we had these sweet little moments. He was on my beach the morning of my birthday. I was happy, doing cartwheels. He laughed at me. Videotaped me. Teased me about recreating my mom's movie poster. I redid it for him my way. Turned around, tossed water at him, then blew him a kiss over my shoulder. I invited him to my birthday party. I was shocked when I figured out it was him who was trying to kidnap me. And, since then, I've questioned everything I've felt."

"Even with me," Aiden says.

"Yeah, mostly with you."

"So what does your heart tell you now about Brooklyn?"

"That he'll be okay for a while. But not for long. I think his having Brooklyn will be both motivation to get me and a reminder of the fact that he hasn't yet."

"That's a fine line."

"Yes."

"Do you think he has the seven days Garrett asked for?"

"Probably," I say slowly.

"But what?"

"But I'm probably not going to wait that long."

"You'll go anyway?"

"I think I'll have to."

Aiden nods. "You keep saying that you don't want me to help, but I'll help you find him."

"I'm surprised you'd say that. If I find him . . ."

"If you find him, Vincent will go to jail and you'll have your life back."

"Even if I don't end up with you when I get it back?"

He closes his eyes and takes a deep breath. When he opens his green eyes, they are sparkling with moisture. "I'm trying not to consider that possibility."

WHEN I GET back to my room, Katie gives me a hug and goes to sleep.

My friends have been treating me with kid gloves since I got back.

I'm sure they've all been filled in on what's going on.

And I appreciate it.

A text pops up from Garrett right before I fall asleep.

Garrett: *Remember the girl from the club? She was a message to you. I don't think he's going to hurt Brooklyn until he starts "filming his movie," which we both know he can't do without you. Not finding a body after almost twenty-four hours means we were right. I didn't mean to upset you. It's just a fact. And that fact makes me feel better. It should you too.*

Me: *Thanks.*

Thursday, January 5th
TALKING ABOUT SEX.
7:20AM

I DECIDE SITTING around feeling sorry for myself isn't going to help Brooklyn or Garrett, so I take everyone's advice, get up, and get ready for class.

"I'm glad you're going," Katie says. "How are you doing? Really?"

"Not that well. I'm hoping school helps me not go crazy."

"I heard Whitney didn't come back to school."

The dance was only a few weeks ago but I'd already almost forgotten about what Whitney was going to do to Peyton. So much has happened since then.

"That surprises me."

"Surprised me too," she says as we walk to class. "I heard Aiden sneak in last night. You guys finally doing it?"

"He came to France with me for Christmas. Got to meet my family."

"So you did it in France?"

"Did what in France?" Aiden asks, coming up from behind me and scaring us both.

"Taught you to speak proper French," I say with a smile.

"Katie's blushing. You two were talking about sex, weren't you?"

We both giggle.

"Maybe," Katie admits.

When we get outside my history class, Aiden takes my hand, kisses it, and says, "*Tu es l'amour de ma vie. Je veux être avec toi pour toujours.*"

"What did he say," Katie asks, after he walks away.

"He said, *You are the love of my life and I want to be with you forever.*"

"Oh, that's so dreamy," she replies.

DO GREAT THINGS.
HISTORY

AFTER OUR TEACHER goes over this semester's syllabus and hands back our midterms, he gives us an assignment and tells us to get started on it.

I've been thinking about Grandpa's advice. About listening to my heart.

And the more I think about it, the more sure I am.

If Brooklyn hasn't been found by Saturday, I'm going to Malibu.

I lean over and whisper to Riley, "Hey, where's that map of Stockton's exits? Have you ever noticed if one goes off property?"

"The map is in Stockton's. But, yes, there is one. I'm sure that's how they get everything in and out of there."

"Where does it go?"

"I've never been. Do you want to go see?"

"Yes. Cooper and I—or maybe just I—may need to leave here without anyone knowing."

"I thought you agreed to wait seven days."

"I may have lied. This is all my fault, Riley. I can't just sit here."

"If Cooper doesn't go with you, I will."

"I love you. You're the best friend."

"You just love me because you want me to help you run your new production company."

"I'm serious about that. We'd have a blast working together. And I trust you—maybe more than anyone."

"More than *anyone*?"

I sigh. "I trust Aiden, and he wants to help. But I just can't let him."

"So you'll sneak out of Stockton's?"

"Yes."

"I'm serious. I'm going. I'll do whatever you say. Even if it's just to ride on the plane with you."

"I'm afraid if I let you on the plane, you'd renege on your promise."

"I won't," he says solemnly.

"Riley, if something happens to me, the whole production company is going to you. Do great things with it, okay?"

His shakes his head at me, but agrees.

HELL HAS OFFICIALLY FROZEN OVER.
4:30PM

"I THINK IT'S this one," Riley says, taking me through an exit from Stockton's.

"We should really check this place out sometime when we're not drinking," I say with a laugh. "We'd probably find all sorts of interesting stuff."

We walk along the dimly-lit tunnel.

For a surprisingly short while.

When we get to the end of the tunnel, we find a ladder, climb up, and open a trap door in the floor of what appears to be a small cement block building.

"You stay down there," Riley instructs. "I'm going to close the door and see if I can get back in with the key."

"Come on out. That," he says, showing me a keypad, "must be how they do the deliveries. They can control access through keypad codes. I bet only members get keys."

"It's pretty crazy if you think about it. Someone spent a lot of time and energy on this place."

"I think it's sort of evolved over time to be what it is now. Some of the tunnels look older than the others. Speaking of that, have you ever read any of the names on the walls?"

"I looked at some that first night, but I didn't really pay attention."

"I started looking at them before break. There are some important names on those walls. History-making names. Leaders-of industry-and-state names. People you could maybe call, Keatyn. One is a California judge. I looked him up. He's a big deal. Well-connected. What if you went to him?"

"For what?"

"You said they couldn't get a search warrant. I'm just saying that sometimes it helps to know the right people."

"Garrett knows a lot of people. If he couldn't pull strings . . ."

"I'm just saying . . ."

"Yeah, you're right. Let me think about it. Let's go look outside."

We walk out of the little building and find ourselves just on the other side of the Eastbrooke fence.

I point to a plaque above the door. "This was a gift from the class of nineteen seventy-eight."

Riley smiles. "We have a year and a half to figure out our gift. We need to make it epic."

I look up at him, tears filling my eyes.

"Don't give me those eyes. You will be back here for our senior year. Promise me."

"I can't promise that."

"No. Don't say you can't or you won't. Say *I will be back for my senior year, Riley. I want to come back for my senior year.*"

"I want to come back for my senior year, Riley," I say.

And I mean it.

"Now, I think you should call that judge."

"I don't know his number."

"Lucky for you, I already looked it up." He takes my phone and enters a number.

"What am I going to say?"

Riley chuckles. "Tell him you took the oath of silence swore."

"This is crazy."

"Crazy is usually what works."

"You're right. Here goes nothing," I say as I hit send.

A receptionist answers and asks if she can help me.

"I'd like to speak to Judge Waters."

"I'm sorry, he's not available. May I take a message?"

"Um, can you just tell him my name is Keatyn and that I took the oath of silence swore. Would you write that part down, please? It's important."

"Uh, sure, Keatyn," she says, humoring me. "I'll tell him

that you took the oath of silence swore."

I hear a deep voice say, "Silence swore?"

And the assistant goes, "Yes, sir."

Then the deep voice goes, "Transfer the call to my office. I'll take it in there."

The assistant comes back on the line and says, "Judge Waters just arrived and will speak to you now."

I'm put on hold, classical music playing in the background for a few moments until the deep voice says, "This is Judge Waters. Tell me the rest of it."

"The rest of the oath?"

"Yes."

"All who pass through Stockton's door, take an oath of silence swore. In this place of legend and lore, party on, friends, evermore."

"How can I help you, Keatyn?"

"I need a search warrant."

"Are you an attorney?"

"No, sir. I'll try to keep this brief. I'm a current Eastbrooke student. My mom is Abby Johnston, and I was sent to Eastbrooke this fall because a man tried to kidnap me. That man was questioned by the police on August twentieth and released for lack of evidence. Later, I remembered that during the kidnapping, he said he was taking me to a van out back. They found the van—a rental with millions of fingerprints—with duct tape and drugs in it, but nothing leading back to the man. The man is rich and good-looking."

"Who is it?"

"His name is Vincent Sharpe. He's been obsessed with my mom for years and owns a production company."

"Is he the guy doing the nationwide search for the next Abby Johnston?"

"Yes. He was trying to find me."

"I see. What's the search warrant for?"

"He kidnapped my boyfriend, Brooklyn Wright—well, ex-boyfriend, but Vincent doesn't know that. I pissed him off."

"How?"

"On Monday, at his board meeting, I announced that I was the new majority owner of his company and fired him. He threatened me. Told me that no one I loved was safe. Our family dog was taken yesterday morning and Brooklyn has been missing since around eight last night. Vincent video chatted with me on Brooklyn's computer. I made him prove that he'd taken Brooklyn, so he turned the laptop around and showed me Brooklyn, tied up and lying motionless on a mattress. I have a screenshot of that, but nothing else. No proof that I spoke to him. We need to search his properties, but the judge turned us down for the warrant because we don't have any proof and, according to him, I'm not credible."

"Was the board meeting recorded?"

"Yes."

"I'd say you go at the warrant from that angle. Submit a copy of the recording of the board minutes along with written statements from at least two of the board members stating they heard him threaten you. State that Brooklyn has been missing and is presumed to have been kidnapped. Include the screenshot. Then, have the warrant request sent to me. Do you have a pen? I'll give you an email address. We'll be waiting for it."

"Yes, sir," I say, taking down the number. "Thank you, sir."

"You're welcome. Anything else I can do for you?"

"Um, actually, there is. If they don't find Brooklyn soon, I'm going against the wishes of my security counselor."

"Who's that?"

"Smith Security."

"Garrett Smith is the best in the business."

"I know. But he wants me to hide, and I'm afraid one of my little sisters will be next. Vincent told me to come home. If they haven't found him by Saturday, I'm going home. If things don't go well—like, if I don't survive and he does . . . Please contact my family and help them put Vincent away for a very long time."

"You have my word." He gives me his private cell number. "If you come back to California, call me before you do anything."

"Okay."

I give Riley a high five. "You are brilliant!"

He grins. "That was too easy. I'm totally looking up everyone on the walls now. You never know when something like that could come in handy."

"Obviously."

I call Cooper.

"Where are you?" he asks. "Aiden was looking for you."

"I'm at the, uh, chapel with Riley."

"I'm on my way," he says.

"Wait a couple minutes. I need to call Garrett. I know how he can get the search warrant."

I CALL GARRETT and give him all the info from the judge.

Then Riley and I rush back through the tunnel, into Stockton's, and upstairs.

Aiden and Cooper are waiting for us in the back of the chapel.

Cooper hands me a printout of a story about Vincent. Apparently, he's spoken to the press about the takeover. The article goes on to mention that he's seriously concerned about the company he founded in the hands of a seventeen-year-old. About how it's a disgrace to the industry.

I shake my head. "We need something that will bury this story. I don't want it to get legs."

"What kind of story would do that?"

Aiden smiles at me and points to my finger. I look at the four-leaf clover on it. "Ohmigawd, Aiden. You are brilliant!"

I call Mom, get her permission, and have her email me what I need.

A SHORT TIME later, the news is out.

```
     HOLY SHIT!! STOP THE PRESSES!!!!!
              THIS JUST IN!
     HELL HAS OFFICIALLY FROZEN OVER.
```
Keatyn Douglas, our new obsession, just emailed us.

One.

Single.

Beautiful.

Precious.

Photo.

(Okay, so her publicist probably sent it to every media outlet at the same time, but whatever.)

And what a photo it is.

Keatyn, dressed in an adorable strapless pink Sherri Hill high-low dress and cowboy boots, standing up for her mother, Abby Johnston, wearing Versace at her wedding to one of the sexiest men alive, Tommy Stevens.

We'll give the ladies of the world a moment to mourn their loss.

Okay, we're back.

```
Here is the official press release:
```
Abby Johnston and Tommy Stevens were married over

the holiday in a small, surprise ceremony attended by the couple's family and closest friends.

And the real story:

Long-time friend and multi-mega-hit director, Matthew Moran, loaded up a plane full of guests and took them to his mansion in the Italian countryside. Tommy proposed on Christmas Eve with a stunning sparkler hidden amongst his gifts to Abby, and the couple was married the following day in a lavish outdoor wedding. Guests later noshed on a Christmas Day feast where they toasted the happy couple.

P.S. Guess that sort of kills off the rumors of their imminent split.

P.P.S. Rumor has it Keatyn danced the night away with none other than Damian Moran, who has been writing love songs about her for years.

HOPING.
NIGHT

I'M LYING IN bed, trying to go to sleep. But I can't.

So, I do what I've been considering doing all day. I grab my computer and take it into the stairwell.

I hit the video conference icon and call Brooklyn, hoping that Vincent will answer.

I need to know that Brooklyn's still okay.

And to let Vincent know that I'm coming home.

HE DOESN'T ANSWER.

Friday, January 6th
THEY'LL FIND HIM.
1PM

FRIDAY IS THE longest day of my life.

I go through the motions, slogging from one class to the next.

I skip lunch, going to Cooper's office, instead.

"You look as tired as I feel," I tell him, noting his bleary eyes and the scruff he always shaves.

"So do you. I just got off the phone with Garrett. Still nothing."

"He's been planning this for a while. Are they checking basements and closets? For secret rooms, trap doors? On my birthday, he had to have somewhere he was taking me. He planned everything else out. Think about it. He wants to make a movie. There has to be a set somewhere."

"Garrett has brought in some of his top men to help with the search, Keatyn. These guys are all ex-special forces. They know how to find people who don't want to be found, if you know what I mean. And they're utilizing technology to scan the buildings for heat sources and using search and rescue dogs."

"Heat sources? Is that like in the movies? Where they can find people who are hiding by tracking their body temperature?"

"Exactly."

"And what do the dogs do?"

Cooper just looks at me.

And it hits me.

The dogs find people who don't have any body heat.

ISN'T NORMAL.
2AM

I WAKE UP because I hear a noise.

The kind of noise I know isn't normal.

I reach out for Aiden and remember he wasn't coming over tonight. Something about hearing there was going to be some sort of late-night dorm check.

Just as I open my eyes, a hood is thrown over my head and I'm being pulled out of bed and down the hall.

It takes me a few moments to get my wits about me.

This is it.

Vincent has found me.

I think about fighting him here in the dorm, but decide against it. The noise would wake people up and then they would all be in danger.

As soon as we get outside, I attack.

I use my elbow to give him a shot to the ribs, then pull his arm down hard, knocking him off balance. When I feel him start to fall, I push my shoulder into him, knocking him down the stairs.

I quickly pull off the hood.

"What the fuck are you doing, Monroe?" Jake yells at me.

My insides stop shaking.

"Jake!? What the *hell* are you doing?!"

"I'm trying to kidnap you."

"Why?" I say, suddenly looking around in every direction. Did Jake out me to Vincent?

"Because I'm taking you somewhere special. I'm sorry, I've just been excited to do this since I got kidnapped last year."

"Jake, what the fuck are you talking about? When did you get kidnapped?"

He sits up and rubs his back. "I just told you I got kidnapped last year. It's an honor."

"Getting kidnapped is an honor? Are you serious? You know why I'm here, right?"

"Oh my god. I didn't even think of that. I'm sorry. I'm not supposed to tell you. But maybe, under the circumstances, I'd better."

"Ya think?"

"You are about to be kidnapped, teased, and then inducted into Eastbrooke fame."

"Fame?"

"Yes. You, Monroe, are about to become a prefect."

"But, I . . ."

"No buts."

"I don't know if I'll even be here next year."

"Whatever. If you don't come back, we'll deal with that later. Enjoy tonight. It's kinda corny, but it's kind of special too. And I'm not telling you anything else. I don't want to ruin the surprise. Now, will you let me put the hood back on you without kicking the shit out of me?"

"Sure."

He puts the hood back over my head and leads me down the sidewalk.

"I have to spin you around," he whispers. "So you don't know where we're going. The prefect room's location is supposed to be a secret."

"But you know where it is. If I'm a prefect, I'll know where it is. Why the secrecy?"

"Fuck if I know. But if you don't play nice with the all the old prefects who are here for the ceremony, they might change their minds."

"Okay, fine. Spin me."

Jake spins me around a few times and then leads me up the hill on the concrete, which makes it quite obvious what direction we are heading.

And, now that I have my wits about me and my heartbeat has slowed down to a reasonable rate, I kind of want to jump up and down and scream.

Because, me . . . a prefect?

I'm led into a building that I'm pretty sure is the student center and then down a set of stairs. We go into a room and then down another set of stairs.

Jake leads me a bit further then grabs my shoulders, turns me around, and positions me in a line. I can feel someone's shoulder next to me. Based on his cologne, I'd guess it's Dallas.

"Brothers and Sisters of Eastbrooke," a deep voice announces, "we welcome Keatyn Monroe into the fold."

My hood is pulled off, revealing a huge stone room, lit only by the candles being held by what I assume are years' worth of prefects, all dressed in red robes.

It's like a scene out of a movie where college students are taken to a dark basement and inducted into a secret society.

They take the hoods off the students one by one and

announce them.

"Brothers and sisters of Eastbrooke, we welcome Dallas McMahon into the fold. Brothers and sisters of Eastbrooke, we welcome Logan Pedersen into the fold. Brothers and sisters of Eastbrooke, we welcome Ariela Ross into the fold. Brothers and sisters of Eastbrooke, we welcome Riley Johnson into the fold. Brothers and sisters of Eastbrooke, we welcome Maggie Morgan into the fold. And, lastly, brothers and sisters of Eastbrooke, we welcome Aiden Arrington into the fold. Seven prefects. A divine number for a divine responsibility."

He moves to address us directly. "Prefects, you have been chosen because of your leadership and sense of community. You are the new faces of Eastbrooke. The hearts and souls of this magnificent place. Those who will guide our students, be their collective conscience, and uphold all the traditions that define Eastbrooke. The video with the seven of you has given our school faces for students to identify with for years to come. That, combined with your philanthropy, leadership, and social efforts are why you were chosen to best represent our school for the coming year."

Each of the current prefects move to stand in front of the student they brought, with Jake stopping in front of me.

The main prefect announces, "Current prefects, please remove your robes and present them."

Jake unzips the black robe he's wearing and helps me put it on. Then he receives a red robe of his own.

"This is the changing of the guard. For the next semester, you will work alongside your prefect guides to help prepare you for the coming year."

As a circle of red robes forms around us, I'm handed a candle and instructed to get in a circle with the other new prefects.

Everyone sings Eastbrooke's school anthem.

Tears fill my eyes as they sing about tradition, honor, and glory; friendship, bonds, and love. All things that resonate clearly in my heart in a way they never have before.

Standing here, in a circle with my best friends, has solidified what Eastbrooke means to me. It's love, friendship, and bonds that I pray will never break. It's the parties, the late nights, the sneaking out, the homework, the sports, the planning, the clubs. All of those things have introduced me to a world I love. A world that, no matter what happens to me next, will always be in my heart.

I'm beaming with pride when the song finishes, then our candles are taken away and Eastbrooke prefect pins are placed on our lapels. "We proudly present you with this badge," a prefect says. "A symbol of all that is Eastbrooke."

Another prefect speaks to us. "The word prefect is from the Latin *praeficere*, meaning 'make in front.' The prefect tradition began here in nineteen forty-eight with two male prefects. In nineteen sixty-seven, we opened our doors to a co-ed population and were ahead of our time when we honored our first female prefect in nineteen sixty-nine. For the last sixty-six years, students have been chosen in twos, fours, sixes, and this year, sevens, for their prowess in scholarship, leadership, and philanthropy. Tonight you join a society with only two hundred sixteen members. Now, we'd like for you to meet some of those who have gathered to welcome you tonight."

The former prefects create a receiving line. The first hand I shake is that of Regina Bosworth, prefect, 1972. Then Alfred Norman, prefect 1952, and the oldest prefect here.

We shake hands with nearly one hundred former prefects. Many whose names I recognize from Stockton's walls, including two of its founders.

Then we're escorted back to our dorm rooms, where I find a prefect's polo and sweater laid on the end of my bed.

I'M WIDE AWAKE after the ceremony, so I lean against my headboard and start going through all the millions of emails I've gotten announcing January sales at all my favorite retail stores.

I delete them and go through my spam folder.

I'm bulk deleting crap emails when one catches my eye. I quickly click it.

RE: Warren Taylor Agency script request.

Keatyn—

Sorry it took so long, but here's the script you requested for A Day at the Beach, *the working title for the remake of* A Day at the Lake. *Please see attachment.*

Cheers.

I'm just opening the script when a notification pops up telling me I have an incoming call from Brooklyn.

I immediately answer it, praying it's actually him.

That's he's overtaken Vincent and is free.

Or that Garrett found him.

I say a quick prayer then open my eyes.

To find Vincent staring back at me.

"You called yesterday?" he asks.

"Uh, yeah," I reply. My eyes are fixed to the screen, trying to scan the background for any possible clue or indication to where he may be keeping Brooklyn.

At the same time, I'm patting the bed, searching for my phone. I have to record this.

Put your hands where I can see them," Vincent orders.

I hold my hands up. "Why?"

"Because I need to know you're not recording this."

"Why, are you going to say something incriminating?"

"No, I was seeing what you wanted. You called me last night."

"I'm coming back to Malibu. I'm ready to make the movie."

He smiles a genuine smile, looking like the Vincent who I thought was my friend. "Really? When?"

"I'm flying in from New York on Sunday," I lie. "Where should I meet you?"

"I think you know."

"On the beach?"

He nods.

"I want to talk to Brooklyn."

"I'm afraid he's unavailable at the moment."

"Is he alive, Vince?"

"Yes, Lacey, he's alive. We're just waiting for you to join us."

I nod, end the call, and immediately open the script and read the ending.

EVEN THOUGH IT'S late, I call Garrett.

"I just got the new script!" I tell him.

"Keatyn, what time is it there?"

"I don't know. Late. Were you sleeping? Did I wake you?"

"I was taking a quick nap. It's okay. What did you learn?"

"Well, first off, Vincent changed the name of the movie to *A Day at the Beach*. He added a bunch of special effects things that I sort of skimmed over but—have you ever seen the original?"

"It's been quite a few years but, yes."

"So, in the original, Vince was the killer. He had a major crush on Lacey—Mom's character—and it was his house on the lake. At the end, you figure out he's the bad guy because he tries to kill Matt, who is Lacey's boyfriend. You think Matt is dead and Vince is being all creepy and trying to get Lacey. You find out that he wants Matt gone because he wants Lacey to go on a semester abroad with him. But Matt staggers back up, kills Vince, saves the day, and rides off with the girl."

"How is the new script different?"

"Well, first of all, it's set on a beach, not a lake. Vince now has a dog, which is a classic writer's trick for making a bad character more lovable. The big twist, though, is that Vince kidnaps Matt, kills everyone, frames Matt for the murders, has him arrested in front of Lacey, and when the police take him away, Vince professes his love to Lacey and they kiss. The end. The bad guy gets the girl. Bring on the sequel."

"And you think his script translates to real life?"

"Yes, I think Vincent thinks the movie is real life. He told me he had the dog and he had Matt."

"So you think he's going to kill people and set Brooklyn up to take the fall?"

"Yes."

"And then he's going to ride off into the sunset with you?"

"Something like that, yes."

"Do you still think he'll kill you?"

"If he does, I think he'll kill himself too. Just know that no matter what the evidence looks like, Brooklyn didn't do it."

"Got it. Now get some sleep."

Saturday, January 7th

JUST ME.
NOON

I'M IN MY room, packing a few things in my backpack. I stop to run my hand across the prefect badge on the shirt that's still lying on my bed, trying not to cry. I wish I was coming back to use it.

I shake my head and focus on the task at hand.

Then I go meet Dallas. He's walking with me to the chapel, where we'll sneak down to Stockton's.

Riley and Aiden went into town to get pizza, so I have a small window of opportunity to stash my backpack down there without anyone knowing I'm planning to leave tonight.

"You're not thinking of running away, are you?" Dallas asks.

I hate to lie to him, but I do. I hold up my backpack and say, "I'm taking this down there, just in case."

"Just in case what?"

"Garrett reneges on his promise. We agreed to seven days. But I can see him trying to keep me here longer than that."

"And if he does?"

"Then I'll sneak out of Stockton's, go home, and try to find Brooklyn myself."

"Ugh," Dallas says.

I turn around and see him crumpled on the ground. "Dallas! Are you—"

"Keatyn!" I hear Cooper yell.

As I turn toward his voice, a booming sound assaults my ears. I watch in horror as Cooper takes two bullets to the chest and falls to the ground.

And I know.

Vincent is here.

A strong arm wraps tightly around my neck, choking me. "Eastbrooke Homecoming Court, huh?" Vincent says. "Congratulations."

Oh my god. I forgot all about the homecoming court sash that's been hanging off my bedpost since October. He must have seen it during our video call last night. I was so focused on trying to find a clue on his screen that I never even looked at mine.

I'm an idiot. I led him straight to the one place I wanted so badly to protect.

"This looks like a fancy place," Vincent continues, "but their security is pretty lax. I drove right through. I mean, after I shot the three guards."

Ohmigawd.

He's going to shoot anyone who gets in his way.

I have to get him out of here—and fast.

"Where's Brooklyn?" I ask him.

"He's fine. A little tied up at the moment," he says again with a maniacal laugh, pressing a gun into the small of my back and pushing me toward a white delivery van.

"You don't have to push me, Vincent. I want to come

with you."

"Don't move," he says, keeping the gun trained on me while he lifts Dallas up and puts him in the back of the van.

I've got to convince him not to take Dallas, I think, as I'm hit on the back of the head and everything goes black.

RILEY
12:35PM

AIDEN AND I picked up a bunch of pizzas and are turning into the Eastbrooke driveway when a white delivery van barrels around the corner, almost hitting us.

"What the hell?" Aiden yells.

"Wonder what delivery he needs to make in such a big hurry?" My phone rings with a call from Dawson. I answer it as Aiden flips a U-turn. "What's up, bro?"

"Keatyn and Dallas were just kidnapped! Thrown in the back of a white van! The guy shot Cooper when he tried to stop it!"

"A white van almost hit us . . . Wait!" I see that, somehow, Aiden already knew. He's racing down the road. But I still say, "That delivery van. Keatyn and Dallas are in there. Kidnapped. Cooper shot!"

I know what I say doesn't make a lot of sense, but I'm all hyped up. Panicked. "Follow them! We can't lose them!"

"Tell me what happened!" Aiden yells as he's gunning the engine and slamming through the gears.

I plug my phone into Aiden's car, so we can both hear Dawson.

"Dawson, you're on speaker. Tell us what happened."

"All I know is I heard gunfire, ran toward it, saw Cooper

hit the ground. Dallas was already down. The guy was talking to Keatyn. He held a gun on her as he put Dallas in the van and then hit her on the back of the head with the gun, threw her in the back, and took off. Brooke called nine-one-one and the school is on lockdown."

"He got a head start on us, but we'll catch him if we go the right way," I say to Aiden.

"We have to go the right way," Aiden replies. "Think. Where would he take them?"

"Keatyn was going back to Malibu tonight to find Brooklyn."

"What do you mean? They wouldn't let her leave."

"She found a secret way out of school through Stockton's."

"Was she going to tell me?" He stops staring at the road and turns to me, fire in his eyes. "Were *you* going to tell me? Were you going to *let* her go?"

I hang my head a little. "I was going with her."

Aiden shakes his head. "She said he wanted to film a movie with her. The script she got was set in California. She didn't think he'd hurt Brooklyn until after they filmed the movie. So, if she was right, he'd take her back to California. So the airport?"

"I think so, but the highway's right there!" I point to the turn off, which we are closing in on way too fast. "Slow down!"

Aiden handles his car perfectly, tapping the brakes, and then veering us onto the highway.

He barely even slowed down.

Fuck if I'm not impressed with his driving skills.

"We have a problem," Aiden says. "I'm almost out of gas."

"Then we have an even bigger problem," I tell him.

"Keatyn may not have on her tracking necklace. She didn't want anyone to know when she'd left. God, why did I go along with her plans?"

"Because you're a good friend," Aiden says. "But we can't worry about that now. We've got to find that van or they'll both be dead. They've been searching for Brooklyn for three days with no luck."

"We can't call Cooper. He got shot. I don't have Garrett's number. Do you?"

I watch as Aiden takes one hand off the wheel and runs his finger over the clover keychain Keatyn gave him. When I look back at the road, I see it in the distance, up ahead.

"The van!" we both yell at the same time.

"Get close to it so we can get the license plate. I'm calling Senator McMahon."

"You know he didn't come for Dallas."

"It doesn't matter who he wanted. Kidnapping Dallas was the wrong move."

The senator answers his private line after a few rings.

"Riley," he barks. "This is the number you are supposed to call only in an emergency."

"It is an emergency, sir. Dallas and Keatyn have been kidnapped from Eastbrooke and are in the back of a white van. A teacher was shot."

"I need to make a call on the other line. Hold on."

"Grab my phone," Aiden says. "Take a picture of the back of the van and the license plate."

"Are you sure it's the same van?"

"Yep. It says Charlie's Produce on it. But, look, there's no plate."

"Riley," Mr. McMahon's voice booms through Aiden's speakers. "I have the Service on the line. Did the van leave school? Do you know what direction it was headed? License plate? Description of the assailant?"

"We're following the van right now. Keatyn usually wears a tracking device, but we don't know if she has it on. We need to reach Garrett Smith, but don't have his phone number. We believe the kidnapper is Vincent Sharpe, Keatyn's stalker; the guy from the club in Miami. But we're not sure."

"Doesn't matter who or why, son. We need to get them. Where are you?"

I give him the mile marker of the highway we're traveling on. "If it is Vincent, we think he will be headed to an airport, but we don't know which one."

"Help is on the way, boys. Don't lose the van. What are you driving?"

"White Maserati," I say. "California plates: Golf, Oscar, Alpha, Lima, India, Echo, One."

"We can't keep up this speed," Aiden says frantically. "I'm burning through fuel. We're going to have to do something else."

"Like what?"

"Hit them," he says.

"Hit them? This car against a full-sized van? It will crumple."

"I sat in on a stunt planning meeting while Keatyn was filming. They talked about what would happen in real life as opposed to what would happen in the movie. I'm going to do the stunt. I'll speed past him. Double back. T-bone the driver's door."

"You'll kill us. Them too, probably."

"Not if I do it right. And we don't have another option. The cops aren't here. The feds aren't here. It's just him and us. Besides, we have airbags, right?"

"I'm more worried about my head."

"Helmets!" he yells. "Keatyn bought them for my birthday. They're behind the seat."

I strap on a helmet, then hold the wheel while Aiden does the same.

"You look ridiculous," I tell him. "I totally have to record this."

I grab my video camera out of my pocket and mount it to the dash. "One DashCam coming up."

After getting it in place and hitting record, I'm feeling claustrophobic. "This must be her helmet. It's too tight."

"It will protect your head. That's all that matters. Okay, so I'm going to speed way up. Pass them. Come back. We'll time it so we hit the driver's door."

"Where the hell is the Secret Service? In Miami, they were there in minutes."

"It's just us, Riley," Aiden says solemnly. "And I'm on fumes. Just before we hit, I want you to pull the emergency brake. It'll spin us around and we'll hit him with the back of the car. It will protect us."

"Do you think you can do that? Drive right into the side of it?"

"I don't have a choice. Here we go."

Aiden pushes the pedal down, slamming through the gears.

We pass the van.

Trees and power poles fly by us.

"How far do we have to go before we turn back?"

Aiden's screeching brakes are the answer to my question. He flips the car around and drops the clutch.

Then it's rev the motor, shift, rev, shift, rev, shift.

"One-forty!" Aiden yells.

"One-sixty!" I yell back. "What's her top speed?"

"Stock is one eighty-five, but I have a chip. I've never

tested it, but they say it'll go two hundred. Just pray we don't blow a tire."

"Oh, great. Like we need something else to worry about. This is like one of those math problems. A car is traveling toward you at seventy miles per hour. You're going the opposite direction at a hundred ninety miles per hour. If you want to hit the van, when should you cross the median?"

"You know the answer?"

"No. I suck at math. The van is getting closer. Now!" I scream.

Aiden cranks the wheel.

"Ahhh!!!" I scream again as we bear down on the van.

Just when I recognize the driver as the guy from the club in Miami, Aiden yells, "Pull it, Riley! Pull it!"

I wait a heartbeat longer and then pull the emergency brake.

Tires scream.

Metal crunches.

The car does a flat spin and we hit again.

GET AWAY.
12:40PM

I'M DISORIENTED AND feel like I'm being tossed from one metal hand to another.

I rub a bump on my head as I crash into something softer.

Dallas.

I quickly remember the events. Dallas falling to the ground. Cooper yelling my name. Vincent firing shots to his chest. Him going down. Vincent's voice behind me. Dallas being thrown into the van.

Which, I'm pretty sure, is rolling.

I hit my shoulder hard and hold on tight to Dallas, trying to cover his head with my arms. I feel his breath on my face, but he doesn't respond when I say, "Dallas, wake up."

After what seems like an eternity, the van teeters to a stop.

I hear Vincent moan.

Somehow, I've got to get Dallas away from him. So he doesn't shoot him like he did Cooper.

Poor Cooper.

I relive the moment. The noise. Cooper's body thrown back when the bullets hit him.

I want to cover my head and bawl. I can't believe he's dead because of me.

He was more than a bodyguard.

He was my friend.

I shake my head to clear it and everything he taught me rushes into my brain.

I need an advantage. A weapon.

Anything.

The van is completely empty in the back. Just me and Dallas surrounded by white metal and gray carpet.

Vincent has switched from moaning to cursing.

And I can tell he's pissed even though I can't understand what he's saying.

He must've been driving too fast and crashed.

I hear a slicing sound and the pop of what I assume is the airbag.

Meaning he's got a knife.

Wrists. Face. Crotch.

Disable him.

Get the gun.

Grab Dallas.

Get away.

But then how will I find B?

My head is throbbing. My shoulder is sore.

Think, Keatyn.

New plan.

Get the gun. Use it to make Vincent tell me where B is.

My eyes are darting across the van, looking for something to use as a weapon, when I spy my backpack. Dallas and I were headed to Stockton's so I could drop it off. So it would be ready when I left tonight.

And there's something heavy in it, I remember.

The rock Avery gave me!

I slowly inch toward it, hoping Vincent can't hear me moving.

Cooper always said to use the element of surprise whenever possible. He said the fact that I'm a girl adds an element of surprise in and of itself. That a man wouldn't expect me to be a threat.

Maybe if I pretend to still be knocked out.

I look toward the windshield. It's smashed and, based on the fact that the trees are pointing the wrong direction, I determine that the van is lying on its side.

Vincent yells loudly, crawling toward me. "Keatyn! Are you okay?"

I keep my eyes shut as he touches my temple and cries out, "You're bleeding!"

I'm bleeding?

I will myself not to open my eyes.

"Abby," he says, and he does something I totally don't expect. He pulls me into his lap and caresses my face. But then he slaps me, causing my eyes to involuntarily open.

I assess his condition.

His pupils are huge. His face is banged up. A gash above his eye is bleeding. And, most importantly, there's neither a knife nor a gun in his hands.

I punch him right in the face.

He backs up, surprised, but quickly recovers.

He pounces on top of me, grabbing my wrist and ripping off my wish bracelet in the process.

I look at the little seashells—my hopes and dreams of getting my life back—scattered across the floor.

A moment of panic takes hold as the reality of what Vincent has already accomplished sets in.

He has Brooklyn and no one can find him.

I reach for my locket, grasping it and praying the cavalry is on the way.

But with the gunshots, the school would have immediately gone on lockdown.

How long would it take for them to realize we're missing?

"What's that?" Vincent says, taking the necklace out of my hand, ripping it off me, and tossing it aside. "That's not from wardrobe. You can't wear it."

"But . . ."

He gives me a smug grin as he grabs my free hand, then pins my arms above my head.

"It's just you and me now, Lacey," he says, reciting a line from *A Day at the Lake*. "You want this as badly as I do, don't you?"

He's lost it. He doesn't even know who I am.

I definitely pushed him completely over the edge.

I close my eyes, relaxing like Cooper taught me to do in a situation like this.

But then I decide to take a different approach first.

Because if it's a scene from the movie he wants then that's what he's gonna get.

"I changed my mind, Vincey," I say the lines I read last night in his new script.

"No! Don't give me that bullshit," he says, reciting the next line. "Matt changed your mind! You came crying to me about it! I told you to figure it out."

Even though he's acting pissed, his hold on me has completely relaxed.

It's time.

I knee him in the crotch with as much force as I can muster then grab my backpack and swing it into the side of his head.

The force of the blow knocks him off me.

I move quickly, knowing I need to get Dallas out of here. I don't want him to become Matt or dead partier number whatever in this crazy charade.

I kick the van's back door open.

Vincent sits up.

Just like in the original movie.

He's beaten, bruised, broken, and he still keeps getting up.

But that's good, because I have to get him to tell me where the hell he's keeping B.

Vincent grabs my hair, pulling me back into the van and causing the doors to swing shut.

"No! Don't give me that bullshit," he says, repeating the line. "Matt changed your mind! You came crying to me about it! I told you to figure it out."

I manage to flip my body around, kicking Vincent's arm in the process.

"Ow! Fuck!" he yells. "Abby, stop it. Stop screwing around! You aren't being very professional."

"This isn't part of the movie, Vincent," I say softly. "Tell me where Brooklyn is."

Vincent's face softens and he smiles at me. When he leans in to touch my face, I smash him in the head with the rock I managed to pull out of my bag.

He crumples to the ground.

I don't waste any time. I grab Dallas under his arms, pull him out of the van, across the grass, and to what I hope is a safe distance away.

"Lacey!" Vincent wails from inside the van. His voice sounds horrific. Like a wounded animal's.

I leave Dallas in the grass and run back to the van.

Throwing the door open, I find Vincent waving a gun at me.

"You didn't fucking listen to me. You listened to him."

"Tell me where he is!" I yell back.

"You'll find out our location when we get there. Filming will commence immediately."

"You're hurt. The van is wrecked. How are we going to get there?"

He moves toward the door. "We'll find alternate transportation. And if you don't do what I say, I'll kill him."

I realize I have no option. I knew it would come to this.

And I knew, when the time came, that I'd go willingly.

"I'll come to Egypt with you, Vincey. You're right. I want you. All to myself."

Vincent squints, knowing I recited the script but that they were his lines. It seems to perplex him for a moment.

He gets out of the van, waving the gun at me. "Get back in the van. We're leaving."

I have no idea how in the world he thinks we could leave. Is he going to flip the van upright with his brute strength?

That only happens in the movies.

That's it!

I look him straight in the eye and imitate my mother when she's mad. "Vincent Sharpe! How am I supposed to look good on set if you won't tell me where to send my hair and makeup people?"

Screech!

I turn around as three black SUVs stop and a swarm of agents jump out, their guns pointing at us.

"Drop the gun and put your hands up," one of them shouts.

Vincent turns and shoots, causing the agents to duck behind their cars and return fire.

"Stop!" I scream, rushing in front of Vincent so they won't kill him. I feel a burning sensation on my side and my arm before the shooting stops.

I scream again as Vincent drops to the ground behind me, bleeding profusely.

Dark blood is pumping out of his chest with each shallow breath.

A guy in a black suit tries to pick me up, but I react by throwing my arm backward and connecting with his face.

I look down at Vincent.

And know he's dying.

"I love you, Lacey," he whispers.

I fall on my knees in front of him, crying.

Trying to be gentle, I pick his head off the concrete and cradle it in my lap.

His eyes are shimmering with the love I saw that day on the beach when he talked about his grandmother.

"It'll be okay, Vincent. You'll get to see your grandmother now."

"I miss her," he says, his voice raspy.

Blood is spurting out of his chest. I take my scarf off and shove it against his chest, trying to make it stop.

"Please tell me where Brooklyn is. Where Matt is. So we can finish our movie."

"Don't cry," he says. "I love you."

The color drains out of his face and I know he's almost gone.

"I love you too, Vincey," I say, as tears stream down my face.

He looks into my eyes and mutters something that sounds like, "Grandmothers."

He stops breathing. His eyes becoming fixed.

And I know he's dead.

I wanted him out of my life, but I didn't want this.

I bury my face in his hair and cry.

ONE OF THE men, who I recognize from Miami, picks me up and moves me away from the body. I sob into his suit as I hear sirens wail.

"Dallas is awake and will be fine," he says. "Probably just a mild concussion. We're working on the other boys."

What other boys? Does he mean Brooklyn? Did they find him?

No, he couldn't know about B. I haven't told him where he is yet.

"I need my bag!"

I run to the van, grab my backpack, retrieve my phone, and make a call.

"Damian! Damian! Have you left for Miami yet?" I say, remembering that he was leaving soon.

"No, I took Peyton out for lunch and just got to the airport."

"Whatever you do, do not leave without me!" I yell over

the sirens.

"Where the hell are you? And why are there sirens?" he asks, but I hang up and rush over to Dallas, who is now sitting up.

"Are you okay?"

"I feel like I was rode hard and hung up wet."

I laugh. "My grandpa says that."

One of the agents helps Dallas to his feet, saying, "We need to get you checked out by the paramedics."

He leads us around the van when I see it.

Aiden's car.

Barely recognizable.

Smashed beyond belief.

Oh my god!

Is that what he meant by *other boys*?

I panic and start screaming at the top of my lungs, "Aiden! Aiden! Aiden!"

I run to the car.

He's not there.

My heart nearly stops beating.

My eyes move quickly across the debris, searching for him.

"Aiden! Aiden!"

"Keatyn," I hear him say.

I turn around and, there, on a stretcher by the ambulance, I find a tuft of blond hair and the greenest eyes I've ever seen.

I rush to his side. "Aiden, what happened?"

"Thank god you're okay," he says, grabbing my hand. "I heard gunshots. Riley and I were freaking out because we couldn't get out of the car."

"Did Vincent crash into you?"

Riley holds up a little camera from a neighboring

stretcher. "Not exactly. I recorded it, so you can see what happened later."

I rub the bump on my head, not really understanding how he could have recorded an accident, but there's really only one question I want answered. "Are you two okay?"

Riley points down. "My foot's messed up. Maybe broken. They want to X-ray it."

"Aiden?"

"Probable clavicle fracture," the EMT working on him says. "We're taking them to the hospital, but they appear to be in pretty good shape, considering the way the vehicle looks. They're lucky they were wearing seat belts and helmets."

"Helmets?"

"The ones you bought at the track," Aiden says.

"You mean he didn't hit you?" I ask. As soon as I do, it dawns on me. "Wait?! You crashed into the van *on purpose*?!"

Aiden gives me a sheepish grin.

"You promised not to interfere!"

"It was our only option. No one was coming. Riley didn't think you had your locket on. And we knew if we lost you . . ." He reaches up and touches my face.

"But your car—and you're both hurt."

"It's just a car. It can be replaced."

"Aiden was on fumes. Almost out of gas," Riley continues. He's all pumped up. "Between his driving lesson and him sitting in on some movie planning, he thinks he's a stunt man!"

I'm listening to Riley, but Aiden has me caught in his tractor beams and I can't look away.

Tears fill my eyes again. "The prince isn't supposed to crash his white steed to save the princess."

"I couldn't risk losing you."

I close my eyes.

I hate that I have to say this.

I hate that I have to leave.

Like this.

Right now.

But I have to.

I bend down and kiss his cheek. "Thank you so much for rescuing me. Vincent is dead, and I know this is really bad timing, but, um, I have to go."

"To the hospital?"

"No, home. Damian's holding the jet for me. I have to go find B. It's my fault he was kidnapped in the first place. Please understand. I have to."

"You're hurt," he says. "You need to be looked at."

I shake my head, knowing I'm being pulled in another direction.

I'm listening to my heart.

And my heart is telling me I need to get my ass to Malibu and find him.

"I'm sorry," I say.

Aiden doesn't reply. He turns to Dallas, who has joined us. "Dallas, go grab my keys."

"I hate to break it to you, dude," Dallas says, "but I don't think you'll be able to drive her again."

"It's important."

Dallas nods his head, hobbles over, gets the keys out of what's left of the car, and brings them to Aiden.

Aiden separates the key from the keychain and presses it into my hand. "Luck and fate. Take them with you, find him, and then come back to me." He looks deep within my soul and says, "Promise me you'll be back."

Tears fill my eyes as I shake my head and turn away from him.

Because I know I can't promise anything.

"CAN YOU TAKE me to the airport?" I ask one of the black-suited men.

He shakes his head. "The police will need you to give them a statement."

"But you shot him. I didn't."

"I think you might be going into shock," he says in a patronizing voice. "Let's get you back over to the ambulance."

"If you don't find someone to take me to the airport right this second, I'm going to call Senator McMahon and throw the biggest temper tantrum you have ever seen."

The guy from Miami walks over. "What's the problem?"

"Vincent, the guy who you shot, kidnapped my friend three days ago. They've searched Vincent's properties but haven't found him. That's why I didn't want you to shoot him. I needed to find out where he was."

"Did he tell you?"

"I think so. I'm so worried about him. There's a plane waiting for me. I can drive myself if you'll just let me borrow a car."

"Are you sure you don't need medical attention?"

"I'm positive."

"Come on," he says. "I'll take you."

CATASTROPHIC EVENTS.
1:35PM

THE AGENT PULLS out on the tarmac and Damian comes out of the terminal to greet me.

"What is going on? Why do you need to come with me to Miami? And what was with all the sirens—oh, my god. Is that blood?"

I look down at my shirt and realize it's covered in it. I nod at him, too tired to explain.

"Is that *your* blood?!" he yells.

"No. Let's take off and we'll deal with my wardrobe later."

I close my eyes and say a prayer.

Please help me find Brooklyn.

"Is there anyone you need me to call?" the agent asks as he carries my backpack to the plane.

"Uh, what?"

"Is there anyone you need me to call?"

"No, thank you," I say to the agent, but to Damian I say, "but I do need to call Garrett and tell him what happened."

"You need to tell *me* what happened," Damian says.

"Hang on," I say, as I pull my phone out of my backpack.

I see that I have a text and numerous missed calls from Garrett.

I read the text from earlier today first.

Garrett: *Two concurrent catastrophic events have just occurred. Get Cooper and run. You must leave Eastbrooke now.*

I call him as Damian and I board the plane.

"Keatyn, where are you? Does Vincent have you?"

"Vincent is dead."

"Vincent is dead?" both he and Damian say.

"Yes, but I know where he was keeping Brooklyn. I need you to go rescue him. I'll be there soon."

"Where is he?"

"At Vincent's grandmother's house."

"Vincent told you that?" Garrett asks.

"Yes, right before he died in my arms. Wait. What two catastrophic events?"

"Are you with Cooper? Can I speak to him, please?"

"Vincent shot Cooper in the chest. He fell to the ground." I start crying again. "I'm sorry. I think he's dead. Damian and I are getting ready to take off. We're coming home."

"Not Cooper," Garrett says sadly. "He was a good man."

"I know he was. I'm sorry."

"You're *positive* he said Brooklyn was at his grandmother's?"

"Yes, the Secret Service was shooting at him, so I ran in front of him, trying to get them to stop. But it was too late. There was blood everywhere. He told me he loved me, and I asked him to tell me where B was. As he was dying, he told me B's at his grandmother's."

Garrett lets out a huge sigh. "Keatyn, I'm afraid I have some bad news. There was an explosion at his grandmother's house. Firefighters are on the scene, but it doesn't look good. I'm there now."

"What are you saying?"

"I'm saying Brooklyn couldn't have survived the blast. Or the subsequent fire."

"No!" I scream. "No!"

I drop the phone.

It can't be true.

Damian wraps me in a hug. I sob into his shoulder as he picks up my phone.

I hear him say, "Are you sure? What? Two events?"

I pick my head up and grab the phone out of his hand. "Garrett, wait. Your text said there were two events that made you think Vincent was coming for me. What else happened? Is my family okay?"

"Why don't you put me on speaker, so I can tell Damian too," Garrett says defeatedly.

"Something else bad happened, Damian," I say, gripping his hand tightly. "He wants me to put it on speaker."

"You're on speaker, Garrett," Damian says.

"This is difficult for me to tell you both, but there has also been an explosion on the *Retribution* movie set."

Damian squeezes my hand back as Garrett continues. "There was a bomb in Tommy's trailer. Damian, he and your dad were said to have been inside at the time and are presumed dead."

"Oh my god," Damian says, tears flooding his eyes.

I cry too.

And hug him.

Not Matt and Tommy, too.

"I'm sorry, Damian," I say as we hear Garrett say, "What the fuck?! Are you kidding me?"

I hear a fist hitting metal.

His voice cracks when he comes back on the phone. "There was another bomb. One of my men at the France location just reported that a bomb exploded there, too."

"At our house? Is Mom okay? My sisters? Grandparents?"

"I don't know. Fuck!" he says again. "I'll call you back as soon as I know something."

"We're ready to go," the pilot says over the intercom. "Attendant, please close the door."

"Damian, shit. I need you to have them change their flight plan. We need to go home."

He rubs his eyes, shakily stands, and is going toward the cockpit when the pilot comes over the intercom again. "Hang on. The tower says there's some confusion. There's a bright green Viper causing some problems. Actually, the idiot is heading straight towards us."

"Wait!" I scream, knowing it's got to be Riley's car.

Except Riley is on his way to the hospital.

I stick my head out the door just as the Viper screeches to a halt.

Cooper jumps out of the car, waving a gun.

"Cooper!" I scream.

"Where is he?" Cooper yells. "Where is he?"

I fly down the stairs and launch myself at him. "You're alive!" I say, crying harder.

"I am. Where's Vincent?"

"He's dead."

Cooper holsters his gun, relaxes, and hugs me back.

"I was afraid I had lost you," he says. "Where are you going?"

"Home," I cry, grabbing his hand. "Please come with us. I need you."

As we board the plane, the attendant gives me an expectant look. "Just picked up another passenger," I tell her.

"Get buckled up," she says. "We'll be taking off for California shortly."

I sit back down and hold Damian's hand.

"Tell me what happened," Cooper says.

"Bombs went off," Damian says flatly. "Brooklyn, Tommy, and my dad are dead. We're waiting to hear if Keatyn's family in France is okay."

"What?"

I tell him about the bombs.

"I never expected him to do something like that,"

Cooper says.

"Me either. I got his new script last night but only read the end. I bet anything bombs were part of the big action scenes. I should have stayed up and read it all. I could have stopped it from happening."

"Tell me what happened with Vincent. Did you kill him?"

"No. Aiden and Riley saw the van tearing out of school and chased it. I guess they were almost out of gas. Riley was afraid I'd taken off my locket because I had planned to sneak back home tonight." Cooper gives me a pointed look, but I ignore it. "They crashed into the van; it rolled. Vincent and I fought. The Secret Service showed up and shot him. I thought you were dead, Cooper. I saw him shoot you in the chest. You went down."

Cooper pulls up his shirt, revealing a bulletproof chest protector. "The shots knocked me over and knocked the wind out of me. When I got up, you were already gone. The school was on lockdown. I came here because I figured he'd fly you back to California."

"I'm so glad you're alive." I start sobbing again. "I caused all of this. Everyone's hurt or dead because of me. All I wanted to do was protect them. I tried to protect them."

My head wobbles a bit; I feel woozy.

"I don't feel very good."

"Did you hit your head?" Cooper asks.

I nod, but then I touch my side and feel warmth. Pulling my hand away and putting it in front of my face, I see blood.

Cooper yells at me. "Are you bleeding?"

As my vision blurs, I have a fleeting memory of a bullet hitting my side.

"Keatyn. Keatyn! Wake up!"

When I open my eyes, I see Damian. His eyes are red and teary.

I shouldn't have fought Vincent. I should have let him get me a long time ago.

I may have my life back, but how many lives did I ruin in the process?

Brooklyn's. Damian's. His family's.

And mine.

I don't have anyone to go home to.

Tears fill my eyes.

"Did you not notice you were bleeding?" Cooper asks me.

"They're okay!" Damian blurts out.

I sit up quickly but then feel dizzy again.

Damian pulls me into a hug.

"Who's okay?"

"Your family."

I start crying with relief. "Are you sure?"

"Yes, Garrett messaged Cooper while you were passed out. The bomb was inside a package that was delivered to your mom. The nanny was opening it on the kitchen island when it exploded. The nanny, unfortunately, is dead. Your mom was standing, looking in the fridge when the blast occurred. The heavy door shielded her. She has a concussion and some cuts, but she's fine."

"And the girls?"

"They were outside playing with James. They're all fine."

"And my grandparents?"

"They were outside too."

"Oh, thank god."

"It's gonna be okay," Damian says.

"But the nanny. And your dad and Tommy. And Brooklyn. I didn't win, Damian. I lost. I lost them."

"You lost quite a bit of blood, Keatyn. Try to stay calm."

"We're about to land," Damian says.

I reach down and touch my side, not far above my chaos tattoo, and feel a bandage. "I think I got shot."

"You did," Cooper says. "Fortunately, it just nicked you. I stopped the bleeding but you probably need a few stitches."

"How's your chest?"

"I'm gonna have a hell of a bruise, but that's better than the alternative."

As soon as the wheels hit the ground, I call James.

"How is Mom?"

"We heard Vincent's dead. That you were in an accident *and* a gun fight? How are *you*?"

"It just grazed me. I'm fine. Can Mom talk?"

"Of course. Hang on."

"Keatyn!" Mom says. I can tell she's crying. "Sweetie, are you really okay?"

I lose it and start bawling. "I'm so sorry about Tommy and the nanny. I'm so sorry. It's all my fault. It's all my fault."

"Honey, Tommy and Matt aren't dead. Tommy just called me. They weren't in the trailer when the bomb went off."

"They weren't?"

"No. You know those two. They made everyone think they were in there discussing business when they had really snuck out to smoke a cigar."

"Ohmigawd! Damian! Your dad and Tommy are fine!

They weren't in the trailer!"

I hug Damian while my mom says, "Honey, I have to go. The doctor is here, and I need a few stitches. As soon as I'm allowed, we're coming home."

"To Malibu?"

"Yes. As soon as possible."

"I can't wait to see you. I love you."

"I love you too. And I heard about Brooklyn. Keatyn, none of this is your fault."

COOPER HERDS DAMIAN and me into a car when we land.

"Cooper, we have to go to Vincent's grandmother's house. We have to."

Damian nods in agreement.

Cooper calls Garrett, who advises us against it, but gives us the address.

We're all quiet on the ride there. Somber.

I feel like I'm going to a funeral.

It's easy to know when we're close.

The air is dark and smells of fire.

We get out where the street is blocked off and walk up the hill.

The police have the area cordoned off, but Cooper says, "We're looking for Garrett Smith."

The policeman lets us through and points us in his direction.

I get my first glimpse of what's left of the mansion.

Which isn't much.

Just four brick fireplaces standing at attention and a side portion of the home, the wood black and charred. Water is rushing down the street and there are numerous choppers flying overhead.

Garrett points at the burned trees.

"The fire was very hot, and they were worried it would spread. The firemen couldn't even get inside because it was so hot." My face takes on a pained expression as I think of the horror of Brooklyn burning to death. Garrett stops talking and puts his hand on my shoulder. "If he was in there, he didn't suffer. He would have died when the bomb went off, not in the secondary fire."

I nod gratefully. At least there's that, I guess.

"How are you?"

"I'm fine."

"You were in a car accident and got shot."

"I'm fine. Um, I just need a minute."

I move away from the group and walk closer to the house, close my eyes, and take a deep breath.

And use my heart as a guide.

I've felt this way since we arrived.

I'm detached.

Honestly, I feel like B isn't here.

Is it because he's dead?

"I don't think Brooklyn is here," I say out loud.

The second I speak the words, I become even more convinced. "They aren't going to find him. He wasn't here."

"Keatyn, you've been through a lot today. It's understandable that you'd be in denial," Garrett says.

"I'm not in denial. He's not here. I know it. He's alive and he's—I don't know, but we need to find him. I want a list of every single property. I'll go search them all myself if I have to."

"Keatyn, you need to rest," Damian says, looking really drained himself.

"I can't rest!" I yell. "Not until I find him."

"Keatyn, honey," Cooper says. "You need to calm down."

"I'm not going to calm down until we find him. So, if you want me to calm down, help me!"

"If you go home and take a shower, I'll meet you there in a half hour with the list of every property his grandmother owned along with all of Vincent's holdings," Garrett says, patronizing me.

I'M HOME. IN my room.

Looking at myself in the mirror.

I'm a complete wreck. There is blood and dirt—and probably other gross things I don't want to know about— matted in my hair. One of my cheeks is swollen and red. I have bandages on my side and across my arm where bullets grazed me.

I hear Garrett talking to Cooper outside my door.

"She needs a sedative," Garrett says.

I swing my door open with such force it bangs against the wall and almost shuts back on me. "I don't need a sedative. I need you to find B. And that's what you should be doing, rather than plotting to drug me against my wishes!"

"She doesn't need a sedative, Garrett," Cooper says. "She just needs this."

He walks into my room and pulls me into a hug. A nice, tight hug.

And I start crying.

Again.

I don't know how long I cry.

But Cooper never lets go.

All the emotions I've felt today, all the sadness and sorrow, come running out of me.

I finally stop then look at Cooper and smile.

"Thank you. That is what I needed."

"Why don't you get cleaned up? I'll get us some food. And we'll make a plan."

"You know, officially, you don't have to spend any more time with me. I'm safe."

"Are you firing me?"

"No, I just love that you didn't want to leave. That you still want to help me. You're way more than a bodyguard, Cooper. You've become someone I trust. You've become my friend."

Cooper smiles and pats my back. "You've become my friend too."

"When this is over, what are your plans? Do you want to go back to work for the government? Or would you ever consider personal security?"

"You offering me a job?"

"Yes. I think the press is going to be insane when this all gets out."

"As long as I don't have to grade any more papers."

"Deal. I'm going to shower and then just lie down for a minute."

"Okay," Cooper says.

Sunday, January 8th

FACE FACTS.
8AM

I WAKE UP with a start.

I was just having a horrible dream.

And I can't shake the feeling something bad is going to happen.

I rub my eyes and look at the clock. It's eight in the morning! Shit. Why did they let me sleep so long?

I have to find Brooklyn.

Brooklyn.

That's what I was dreaming about.

He was trapped.

Dying a fiery death.

I jump out of bed and the towel I wrapped around myself after my shower falls to the ground.

I leave it on the floor, run into my closet, throw on some sweats, then nudge Damian, who is sleeping on the couch in my room.

"Damian, wake up. We've got to go find Brooklyn."

A few minutes later, I have Garrett and Cooper awake and sitting at the kitchen table with me while Damian makes us breakfast.

"We revisited every property on this list yesterday," Garrett says. "It doesn't look good, Keatyn. You're going to have to face facts."

"And what facts are those?"

"That either he was in Vincent's grandmother's house when it exploded or that Vincent killed him before he came to get you and disposed of the body."

"No. It doesn't make sense. It goes against everything we know. He wasn't going to hurt Brooklyn until we did the movie. Vincent was coming to get me! He was close to having everything he wanted. There's no way he'd ruin our movie by killing him before he'd realized his dream."

Cooper holds up his hand. "I hate to say it, but you told us that Vincent kidnapped Dallas too. Why do you think that was?"

"Because he was there?"

"Or because he needed a new Matt?"

His comment is like a sucker punch straight to my gut.

I get up, run out of the house, and down to the beach.

I plop down in the sand, watch the waves rush into shore, and think about crying.

But no tears come.

I know it's not over.

It can't be.

I refuse to believe it.

I think about Vincent's rewrite of the movie. How he framed Matt.

He told me that all he needed was me. That he had everything ready.

I know we're missing something.

What am I missing?

I try to clear my head by focusing on the waves.

I think about the new ending to movie. How it was exactly like his grandmother's old movie, Vince and Lacey passionately kissing in the sand.

I remember Vincent telling me about it when his . . .

A word suddenly pops into my head.

One single word.

Ashes.

Ohmigawd!

That's it!

I get up and run into the house yelling. "Cooper! Damian! Garrett! I know where he is!"

Cooper and Damian are sitting at the kitchen table scouring over the property lists for the millionth time.

"Let me see the list again!"

Damian hands it to me and I quickly scan it.

"Is this list current?"

"Yes," Garrett says.

"What about the house he bought down the beach?"

"There's no beach house on here. Let alone a property down the street."

"The old man, Damian. The one who gets up early and watches ladies jog down the beach. Vincent had coffee with him. I don't think he made it up. Come on!"

"There's an old guy about seven houses down I used to see on his deck sometimes when we were out surfing," Damian says, and follows me to the beach.

We take off running.

I count the houses as we run by.

One.

Two.

Three.

Four.

Five.

Six.

Seven.

I run up to the deck and bang on the glass door. A startled woman answers in her robe. "Can I help you?"

"This is the wrong house," Damian says, stating the obvious.

"An old man. Gets up early in the morning and has coffee on his deck. Have you seen him? Do you know where he lives?"

"Mr. Richards lives next door," she says. "Although, come to think of it, I haven't seen him in a few days."

I tear down the stairs, back through the sand to the next house, and then take the stairs up to the deck.

When I bang on this door, a dog barks loudly and comes to the glass.

"Kiki!" Damian and I both yell.

"This is it! They're here!" I scream.

I pick up a ceramic pot from the deck, yell at Kiki to move, and then throw it through the window.

The living room is large and open, cluttered with cameras, sound booms, lighting.

A movie set waiting for me.

"Where's B?" I ask Kiki.

She runs to a bookcase in the living room and spins in a circle. Almost like she's chasing her tail.

"Search all the rooms," Garrett commands, coming in behind us.

Kiki barks and follows him down a hall.

I follow Kiki.

I round the corner to a bedroom and see a man lying on the floor, Garrett bent down next to him.

"This must be the old man who owns the house," Garrett says. "He's dead."

I close my eyes and pray that B's still alive.

Cooper and Damian meet us back in the hall.

"We've been through all the bedrooms down this hall. No one in them," Cooper says.

"Upstairs," Damian suggests, taking off running.

I go back to into the living room and start yelling, "Brooklyn! Brooklyn! Brooklyn!"

Kiki jumps on me, her big paws hitting my thighs and almost knocking me down.

"What is it girl? Do you know where he is?"

She runs back to the first place she took me. The book-shelf.

Only this time, she starts digging and barking.

"B!!" I yell again as I try to figure out what's behind the bookshelf.

A secret room, maybe?

I look for a latch. A button.

And the whole time, I'm yelling for B.

Finally, I put my fingers under the edge of the trim and pull, causing the whole bookcase to swing out toward me and revealing a steel door.

I pull the big handle, but it's locked and won't budge.

I bang on the door as Kiki starts digging and barking.

"B!" I scream, still pounding.

"Garrett, Cooper, Damian! I found a secret door!"

They are rushing back into the living room from different locations when I hear B's faint voice.

"Keats?"

"B! Ohmigawd! Are you okay?"

"Am I in heaven?" he asks.

"What? No. Vincent kidnapped you. He's dead. We've been trying to find you!"

"What about the bomb?"

"What bomb?"

"He said that if he didn't make it back with you, I'd burn."

Garrett goes, "Holy shit. We have to get out of here! Now!"

I turn around to see him staring down in disbelief at what appears to be a briefcase.

"This is a bomb. It's going off in twenty-seven seconds! We've got to get out of here!"

"We have to get B, first!" I yell.

"There's not time," Cooper says, pulling me toward the door. "If we don't leave now, we're all going to die."

The scene is surreal.

Looking like a movie set, but feeling way too real.

Damian and I share a look.

"You go. I'll stay with Brook," he says bravely. "Maybe it won't go off."

"No!" I yell as both Garrett and Cooper try to drag me out the front door.

Damian says, "Tell Peyton I love her."

My eyes fill with tears as Cooper pulls me closer to the door.

"No!" I scream.

I can't believe after everything we've been through that it's going to end this way.

My body goes limp in defeat.

As it does, a single word pops into my head.

The same word from the beach.

Ashes.

And I immediately know what I have to do.

I PUSH COOPER against the wall and shove Garrett out of the way.

I run back to the bomb, see there are twelve seconds left, slam the briefcase lid shut, grab the handle, and take off with it.

I hear shouts of protest coming from behind me, but I ignore them.

00:11

Sprint across the living room as my life flashes before my eyes.

Floating in the waves. Salt. Sand. Freedom.

00:10

Crash through the broken window to the deck.

A hand on mine. Keats poetry. Sadness. Ribbit.

00:09

Run across the deck.

Pink blanketed bundles. Thirty perfect stubby fingers. The softest hair ever.

00:08

Hurdle a chaise blocking my way.

Fall leaves. Old Bricks. Green grass. Feeling safe.

00:07

Unlatch the gate.

A flash of green. Heartbreak. Love.

00:06

Bound down the stairs.

Tie-dyed tutu. Ballet shoes. A handsome grin.

00:05

Tear through the sand.

Hammock blowing in the breeze. Three little words.

Happy tears.

00:04

Feel the ocean rush onto my feet.

Stacks of hay. Cowboy boots. Lemonade.

00:03

Swing the briefcase back.

Ferris wheel. An arm on my shoulder. A perfect kiss.

00:02

Fling it into the ocean with all my might.

Stranglehold hugs. Baby powder and chocolate. Falling asleep in my arms.

00:01

Turn around and run like hell straight into Damian and beat feet back toward the house.

Shining lights. An audience. Performing.

00:00

An explosion knocks us both into the sand.

Blond hair. A hug. Lavender, honeysuckle, and the ocean.

Fish, water, and seaweed rain down on me.

I push myself up off the sand, ignoring my protesting body. Damian looks a bit dazed, but Kiki licks my face.

"Holy fuck, Keats! I can't believe you just did that. You're fucking nuts."

I ignore him and say, "Let's go, Kiki!"

As we run into the house together, the police and firemen arrive.

But I don't care.

They aren't moving fast enough.

What if there's another bomb in the room with B?

One we don't know about?

It could go off at any second.

"B!" I scream, pushing through the firemen who are discussing the best way to get through the steel door.

"Did the bomb just go off?" he asks.

"Yes, I threw it in the ocean."

"It shook the room so hard there's drywall dust everywhere."

"Drywall dust? Where?"

"Looking at the door, it's on my right."

I shove through whoever all these people are. At this point, I don't care.

I have but one goal.

Get to B.

I.

Have.

To.

Get.

To.

Him.

Working my way around the corner from the steel door, I find a bedroom.

And on the wall surrounding the room is a closet.

I throw the doors open, grab the clothes hanging there, and toss them out of my way.

Kiki starts digging and barking, her claws marking the drywall and spraying up dust.

"That's it, Kiki. Good girl. Good girl!"

I pay attention to where the screws are in the rack holding up the bar, assume that's where the studs are, and use my fist to start punching the drywall in between them.

I punch as hard as I can.

The drywall crumples but I can't break through.

Cooper flies in the room. "What the hell are you doing?"

I stand back slightly, giving way to him, and scream, "Punch it Cooper. Punch it!"

"You're hysterical and you need to calm—"

"Punch!"

"It!"

"Now!"

He shakes his head, but then stands back and hammers the wall with his fist, cleanly breaking through.

I see light and push him out of the way, shoving my arm through the hole and yelling, "B!"

All of a sudden a hand grabs mine.

I start crying.

And I know.

I am finally home.

AT SOME POINT the firemen come into the room. I don't let go of B's hand until the wall comes down around us.

I start crying again when I see him.

His blond hair is matted, his skin looks pasty, his grip is weak, but those blue eyes reach way down and grab my soul.

Kiki jumps on B, showering him with wet, sloppy kisses.

And I wrap my arms around him and hug him with all my might.

"Are you okay?"

He hugs me tighter than he ever has before. "I am now. Is he really dead?"

"Yes. It's over, B. It's finally over."

Damian is crying too as he wraps his arms around both of us.

"I thought we were all going to die," he says. "Keats,

you are absolutely crazy, but thank god you are."

The three of us continue our group hug and the rest of the world fades away.

"How did he get you here?" I ask B.

"I'm not sure. All I remember is walking to my bike. Then I woke up here. He's seriously deranged. And obsessed with your mom's movie. He talked about Lacey, Abby, and Keatyn as if they were one person. Did you see the walls?"

Brooklyn motions around to the walls of the room, which are covered with photos.

Stills from *A Day at the Lake*.

A poster of my mom.

Photos of her and my dad.

A newspaper article about his mother and stepfather's mugging and death.

A press release about A Breath Behind You Films.

A still shot of the ending of his grandmother's movie, where they are lying in the sand kissing.

Brooklyn points to an article about my dad's plane crash. "He admitted to tampering with your dad's plane. He wanted Abby for himself."

My eyes fill with tears again. "That's why my dad talked to me," I say out loud.

"What do you mean?" Damian asks.

"When Vincent tried to kidnap me, a voice—a voice that I recognized as my dad's—told me what to do. It was just a few words. But they calmed me and helped me get away from Vincent. And, today, it was the word *ashes*. Twice. Once to help me find B and again before I grabbed the bomb."

"How did the word ashes help you find me?" B asks.

"When Vincent's grandmother died, I helped spread her ashes. He told me her love story and how he was buying the house up the beach—this one—for her. When it wasn't on the list of properties where they had searched for you, I knew it's where you were. And then when I heard it again, it reminded me of how he tossed the urn out into the ocean. I did the same thing with the bomb."

Brooklyn rubs his face, trying to take it all in.

"He drugged me. Told me about all the bombs. Are your mom and Tommy dead?"

"The bomb in France killed the girls' nanny, but everyone else is okay."

"And Tommy's trailer?"

"For a while we thought he and my dad were dead," Damian says somberly. "Fortunately, they weren't in it and there were only some minor injuries to a few people in the vicinity."

Brooklyn turns me around to face the wall dedicated to me.

Photos of my life.

A large poster made from the still of me turning around and blowing Vincent a kiss.

There are notes, scripts, character profiles, and story arcs.

"Right before he drugged me the last time, he told me he was going to get you. That if he made it back, I'd be famous. That we'd all star in the most epic reality movie ever. And that if he didn't make it back, I'd be famous too. Because I would die when the bomb went off."

Tears stream down my face, thinking of what he must have gone through.

He hugs me, says, "I love you," and kisses the top of my head.

Cooper says, "The medics need to check you out."

B shakes his head and says, "I wanna go home."

"We are home," I say. "Let's get you looked at."

"You too," Damian says. "You're bleeding again."

The medics check us all out. Brooklyn is still a bit woozy, but they determine it's just the lingering effects of the drugs and release him.

"We'll handle everything here," Cooper tells me, nodding toward Garrett. "You guys go home. If the police want to question Brooklyn, they can make an appointment."

"That sounds good," B says.

Damian, Brooklyn, and I make the familiar walk down the beach with Kiki in tow. She's running ahead of us, prancing through the waves and digging in the sand.

It's a beautiful day and it almost feels normal, like we're walking home after a day of surfing.

We walk by B's house and down to mine, file up on the deck, collapse on the day bed, and stare quietly out into the ocean.

Each of us lost in our own thoughts.

And happy to be alive.

IT DOESN'T TAKE long for our few moments of solitude to be interrupted.

Brooklyn's mom and dad arrive together, whatever issues they had in the past seemingly forgotten amidst concern for their son.

The police have lots of questions.

Tommy and Matt arrive from New York.

Cooper contacts the reporters from the dance, who hop on planes immediately.

I do their interviews as promised, telling them everything up until the point when Vincent died.

THE BEST PART, though, is late at night when Mom, James,

my grandparents, and the girls arrive home from France.

Brooklyn, Tommy, and I get hugs and kisses, but the girls seem even happier to see Kiki.

"My bad Kiki! I'm home! I was on an adventure just like you!" Gracie yells.

"A little too much adventure," B says to me under his breath.

"You can't call her Bad Kiki anymore," I tell them. "She's a hero and a very lucky dog."

"Let's call her Lucky!" Avery suggests.

Gracie gives the dog a strangling hug. "Bad Kiki, do you like the name Lucky?"

The dog gives her a sloppy kiss up the side of her face.

"She likes it!" the girls shout.

"Lucky! Lucky! Lucky!" they yell.

"I like that name. You girls are pretty wound up."

"They were awake the entire flight," Mom tells us, looking exhausted. "We need to get them to bed."

GRACIE PULLS ON my hand, leading me toward her room. "I show Kiki something!"

"I wouldn't show her, Gracie," Avery says. "She's gonna be mad at you."

Grace sticks her tongue out at Avery, then turns to me with a grin and pulls me through the living room, down the hall, and into her closet.

She waves her hand at five pairs of my high-heeled shoes.

"Why do you have my shoes in here, Gracie?"

"Cuz when Kiki went on adventure, I go in Kiki's closet. These shoes missed you."

"We never told Mommy on her," Ivery confides.

"I took care of Kiki shoes," Gracie tells me. "I pet them.

Talk to them. Wear them."

I give her a big hug. "Thanks for taking care of my shoes, sweetie. I really appreciate it."

She gives me a satisfied grin and says quietly, "They want to live with me now."

"Hmm," I say, pretending to deal with her. "Is it okay if I borrow them sometimes?"

She nods, her little curls springing around her face. "I let you wear them. I told Mommy I want to be on TV. That I promise to be good." She picks her Pooh Bear off the floor. "Watch." She sets Pooh on her bed and says, "Mr. Pooh, I think you should change your name, because it's like dog poo. And dog poo is yucky." Then she pretends to be Pooh, holding him up in front of her face and talking in a deeper voice. "I don't want to be named Pooh. I want to be called Mr. Bear." Then she puts Pooh out in front of her and replies in her voice. "I think Mr. Bear is a lovely name."

She shakes Pooh's hand and turns toward me and bows.

Of course, I clap.

"You will be a brilliant actress, Gracie, if that's what you want to be."

She gives me a neck-crushing hug, then screams when Brooklyn brings the triplets in to get ready for bed.

"Tell us a story!" Avery yells.

"Yes! We missed your princess stories," Emery agrees.

"Fine. Everyone on the bed!"

I smile at Brooklyn as Gracie sits on his lap.

Then I start telling the girls our story.

"Once upon a time, there was a girl."

"No!" Ivery says. "She can't be just a girl."

"Yeah," Emery chimes in. "She has to be a princess."

"Okay, fine. She was a Hollywood princess."

"Like me?" Gracie says.

"If that's what you want to be, Gracie, sure."

"Wait," she says as she leaps off his lap. "I need something!" She digs in a toy chest, pulls out a pink-jeweled tiara, and puts it on her head. Then she runs out of the room and comes flying back in with one of Mom's faux fur vests.

She does a little bow. "Okay, I ready!"

"So the Hollywood princess went to school, where she was popular, dressed nice, and dated the perfect boy. But the princess was sad."

"Why was she sad?" Avery asks.

"Because the princess worried too much about what everyone thought about her and not enough about what she thought of herself. And sometimes the princess was kinda mean to people."

"Was she a bad princess?" Ivery asks.

"Princesses can't be bad," Emery says sarcastically, shaking her head at her sister.

"So, one night after a big ball—"

"Was Prince Charming at the ball?" Gracie yells and does a twirl. "Did they dance and kiss?"

"Did she lose her shoe?" Avery asks seriously.

Gracie turns and looks up at Brooklyn. "I hate when I lose my shoe. Bad Kiki chewed up my red glitter shoes and I was very mad. I say, *Bad Kiki!* But, now, Kiki—I mean Lucky—is a good puppy. She very brave."

"I agree. She's very brave. But, no," I continue. "Prince Charming wasn't at the ball. And the princess was sad, so she went outside and sat on her beach. She wondered where her prince was. Sometimes she almost felt like she could feel him. So she made a wish on the moon. She wished she would find him."

They all speak at the same time:

"Did a bad guy keep them apart?"

"Was the prince in a dungeon?"

"Did she go rescue him from a dragon?"

"No, silly. The prince is supposed to rescue the princess."

"Well," I say. "There was a very bad man. He wanted to lock the princess away in a tower and keep her all to himself."

"Like Rapunzel?" Avery asks.

"Kinda. The princess was afraid of the bad man, so, to protect her family and her adorable little sisters, she ran away and hid."

"Where did she go?"

Emery raises her hand. "I know. I know! She went on an adventure!"

"She did. To a school where no one knew she was a princess."

Gracie grabs my face in her little hands. "Did she lose her crown?"

"Kinda. But she found herself."

"What do you mean?" Ivery asks, looking perplexed.

"When she didn't have to behave like a princess anymore, she got to just be herself."

Brooklyn touches my hand and says, "And she learned that she was smart, and strong, and a good friend."

"What about her prince? Did he rescue her? Did the bad man find her?"

"Well," Brooklyn says. "The bad man kidnapped the prince, so the princess rescued him."

"No," Emery interrupts. "That's not how it works. The *prince* rescues the princess."

B looks at me and grins. "Maybe the princess knows how to kick ass."

Avery pulls on Brooklyn's sleeve and whispers, "Ass is a

bad word."

"So, did the princess give the prince true love's kiss?" Ivery asks.

"Under the stars?" Avery continues.

"No, I like it better when they kiss during the day. That's what makes the birdies happy. They chirp and fly around their heads," Emery says.

"Let's just say the story is still being written," I tell them. "But what's important is that the princess vanquished the bad man and now she's back home. With her little sister princesses."

The triplets leap on me in a group hug.

"Time for sleep," I tell them. "I love you."

As I kiss them each on the forehead, I'm overcome with emotion. This is what drove me. This exact moment. My sisters safe, happy, and home.

B grabs my hand and leads me out of their room. "So, would kick-ass Princess Keatyn like to go out on the beach with me?"

"Princess Keatyn would love that," I tell him.

"I'll grab a couple beers. You go find us a good spot."

I GO OUT the back door and wander down to the beach.

They're all good spots, but I'm drawn to one place.

The place I sat that night.

The night that seemed to set everything in motion.

The night I believed in true love and fate.

The night I wished for my perfect boy.

A lot has happened since then and I know I'm not the same girl. But, as I look up at the moon, I know that I got my wish.

B plops down next to me and hands me a beer.

We clink our bottles together and he says, "To being

home." He looks out at the ocean for a moment and when he turns back to face me, his eyes are shimmering. He clinks my bottle again and says, "And to you. Thank you for saving my life."

"You're welcome," I say with a smile.

He shakes his head. "I still can't believe you picked up a live bomb and threw it in the ocean. Do you have any idea what it weighed?"

"It wasn't that heavy; like, five pounds, maybe."

"More like twenty."

"Hmm. Must have been the adrenaline."

"You didn't just save me, you know. They say that had the blast happened in the house, it would have taken out at least three homes—possibly more from the fires. Have you seen the crazy throng of reporters outside the gates? My dad says we should be out there talking about all of it. That you can't buy publicity like this."

"And how do you feel about it? Do you want to be interviewed?"

He shakes his head. "No. I don't."

"Other than the story I owed those reporters, I don't want to talk about it either, B."

"Were you serious about sponsoring me?"

"Absolutely. In fact, I have this production company. We're looking to sponsor a hot young surfer. Although, I seriously have to come up with a new name for it."

"What's it called now?"

"A Breath Behind You Films. The acronym of which is Abby."

"Pretty creepy."

"Exactly. I think the new name should remind us of this. Of all we went through. Of how we've both changed. I don't ever want to lose sight of what's important in life again."

B reaches in his pocket and pulls out a joint. "Haven't had one of these in a while; what do you think?"

"I think I love you."

"I love you too." He lights up, takes a few puffs, and passes it to me.

"Ahhh," I say, relaxing completely.

We don't say anything.

Just smoke in a comfortable silence.

"Captive Films," he finally says.

"Captive?"

"Yeah. Vincent held our lives captive."

"And we wanna hold our audiences captive."

He grins. "Exactly."

"That's perfect. You cool with having that name on your surfboard?"

"I'd be honored." He laughs. "You know, tonight reminds me of that night. Your prom night. A lot has happened since then."

"I'm so sorry for everything, B."

He shushes me. "Stop feeling guilty. Vincent screwed up our lives, not you."

"I know. But you managed to get through it and become an amazing professional surfer."

He shakes his head. "It's hard to believe, isn't it? I can't wait to share it with you. Will you come to my next tournament?"

"I wouldn't miss it."

He looks at me wistfully. "You always look so pretty in the moonlight." He reaches out and touches my face. "Want to hear something silly?"

"Yeah," I say, leaning my cheek into his hand. His touch feels like it always has. Gentle and sweet.

"Remember your prom night?"

"Yeah."

"I'll never forget seeing you sitting here in your beautiful dress. The breeze blowing through your hair. You were staring at the moon, and I stopped right then and made a wish on it. I wished for you. Wished that you and I could end up here on the beach together."

Hang on.

I'm trying to process this.

Just give me a minute.

Two boys.

A country apart.

Who share the same birthday.

One whose name means fire.

The other, whose name means water.

Both made a wish when I did?

Except that B actually wished for me.

And, really, even though I wished for my perfect boy, technically, I was thinking of B when I made that wish. He was who I wanted to be my perfect boy.

"We've been through a lot to get back here, huh?" I say.

"Yeah."

He wraps his arm around me and I lean my head on his shoulder.

Like I've done so many times before.

He lifts my chin and kisses me. It's a good kiss. A kiss that speaks to me. A kiss full of *what ifs*. A kiss full of love and regret. A kiss that sums up our entire relationship.

A million emotions run through me. Each one hitting me like a wave. Happiness, sadness, regret, hope, and love. Lots and lots of love.

"I need you in my life, B."

"I need you, too," he says, wiping tears from his own eyes. "We've been given another chance at life, Keats. Let's do it right this time."

Tuesday, January 10th

GOOD TO BE HOME.
6:45AM

I WAKE UP to my alarm, wrap a blanket around my shoulders, and go out onto the deck.

The sky is still dark, but you can just see the sun's rays peeking up behind the house. I love the way the ocean looks as the sun rises, splashing color across it.

There's something so peaceful about this time of day. Something that calms me.

Sunrises symbolize new beginnings.

So I thought it was only fitting that I start my new beginning with one.

My new beginning.

Another chance at life.

The kind of life I've dreamed about.

And it all starts today.

A WHILE LATER, Mom and Tommy join me.

Mom hands me a mug of steaming coffee and curls up on the love seat with me.

"It's a really pretty morning," she says as she steals part

of my blanket.

"It is. Thanks for the coffee."

"You going surfing?" Tommy asks.

"No, B wanted to sleep in."

"Is he doing okay?"

"He is. He went through a lot more than I did. Being kidnapped. Drugged. Thinking he was going to die."

"He told me it's brought clarity to his life," Tommy says.

"He told me that too."

"Tommy," Mom says, "I can't keep it to myself."

"Keep what to yourself?" I ask.

"What we went through as a family brought some clarity to our lives, too," Tommy says. "Your mom and I have made some decisions."

"We're going to make an offer on a house in Hidden Hills," Mom continues. "There's lots of land. The girls can ride horses."

"And, most importantly, it's a very secure community. No one can just walk up to your back door like they can here," Tommy adds. "I've been thinking about it for a few months. And there's a house I've seen online that looks perfect. We want somewhere safe, where we can all be together."

"I missed all of you. It's so good to be home."

"Back on your beach?" Mom says with a smile.

"Do you remember when you told me one Thanksgiving that it doesn't matter where in the world you are, it only matters who is sitting next to you?"

Mom shakes her head. "I don't remember saying that. But I like it."

Tommy laughs at Mom and says, "Everything you say is so brilliant, you can't even remember it all," causing Mom to laugh too.

"So, tell me more about the house."

"The big draw, besides the security, is the land. A place for the girls to have a swing set. A big pool. A playhouse."

Tommy smirks. "Don't forget a place to kick a soccer ball and throw a football. Maybe I'll build a baseball diamond."

"Tommy," I say with a grin. "Do you think you're going to have a boy? Or are you planning on playing football with the girls?"

"Of course, I'd be thrilled with another healthy baby girl, but Inga said a long time ago that this one would be a boy."

"He didn't believe any of what he called *that nonsense* when I was pregnant with the girls, but now that it's what he wants to hear, he's a believer," Mom says, laughing.

"I'd love to have a baby brother. Although, if he's like you, he'll be trouble."

"Only if we're lucky," Tommy grins. He loves his former bad boy reputation. "Anyway, I think we'll all like the new house. And, of course, you'll have your own suite."

"What about this house?"

"Once we get moved, we thought we'd put it on the market."

"I'll buy it," I blurt out. I can't let go of this house.

"Really?" Tommy says. "You don't want a fresh start?"

"Speaking of that," Mom says delicately. "It was suggested that we have a psychiatrist come talk to you. With everything you've been through, you seem entirely too normal. And this morning you seem exceedingly happy. Is it all just an act?"

"No, Mom. I'm happy. I'm home. With my family. With B. And I'm going to call Vanessa and RiAnne today. I owe them an explanation. And a few apologies."

"What about Aiden? Have you talked to him?" Tommy asks.

"I've texted him some. I let him know what happened. He knows we're all back together. He's back home healing up. He said his shoulder is feeling better."

"You seemed really close in France," Mom says, using her gentle voice again.

"We are really close."

"Don't you think you owe him more than just a few texts?" Tommy asks.

"Of course, I do. But he understands that I just got my life back."

"Yes, but does he know about you and Brook?"

"He knows I promised B another chance." I study both Mom and Tommy's faces then ask, "Do you think I'm being selfish taking a few days for myself?"

"No, but Aiden's in love with you," Mom says.

Tommy adds, "I just feel bad for him. I mean, the wait. The not knowing who you've chosen has got to be killing him."

"I didn't expect to know right away. When Aiden and I talked about it, he said he was okay with me dating them both when I got my life back, so he's not expecting an answer."

"Still . . ." Mom says.

"It's just not something I want to say in a text or over the phone. I need to tell him this in person. He deserves to hear it from me that way."

"You're right. Your life," Tommy says. "We'll butt out."

"You know, for the first time in my life, I actually feel like it *is* my life. And I can't wait to live it. I'm so excited Knox and I are taking over the *Trinity* franchise roles."

I get a grin somewhere in size between his I-think-I'm-having-a boy-smile and the one he gets when you offer him a good glass of scotch. "That's still supposed to be a secret. Matt's so freaking excited, he's already hired a writer. He's hoping to start filming next year in the fall. Have you thought about that? What you'll do about high school?"

"I really haven't thought that far ahead yet. All I know is that I'm going out for Chinese with B today. I can almost taste the egg rolls. Do you want to join us?"

"We're supposed to tour the house before we put in an offer. But we thought we'd have a few people over for drinks and to watch the sunset. Millie, Deron, Matt and Marisa, Damian. Will you be back in time? I know they want to see you."

"I'll make sure we are. Speaking of food, I think I'll make some waffles and then wake the girls up."

AIDEN
2:30PM

DAMIAN CALLS ME.

"Hey, Crash Gordon," he says.

"Very funny."

"How are you feeling?"

"I'm fine. Hate having my arm in a stupid sling, though."

"So could you come to Malibu today?"

"I told her I'd give her time." I let out a sigh. "With him."

"When did you tell her that? And why?"

"When we were in St. Croix, after he called. She said she

promised him another chance. I told her I was up for the challenge, but I thought I had until August with her. I wasn't prepared for all this. How is she? She's been texting me some. She sounds normal, but how could she be after everything she's been through?"

"There are a lot of reporters dying to know those answers too. So far, she and Brooklyn have refused to talk to anyone other than the reporters Keatyn made the deal with at the dance. I just spoke to her. She's really happy to be home with her family."

"I know. That's the other reason I don't want to intrude. And . . . I really don't want to know the answer to this, but what about her and Brooklyn?"

"They're closer than ever because of what they went through."

"Shit," I say.

"Dude, do you love her?"

"You know I do."

"Then come to Malibu and ask her that question yourself. Or are you the kind of guy who will go down without a fight?"

"I promised."

"Fine, do what you want. But I'm just gonna say there's a plane sitting on the tarmac with your name on it. Like, you know, in case you wanna come. I'm texting you her address and approving you at the guard stand. We're going to have drinks there tonight and watch the sun set."

"The sunset?" I say, immediately remembering the first one we watched together. On the bench in front of the library. "Okay. I'll think about it."

"Bring your sister with you. I miss her."

"Is that what this is really about?"

"No, it's not what this is really about. Keatyn is my best

friend. I've seen how she is with you. I've seen how she is with him. I don't think you should give up. But it's up to you. Take me up on my offer or don't."

He hangs up.

"What the hell is there to even think about?" I say out loud as I grab my wallet, toss a few clothes in a bag, and yell to my sister. "I'm going to Malibu. You wanna come?"

"Uh, yeah! When do you want to leave?"

"You've got five minutes," I reply.

Now that I've decided to go, I can't get there soon enough.

PEYTON RUSHES OUT to the truck my parents bought yesterday to replace my car. It's not exactly an even replacement, but I couldn't care less what I'm driving as long as it gets me to the airport.

"Text Mom and Dad and let them know we left."

"Why are you in such a hurry? Malibu isn't going anywhere."

I raise an eyebrow at her.

She bobs her head back and forth. "I mean, I know a bomb went off there recently and all, but everyone's okay."

"I need to see Keatyn," I say.

I also need my sister to stop talking.

"How's the shoulder?"

"It's fine."

"What the hell is up your butt? You talk to Keatyn like that and she's going to send you back home."

"I'm sorry. I'm nervous. No, I'm excited. I'm nervous and excited. Worried. Freaking out, mostly. I have no idea what I'll say to her. She has no idea I'm coming."

"Aiden, if Keatyn loves you the way I think she does, it will all work out. Damian told me about her promise to her ex-boyfriend. Are you sure you shouldn't give her a little time? I mean, she just got her life back. Her family is finally together."

"Damian is the one who suggested this trip."

"Oh," she says, glancing down and looking interested in her cuticles.

"What?"

"Uh, nothing."

"Tell me what you're thinking."

"I'm thinking if Damian made you come, it's bad."

"That's what I'm afraid of. I know nothing about them. Why didn't I ask more about him? About their relationship."

"Probably because you didn't want to know," she says. "I know some. I know that he hurt her. I know that Damian didn't like the way he treated her."

"When she went to her little sister's birthday, he was there. He's probably practically part of the family."

DAMIAN MEETS US outside Keatyn's house and gives my sister a kiss that's too long for me to be able to wait until it's finished.

I can't wait any longer.

I ring the bell.

Keatyn opens the door, laughing. She looks more beautiful and happier than I've ever seen her.

But her smile turns into something else the second she sees me.

"Aiden!" She shakes her head. "I wasn't expecting you tonight. Sorry, come in."

I want to just scream at her.

Pick me.

Love me.

Tell me.

But before I can say anything, Brooklyn, who I immediately recognize from his social media, walks into the hall with one of the triplets on his back, looking entirely too cozy here.

Why the fuck did I do this?

"Aiden! Aiden!" her little sisters chant.

At least someone is happy to see me.

Gracie stands in front of me and says, "Bad Kiki no bad no more. She's Lucky now. My furry, good puppy saved Bwooklyn."

"I think it was Keatyn who did the saving," Brooklyn says, picking Gracie up and tickling her.

I watch as Keatyn and Brooklyn share a smile.

An intimate one.

Oh, god.

Did she sleep with him?

Already?

"We taking this action film star stuff a little too seriously?" I ask. It doesn't come out in the funny way I mean it to.

She gives me a precious pout and says, "I killed fish."

I want to reach out and touch her face. Say, *Baby, it's okay,* but she turns toward him.

"I'm sorry. Um, Aiden, this is Brooklyn. Brooklyn. Aiden."

Brooklyn reaches out and shakes my hand. He's confident.

I hate him.

Keatyn says, "Everyone is out on the deck. Come join us."

Her mom and Tommy are polite as is everyone else who's here and that I already know. Cooper, James, Kym, Millie and Deron, the Morans.

They are happily celebrating and chatting about stuff that I should probably be paying attention to.

Lots of details she hasn't told me.

But I can't focus on their conversations.

I can only focus on her.

She's walking toward me, holding a glass of wine.

Her long blonde hair is blowing in the breeze. Her hips have that easy, sexy sway.

When she hands me the wine, her smell invades my senses.

She smells different here. There's salt and something fruity mixed in with her normal sugar-sweet smell.

"The sun's getting ready to set," she whispers, sliding into the chair next to me. "I know when we watched sunsets together you were thinking about your mom surviving another day, but they touched me because it also meant that my family had survived another day. You helped me so many times when I was upset. I really appreciate it."

Brooklyn sits down on the other side of me and says sincerely, "I appreciate all you did for Keats, too."

He's *thanking* me?

Fuck.

That's bad.

It's so bad I can't speak. I just nod and wonder why the fuck I'm doing this to myself.

THE SUNLIGHT FADES, but the party continues.

And why the hell does Brooklyn have to be so cool? Like, if I didn't hate him, he's the kind of guy I could be friends with.

Actually, he reminds me of Dallas.

But then I realize why he's being so cool.

Because he knows.

He knows she chose him. Knows there's no competition. It's over. He's won.

He touches her arm.

She laughs.

And I want to kill him.

Gracie is sitting on his lap. Apparently, she knows too.

Why did I agree to this torture?

And why the hell did Damian tell me to come?

Speaking of the fucker, he walks in the door with my sister on his arm. I don't even want to know where they've been or what they've been doing for however long this nightmare has been going on.

My sister is glowing and happy. In love.

Damian and Peyton greet everyone and chat while I think about my tattoo.

The one hiding under my shirt in shame.

I was so sure of our love when I got a pair of cowboy boots wrapped in a heart on my side yesterday.

Now, I feel like a fool.

Everyone is laughing. Drinking.

I can't drink.

I feel like I'm going to explode.

Can't they see?

The time bomb app is going off inside me.

She saved him.

She loved him for more than two years. How did I think I could ever compete with a foundation like that?

FINALLY, AS THE sky turns from dusk to night, Brooklyn stands up, touches Keatyn's shoulder, and says, "Thanks for dinner. I'm gonna head home. I know you and Aiden need to talk." He looks at me, gives me a wave, and then kisses her on the cheek.

She stands up and hugs him way too tightly.

Then she beams at him and says, "Sunrise together? Surfing, as usual?"

Sunrise?

What about sunset? The million sunsets that we were supposed to watch together?

"Although, I don't have my board," she continues. "It's still in St. Croix."

Brooklyn smiles at her. "I'll bring you a board. Don't forget your skirt. Damian, you up for it?"

"Absolutely, man, it's about time we're back here together. I already texted all the guys."

Okay, it's official.

I hate Damian too.

Especially as he says to Keatyn, "Your board is at my house. I brought it home with me."

She runs over and gives him a hug. "You did? That was so sweet!"

"Yeah, yeah," he says, embarrassed by her outpouring of emotion.

That's one thing I love about her. Her emotions. They always seem so raw. So real. Like everything just affects her more than other people. And that face. God, I love that face. The way her every emotion is practically written across it.

You always know exactly what she's thinking and feeling.

Except tonight.

With me, she's guarded.

And that can't be good.

Brooklyn gives me the once over, then asks, "You surf?"

No.

No fucking way I'm going to surf with him.

But, of course, the competitor in me says, "Absolutely."

"Can you surf with the sling?"

"Aiden is just learning," Keatyn tells him. "But he's a natural." At least she's sticking up for me a little. She turns to me. "And, no. You're not surfing with a broken collarbone."

Then she grabs my pinkie.

It's a simple, small gesture.

But her touch is like a jolt of lightning to my body.

Bringing all the feelings I've been trying to push down right back up to the surface.

SHE KISSES HER sisters goodnight and then leads me down to the beach.

Their beach.

I look up at the moon, shining brightly above us.

My life was a mess when I made a wish on it.

A lot of girls who only needed a smile from me, a few shots, or a good game.

My dad says success is a string of failures.

She was a string of failures. Of wrong moves. Of saying stupid stuff.

She infuriated me to no end.

Pushed me to my limits.

I know the moon brought her to me. I know she saved me from myself.

Showed me what love is supposed to be.

Not the shallow, immature love I used to believe in. Love that was nothing more than hormones and ego.

When she kicked the soccer ball at my head, it was like she woke up my soul.

At that moment, I knew.

As naturally as I knew the sound of my own heartbeat.

Knew we belonged together forever.

When I told her she had my heart, I meant it.

And, now, she might choose him. Probably already did.

There were so many times she told me she didn't know where things stood with him. That he still held a piece of her heart.

All I know is this. If she chooses me, I'll sure as hell dance with her on her birthday.

I take a deep breath and tell myself to stop freaking out. To believe in our love.

And when I do, I feel the innate pull she has on me— like gravity, constantly drawing me to her.

I really don't know how I'd ever be okay without her.

I want to scream at her to tell me she loves me. That there's nothing holding her back anymore.

But I can't, because I stupidly promised to give her time.

I can't give her any more time. I have to know now.

She stands in front of me, taking my breath away.

"You seem stressed," she says.

"That's because I'm ready to fucking explode!" I yell at her. *Shit.* I didn't mean to yell. "I'm sorry. I just need you to tell me. Are you still in love with him? Do you just want him? Or me? Will you date us both? How's this going to work? Did you sleep with him? Wait. No, don't tell me."

She was looking into my eyes, but now she looks down and kicks at the sand nervously.

"Aiden, there's something I need to tell you. Do you remember what Logan told Maggie? About how it doesn't matter where you've been, but only where you end up? Brooklyn told me that. I didn't get it back then. But I do now. This whole mess. Almost being kidnapped. Going to Eastbrooke. Making new friends. Meeting you. Fighting for my family. It was all part of shaping me into who I've become. It's so weird. I'm back here on my beach. I'm home. Exactly where I wanted to be. But I'm not the same girl."

She gives me a wide, dazzling smile. The same smile she gave me the first time I saw her. Cocky. Confident. That ha-ha-I-totally-just-scored-on-you-wearing-cowboy-boots smile.

"Not everything has changed, though," she continues. "I still believe in fairy tales."

It takes everything I have not to roll my eyes, because if she tells me Brooklyn is her prince, I'm seriously going to puke.

SHE TAKES MY hand and leads me closer to the ocean.

Her hand is shaking and I can't tell if it's from nerves or excitement.

"I should've told you this in St. Croix," she says, "but I didn't because I thought I might never see you again. And I wanted you to be able to move on without me."

Is she trying to tell me that I should move on? That she's home with Brooklyn where she belongs?

Doesn't she know that I'd never get over her?

I look deep into her eyes, hoping mine convey the love I feel for her.

She takes a deep breath, turns away from me, and looks up at the moon.

I don't want to hear it yet.

I can't hear it yet.

"Dance with me," I say. "Before you tell me. Please?"

I know I sound desperate, but maybe if we dance it will remind her of all those nights we danced under the twinkle lights in my room.

And the night under the gazebo when a simple dance turned into something so incredibly hot.

And then afterwards.

The way our bodies fit together perfectly.

I'd never felt more perfect in my life.

I cling to her, taking in everything.

The way her hands are laced together behind my neck.

The smell of her hair.

How her chest feels when it's pressed against mine.

How we're so close that I can feel her heartbeat.

Feel her chest rise with each breath she takes.

How there's no music, but we're somehow swaying to the same song.

When she lays her head on my shoulder, I feel cool tears trickle down my neck.

I want to push her away from me and ask her why she's crying.

But I don't want to know the answer.

I'm so afraid of the answer.

Maybe we can just stay here forever, dancing.

But then her lips graze my neck.

She kissed me.

Hope floods through me.

Please, let her say she loves me.

She pulls out of my arms—well, arm, since I have this stupid sling—ending our dance, and says, "Remember how I told you about my prom night? How it didn't go according to my script and I sat on the beach afterward?" She points down. "This is where I was sitting."

"And Brooklyn was sitting here with you?" I snap.

I don't mean to snap at her, but, fuck. Why the hell is she dragging this out?

She turns around, looking surprised by my question. "Well, *later* he came out to talk to me. That was the night when he and I sorta got started. But, I meant before that. When I was sitting here alone. It was about two in the morning. I was sad and, it sounds crazy, but I was sort of talking to the moon. Telling it what I wanted. What I didn't tell you in St. Croix, Aiden, is that I made a wish on the moon, too."

"What did you wish for?"

"My perfect boy. And I thought he was staring at the moon at that very moment, wishing for me, too. I swear, I could almost feel you."

"What are you saying?"

"I'm saying we wished on the moon at the same time. If you had told me about your wish the night we first danced, I would've let myself fall in love with you right then because I so desperately wanted it. I would've loved you even if we weren't right for each other. When I made my wish, I didn't really understand what love was. What it should be. What it could be. I just knew I wanted it. It was like the green flash. I didn't know I hadn't felt it until I experienced the real thing."

There are tears shimmering in her eyes.

Mine too. Because I swear that night I felt her too.

She smiles and takes my hand, causing my heart to soar.

"Through all of it. Taunting Vincent. Taking over his company. Fighting him in the van. Trying to save him from getting shot at. Finding B. Throwing a bomb in the ocean. Getting my family back home. *You* motivated me. Because every time I closed my eyes and wondered if I could—if I would—survive, all I would see is you. You're my green flash, Aiden. Our moon wishes may have brought us together, but it's our hearts that led us home. To each other. I know with everything I am that you're it. My true love."

"Really?" I say. "But, um, I thought you needed to see how things were with Brooklyn."

She shakes her head as she puts her hands back around

my neck. "Aiden, when you took my hand and led me to the Ferris wheel, I knew my hand belonged in yours forever. I just didn't think I'd get a forever. I didn't think I'd survive *my* kiln. But I did. And I want forever with *you*."

We kiss.

If this were the movie of our life, this would be our happy ending.

Our fairy-tale kiss under the moon that used to mock us both—but that may have actually brought us together.

Like, if you believe in that sort of thing.

Even after the kiss, part of me still doesn't believe I could be so lucky.

"You aren't wearing your ring."

She looks down at her hand. "Oh. I took my jewelry off when I showered after the whole bomb thing. Then there were police and reporters and family. It's been a blur since."

"Your wish bracelet too?"

"No, that got ripped off when I was fighting with Vincent."

"What did you wish for?"

"That I'd get my life back."

"I'm glad you got your life back."

"Me too, Aiden."

"So does that mean you'll finally go out with me?"

"I'd love to be your girlfriend, Aiden, but I'm not sure if I'll be going back to Eastbrooke. Matt told me earlier that with the script changes they've made expanding my and Knox's roles, we'll have a full filming schedule this spring. I haven't really had a chance to think it all through." She hesitates. "Or what it might mean for us."

"What it might mean for us? Boots, we survived this. I think we can survive a few days apart. I'll come to the loft every weekend. You need to follow your dreams."

"Wherever they take me?"

"Wherever they take *us*," I reply, grabbing her and hugging her tighter than I ever have before.

God, I love this girl.

And she wants me.

"I love you," I breathe into her hair.

"I love you too," she says.

And then she kisses me. It's a perfect, time-stood-still, fireworks kind of kiss. The kind of kiss that speaks to my soul.

And always will.

She leads me through the sand to her room, carefully locking the door before she starts undressing me.

Wednesday, January 11th
AIDEN
6:30AM

I WAKE UP to her kissing my neck. "Get up, sleepyhead. Time for surfing. You have to come watch."

I look at the clock. It's six-thirty. "Sleepyhead?" I say, grabbing her waist and pulling her on top of me. "You didn't let me sleep last night."

"I'm pretty sure the Titan proved to me just how much of a god he really is," she laughs. It's a beautiful laugh. One I want to hear every day for the rest of my life.

I lie in bed, taking it all in. What it's like to be in her room. In her house. In her bed.

She comes out of her closet dressed in a teeny bikini. One that makes me want to grab her and not let her out of this room for a few more hours.

She tosses a pair of board shorts at me. "They're Tommy's," she says.

I nod thankfully at her. I'd be okay with borrowing one of Brooklyn's boards, but I'll be damned if I'm wearing his shorts.

GOING TO BE OKAY.
10AM

I'M TAKING A break from surfing, lying in the sand, and watching the boys play in the waves, when Cooper brings me a phone.

"This was found inside the house down the beach. It was dead, so I charged it last night. We think it's Brooklyn's."

I enter B's usual passcode, bringing the phone to life.

I hold it up and yell, "Hey, B! They found your phone!"

He rides a wave straight in, sticks his board in the sand, and sits down next to me while Cooper heads back into the house. I know he and Garrett have a meeting this morning.

"It looks like you have a lot of missed calls and texts."

As he reads through the texts, a lot of emotions cross his face. He shakes his head. "I don't know what I'm going to say to her."

"You told me a little about her when we talked on the beach. I know you care about her."

"She's pretty. Models swimwear for one of my sponsors. At first, she reminded me of you and we became fast friends. It sorta grew into more than that. We'd hang out together. Talk about life. Things had gotten kinda hot and heavy between us right before Thanksgiving. But then . . . you know . . . I said what I did."

"That you loved me."

He nods but stares out at the waves, his mind clearly elsewhere. "Yeah. When our call dropped, I looked out into the crowd and our eyes met. She looked so hurt. She shook her head at me, turned around, and walked away. I left my trophy onstage and ran after her. I told her all about you. How you encouraged me. I told her you were seeing other people, but that we promised to give each other another chance when I came home."

"What'd she say?"

"That she'd take me for as long as she could have me."

"She sounds like Aiden," I say, looking out at the water, where he, Damian, and Mark are floating on boards and chatting.

"I didn't tell her about the stalker. I couldn't. I tried to keep it casual. Right before I came back to Malibu, she asked me why I kiss my tattoo before I go out. I told her that you and I have matching tattoos. She left mad. That's the last time we spoke. Honestly, I don't even know why I kiss it. It's habit, you know?"

"I know why you do it. That tattoo symbolizes living your dream. Because that's when it all started. Our trip. My birthday. Our tattoos."

"You'll always be a piece of me," he says, leaning his shoulder against mine. "You were my first love."

"You were my first love, too. I missed you so much."

"I missed you too." He looks out at the water again and says, "I like Aiden."

"I like Aiden, too."

He shoves his shoulder into me. "I told you it was fate you went to school there. That there was someone you were going to meet."

"I feel old, B. I must be out of surfing shape."

"Or maybe it's because you were hit over the head, in a car accident, got shot, flew across the country to find me, and then just about blew yourself up."

I laugh. "Well, at least that makes me feel better."

"Her last text says we're through."

"I'm gonna call her," I say.

"Why?"

"She's never going to believe your story. *Oh baby, I lost my phone when I was kidnapped by a madman, held captive, and almost died in an explosion. But, thankfully, my Keats threw the bomb in the ocean and saved me.*"

"Yeah," he laughs. "It does sound totally made it up."

I take his phone.

"What are you doing?"

"Calling her. I'm serious."

"What? No!"

"Watch me."

"What are you gonna say?"

"I don't know."

"You're not going to script it first?"

"I'm done scripting my life, B. I'm just living it. What's her name?"

"Jaida."

She says, "Hello?"

"Hey, I'm, um, this is Keats."

"Ohmigawd. Do you know where Brooklyn is? First, I was pissed. Now, I'm just really worried. Is he okay?"

"Where are you?"

"Malibu. I thought he might be here. We had a fight. And then he was gone."

"He was kidnapped."

"What?" she says, sounding like she doesn't believe me.

"Why don't we explain it to you in person?"

"Is he with you?"

"Yeah, and he's going to be okay. We're all going to be okay."

Seven months later . . .

Saturday, August 18th

THE DRESS OF YOUR DREAMS.
3PM

"THEY'RE LATE," KYM says, checking her watch for the hundredth time. "Did the boys really need to golf today?"

"Apparently," I say, knowing Damian, Tommy, Aiden, and Matt Moran will come home with seconds to spare, but happy to avoid the chaos of their dates getting ready.

Peyton is getting her nails and hair done at the same time. She's escorting Damian on the red carpet tonight, and Aiden, as promised, will be my arm candy.

Red carpet appearances are all timed so that each star arrives at a different time depending on their clout, role in the movie, etc. We'll walk the carpet, see the premiere of the movie Mom and Tommy filmed together in Vancouver, make our appearance at the after party and then go to my birthday party, which is being held at the same place as last year.

Troy bought the club, known as The Side Door, a few

months ago. He renamed it Chaos, upgraded the DJ facilities and dance floor, and—with his *Twisted Dreams* connections—has been bringing in some of the world's hottest DJs while he's out touring.

I've had my premiere and party dress picked out for a month, so I'm flipping through a magazine while Kym divides her time between looking at her watch, reminding Peyton of red carpet etiquette, and making sure Mom and I will be ready on time.

Damian strolls into the house and Kym immediately questions him. "Where are they?"

"They stopped for a beer," he says with a shrug. "They said they have plenty of time."

"If your father says all he has to do to get ready is shit, shower, and shave, I might just punch him in the face."

AFTER SHE'S GOTTEN Damian and Peyton ready and out to the car, she rolls another rack of dresses in.

"Keatyn, I know you already have a dress picked out, but let's go through these and see if there's anything that can top it."

"Okay," I say, even though I have no intention of changing what I'm wearing. I love my slinky gold gown.

I flip though the dresses, going through the motions to make her happy.

But then I come to a dress that looks familiar.

"Oh my god. It's my dress."

"Your dress?" Kym asks.

"Yes, the dress from my dream."

I examine the dress closer, shocked at how closely it matches the one from my dream.

Sweetheart neckline. Corseted bodice. Tiered bottom in an ombré of pinks.

I look at the label to see who designed it and find a note.

I thought on the night of your dreams, you should wear the dress of your dreams.
    Hope this is close.
    Happy Birthday!
Love,
Aiden

"How did he do it?" I ask Kym, quickly taking the dress off the hanger, holding it up to me, and twirling around.

"He told me about your dream. I called in a favor and this is what we came up with. Is it close?"

"It's like the dress of my dreams on steroids. This corset and these feathers. They're ridiculously beautiful. I can't believe he remembered."

As I spin around, I get tears in my eyes remembering how he went to all my rehearsals. How I trusted him enough to tell him my dreams. About my scripts. About wanting to act.

"Don't cry," Kym scolds. "We don't have time to redo your foundation."

While I quickly change to a strapless bra and slip into the dress, Kym sets out diamonds.

"This thirteen carat pink diamond is surrounded by cushion-cut diamonds, adding another eight carats. Price available on request," she reads off the card that arrived with them from Harry Winston. The diamonds have their own guard who will follow me tonight.

"All right," Kym quizzes, "Diamonds by?"

"Harry Winston," I reply.

"Shoes?"

"Louboutin."

"Bag?"

"Fendi."

"Favorite stylist?"

"Aiden," I reply, teasing her.

"You say my name?" Aiden asks from behind me.

He's dressed in a black Gucci tuxedo, a pair of aviators perched on the top of his head. He looks like sex on a stick.

Seriously, no one is going to look at me.

Gracie and the girls are dressed up too. They're having their own pretend red carpet with their new nanny, Miss Praline, who, with a little time and some luck, may just end up Mrs. Garrett Smith.

Aiden looks me over. "I don't know, Kym. I'm not sure those are the right shoes for the dress."

Kym scoffs at him as he pulls a box out from behind his back.

It's a box I recognize.

My eyes fill with tears as he opens the lid.

I delicately lift them up. "You had the heel fixed?!"

"Yeah," he says, pulling me close. "Seems like the perfect night to wear the shoes that are the real you."

He takes my hand, leads me over to a chair, then bends down and puts the shoe on my foot like he's Prince Charming.

Actually, he *is* my Prince Charming.

Yesterday, on my actual birthday, he spoiled me rotten, giving me a gorgeous, not-for-a-rainy-day dress and taking me to a beautiful restaurant overlooking the ocean for dinner. I was shocked to find our families and closest friends waiting there to surprise me. It was a truly celebratory night.

Afterward, all dressed up, he took me to the Santa Monica pier for cotton candy and a ride on the Ferris wheel.

Gracie interrupts my thoughts. "Kiki, are you Cinderella tonight? Did Aye-den find your shoe?"

"Yes, he did."

"No," Avery says. "You can't be Cinderella. She has a blue dress. Sleeping Beauty wears pink."

"All right. Chop. Chop. You two need to be in the car in thirty seconds," Kym says, interrupting.

I take Aiden outside where Tommy's driver pulls up in a new beautiful white Maserati. It's similar to the one Aiden crashed when he saved me, but with a few upgrades.

He tosses Aiden the keys. "Looks like you get to drive Cinderella to the ball."

Aiden immediately notices the keychain. The one I gave him in St. Croix. And the one he gave me for luck when I left to find B.

"This is my keychain," he states.

"Your car, your keychain," I say with a shrug.

"My car?"

"Yep. It's a gift from Mom and Tommy. You know, for saving my life. It took a while to have it customized."

Aiden walks around it. Then he looks under the hood and whistles.

I frown.

"Ah, Boots, what's the pout for?"

"How come I don't get a whistle when you look under my skirt?"

He gently shuts the hood and grins. Then he grabs me around the waist and kisses my neck.

"Because she won't smack me," he teases, gesturing toward the car.

Kym yells out the front door, "For god's sake. Go! Or you're going to be late!"

"Mom said the red carpet always runs late."

"Aren't we supposed to be in a limo?" Aiden asks.

"Yeah, probably, but Prince Charming rides a white horse to the ball. We can't screw that up."

He pulls me back into his arms. "You look beautiful tonight."

WE ARRIVE AT the premiere on time, only to have to sit and wait.

Damian and Peyton arrived earlier. Knox is in line right ahead of us. Tommy, Mom, and Matt will be the last to arrive.

When we're finally waved ahead, I look at Aiden. "It's our turn. You sure you're up for this craziness?"

"I promised to be your arm candy. I'm a man of my word."

"Yeah, you are. So, you're going to get out first, the valet will get in to park the car, you'll come open my door—" He grabs my face and kisses me, effectively shutting me up.

"Kym has drilled exactly what I'm supposed to do into my head by repeating it about seven hundred times. Then your publicist told me the same thing a few thousand times more."

"People think Knox and I are an item. It's a big deal that I'm showing up with you."

"Is this what you want?" he asks.

"More than anything."

As soon as I get out of the car, the cameras flash.

Almost blinding me.

It's my first public appearance since everything happened with Vincent. Mom wanted me to go to the Academy Awards with her and Tommy, but I only went to the after parties to help celebrate.

I didn't want the night she won her first Oscar to be

about anything other than her.

And, thankfully, without me there, the press respected that.

I still haven't spoken publicly about what happened with Vincent.

The reporters from Winter Formal did that for me. They got their interviews and did the talk show circuit.

I gave them everything that happened up until the point that Vincent was shot and killed.

And, since B refused all interviews too, the public doesn't know about him being kidnapped or about the bomb.

It's just too personal.

Aiden holds out his elbow, and I can't help but smile widely.

And not because I'm posing for the cameras, but because I'm really, truly happy.

I STOP IN front of the bleachers full of fans and sign autographs with my purple glitter pen. Just like the one that Avery gave me when I went to Eastbrooke and just like the one I used to sign my very first autograph for Aiden.

Next, we work our way down the line of reporters assembled behind the barricades of the red carpet.

Their lights are bright.

Their flashes even brighter.

They're all calling out my name, so I stop to answer their questions. Most of them are the same.

Are the rumors about you and Knox true?

Show us your shoes!

Who's your date for tonight?

Why are you and Knox pretending not to be together?

Keatyn, can I get your autograph?

AIDEN HOLDS OUT his elbow, so I take ahold of it and he leads me up the stairs where all the big entertainment shows are set up. They get longer individual interviews as most are doing live streaming.

"I just wait for you at each one, right?" he asks. We're waiting for Knox to finish his interview.

"I'd rather you were with me."

"I don't belong on TV. But you do. You're like a shooting star. Hell, I should make a wish on you."

"You're silly. I'm so glad being apart last semester didn't hurt our relationship."

"I told you," he says with an adorable grin. "Wherever you go, I go."

"You did spend a lot of time at my loft. But it was still hard being apart during the week."

"You mentioned another project earlier . . ."

"They're ready for us, now," I say, interrupting him. "And you're sticking with me for these."

Even though Knox was just interviewed a few seconds ago and I'm standing here on Aiden's arm, the reporter delves right in.

"Knox just mentioned how close the two of you are."

"We've been working together, so we've gotten to be good friends."

"There are rumors that you're dating. Photos of you clubbing in New York."

"Do you ever go out with the people you work with?" I ask the reporter, who is married and stars in her own reality TV series.

"Well, of course," she says.

"But, yet, you're happily married?"

"Uh, well, yes."

"Exactly my point."

We move to the next network. This reporter's name is Stacey and she's known my mom forever. They waited tables together when they first started out.

"Keatyn," she says, giving me a hug and air kisses, "you've grown into such a beautiful young woman."

"Thank you."

"And your dress is gorgeous. Who designed it?"

I rattle off the name of the designer.

"How about your shoes?"

I show off my gorgeous shoes. "Tabitha Simmons."

"There's a big ring on your finger. Does it mean anything? There were rumors that you and Knox were recently engaged."

"Really?" I laugh. "I'm only eighteen. I don't plan on getting engaged for quite a while. But this gorgeousness," I hold up my borrowed diamonds, "is on loan from Harry Winston."

"The diamonds pale next to your beauty," Aiden whispers into my ear. I know his sweet gesture will be all over the internet in a matter of moments.

I can feel the flashes around me but when Aiden is this close everything else fades away and I'm just a girl.

In love.

"You're being awfully complimentary tonight," I tease him.

"Well, you did just give me a new car," he teases back.

We move on to the next big-name reporter.

After an appropriate amount of discussing my wardrobe choices, she asks, "We understand you're doing a remake of your mom's cult classic, *A Day at the Lake*. When do you expect it to be in theaters?"

"We just wrapped filming this week and are hoping to get picked up for distribution soon. But tonight is all about my mom and Tommy's film."

"Speaking of Tommy," she says. "We know that your film debut, *Retribution*, is slated for a highly-coveted Thanksgiving release."

"That's correct."

"And rumor has it the studio is creating a new spin-off franchise for you and Knox."

I smile, because they are. I'm even helping revise the script.

"That would be pretty awesome," I say, unable to comment because the studio hasn't officially announced it yet. They're waiting for people to see *Retribution* first.

"Then, tell me, after you were kidnapped, why wouldn't you do any interviews? You could've had instant fame. Your publicist must've been going crazy."

"I hope if I ever have fame it'll be because of my acting ability," I reply, as Knox photobombs us.

He and Aiden are cracking up about it when the reporter asks another question. "So, what's next for you?"

"What's next is kind of a secret."

"I think we'll cut with that," she says, quickly moving on to Matt Moran, who has caught up to us. He's a man of very few words on the red carpet.

As Aiden and I walk down the stairs to make our way toward the last row of reporters and fans, he whispers to me, "So, did you decide if you're going to do that book to film project? Didn't they want you to start next month? Is that what the secret is?"

"No, I turned it down."

"Why?"

"Well, Knox and I will start working on the *Trinity* project next summer."

"I know. That's why I'm surprised you turned it down.

The timing worked out so that you could do both."

"Except that I have another project I'm way more passionate about."

"What's that?"

"I'm going to be starring in the movie of my life. It will be filming at Eastbrooke, and I'll have the hottest co-star. His name's Aiden Arrington. You may have heard of him."

Aiden's grin blinds me.

I lean close to him and whisper in his ear. "And I can guarantee you that rumors of our off-screen romance will be completely true."

"You're really coming back? For our whole senior year?"

"Yep. I am a prefect, after all. And I'm wearing cowboy boots to New Student Orientation."

FOLLOW YOUR HEART.
10PM

WE QUICKLY MAKE the rounds at the after party, and then go back to my house. All my closest friends are meeting here, so I can introduce them before heading to the club for my birthday party.

Aiden offers to greet everyone as they arrive while I go change.

But when I return in my party dress, I find my friends all congregated in groups with the people they already know.

That will not do.

I grab Dallas and Dawson.

"RiAnne, I'd like you to meet Dallas, my friend from Eastbrooke." I wink at her and whisper, "He's a really good kisser."

She gets a huge smile on her face and giggles when Dallas says, "Howdy. And Keatyn's right. I am a good kisser. You wanna find out?"

RiAnne bites her lip like she's actually contemplating it and nods. Dawson and I both raise our eyebrows at each other and laugh when they just start making out.

"Dawson, I think you need to meet Vanessa."

Vanessa turns around when she hears her name.

"Keatyn, you look gorgeous." She eyes Dawson and says, "And so do you."

"Vanessa, this is Dawson Johnson. He's headed to NYU this fall and plans to major in luxury marketing."

"We have a lot in common, then," she flirts, putting her hand around his buff bicep and purring, "because I plan to major in luxury spending. Let's go in Tommy's office and have some of his good scotch, shall we?"

Dawson doesn't reply. He's busy taking her in, studying her long dark hair, aristocratic face, long eyelashes, authoritative stance, killer body, and couture shoes. He turns to me and says, "She's the Alpha of all Alphas, right?"

Vanessa and I both laugh.

"What a sweet sentiment," Vanessa says, "but I kinda like it when a man takes charge."

Dawson smirks and replies, "Let's go find that scotch."

"Did I hear the word scotch?" Damian asks, and he and Peyton follow them into the office.

I'm introducing my surfer friends to my Malibu party friends and all of them to Katie, Annie, and Maggie, when Cush walks in.

"Damn," Katie and Maggie say at the same time. "Who is that?"

"Cush!" I yell.

He strides over, hugs me, and then puts my hand on his

stomach. "Got them back."

"It's about freaking time. How's Oregon?"

"I'm over Oregon and moving back. I miss the beach and girls in bikinis. Plus, we need to party it up our senior year."

"Hell yeah, we do," RiAnne says, joining us with Dallas in tow. "I miss dancing on your bar with Keatyn. You should see us, Dallas."

"Oh, I'd like to," he flirts.

Cush gives me a casual once-over, then grins, showing off those sexy dimples, and causing Katie to practically swoon.

"I gotta say, I miss Keatyn dancing on my bar too," he says.

"Can't be as hot as the pool table," Aiden says from behind me, wrapping his arms possessively around my waist.

"It definitely isn't," I say to Aiden. Then I make introductions. "Cush, these are my friends from boarding school, Dallas, Aiden, Katie, and Maggie."

They shake hands as Kerri Sampson and Walker Rhodes walk by, heading toward the bar.

"Cush, have you ever met Kerri? She's the daughter of—"

"We *all* know who her dad is," RiAnne says.

"Who?" Katie and Maggie ask.

"Howard Sampson is a big-time producer. *Everyone* in LA knows his name," RiAnne replies.

"And this is Walker Rhodes."

"Walker Rhodes," Maggie says. "Why does that name sound familiar?"

"He'll be performing at my party tonight. He's music's next big thing."

Walker blushes. "Here's hoping so." He turns toward Aiden and gives him a fist bump. "Good surfing with you and Damian this morning, man. You keep it up, you'll kick my ass pretty soon."

"Well, I can't sing like you," Aiden says, giving me a squeeze. "I gotta do something besides stop a soccer ball to impress this one."

"You a goalie?" Cush asks him.

"He's one of the best," I reply. "It'd be fun to see the two of you face off."

"I vote for a shirtless face off to commence immediately," Katie giggles.

We all laugh as Jake, Sander, Paige, and some of the cast members from the remake of *A Day at the Lake* arrive.

"Jake. Sander. Making the movie star entrance, I see."

Sander nods as Jake rolls his eyes at me. "We were waiting for Paige to finish getting ready."

"Well, it was worth it," I say, giving Paige a hug. "You look beautiful."

Riley and Ariela also arrive.

"Mr. And Mrs. Director," Sander says, slapping Riley on the back. "Don't you make the most beautiful couple? All that gorgeous dark hair."

"Happy Birthday, Keatyn," Ariela says to me.

Riley kisses my cheek. "I'm here, baby. Time to start the party."

"Not so fast, Riles," Knox says, walking in the door for his perfectly-timed, fashionably late entrance. "Not without me."

I look around for B. I really hoped he would come tonight.

But they're right. It is time to get the party started.

I grab Aiden's hand, whisper in his ear, and lead him into the kitchen with me. He helps me up onto the kitchen bar then grabs the trays of shots out of the fridge, giving me one before he passes them around.

"The buses will be here soon, so it's time to get this party started with a few shots!" I smile as they raise their glasses in the air. "For those of you who came to my party last year, thank you for still being my friends, even though I left with no explanation. For those of you I've met since then, thank you for understanding why I had to lie to you, and for still being my friends. The party we're heading to is the same as last year's in so many ways. Same club. A lot of the same people. Last year, I had hoped all my friends— from surfing, partying, and school—would come together and instantly become friends. But you didn't. And now I know why. It was because of me. I wanted to keep you separate because I didn't know where I fit in or who I wanted to be. So, raise your glasses and toast each other. This is for you. Love yourselves. Find control in your chaos. Follow your heart. And don't be afraid to wish on the moon."

Everyone downs their shots.

As Aiden cranks up the music, I pull Peyton, Maggie, RiAnne, Keri, Paige, and Vanessa up on the island to dance with me.

I'M DANCING LIKE a maniac with Aiden—and, well, everyone—when Brooklyn surprises me by cutting in.

He says to Aiden, "Do you mind? This dance is long overdue."

Aiden graciously bows out and Brooklyn wraps his arms around me.

"I'm glad you came tonight."

"I am too. Keats, I'm really sorry I didn't dance last year. This is my feeble attempt to make it up to you."

"It's okay, B. We were both going through some big

changes."

"I got to your house just as you were giving the toast."

"What'd you think of it?"

"I think fate is a tricky bitch," he says. "What a fucking year."

I hug him tightly and laugh. "I'll toast to that. Hell, let's go get a drink!"

Sunday, August 19th

AIDEN
12:55PM

KEATYN IS SHAKING my shoulder. "Wake up, sleepyhead. We have somewhere to be."

I look at the clock, noting that it's nearly one. We didn't get to sleep until six this morning and I'm still tired.

But the sight of her wearing nothing but my boxers perks me up.

"Are those my boxers?" I tease.

"Maybe," she says with an adorable smile.

She runs her hand across my bicep. Then across my cowboy boots tattoo, giving me a naughty grin. "We need to get going."

"Where are we going?"

"A little surprise trip. But I was just thinking . . ."

"What?"

She winks at me, runs into her closet, and then tosses my boxers out the door behind her.

The Titan jumps to attention before I do, urging me to get my ass in there.

I round the corner and find her naked, sprawled across a

white furry rug, surrounded by all her clothes and shoes.

I pounce on her.

What else would I do?

HILLY. LUSH. GREEN.
2PM

I TAKE AIDEN to the plane that's waiting for us, praying I've timed it right.

The flight is quick and when we land he asks, "Where are we going? Are we seeing my parents?"

"No, we're not. I have something I need to show you."

I jump in the Mercedes convertible that I got for my birthday last year.

"How'd your car get here?" he asks.

"I had it brought up here, so we could drive it."

He narrows his eyes at me, trying to figure out what's going on, then hops in the car.

IT'S A BEAUTIFUL drive. Hilly. Lush. Green.

Aiden lowers the convertible top even though it's chilly. "I love the way it smells so clean just after a good rain," he says.

I make a left turn, winding up the rock path.

"Wow," Aiden says, admiring the scenery. "It's gorgeous up here. Are we going to get in trouble for trespassing? There were warning signs back there."

"I don't think so," I say, parking at the top of the hill and grabbing a bag out of the car.

I take his hand and lead him toward the spot with the best view.

"You can see the ocean from here!" he says. "And, look, the sun is starting to set."

I look out at the sky and wonder why I was so worried. I couldn't have timed it more perfectly.

"What do you think of it up here?"

"It's beautiful," he says, turning around and taking it in from all directions. The rows of grapes. The hilly land. The view of the ocean.

I hand him a piece of paper.

"A deed?"

"Yes, this, pretty much as far as your eyes can see, is yours."

"What do you mean, mine?"

"Remember how upset I was when that girl from the club was killed? And I went back a few nights later and danced?"

"Yeah."

"Things were heating up with Vincent, and I was afraid that . . . well, that I wouldn't survive. I bought this land for two reasons. If something happened to me, I wanted to be cremated and have my ashes spread here. Then the land was going to you," I say, tears prickling my eyes. "So you would have something to remember me by. It's a working vineyard. Twelve-hundred acres. Already producing high quality grapes. I left you this deed and a letter in my will. Sam was supposed to bring you up here and give it to you. I decided I'd give you the letter myself. Since I survived and all, and because I want you to know . . . well, I just want you to know."

I hand him the letter and watch as he reads it, tears filling his eyes.

My dearest Aiden—

If you're reading this, then by now you know the truth about me and that I didn't survive the showdown with my stalker. But I want to live on. Here. With you. My hope is that this land will allow you to live out your dream of creating a wine label that will make millions for charity.

It's not that I didn't think you could buy it for yourself someday. I just wanted to make sure you followed your dreams. I didn't want anyone—your friends, your parents, whoever—to say that it didn't make sense financially. That you were too young. Whatever.

And it's my sincerest hope that you'll find someone to love and share all this with. Someone who you will watch a million sunsets with. Here. In this spot.

Because even though I didn't always tell you, you've had my heart since the day I met you. Your lips were always my bliss. And I know we weren't sorta like fate. We were exactly like fate.

Always. Only. Ever yours,
Boots

He's crying, hugging me, and shaking his head.

"We're building our love mansion right here," he says determinedly. "In this very spot."

I smile at him and take the jar out of the bag. "I was hoping you'd say that. Cuz I brought the dirt."

(Pan shot of couple kissing and the land.)

Aiden puts his hand on my knee and whispers to me as *The End* rolls across the movie screen in front of us. "Hard to believe your journals were turned into three movies."

"It's even harder to believe it's been over ten years since we met. I'm so glad we decided to show all three movies back to back for this premiere. It was so fun to see the growth of the characters."

"You mean *our* growth? That was the amazing story of us. How our love survived it all. We really are lucky, you know."

"I loved seeing the first movie again. It's still my favorite."

He smirks at me. "Cracks me up to hear all the stuff you thought. Especially since I was crazy about you right from the start."

"It sure didn't seem like it then. Damn Logan," I tease.

The movie we just watched was a combined Special Edition of all three films in *The Keatyn Chronicles*. Riley had the brilliant idea of stringing them together and saving all the credits for the end.

The audience is clapping and cheering for their favorites. Cush, Brooklyn, Dawson, and the entire Eastbrooke crew.

I think the audience feels the same way we do.

We can't believe it's over.

It feels like an era has ended. Three movies in three and half years.

All box office successes.

All produced by Riley and me. Hard to believe our working together started with a slutty video on a plane.

The biggest cheers of all, though, are saved for the actors who played Keatyn and Aiden.

I clap loudly and whistle, thrilled at how much everyone loves them together. Although, in the first movie, most viewers were torn between Cush, Brooklyn, Dawson, and Aiden, by the second one, so many were Team Aiden. It's kind of funny that many moviegoers didn't even realize the movies were based on a real couple. They've been heating up social media sites and online forums claiming that if Keatyn didn't choose Aiden they would all die. Millions wore four-leaf clover t-shirts and tweeted #ifly.

Next on the screen is a musical montage of Aiden and me; of our real life together. Though I wasn't sure about including shots of us, Riley offered me two options. He was either going to make up a happily ever after for the movie, or I was going to show that the real Keatyn and Aiden got their happily ever after. He said people would love the dirt ending, but they'd want more. They'd want to know if our love, that seemed so strong at eighteen, actually did survive the kiln. He threatened to do a scene where college-aged Keatyn and Aiden get engaged at an Eastbrooke Homecoming. Aiden put his foot down. So we settled on this.

I cried during the movie because I got so involved with the characters and what they went through, but I was able to separate the movies from my real life.

Until now.

I smile and cry happy tears as I watch bits of our life since I gave Aiden the vineyard.

Being crowned Homecoming King and Queen at East-brooke our senior year.

A photo of Aiden being silly and carrying me over the threshold of our senior prom.

Aiden scooping me up into his arms and twirling me around at our Eastbrooke graduation.

A photo of us with the cast and crew who worked on A Day at the Lake.

Aiden with me and Knox after winning Best Kiss at the MTV awards for our memorable kiss in Retribution.

Aiden escorting me to the Academy Awards.

The two of us dancing cheek-to-cheek at Damian and Peyton's lavish rock star wedding.

Both our families running in a 5K fundraiser to celebrate Aiden's mom still being cancer-free.

Us standing on a balcony in Greece in the exact spot Aiden said we would during our Greek-themed weekend.

Then there are numerous travel photos of us. We started a trend with the hashtag #SunsetSelfies and are still working toward a million sunsets together.

Aiden starts to say something as the song ends and the last photo fades away, but Riley leans forward from the seat behind us. "Keep watching. I added something to the end."

What flashes on the screen next is a cute photo of me and B from our summer of waves. We're on a beach in Spain, both of us making hearts with our hands as the sun rises.

But it's the video of him surfing in the final heat of his last tournament that causes my heart to ache. It was the most amazing I'd ever seen him surf. It was where he clinched his third world title. My whole family was there and I cried when he hoisted Gracie up on his shoulders and let her hold the huge trophy above his head.

The next photo is one that graced the cover of *Sports Illustrated*. It's a beautiful action shot of him from that tournament, with the words *In loving memory of Brooklyn Wright, three-time world champion surfer* on top of it.

I'll never forget the moment when I heard. It's been over two years, but it still feels like yesterday. I was filming in Paris. Aiden saw it on ESPN and rushed on set to tell me. Witnesses say that his dad never should have been out surfing in the storm. That the waves were too much for him. When his dad went down, B died trying to save him. Both perished that day.

People try to tell me that B died doing what he loved, but I disagree. Even now, I want to call him and say, *What were you thinking? Why did you let your dad go out into waves he couldn't handle?* But I can't.

His death left a void in all our hearts.

Gracie, who is sitting on the other side of me, squeezes my wrist.

I look at her and know B would have appreciated one thing. That his fate brought two people together.

Gracie has a skinny but buff arm wrapped around her shoulder. Brooklyn's nephew, Brady, and his family moved into the beach house when, at the age of fourteen, he inherited both B and his dad's millions. He and Gracie have been together ever since. First as friends; now as more. And, although they are still young, I'm pretty sure he is her forever love. He's the yin to her yang. Completely laid-back. He adores every part of her spunky personality and bossiness. But, unlike B, when she steps out of line or goes diva on him the way I used to, he just stands there and grins at her, raising an eyebrow that lets her know she's not the boss of him. I love his quiet confidence.

And he's pretty damn good on a surfboard, too.

I grab the hand of the boy who has always been my fate. We've been together ever since I told him he was my green flash.

There's no relationship status.

We just are.

And we're happy.

And that's all that matters.

At least, it did.

Until this morning.

When a little pink line appeared on a stick.

One little pink line that's going to change both our lives.

Suddenly, I want what we keep saying we're too busy for. The fairytale wedding. The ribbons blowing in the trees. Twinkle lights to dance under.

"What'd ya think?" Riley asks.

I turn around and hug him, ignoring the blonde attached to him.

"I didn't know you were adding the dedication at the end." I smile a sad smile. "Thank you. It means a lot to me."

"He was a good friend to all of us. I miss him every day," Riley says, his eyes looking glassy.

"Baby, I need to pee," the blonde says at a completely inappropriate time.

"So, go," he says, shrugging her off.

"It meant a lot to *all* of us," Gracie says, throwing herself into Riley's arms.

Gracie looks so pretty tonight. Her hair is in a cute little pixie cut, a style she's been growing out since she shaved her head to play a girl dying of cancer in a role that was recently nominated for an Academy Award. She spent hours at the pediatric cancer ward immersing herself in the character. And, even now, she goes back as often as her schedule will permit. I can't tell you how many times Mom about shut down the whole movie. Watching your daughter die on screen is not easy. I can't imagine how horrible it would be in real life.

Because of both their experiences, she and Mom started working with Aiden to add another Moon Wish label wine to raise money for families whose children are affected by the disease.

I'm so proud of her.

I'm proud of all my sisters, all but one of whom are sitting in the front row with us.

The triplets, now seventeen, are following their dreams as well. Emery isn't here because she's getting ready to grace the catwalk tonight to kick off this year's Paris Fashion Week. Her schedule is the reason why we decided to have a daytime world premiere in Paris for *The Keatyn Chronicles* trilogy. We're all attending the fashion show and then going to an after party. Ivery's highly anticipated sophomore album is due to release next month. Her angelic voice combined with Troy's DJ mixes have catapulted her to the top of the dance charts. And Avery designs a brand of mass-market clothing called *Stevens*. All four girls were recently featured on the cover of *Teen Vogue* wearing pieces from the line.

"What'd you think of the parts Aiden and I added?" Riley asks.

"I know I fought you on them. But, you were right. The chase scene was amazing."

"It should have been. We used a lot of my real footage—digitally enhanced."

"And, more importantly," Aiden adds, "no Maseratis had to be sacrificed during the making of the film."

"I thought Aiden's point of view was perfect," Gracie says. "I cried so hard. Even knowing that you chose him, I was worried in the movie that you weren't going to. It was so poignant. How he wanted to hate B. Did he really stop and make you dance with him before you told him?"

"Yeah, he did."

"I can't believe you put him through that," Ivery agrees.

"Oh, give me a break," I say. "He and Riley totally embellished that part to pull at your heart strings. And the part where he says it was a fireworks kiss; he totally copied me."

"Girls, don't listen to her. I was a mess. My heart was nearly shattered," Aiden says dramatically.

Ivery says, "I cried so hard, too."

Aiden gives me a smirk.

Mom and Tommy join the conversation. Little Lincoln Stevens is almost eleven years old now, but he didn't come with them. Not when the movie ended up with an R rating. I tried to get Riley to cut out some of the swearing so it could be PG-13 like the first two, but he stood his creative ground, citing all the f-bombs in my later journals. And I couldn't for the life of me cut out the *I fucking love you* scenes. They were too special.

"I felt bad for Aiden in the movie too," Mom agrees. "I remember that morning we talked about it. I told you to call him."

"I didn't want to tell him on the phone."

"I'm glad she didn't tell me on the phone," Aiden says, finally sticking up for me. "So, Boots, I hate to break up the trip down memory lane, but we need to head out."

I glance at his watch. The ridiculously expensive one I bought him when I wasn't sure I'd see another Christmas. "We have plenty of time before the fashion show. Speaking of memory lane," I say to Riley. "I was surprised to see you added a photo with Ariela in it. Maybe you should call her sometime. See how she's doing. It'd be nice to see you with the same girl more than once. I swear, you must have a stable of blondes hidden behind your house."

"No fucking way," he replies. "I'm perfectly happy with Shelly."

I bite my lip, holding back a smile.

"What?" he asks.

"Her name is *Shelby*," Gracie and I say.

He rolls his eyes as everyone laughs. "Whatever. Close enough."

The actors who played Keatyn and Aiden join us. I congratulate them on another success and give them huge hugs.

I watch Riley pat Aiden on the back and discreetly say something to him.

"All right," he says, "we really have to go now."

"You and Riley looked sneaky. What's going on?"

"Nothing," he says, dragging me toward the exit.

"I heard him say something about luck."

"He just said with any luck, he'd accidentally lose Shelby somewhere between the premiere and the party so he could hang with all the models."

"Are there any models left that he hasn't already dated? Or any aspiring actresses? I wish he'd aim a little higher, age-wise. Maybe find someone who's already successful. Maybe I should set him up with—"

"Riley doesn't want strings. Ariela broke his heart when she wouldn't come to California with him after graduation."

"Did you talk to him about it? I was shocked he added that photo from the *Day at the Lake* cast party. They looked so in love in that picture."

"I tried to talk to him, but he just turned it around and gave me shit."

"About what?"

"Us. He said I couldn't give relationship advice until I'd put a ring on it."

"You did put a ring on it. In the gazebo. That's all we've ever needed," I say with conviction, realizing I've been silly. I don't need a piece of paper to tell us we're in love. We can have a baby and not be married. Our love is all that matters. It's all that's ever mattered.

The corners of Aiden's beautiful mouth turn down for a second. I'm about to ask him why, but am interrupted by him telling our temporary bodyguard that we're going straight to the car and not stopping for autographs.

"Cooper always lets me stop," I say, already missing him. He left a few weeks ago to go help out an old friend with something he said he couldn't really talk about.

"No autographs," he says firmly. Which is weird, because he's always so supportive.

As he drags me toward the car, I'm trying to at least wave to the fans yelling my name.

"Stop rushing me, Aiden. You're starting to piss me off."

When the limo door shuts behind us, he gives me a hard kiss, which manages to both cool down my temper and heat up my insides at the same time.

I move my hands to the front of his pants, forgetting I'm mad and thinking about the hotness behind his zipper, when his phone rings.

He pulls it out of his jacket pocket, checks the display, and hands it to me. "It's Dallas. I'm sure he wants to talk to you."

"Hey, Dallas," I say.

"Riley's predicting box office success."

"He always does."

"What do you think?"

"I think I agree with him. He outdid himself on this last installment and releasing the full three-movie version was brilliant."

"Wait. Did I hear that right? Is this history in the making? Did you just admit to being wrong?"

"Yes, I said it. The alternating POVs he stuck in there that seemed so jarring in the script were seamless in the movie. You'll be busy adding up the money." Dallas is Captive Films' chief legal counsel and a partial owner. "How's RiAnne feeling? Baby five cooperating?"

"I can't tell you how many times this week she's said she needs this baby out of her. She's pouting because she couldn't come to Paris and is now craving macarons."

"Are you getting her some?"

"Of course."

"You're a good man."

"Always have been."

"Damn straight. Tell her we'll celebrate with dinner at the beach when we get back."

"Sounds good. Tell Aiden good luck tonight."

"Okay," I say. "Bye."

But as soon as I hang up, I turn to Aiden. "Wait. Why did Dallas just tell me to wish you luck?"

He gives me a smirk. "Probably thinks I'm going to need it. You know, holding off all the models that will be hitting on me at the fashion show."

I kiss him. "You're bad."

"So are you. You never told me Brooklyn wished on the

moon too. Was that part added just for the movie?"

"Nope. It's totally true."

"And you still chose me?"

"I didn't have a choice, Aiden. You've had my heart from the second I met you. I just had to make things right with him. And I had to be sure. After everything I'd been through, I didn't trust myself. But when it came down to it, B and I both knew. We were great first loves. We weren't forever loves. It happened exactly like that."

"What was your favorite part?"

"Oh, gosh. I have so many. The heartbreakingly beautiful love. The *I fucking love you*. The first time we said I love you. The Christmas tree."

The limo stops at the base of the Eiffel Tower.

"What are we doing here?"

"Thought we'd take in the view. It's a gorgeous evening."

HE USHERS ME out of the car and we meet a concierge who takes us to the top.

Aiden pulls his phone out and quietly plays the first song from our 29-song playlist.

"It still pisses me off that Riley didn't use our original playlist."

"Our songs are over ten years old. We had to use current music and fashion in the movies."

"Yeah, I suppose you're right. I just like ours better."

"Me too. Although, I did manage to sneak a few of our favorites in there."

He smiles at me. "I noticed."

We lean against the railing and take in the view of Paris.

"You can see our apartment from here," he says, pointing it out.

"The view is the reason we bought it, remember? It had great bones but was such a mess."

"But it's beautiful now, which makes it worth it."

"We've done a lot in the past ten years," I say. Watching the movie of our love has left me feeling very nostalgic.

"You're right," Aiden says, and starts naming off our accomplishments. "Two college degrees. Twelve movies. Thousands of sunsets in twenty-six countries. We built our mansion of love as well as survived the renovations of the Paris apartment and the Malibu beach house."

"Thank goodness we didn't have to do anything to the loft in New York. It's always been perfect."

He smiles at me and touches my face. "Your loft has that one important piece of decor we've added to every one of our homes."

"And what is that?"

"Don't be naughty," he says, giving me a little smack on the butt. "You know it's the glow-in-the-dark moons on the ceilings of our bedrooms."

"I'm just teasing you," I say. "And don't forget the millions your wines have donated to worthy causes."

"Well, it certainly helps sales when we have the hottest actress under thirty in all our advertisements."

"I'm thinking it might be time for us to slow down a little," I say with a sigh as he wraps his arms around my waist.

"I think that's a good idea. You could use some time off."

"I have something I need to tell you, Aiden."

"Not yet," he says, kissing my neck. "I'm not done with memory lane. Remember when you were first tutoring me and I told you I was going to ask you to marry me here someday? How I asked you to go to Winter Formal with that lame Eiffel Tower we made."

"It wasn't lame. I loved it. It was so romantic. I'll re-member the way you looked that day for the rest of my life. It was one of those *take my breath away* moments."

He whispers in my ear. "I hope this is another one of those moments."

"What do you mean?"

I glance over my shoulder, not seeing him.

I turn around.

And.

Ohmigawd!

He's. Down. On. One. Knee.

He takes my hand.

I hold my breath, trying to capture every feeling. Every single thing about this moment. The smells of Paris, the sunset, Aiden's sexy voice, the way my hand still feels like it belongs in his forever. How he makes me feel like anything and everything is possible.

"You and I are like a promise," he says. "A wish. Proof that fate and luck bring people together. Proof of love at first sight. Proof that true love can survive the kiln. I promise you a life that's better than anything you've ever scripted. So, what do you say, Boots? Wanna get hitched?"

"Hitched?"

"Yeah. Get it—boots, hitched?"

I laugh. "You're silly."

"And you're beautiful. Seriously, will you marry me?"

"Yes, I will."

As he stands up, I throw my arms around his neck and kiss him.

"That was easier than I thought," he says, an adorable smile playing on his face. "Dallas said I'd need the ring to get you to commit to planning a wedding."

"Is there a ring?"

"Is there a ring? Of course, there's a ring. Wanna see it?"

"Hell yeah."

He pulls a velvet box out of his jacket pocket and opens the lid.

The ring is ablaze with color.

A large round canary diamond set into a thick band, baguette stones ringing the band in rows, starting with clear brilliant diamonds then moving across the band in graduating shades of light yellows and pinks.

"It looks like a sunset!" I gasp.

"That's by design." He slides the vintage four-leaf clover ring he gave me in the gazebo so many years ago off my finger and replaces it with the engagement ring.

I admire it for a moment.

"Turn your hand over and look at the back."

I flip my hand around. The back is also ringed with stones, graduating to brighter shades of oranges, hot pinks, and reds.

And one single emerald.

"You're my green flash too," he says, giving me another kiss. "Always. Only. Ever yours."

"Um . . ." I say.

"Um?"

"Yeah, we might need a rewrite on that part."

"*What* part?"

"The *only* part."

"You don't want *only* me?"

"It's not going to be just us anymore."

"What do you mean?"

"I'm pregnant, Aiden."

"How?"

I laugh at him. "Um, I think you know *how.*"

He lowers his voice. "But you're on the pill."

"Remember about six months ago when you said I should go off it and see what happens?"

"You did?"

"Yeah, I didn't say anything because I didn't want the pressure of trying. I was hoping it would just happen. Honestly, I was starting to worry that I couldn't get pregnant."

"You shouldn't have worried," he says, holding up my palm. "You know we're having four kids. It's fate."

"Maybe sorta like fate," I add with a laugh.

He holds my hands tightly and looks into my soul. "Are you really pregnant?"

"Only a few weeks, but, yes, I took a test this morning and it was positive."

He has the same shocked look on his face as he did when I kicked the soccer ball past him.

Then a smile starts to form, the corners of his mouth turning upward.

Which turns into the full-wattage powerful godlike smile that still makes me swoon.

"Come on, beautiful. Let's get going so we can tell everyone the good news."

As we drive to the fashion show, the moon slides into view.

I make another wish on it.

That my little hottie baby gets daddy's smile.

Exclusive Interview:
Captive Films' Keatyn Douglas and Riley Johnson

"Keatyn, tell us how Captive Films got its start."

"Our first project was a remake of A Day at the Lake, *starring Luke Sander as Vince, myself as Lacy,*

and Jake Worth as my boyfriend, Matt."

"That movie was a box office hit. And you were both how old at the time?"

"Almost eighteen," Riley says. "We filmed it over our summer break."

"How did you come up with the name Captive Films?"

Sexy Riley rubs the scruff on his face and says, "It was a nod to both holding our audiences captive and how we met."

"How you met?"

They share an inside joke, then Keatyn says, "You'll just have to see the movie."

So there it is, folks. Go see the trilogy that's taking box offices around the world by storm.

The End

About the Author

Jillian Dodd® is a USA Today and Amazon Top 10 best-selling author. She writes fun binge-able romance series with characters her readers fall in love with—from the boy next door in the That Boy series to the daughter of a famous actress in The Keatyn Chronicles® to a spy who might save the world in the Spy Girl® series. Her newest series include London Prep, a prep school series about a drama filled three-week exchange, and the Sex in the City-ish chick lit series, Kitty Valentine.

Jillian is married to her college sweetheart, adores writing big fat happily ever afters, wears a lot of pink, buys way too many shoes, loves to travel, and is distracted by anything covered in glitter.

Made in the USA
Middletown, DE
13 July 2022

69171125R00234